Two wome
but findi

20 Amber Court,
or did it?

Elizabeth Bevarly and Katherine
Garbera bring you the first two
wonderful books in this series about
four women sharing an address; and
each finding the man of their dreams!

Enjoy

When Jayne Met Erik

and

Some Kind of Incredible

Dear Reader,

Welcome to the fire-cracking world of Desire!

Our first volume presents the initial two books of the mini-series 20 AMBER COURT where four women, who live in the same place, chase their dreams to surprising effect. Elizabeth Bevarly brings us *When Jayne Met Erik* and Katherine Garbera follows up with *Some Kind of Incredible*. Watch out for the final two books next month.

We not only have a millionaire for you this month but a billionaire, too! *Billionaire Bachelors: Ryan* by Anne Marie Winston is the first in a trilogy about three very sexy brothers, and *Jacob's Proposal* by Eileen Wilks is the first book in her trilogy called TALL, DARK & ELIGIBLE—yes, also about three drop-dead-gorgeous brothers!

Finally, we have two kissable, very eligible doctors in *Dr Dangerous* by Kristi Gold and *The MD Courts His Nurse* by Meagan McKinney.

As you may have noticed this is the first month of our new-look covers, so if you have any comments please feel free to drop us a line—we love to hear from you.

Happy Bonfire Night!

The Editors

When Jayne Met Erik
ELIZABETH BEVARLY

Some Kind of Incredible
KATHERINE GARBERA

SILHOUETTE®
DESIRE™

*First published in Great Britain 2002
Silhouette Books, Eton House, 18-24 Paradise Road,
Richmond, Surrey TW9 1SR*

The publisher acknowledges the copyright holders of the
individual works as follows:

When Jayne Met Erik © Harlequin Books S.A. 2001
Some Kind of Incredible © Harlequin Books S.A. 2001

*Special thanks and acknowledgement are given to
Elizabeth Bevarly and Katherine Garbera for their
contribution to the 20 Amber Court series*

ISBN 0 373 04766 5

51-1102

*Printed and bound in Spain
by Litografía Rosés S.A., Barcelona*

WHEN JAYNE MET ERIK
by
Elizabeth Bevarly

ELIZABETH BEVARLY

is an honours graduate of the University of Louisville and achieved her dream of writing full-time before she even turned thirty! At heart, she is also an avid traveller who once helped navigate a friend's thirty-five-foot yacht across the Bermuda Triangle. Her dream is to one day have her own yacht, a beautifully renovated older-model forty-two-footer, and to enjoy the freedom and tranquillity sea-faring can bring. Elizabeth likes to think she has a lot in common with the characters she creates, people who know love and life go hand in hand. And she's getting some first-hand experience with motherhood as well—she and her husband have a seven-year-old son, Eli.

For Joan Marlow Golan,
Gail Chasan
and Allison Lyons.
With many thanks.

SILHOUETTE® DESIRE™

welcomes you to

2O AMBER COURT

*Where four women work together,
share an address...and confide in each
other as they fall in love!*

November 2002
WHEN JAYNE MET ERIK
by Elizabeth Bevarly

&

SOME KIND OF INCREDIBLE
by Katherine Garbera

December 2002
THE BACHELORETTE
by Kate Little

&

RISQUÉ BUSINESS
by Anne Marie Winston

One

Jayne Pembroke was *not* having a good day.

She began it by oversleeping, a development made even worse by the fact that she awoke from the most wonderful dream she'd had in a long, long time—a development made even worse when she confronted the reality to which she did, eventually, awake. Because in her dream, Jayne had had company. Really nice company, too, in the form of a handsome, dark-haired, dark-eyed stranger, who had been performing the most wondrous—and erotic—activities with her.

At least, Jayne *thought* they were wondrous, erotic activities. She was pretty sure they were, anyway. She did have cable TV, after all. Admittedly, though, she didn't have much personal experience with wondrous, erotic activities by which to judge…or *any* personal experience, for that matter. But whatever it was that the dark-haired, dark-eyed stranger had been doing to her in her dream, it had felt really, really good.

Her reality, on the other hand, was…not. Not wondrous. Not erotic. And certainly not good. Because in addition to being late, Jayne was, as always, alone.

When she finally did glance over at the clock and noted the time, she tumbled out of bed—literally—bonking her head on the nightstand in the process. So she kicked the nightstand in retaliation…and banged her little toe in exactly that way that made it hurt the most. Then, as she hopped on one foot toward her bathroom, Mojo, her sister Chloe's cat, whom Jayne was keeping while Chloe attended college, came gallumphing into the room—doubtless because Mojo knew Jayne would be hopping around on one foot—and tripped her. That, naturally, caused her to fall down, and in doing so she banged her knee viciously on the hardwood floor.

Things just went downhill from there.

The water in the shower was barely tepid by the time Jayne turned it on, thanks, no doubt, to the fact that everyone *else* who lived at 20 Amber Court had already had *their* showers because *they'd* awoken on time. Then the only clean shirt she was able to find did not match the only clean skirt she was able to find, and the only pair of clean panty hose she was able to find had a run in them. As a result, she was forced to don a blinding combination of raspberry top and burnt-orange skirt, along with the only belt she could find in her overly tousled closet—which, it went without saying, was chartreuse.

Not surprisingly, her hair dryer shorted out the moment she switched it on, emitting a dangerous-sounding *zzzt* coupled with the smell of something burning. Immediately she jerked the plug from the wall and dumped the appliance in the wastebasket—which overturned, spilling its entire contents across the bathroom floor.

She bit back a scream—and quite a hysterical one it had threatened to be, too—then methodically wove her long, straight, *wet,* red hair into a thick braid that fell between her shoulderblades, and ruffled her bangs dry as best she could. She swiped a bit of raspberry-colored lip-stick over her mouth—at least *some*thing would match at least *part* of her clothes—and dragged a bit of neutral shadow over her violet eyes. Then she ran into the kitchen for the cup of coffee she absolutely *had* to consume in order to function as a halfway effective human being.

The good news was that the coffeemaker's timer had, amazingly, worked perfectly. The bad news was that when Jayne had filled the coffeemaker the night before, she had neglected to add any...well, coffee. So only a pot of hot water greeted her.

She bit back another one of those certain-to-be-hysterical screams—but just barely. Then, surrendering to the fact that she wouldn't be enjoying her morning cuppa today—or much of anything else, for that matter—Jayne turned her attention to the kitchen window and saw that, inescapably, it was an unusually rainy morning for the first of September. And of course, likewise inescapably, she recalled that she'd left her only umbrella at Colette Jewelry, the showroom of the highly successful Colette, Inc., where she worked as a salesclerk, the last time it had rained.

My, my, my, she thought. What else could the day possibly hold? It wasn't even 9:00 a.m.

As quickly as she could, she hurried through the rest of her morning rituals, doing her absolute best to make completely certain that nothing else went wrong. And really, not much else did go wrong. Except for when she chipped her favorite coffee mug putting it away, broke her fingernail to the quick while performing a quick search for her raincoat—which, naturally, she never found—and stepped on a pile of stray cat kibble, crushing it to a fine powder that she'd have to sweep up when she got home, because there was no way she had time to do that now.

But other than that...

She was locking her front door to apartment 1C when

the door to 1A-B, the apartment next to hers—the one belonging to her landlady—opened. It was the first thing to happen that morning that made Jayne smile. Rose Carson just inspired that kind of reaction in a person, a feeling of good cheer and well-being. She was, to put it simply, a nice lady. She'd even been the one who had helped Jayne find a job at Colette Jewelry. A friend of a friend, Rose had told Jayne, had mentioned an opening in the jewelry store. Jayne had been hired for the salesclerk position the day she had applied.

Judging by Rose's short, dark hair that was just starting to go gray, by the laugh lines that crinkled her dark eyes, and by the older woman's matronly figure, Jayne guessed her landlady's age to be somewhere in her fifties. About the same age Jayne's mother would be now, had Doris Pembroke survived the plane crash that had killed her and Jayne's father four years ago.

Even though Jayne had only lived at 20 Amber Court for a month, she felt as if she'd known Rose Carson forever. Her landlady was the kind of person who inspired immediate affection and fast camaraderie, the kind in whom one felt totally comfortable confiding. Within days of Jayne's move to the apartment building, she'd found herself revealing to Rose all the particulars of her past and current situations. About the loss of both her parents when she was eighteen, about taking on the care of her then-fourteen-year-old twin siblings, Chloe and Charlie, immediately thereafter, about sacrificing her own opportunity to attend college in order to send Chloe and Charlie instead.

Jayne didn't mind the sacrifice, though. She'd always felt responsible for the twins, even when she was a child. And she knew neither of them took her sacrifice for granted. Once her brother and sister finished college themselves in four years, she'd go back and earn her own degree. She had plenty of time, after all. She was only twenty-two, and her whole life lay stretched before her.

She was just looking forward to having a bit of stability in that life for a change. The last four years had been more than a little difficult, seeing to the needs of Charlie and Chloe and herself, making sure all three of them kept a roof over their heads and food in their bellies.

The sale of their parents' home, along with a modest life insurance settlement and social security for the twins, had afforded them the financial boost they'd needed during that time. But now that Chloe and Charlie were eighteen, the social security was gone. And college tuition for two, even with the twins' partial scholarships, was going to prove a challenge. Still, the Pembroke finances were stable and reasonably secure right now. As long as Jayne had her job at Colette Jewelry and lived within her modest budget, everything would be fine.

She hoped.

"Good morning, Jayne," Rose Carson said with a smile as she closed her own door and turned toward her newest tenant. She glanced down at her watch. "You're running a bit late, aren't you, dear?"

Jayne quelled the panic that threatened to rise again. She wasn't *that* late, she reminded herself. Thanks to all her rushing around—and skipping her morning coffee—she could still make it to work with a few minutes to spare. Maybe. If she ran the entire way. Which, of course, she would, seeing as how she had missed the bus, and it was still raining. Colette, Inc. was only ten blocks from 20 Amber Court. And if she hugged the buildings between here and there, the awnings might provide enough shelter to keep her dry. Sort of.

"A bit late, yes," Jayne conceded to her landlady. "It's been one of those mornings," she couldn't help adding with no small exasperation.

Rose nodded, clearly understanding. "Rainy days and Mondays, right?" she asked.

Jayne chuckled derisively. "Rainy days and Mondays, and broken alarm clocks and broken hair dryers, and no clean laundry and uncooperative coffeemakers, and homicidal cats and—''

Rose held up a hand, laughing. ''Say no more,'' she said. ''Oh, my. I've had a few of those days myself.''

Jayne was about to say goodbye and scuttle off when she noticed the brooch affixed to Rose's cream-colored blouse. Not quite heart-shaped and not quite triangular, it was unusual and very beautiful, encrusted with dark yellowish stones set in what appeared to be several different metals. So captivated was she by the accessory, she found herself involuntarily lifting a hand toward it.

''Your pin is so beautiful, Rose,'' she said, speaking her thoughts aloud. ''That's not topaz, though, is it?'' She glanced up after voicing her question, only to find Rose beaming at her as if Jayne had just paid her the highest compliment in the world.

''No, it's amber,'' her landlady replied. ''Amber and some precious metals.''

Jayne nodded as she touched a fingertip gently to the brooch. ''Someone must have given it to you because you live at 20 Amber Court,'' she said.

Rose smiled again, a bit sadly this time. ''No, I've had this for quite some time now. There's a rather interesting history behind it, actually.''

''You'll have to tell me about it sometime,'' Jayne said, dropping her hand back to her side. ''Sometime when I'm not running so late and having such a crummy day,'' she added when she recalled her current situation. She started to say farewell again, when Rose stopped her.

''Wait,'' her landlady said impulsively. She reached for the pin Jayne had just admired. ''Wear this today,'' she told her tenant with a cryptic little smile, her dark eyes sparkling. ''In the past, it's brought me what you might call 'good luck.' Maybe it will help get you through the rest of the day.''

Jayne expelled a single, humorless chuckle. ''The way this day has started, I have a feeling it's not going to be 'one of those days' so much as it's going to be 'one of those months.'"

"Then wear it all month, if you need to," Rose told her, unfastening the pin from her own blouse and deftly fixing it on Jayne's. With a mischievous little smile she added, "You'll know when it's time to give it back."

"Oh, I couldn't—" Jayne started to object.

"Of course you could," Rose insisted. "There," she said, patting the pin in place. "It doesn't exactly match your outfit, but…"

This time Jayne laughed in earnest. "But then my outfit doesn't exactly match much of anything, does it? Remind me if you see me later today that I have a lot of laundry to do tonight, okay?"

Rose nodded. "Will do, dear."

Jayne turned an eye to the large marble foyer of 20 Amber Court, gazing through the big glass windows at the bleak, gray day outside. Thankfully, the rain had ebbed to a scant drizzle, so she closed her eyes for a moment and willed the scant drizzle to *stay* that way, at least until she reached Colette. And then, with one more halfhearted smile for Rose, she lifted a hand in farewell.

"Good luck today!" her landlady called after her as Jayne hastened toward the front door.

"Thanks!" Jayne called back. "Something tells me I'm going to need it!"

On the other side of Youngsville, Indiana, Erik Randolph wasn't having a particularly good morning, either—though for entirely different reasons.

His own sleep the night before had been restful and dreamless, and he didn't wake up late for work. That would be because, simply put, he had no work for which to wake up late. Oh, he *could* go to work, if he wanted to—it was no secret that his father was holding a VP position for him at Randolph Shipping and Transportation. But it was also no secret that Erik wasn't much suited to work. Work required something like oh…a work ethic, for one thing. A sense of purpose for another. Or even a feeling of duty, or a desire to provide. Erik, it was commonly known, lacked all of those things. Though, it was likewise commonly known, that didn't detract from his charm one iota.

So as it stood now, his hour of waking was completely immaterial, because he would spend today as he spent every day—without any specified activities or agenda in mind. And although he awoke alone, it was because he had *chosen* to awake alone, which was his habit when he spent the night at his house.

That, of course, was because he shared his house with his parents, who were the actual owners of the house. But it wasn't because he feared discovery by said parents that caused Erik to sleep alone—in fact, the Randolph estate was so large and so spacious, one could be sharing it with the United Arab Emirates and not run into anyone for months. It was because Erik just never quite felt comfortable when he was at home. Certainly not comfortable enough to entertain anyone there.

And, anyway, entertaining was his mother's milieu. Erik was far better suited to being entertained.

In any case he didn't like to spend any more time at his parents' estate than was absolutely necessary. He wasn't sure why that was. Certainly the house was beautifully and elegantly decorated, filled with only the best that money could buy—the most luxurious Persian rugs, the finest European antiques, the most exquisite works of art. And certainly his parents and his two younger sisters were all likable enough people, and, as a family, they all got along very well. But there was something missing here. The house lacked…something. Erik wasn't quite sure what. And as a result, he was just never all that comfortable when he was at home.

It was only one of the reasons he spent so much time traveling. The other reason, of course, would be that traveling was just so much fun. And still another reason was that traveling introduced him to so many wonderful people, from so many walks of life, many of whom—the female ones, at any rate—he could share serious, monogamous relationships with, often for days on end. Jetsetting playboy, Erik had concluded a long time ago, was just about the best occupation a man could have.

Still, when he was forced to spend time at home in Youngsville, his parents' estate was more than accommodating. Even at 9:00 a.m., Erik was still clad in his burgundy silk robe and pajama bottoms, stretched out in his king-size bed, the remnants of his breakfast lying neglected now on the silver tray that Bates, the true-blue Randolph butler, had placed beside him an hour ago. And although Erik felt restless and edgy, as if he were on the brink of some vague, life-altering experience, he just couldn't quite muster the energy necessary to pull himself out of bed and go greet that experience head-on.

Really, what was the point? he asked himself, dragging an impatient hand through his overly long, dark hair. It was Monday, it was raining, and he could think of no better way to spend the day than idling about. On top of everything else, it was the first day of September, reminding him that his thirtieth birthday was this month, and that—

Suddenly, Erik understood his restlessness, his edginess, his need to go out and meet that life-altering experience head-on. His thirtieth birthday was two weeks away. Damn. This was just what he needed. He'd dedicated his entire summer to zigzagging around the globe, miring himself in denial over the fact that he would soon be thirty years old. Now, suddenly, there it was, staring him in the face. His thirtieth birthday. Only two weeks away. Fourteen days. That was all he had left to his twenties. Two lousy weeks, fourteen lousy days.

Thirty. He was about to turn thirty. God. When had *that* happened?

It wasn't so much the chronological significance of turning thirty that bothered Erik. Although he'd very much enjoyed his twenties, he didn't consider thirty to be the end of his life. On the contrary, he knew several people who were actually *in* their thirties, and they seemed to be having a surprisingly good time. Many of them even claimed that their thirties were actually *more* enjoyable than their twenties had been.

Not that Erik was quite willing to go that far, but he wasn't all that averse to turning thirty. Or, at least, he wouldn't be. Not if it weren't for the fact that he had a familial obligation he needed to meet soon. Like, by his thirtieth birthday. Like, in two weeks. Like, in fourteen days.

Fourteen lousy days.

Because within fourteen lousy days, Erik had to acquire something very specific in order to claim an inheritance, currently in trust, left to him by his paternal grandfather. Certainly it wouldn't break Erik financially if he declined the inheritance—even without his grandfather's riches, the Randolphs were an exceedingly wealthy family. But Erik's father was adamant that Erik take possession of the estate that the elder Randolph felt was his entitlement.

Damien Randolph, Erik's father, hadn't gotten along particularly well with his own father—in fact, the two men had stopped speaking to each other more than a decade ago. As a result, Grandfather Randolph had split his entire estate—his entire estate of $180 million—between Erik and his two sisters, bypassing his own son entirely.

Of course, it was all contingent on one small stipulation. Because Grandfather Randolph had feared that his grandchildren would never outgrow their notorious playboy and playgirl habits—and for good reason, too, Erik couldn't help but think now—the will stated that in order to claim their share of the estate, each would have to meet that one simple stipulation before his or her thirtieth birthday. Not that Erik's sisters had to worry about it for some time—Celeste was four years younger than Erik, and Maureen was eight years younger than he—so Erik would be the test subject. And because he *did* have a good relationship with his own father, Erik felt rather obligated to meet his grandfather's requirement, and keep in the Randolph family as much of the Randolph wealth as possible. Really, it was the least Erik could do for his father.

And hey, his share *did* amount to sixty million dollars.

It wasn't every day that a man acquired an estate that large and that secure. Grandfather Randolph had been a very wise investor. Once Erik inherited, he'd be set for life. Not that he wasn't already pretty much set right now, but a man could never be too sure.

And had he mentioned that his share did amount to sixty million dollars?

Still, there was that one simple criterion Erik was obligated to meet before he could take control of his inheritance, and he had to meet it by his thirtieth birthday. Really, it wouldn't be all that hard to do. What Erik needed to find could be found almost anywhere. He just hadn't gotten around to looking for one yet, that was all. Now that he only had fourteen days, though, he supposed he should get hopping.

But where to look first, he wondered? Did the Yellow Pages have a listing for what he needed? If he looked under *W,* would he find a section labeled Wives?

Ah, well. If not, no problem. Should he find a shortage of wives in Youngsville, he'd just pick one up somewhere else. Chicago was right across Lake Michigan and was quite a bit larger than his own community. If he couldn't find a wife here in town, then surely they had plenty of potential wives over there.

Besides, it wasn't as if he was going to have to *keep* the wife he found. Grandfather's will stated quite clearly that Erik need only remain married for one year in order to collect his inheritance. He supposed his grandfather thought that a year of settling down would be enough to *keep* Erik settled down. Grandfather Randolph had been so utterly smitten by his own wife that the thought of the marriage ending prematurely had never crossed his mind. The old man had probably thought that Erik need only spend enough time in the company of a good woman to become equally smitten himself.

In a word, Hah.

Not only was Erik much too pragmatic to believe in anything as…as…as *silly*…as romantic love, but he was also much too entrenched in his globe-trotting playboy lifestyle—not to mention he liked that lifestyle way too much—to ever abandon it. Still, he could put it on hold for a year if it meant maintaining the family status quo, couldn't he? Especially if it meant maintaining the family status quo *and* inheriting millions and millions and *millions* of dollars.

Sometimes, he thought, one just had to make a sacrifice.

Content with his decision to start wife hunting that very morning, Erik rose from his bed. As he launched himself into a full-body stretch, he began his mental shopping list, making note of all the qualities he would require in his wife. She would, it went without saying, have to be beautiful. And blond. He'd always liked blondes, so that's what he would look for in his wife. Eye color wasn't especially important, but brown eyes on a blonde were always a good thing, in his opinion. His wife would also have to be reasonably intelligent and fairly articulate. He did so dislike empty conversations. Not that she would need to expound on physics and genetics—au contraire—but knowledge of the current fashion climate would be most welcome.

Let's see, what else…? he wondered.

She would need to be demure, perhaps even coquettish, and it would be preferable if she had a mild disposition. She should be a free thinker, but open to suggestions, and she would have to have some working knowledge of the social register, not to mention the ins and outs of proper etiquette. Erik attended a lot of parties, and he expected his wife to be as comfortable in such settings as he was himself. She'd need to have a sense of style, a love of fine wine, an appreciation for the arts...

He really should start writing this down, he thought. So much to do, so little time.

A rousing clap of thunder reminded him that he would be doing it in less-than-agreeable weather, too. Still, that would only add to the challenge, wouldn't it? And Erik did appreciate challenges. Provided, of course, they weren't *too* challenging.

Then again, what could possibly be challenging about finding a wife? He was one of Youngsville's most eligible bachelors. He'd read that himself in the Sunday magazine section of the *Youngsville Gazette* not too long ago. Therefore, it must be true. He was practically a local celebrity. Any woman would jump at the chance to be his wife. He had everything to offer—good looks, wry wit, cheerful disposition, good finances, a nice home. All right, so that last was actually not his, in name. That was a minor technicality. It was still a nice part of his personal package. In fact, the only thing Erik could think of that he lacked as a potential suitor was—

A ring. An engagement ring. He'd certainly need one of those if he was going to attract the right woman. A wife would first have to be a fiancée, and he couldn't have a fiancée without the proper ring. Of course, only the finest ring would be suitable for Erik Randolph's future wife. And everyone in Youngsville, Indiana, knew where you went if you wanted to purchase the best in jewelry.

Colette, Inc.

That would be Erik's first stop on his wife-hunting safari today, he decided. He'd find just the right ring, one that was beautiful without being showy, exquisite without being ostentatious, elegant without being plain. Much like the woman he hoped to find, he couldn't helping thinking whimsically.

Yes, Colette, he was certain, would have exactly what he was looking for.

Two

By the time Jayne entered Colette Jewelers on Hammond Street, she was as wet and limp and bedraggled as a street urchin—a street urchin who had just walked eight blocks in a raging downpour, without an umbrella to shelter her from the storm. Because as soon as she had covered the first two blocks between Amber Court and Colette, the skies had opened up and dumped veritable buckets of rain down on Youngsville. It had effectively put an end to the scant drizzle Jayne had hoped would accompany her to work and had begun a deluge of biblical proportions. Not even the awnings had been able to save her after that. So now, in addition to being mismatched, she was completely wet and limp and bedraggled.

And cold, too, because the air-conditioning in the store was blasting full speed ahead, despite the inclement weather, and the chill breeze against her wet flesh and clothing raised goose bumps on her goose bumps. Although the situation was beginning to look dire, Jayne told herself to buck up. Because, after all, things couldn't possibly get any worse, could they?

Belatedly she realized that thinking such a thing completely jinxed her. Because where she normally arrived at work to find the shop in its empty, preopening state—a condition that would have afforded her an opportunity to at least *try* and tidy herself up before anyone saw her—today, the Colette Jewelry showroom played host to a good half dozen of Jayne's co-workers, who were in the shop because today was Colette employee discount day.

Oh, yes. The day was definitely going to get worse. Before it was over, Jayne, looking as bad as she had ever looked in her life, was bound to run into every last person who worked for the company. Because every last person who worked for the company worked in that very building, and virtually all of them took advantage of their twice-yearly employee discount days.

The building that housed Colette, Inc. was a massive, eight-story brick construction that comprised one full city block, located virtually at the center of Youngsville. A large showroom and shop took up the entirety of the first floor, and the corporate offices commanded the remainder of the building. The furnishings, overall, were quite luxuriant, regardless of where one might find oneself in the establishment. Rich jewel tones of varying hues darkened the walls, upon which were hung priceless works of art. Oriental rugs of equally dramatic color and design spanned the hardwood floors, and expensive pieces of sculpture filled all the spaces that weren't used up in the display of jewelry. Bright track lighting overhead made everything—especially the finely cut gems—sparkle like, well, finely cut gems.

In addition to the offices upstairs, the building housed a formal dining room for executives and an open cafeteria for the other employees. Jayne had never seen the former, but she spent most of her lunch hours in the latter. It, too, was elegantly appointed, and furnished in much the same way as the rest of the building. She assumed the executive dining room was likewise decorated.

But her favorite place in the Colette building—besides the jewelry showroom and shop, both of which she found utterly enchanting—was the lobby of the corporate offices on the second floor, where she'd gone to meet some of her co-workers on one or two occasions. Because in that lobby was the most exquisite piece of jewelry Jayne had ever seen—a single rose crafted of rubies and diamonds and emeralds. She wasn't sure what the history was behind the piece, and she'd never asked anyone at Colette. She only knew that it was lovely, and Jayne, like so many people who worked for the company, simply adored beautiful things.

Which was another reason why she felt so out of place this morning. Beautiful, she knew, was the last thing she looked today. And her co-workers mingling about the store now seemed to agree, because she could see them biting back smiles and stifling chuckles when they took in her appearance.

So much for things not getting any worse, she thought morosely. From here on out, she wasn't about to form any more observations on the state of her day. It could only lead to trouble.

She was much relieved to discover that a trio of employees standing nearest the "New Designs" showcase were women she knew well. Because, like Jayne, they lived at 20 Amber Court. And all three had obviously arrived at work on time today, because none of them resembled a limp, bedraggled street urchin in any way, shape or form—oh, no. Each of them was very well put together, sartorially speaking. Not to mention quite dry.

Lila Maxwell lived on the third floor of Jayne's apartment building and worked on the fourth floor of Colette. She was an administrative assistant to Nicholas Camden, a vice president of the company, in charge of overseas marketing. Lila was dressed today as she always was—

for success. And lots of it. Her long, dark-blond hair shone like finely tempered bronze beneath the halogen lights of the showroom, offsetting her dark-brown eyes as if they were bittersweet chocolate. Her charcoal suit was stylishly cut, hugging her curves with much affection.

She was chatting in low tones with two of Jayne's other neighbors and co-workers—Meredith Blair, who was a jewelry designer for Colette, and Sylvie Bennett, who worked as a marketing manager for the company. Meredith, as always, was dressed in her usual, nondescript style, her long beige skirt and shapeless ivory sweater doing nothing to enhance what could be a very curvy figure and truly spectacular facial features, if Meredith would only give herself a chance. Her long, reddish-brown, curly hair was, as usual, pulled tersely away from her face, held in place with a barrette that was as nondescript as her clothing.

Although she'd only known Meredith for a month, Jayne recognized her neighbor's low self-esteem and knew Meredith went out of her way to downplay her appearance in an effort to make herself invisible. Which wasn't going to work much longer, as far as Jayne was concerned, because Meredith designed some of the most beautiful jewelry Jayne had ever seen. She was sure to go far in the business. People were going to start noticing her soon. And then what would Meredith do?

Not that Jayne was in any position to criticize the other woman's style...or lack thereof. At least Meredith's clothing matched. And was dry. Glancing down at her own questionable appearance again, Jayne found herself wishing *she* could be invisible—at least for today.

Sylvie, on the other hand, despite the quiet, obviously serious conversation in which the three women were engaged, appeared to be her usual feisty self. Her expression was more intense than the other women's, as if she were gearing up for battle. Her stark black curls were swept back at her nape, her dark-brown eyes flashed fire. Cou-

pled with her deep burgundy power suit, she appeared a
formidable force indeed.

Doing her best not to make wet, squishy sounds as she
walked, Jayne strode toward the group. But the three
women were so wrapped up in their conversation that they
didn't even notice her approach. Not until Jayne greeted
them.

"G-g-g-good m-m-m-morning," she said through chattering teeth as she halted, resigned to her fate. "L-l-l-
lovely m-m-m-morning, is-s-sn't it-t-t-t?"

The three women turned to her at once, opening their
mouths to reply. But when they got a collective look at
her, they hesitated. For one taut moment no one said a
word. Then all three of her neighbors responded in unison.

"Jayne, if I'd known you were walking today, I would
have offered you a lift," Sylvie told her.

"I just made it in myself before the skies opened up,"
Meredith added.

"You could have taken the bus with me, you know,"
Lila threw in for good measure.

Jayne lifted a hand to stop the flow of commentary.
After all, it wasn't as if they were telling her anything she
didn't already know. "I overslept, so I was running late
and missed the bus," she said. "Thanks for the offer of
a lift, Sylvie, but I'm sure I missed you, too. Besides, it
was barely drizzling when I left home. I thought the buildings would shelter me well enough. I should have known
better. It's definitely going to be one of those days—I can
feel it in my bones."

Automatically, she reached for the brooch Rose Carson
had pinned to her blouse earlier. "I did run into Rose,
though, before I left. She insisted I wear this pin." Jayne
smiled wryly as her friends leaned in for a closer look.
"She said it would bring me good luck, but I don't think
anything can improve this day. Things are only going to
get worse from here. Mark my words."

There, she thought. By saying that she expected the

worst, surely things would get better. Then she immediately cursed herself, because in supposing things would get better, she had surely just jinxed herself *again*. And on top of just jinxing herself again, she'd just tried to reverse-psychology fate. And that, she was certain, was bound to be a major metaphysical no-no.

Sure enough, in response to her remark, all three of her friends exchanged curious—and clearly very anxious—glances, and Jayne got the distinct impression that things were indeed about to get worse. Again.

"What?" she demanded, her stomach clenching nervously in response to their obvious worry. "What's wrong?"

For a moment she didn't think any of them would answer her. Then, finally, Lila hastily replied, "It's just a rumor."

Oh, that didn't sound good *at all,* Jayne thought. And, just like that, all thoughts of her current state of personal discomfort immediately fled to the back of her brain. "What's just a rumor?" she asked.

This time it was Sylvie who answered. "It's about Colette," she said simply.

"What about it?" Jayne asked.

"Well," Sylvie began again, "it's like Lila said—just a rumor."

Jayne switched her gaze from one woman to the other and back again. "But what, exactly, is *it?*" she demanded more frantically. "What's wrong? Why do you all look like you're expecting the end of the world?"

"It's a hostile takeover of the company," Meredith blurted out with an artist's kind of spontaneity.

"A hostile takeover?" Jayne echoed. "What do you mean a hostile takeover? Why would anyone want to hostilely take over Colette, Inc.? It's such a nice company."

"That's why someone wants to take it over," Meredith pointed out. "Word has it that someone—and nobody seems to know who—is buying up shares of Colette in an effort to have controlling interest.''

''But that won't affect us, will it?'' Jayne asked hopefully—and probably naively, she couldn't help thinking.

''Well, there is that pesky business of our jobs,'' Sylvie said mildly. ''Hostile takeovers have a tendency to lead to downsizing, and downsizing has a tendency to cause unemployment. Oh, but hey, other than that…''

''But…but…but…'' Jayne sputtered. Unfortunately she had no idea what to say.

''Look, there's no need to panic,'' Lila said emphatically. ''It's just a rumor.''

But rumors were almost always at least grounded in truth, Jayne thought. And this one was doubtless no different. ''What happens if Colette is taken over?'' she asked. ''Hostilely or not? What *will* happen to our jobs?''

Jayne was completely ignorant when it came to all things corporate related. Although she genuinely enjoyed her job as a salesclerk, she really wasn't much interested with the workings of the business as a whole. Her familiarity with Colette, Inc., was limited to the history of the company that was common knowledge in Youngsville, what she'd heard from her neighbor co-workers, and what she'd learned herself in employee training a month ago. About how Abraham Colette, whose family had been in the jewelry business in Paris for generations, came to Youngsville from France in 1902 to start over. About how he married a local girl named Teresa and started his own branch of the company, which soon became known for having the most precious of precious gems in the most exquisite of settings.

Even during the Depression, Colette, Inc., had flourished, thanks to Carl Colette, Abraham and Teresa's son, who naturally followed in his father's footsteps, and had had the foresight to bring in investors a decade earlier. As a result, over the years, Colette had become known nationwide, even worldwide, for its unique and elegant pieces, pieces created by only the finest designers and craftspeople.

Which, Jayne thought further, probably went a long way toward explaining this hostile takeover business.

"What will happen to our jobs if someone takes over the company?" she asked again when no one offered a reply—which wasn't exactly reassuring. "I can't lose this job," she said further. "I was lucky to get it in the first place, and that was only because Rose put in a good word for me. I'm not trained to do anything. I'd never find something else that pays as well as this. I need my commissions," she added, swallowing the hysteria she heard bubbling up in her words. "I have a brother and sister to put through college."

"Look, everybody, just relax," Lila said, "it's only a rumor, okay? There's no need for us to go off half-cocked. Everything is probably going to be fine." She glanced down at her watch. "The store's going to be opening in a half hour, Jayne," she said. "And you've got a lot of employees in here who want to make purchases. You and Amy better get on the stick if you want to open on time this morning."

"Right," Jayne said, pushing to the back of her mind for now—well, almost to the back of her mind, anyway—all thoughts of hostile takeovers. "Right," she said again, steeling herself. Work—an excessive amount of it—was exactly what she needed right now, she told herself. Something to take her mind off just how badly her morning…her week…her month had begun.

It can't possibly get any worse, she told herself again. And this time she didn't worry about jinxing herself or offending fate by doing so. Because for the first time in her life Jayne was confident that that was true. Things couldn't get any worse from here. No way. Whatever else the day ahead held, it was only going to be better.

It would be, she promised herself.

It would.

* * *

By mid-afternoon, Erik Randolph wasn't feeling quite
as optimistic about his marital prospects as he had upon
waking that morning. For one thing, the gloomy weather,
which traditionally boded ill, anyway, had dampened his
mood—so to speak. But what had dampened his mood
even more was the fact that, astonishingly, of the three
women to whom he had proposed marriage so far today,
none had accepted his offer. None. Talk about boding
ill…

The first of those women had been his sister, Celeste's,
best friend, Marianne, who was enjoying a few days with
Celeste at the Randolph estate before returning to graduate
school. Erik had known her for years, of course, and rather
liked her, even if he didn't know her all that well. Still,
he had thought it reasonable that she might warm to his
offer of marriage, however temporary, because Celeste
had confided to him recently that Marianne had a huge
crush on him.

Well, all right, so maybe Celeste's revelation hadn't
been all *that* recent. Maybe it had been more than a decade ago, when Marianne was eleven, but that was beside
the point. Erik had still been surprised when she declined,
citing a desire to return to her studies. Her tuition for the
fall semester, she had explained, had already been paid in
full.

Fine, then, Erik had thought. On to prospect number
two: Diana, the daughter of the Randolphs' housekeeper,
Mrs. Martin. Erik had known Diana for ages, too, seeing
as how Mr. and Mrs. Martin had come to work for his
family when he was still in high school. But for some
reason Diana hadn't seemed to think Erik was serious
about his offer of marriage, had simply giggled riotously
when he'd outlined his proposal, and had kept giggling
no matter how hard he had insisted that he was, in fact,
quite serious. Finally, wiping tears from her eyes—and
still giggling—Diana had declined, thanked him, anyway,

and headed off to work. He had heard her giggling all the way down the hall.

Erik's third rejection had come only moments ago, from the waitress at Crystal's on Marion Street, an upscale eatery that claimed one of Indiana's only Cordon Bleu trained chefs. And although said waitress hadn't seemed to take his suggestion quite as lightly as the other women had, she had ultimately declined due to a previous engagement—literally. She'd told Erik she felt obliged to marry her fiancé the following month.

Nevertheless, he held firm in his conviction that his search for a wife would pan out—today. He was even so sure of that, that he had dressed in his best suit, a Hugo Boss charcoal pinstripe, and a Valentino silk necktie with an elegant geometric design, knowing that such an outfit would make an impression. Now, as he approached Colette Jewelry, Erik felt more than optimistic that he was on the right track. Finding a wife with whom he could enjoy wedded bliss for a full year, he was certain, would be a piece of wedding cake.

The whimsical thought made him smile as he pushed open the door to Colette Jewelry and strode into the main showroom. He'd been in the store many times over the years, of course, to purchase baubles for his feminine companions. But where he normally turned left, toward the specialty pieces, now Erik went right, toward the wedding and engagement displays. As he strode in that direction, he overheard two women chatting, and glanced up to see that two of Colette's salesclerks were busily rearranging one of the wedding-and-engagement showcases.

Perfect, he thought. Whatever new inventory the women were putting out, that was what he wanted. He was known for being on the cutting edge of, well, just about everything. So if there was something new happening in engagement rings, Erik Randolph wanted to know about it.

The two salesclerks had their heads bowed in soft conversation, he noted as he drew nearer, presumably about the display they were in the process of putting together. So rapt was their concentration on their conversation, in fact, that they didn't even notice Erik's approach. He was about to clear his throat to make his presence known— after all, this was most uncommon at Colette, to be over- looked by the sales staff—when one of the women's re- marks made him hesitate.

"I don't know what I'll do if there is a hostile take- over," said the woman closest to him, a redhead. "If Co- lette is gobbled up by a rival company, I could end up unemployed. Without this job, I can't possibly pay for Charlie and Chloe's tuition and living expenses."

"It's a bad situation all around," the other clerk, a bru- nette, agreed. "But it's just a rumor, Jayne. Don't borrow trouble."

"I can't help it, Amy," the woman identified as Jayne replied quietly, soberly. "I keep worrying about what would happen to Charlie and Chloe—and to me, too, for that matter—if I lose my job. I'm barely making ends meet as it is."

"Maybe you could go on that *Millionaire* question-and- answer show," the brunette called Amy said lightly, clearly joking. "You're pretty good with trivia. Or, better still, maybe they'll have another one of those shows about marrying a multimillionaire, and you could go on that."

"Oh, yeah," Jayne, the redheaded salesclerk, agreed with a chuckle. "Even though that one didn't *quite* turn out the way they planned," she added, "I'm sure that would solve all of *my* problems. Yeah, I'll just go out and find myself a multimillionaire to marry, if only momen- tarily. Because I'd probably at least wind up with some nice parting gifts, right?"

Erik snapped his mouth shut at hearing both the remark and the woman's laughter. Because the first had been a comment that was simply too serendipitous for words, and the second had been a sound that was simply too musical to ignore. Whoever the woman was, she had a wonderful laugh, one that made something pop and fizz and settle in a warm place very close to Erik's heart.

And what an interesting sensation that was, too.

When she glanced up to find Erik looking at her, he noted that she also had a charming way of blushing. Well, my, my, my. For such a gloomy day, things sure were brightening up all of a sudden.

"Hello," the redhead said softly, her voice as pleasant as her laughter had been. "Can I help you?"

Erik smiled. Oh, if she only knew.

What was it he had been thinking he required in a wife? he asked himself again as he gazed upon the redhead named Jayne. Oh, yes. First and foremost, she would have to be beautiful.

He considered the salesclerk behind the counter again, taking in the wide eyes, the fair complexion, the smattering of freckles, and the…*unusual* wardrobe that appeared to be kind of…damp?

We-ell, he thought, she *was* kind of cute. In a soggy, mismatched, ragamuffin sort of way.

"Actually, Miss…" he began, deliberately leading.

"Pembroke," she told him. Then she asked her fateful question once again. "Can I help you?"

Erik's smile fell some when he recalled that he'd also been thinking earlier that he wanted his future wife to be blond. And preferably brown-eyed, as well. He noted the pale-red hair again and thought, Fine. So she was strawberry blond. It was close enough. And although her eyes were a striking lavender color, he'd never said they absolutely *had* to be brown, had he? No, he had not. He'd simply indicated that it would be preferable, that was all. Let it never be said that Erik Randolph couldn't make compromises. Lavender eyes it would be.

"As a matter of fact, you can help me," he told her. "I'm looking for something very specific."

She smiled at him, and he decided then that he liked

her smile very much. That was going to be so helpful in the coming year.

"Well, you've come to the right place," she told him.

"Oh, I don't doubt that for a moment," he assured her, recalling that the third item on his list of wifely requirements had been reasonable intelligence and a fair amount of articulation. Even if the woman behind the counter had barely spoken two dozen words so far, she did seem to at least have the capacity for both.

Still, he had wanted the future Mrs. Randolph to be knowledgeable about current fashion trends, hadn't he? he further reminded himself. And, noting the woman's outfit once more—however reluctantly—there was no way he could make excuses for her there, could he?

Unless, of course, she was way *ahead* of Erik in fashion sense, he told himself. Which, although unlikely, was certainly possible. Who knew? Maybe a month from now, everyone who was anyone in Youngsville would be wearing burnt orange and raspberry with chartreuse accessories. Hey, it could happen. After all, bell-bottoms and fringed vests were back in style, weren't they?

He mentally tallied the rest of his wife to-do list. A demure and mild disposition had been desirable, he remembered thinking, which, clearly, this woman had. And he'd wanted his wife to be a free thinker, too. Taking in her outfit again, he realized that wasn't going to be a character trait she lacked *at all*. A knowledge of the social register—well, they could study together, he told himself—and an appreciation for the arts. Again, more studying might be required.

Ah, well. No one was perfect, he reminded himself. And they would be spending a year together, so all this studying would give them something to occupy their time. Jayne the salesclerk did, at least, seem to claim the majority of the desirable traits Erik required in a wife.

Which was good, because he decided in that moment that she was exactly the woman he needed. She had just stated quite clearly that marriage to money—temporarily, no less—would solve all of her problems. And having a woman married to his money—temporarily, no less—would solve all of Erik's problems, too. He needed a wife. She needed money. Their encounter this afternoon, clearly, was fate. It was providence. It was kismet. It was destiny.

It was perfect.

He smiled again when he realized just how well this was going to work out. Obviously, the two of them were meant for each other. Now all he had to do was convince Jayne—what was her last name again?—of that, too.

"I apologize for your having to wait," she said, just as the silence was beginning to stretch taut. "We didn't mean to ignore you. We just didn't hear you come in."

"Oh, no harm done," he assured her. "In fact, I found your conversation to be quite intriguing."

Jayne's eyes widened in obvious concern. "Ah…" she began eloquently. "You mean that, um, that stuff about a hostile takeover? Oh, that was all totally false."

"Yeah," her co-worker quickly agreed, with a very adamant nod. "That was a complete fabrication. We were just playing What-if."

Jayne nodded again. "I mean, who'd want to hostilely take over Colette, you know? It's unthinkable."

"I couldn't care less about a takeover," Erik said amiably, honestly. "Hostile or otherwise. That wasn't the part of your conversation that I found intriguing."

The two women exchanged glances, then Jayne directed her attention back to him. "Oh," she said softly.

Erik, in turn, directed his attention to the brunette. "Do you mind?" he said politely. "I think Miss…"

"Pembroke," redheaded Jayne repeated.

"Miss Pembroke, here," he continued, "can see to my needs."

The brunette gaped softly at his less-than-subtle dismissal, but she nodded and strode toward another jewelry case. Nevertheless, her watchfulness, Erik noted, didn't stray far from her colleague. Which he supposed was understandable. You never knew what kind of oddball was going to stumble in from the street and make some bizarre, unacceptable suggestion.

He turned to look again at Jayne Pembroke—*Pembroke,* he reminded himself firmly, lest he forget again; it really wouldn't do to forget one's fiancée's name, would it? *Pembroke, Pembroke, Pembroke*—calling up the most disarming smile in his ample arsenal. "No, it wasn't the takeover part of your conversation that was so intriguing," he said again. "It was the part about you marrying a multimillionaire."

Her expression, he noted, changed not one iota, save an almost imperceptible arching of one eyebrow. So he had no idea how to gauge her reaction. Very quietly she replied, "Oh." Nothing more. Just *Oh.*

So Erik plunged onward. "Because you see, I myself happen to be a multimillionaire," he told her with much equanimity.

"Oh," she said again. And again her expression reflected nothing of what she might be thinking.

Erik took it to be a good sign. Then again, he took most things, short of natural disaster, to be good signs. That was just the kind of man he was.

"Or, at least, I *will* be a multimillionaire," he clarified pleasantly. "Once I get married, I mean."

Jayne Pembroke's expression cleared then, making her look…relieved? Maybe this was going to be easier than he'd anticipated.

"So you've come in to buy an engagement ring for your intended," she said, her smile returning.

"Yes," he agreed happily. "That's it exactly. A ring. A fiancée—and, hence, a wife—will, after all, expect a ring, won't she? Two rings, actually. One to signify the engagement and one to signify the marriage. Which," he added, "when you get right down to it, is a damned nice gift, considering the fact that she will only be my wife for one year.''

Now Jayne's smile fell again, and her expression grew puzzled. ''One year?'' she echoed, sounding disappointed.

''Well, you can't expect me to stay married any longer than is necessary, can you?'' Erik asked, fighting a twinge of indignation. Honestly. They weren't even married yet, and already she was finding fault with him. ''I mean, I do have other obligations, you know.''

Now Jayne opened her mouth to speak, but no words emerged.

''Not that my wife will have to worry,'' he said, jacking up the wattage on his smile. ''Because it goes without saying that, after we go our separate ways, she will end up with some—'' he wiggled his eyebrows meaningfully ''—lovely parting gifts.''

Now Jayne, he noted, was looking at him as if she had just discovered he'd escaped from a hospital for the criminally insane. Hmmm, he thought. Perhaps they weren't quite on the same wavelength as he had assumed they were. Perhaps he wasn't going about this the best way he could be going about it. Perhaps he wasn't making himself as clear as he could be making himself.

So Erik straightened to his full six feet, tossed his head in a way that he'd been told by several women was quite boyish and charming, brushed his dark hair back from his forehead, and smiled what he liked to think was his rogue's smile. ''What I'm trying to say, Miss Pembroke,'' he began in his most enchanting tone of voice, ''is...will you marry me?''

Three

Jayne eyed the man standing on the other side of the counter very cautiously, and debated for a full fifteen seconds whether or not she should stomp her foot down—hard—on the alarm button located conveniently behind the jewelry showcase. He didn't *look* like a psychotic, crazed, homicidal maniac. In fact, she thought upon further consideration of his charmingly disheveled dark hair and kind, bittersweet-chocolate brown eyes, he was actually kind of cute. But one could never tell these days. Ultimately, being the kind of woman that she was, she decided to give him the benefit of the doubt.

And also, being the kind of woman that she was, she decided to speak slowly and not make any sudden moves.

"Uuummm," she began, stringing the single syllable out over several time zones. "That's uh…" She cleared her throat indelicately and tried again. "That's really nice of you to ask, Mr. um…"

The potentially psychotic, crazed, homicidal—but kind

of cute—maniac closed his eyes in what appeared to be genuine embarrassment, pressed his fingertips lightly against his forehead, made a soft tsking sound and looked very sheepish.

"I'm sorry," he said. "I haven't even introduced myself, have I? I can't imagine what you must be thinking of me, proposing this way when I haven't even told you who I am." He opened his eyes again and extended his hand toward her. "Erik Randolph," he said by way of an introduction.

Oh, well, that explained everything, Jayne thought as relief coursed through her. Even though she had only moved into 20 Amber Court a month ago, she had grown up in Youngsville, so she knew all about the Randolph family. They were like local royalty. They kept the society pages of the *Youngsville Gazette* in business. The Randolphs were purported to be one of the wealthiest families in the state of Indiana. And they were rumored to be one of the most eccentric families in the state, too, from what Jayne had heard and read.

If Erik, here, was any indication, the eccentricity thing was no rumor at all.

Still, from all accounts the Randolphs were harmless. They were, in fact, gregarious, magnanimous people, known throughout several states for their wealth, their prominence, their numerous and varied social causes and their limitless philanthropy. But never had she heard anyone refer to any of the Randolphs as psychotic, crazed *or* homicidal. Which, naturally, was quite a relief.

Nevertheless, she still felt a bit cautious as she extended her own hand and shook his. Then he grinned as he gripped her fingers firmly—but not homicidally or maniacally—and Jayne relaxed.

"Mr. Randolph," she said, feeling glad that she had hesitated setting off the alarm. "It's lovely to meet you," she added, uncertain what else to say. After all, she couldn't very well tell him she accepted his proposal, could she? As an afterthought she added, "I've heard so much about you."

He nodded amiably, as if he was in no way surprised to hear her say this. "All good things, I hope."

"Oh, yes," she assured him. "From all reports, you're quite the charmer." *And also quite the odd duck,* she added to herself.

"Well then, you have me at a disadvantage," he told her, still smiling, still relaxing her. "Because I'm afraid I know little about you. Other than the fact that you, too, appear to be quite charming. And that you are in need of a wealthy husband. Which," he hurried on before she had a chance to contradict him, "works out perfectly, because I, in addition to being wealthy, am in need of a wife."

Oh, dear, Jayne thought. They were back to that, were they? Very diplomatically she said, "Well, I wish you luck in your search, and I'll be happy to assist you in finding the perfect ring to present to your fiancée. But I couldn't possibly accept your offer myself." She smiled, too, what she hoped was a kind—and in no way homicidal-mania-provoking, just in case—smile. "Even if I know *of* you, I don't *know* you. So I really couldn't accept your proposal. Not that I'm not flattered," she hastened to add for good measure. "Now about that ring," she hurried on further. "Personally, I think the square-cut diamonds are just so lovely, especially in the white-gold setting, and very—"

But Erik Randolph was not to be dissuaded that easily. "No, no, no," he interrupted her gently. "You don't understand. It isn't necessary for my wife to know me."

Jayne arched her brows curiously. *Eccentric,* she thought, really wasn't an accurate word for Erik Randolph. No, she was beginning to think the term *delusional* might better describe him. "Oh?" she said.

He nodded knowingly. "The marriage will be in name only," he told her. "Oh, certainly, we'll have to live together, to fulfill the terms of the agreement, but that won't be a problem.''

Wondering what it was that made her prolong this discussion, Jayne nevertheless asked, "Um, no?"

"Certainly not.''

Well, naturally, a *man* would think that way, she thought. Especially a delusional—oops, she meant *eccentric,* of course—man like Erik Randolph. But Jayne kept the observation to herself and, in an effort to conclude this part of their dialogue and move on to the next, said instead, ''Well, I'm sure you'll find the right woman soon. Now then, we have a very good selection of square-cut solitaires that you might find—''

Before she had a chance to direct his attention to the jewelry showcase, however, Erik interrupted her again. ''Oh, I believe I've already found the right woman,'' he said.

Oh, Jayne didn't *think* so. She met his gaze again— really, he did have the most beautiful brown eyes, thickly lashed and so dark she could scarcely see where the irises ended and the pupils began and…and…and…

And what was it they had been talking about? she wondered vaguely. Oh, yes. He had asked her to marry him, and she was trying to explain why she couldn't.

It was all coming back to her now.

''Yes, well, as I said,'' she tried again, ''I'm very flattered that you would ask, Mr. Randolph, but I really can't marry you. Truly, I can't. I'm afraid I decided a long time ago that before I married a man, I wanted to, well, know him. And being in love with him would be even more helpful. But thank you, anyway. Now about that ring for your intended, whoever she might turn out to be…''

Jayne tried once more to turn his attention to the array of sparkling diamond rings that lay in the glass case between them. But Erik Randolph would have none of it. Instead of focusing his attention on the exquisite gems, he eyed Jayne with much consideration and interest.

"You don't think I'm serious, do you?" he asked.

Actually, Jayne suspected he *was* serious. Which was entirely the problem. Aloud, however, she only said, "Well, can you blame me?"

"I suppose it does make sense that you would draw such a conclusion," he conceded. "How often do strangers come in from the street and propose marriage, right?"

"I think I can safely say that you're my first."

For some reason, he smiled *very* suggestively at that. Then, "Well, I assure you, Jayne Pembroke, that I am completely serious. I want you to marry me."

"You fell in love with me at first sight, is that it?" she asked playfully.

"Don't be silly," he countered. "I don't even know you."

"Oh."

"Besides, I don't believe in love at first sight. Or any sight, for that matter." Before Jayne could comment on that—not that she had any idea what to say—he continued, "As I said, the marriage I'm proposing would be in name only. A marriage of convenience, if you will. I'll be turning thirty soon. And my grandfather, a lovable old rogue, I assure you, decided a long time ago that I should be married by the time I turn thirty. In fact, he's blackmailing me into it."

"Can't you talk to him? Explain that you don't want to get married?"

"No," Erik said. "I can't."

"Why not?"

"He's dead, you see."

"Oh. I'm sorry."

Erik Randolph looked genuinely bereft as he said, "I am, too. But he was a lovable old rogue, as I said, and I do believe he only wanted what he thought was best for me."

"And what did he think was best for you?"

"The love of a good woman," Erik replied promptly.

"Oh," Jayne said, smiling in spite of the strange situation. "Oh, that's so sweet."

"And also one-third of his $180 million-dollar estate," Erik added, in as matter-of-fact a tone as Jayne had ever heard.

Then his words hit her, and her mouth dropped open slightly, an incredulous little gasp of air escaping. "One-third of…of…of…"

"Sixty million dollars is what it boils down to." Erik did the math for her, in that same matter-of-fact tone, by golly, when Jayne wasn't quite able to calculate—or enunciate—the amount herself.

"Well," she finally got out. "Well. Well, gee. Well, that's pretty doggone good," she conceded with much understatement.

Erik nodded, apparently oblivious to her complete astonishment, as if everyone came into $60 million because their lovable rogue of a grandfather willed it to them. "Unfortunately," he said, "Grandfather Randolph insisted on one small stipulation before I could inherit. That I be married. By the time I'm thirty."

"And you'll be thirty soon," Jayne echoed his earlier sentiment.

He nodded again. "Very soon. In two weeks, to be precise."

This time Jayne's jaw dropped a lot more, and the gasp of incredulous breath that escaped was more like a great big whoosh of air. *"Two weeks?"* she repeated.

He nodded once more.

"You expect to find a woman who'll marry you in two weeks' time?"

He eyed her with much concern. "Do you think that's unreasonable?"

Jayne couldn't believe what she was hearing. He honestly seemed to think he could just waltz right in off the street and ask a woman to marry him, just because he would be coming into $60 million as a result. Then again, she thought, there were probably lots of women out there who would do just that. Especially once they got a look at Erik Randolph in his expertly tailored dark suit, with his silky, dark-brown hair and puppy dog brown eyes and full mouth that was just made for kissing and—

Well, suffice it to say that there were probably plenty of women who would take him up on his offer. Women other than Jayne Pembroke, anyway.

"Um, look," she said, striving for a polite way to tell him he was nuts. "I'm really flattered," she said again, "and I wish you well in your search, and I hope you enjoy your…" she swallowed with some difficulty before finally getting out "—$60 million. But I'm not the woman you need, truly."

He eyed her intently for a moment, saying nothing. Then he asked, "Would you at least let me take you to dinner tonight?"

Jayne shook her head. But she was surprised at how reluctant she felt when she told him, "No, I'm afraid not. Thank you."

"Oh, please," he said. "I can explain things better, and you might change your mind. Plus, it would give you *hours* to get to know me."

She couldn't quite prevent the smile that curled her lips in response to both his cajoling and his own earnest grin. "No, really," she told him. But she could feel her conviction slipping, and she was certain that Erik detected it, too, because his smile grew broader still.

"And once you get to know me," he added, "you'll discover just how charming and irresistible—not to mention what a great catch—I am."

Jayne had no idea why, but she found herself wanting to say yes to his offer. Not the marriage offer, of course— that would be silly—but the dinner offer. Had he been another man who had wandered in off the street and flirted with her, one who *wasn't* rumored to be eccentric, and one who *hadn't* just proposed marriage to a total stranger, she might very well have given his invitation serious consideration. He *was* kind of charming and irresistible, after all. Not to mention cute. And he was seeming less and less like a psychotic, crazed homicidal maniac with every passing moment.

So that was a definite plus.

"I'm not sure it would be a good idea," she said halfheartedly. She told herself she was trying to let him down easily. But she knew she was really only stalling for time, because she discovered then that—surprise, surprise—she really wanted to accept his invitation.

Erik, however, still clearly picking up on her uncertainty, pressed, "Look, if you're worried about my intentions, you don't have to tell me where you live. You can meet me somewhere."

"Gee, I don't know…"

"And I'll let you pick the restaurant."

"But…"

"And choose the time."

"It's just that…"

"Please, Jayne," he said. "You may well be my only hope. And once I explain the situation to you, you might change your mind."

She wasn't sure how she should take that first part of his statement, whether being his only hope was a good thing or a bad thing. But she was absolutely certain about the last part of his statement—there was no way she would change her mind, no matter how well she understood what he termed "the situation."

Still, what would it hurt to have dinner with him? she thought. It wasn't as though she planned to do anything else this evening. Oh, wait a minute. Yes, she did have plans, she suddenly remembered. She planned to do laundry.

Dinner with Erik was definitely looking better now.

"It will all make sense to you when I explain," he promised, swaying her further.

Jayne gazed into his eyes, nearly losing herself in their dark-brown depths. He was allowing her to call all the shots, letting her set up their date—or whatever it was—in any way that would make her feel safe and comfortable. Just because he had a reputation for being eccentric, that was no reason to say no, was it? she asked herself. Were he any other charming, irresistible and cute—did she mention cute?—man asking her out to dinner under the same circumstances, she'd probably say yes.

And he was *awfully* cute.

"Look, I'll tell you what," Erik said when she still didn't reply one way or the other to his invitation. "J.J.'s Deli is right up the street. What time do you get off from work?"

"Five," Jayne said before she could stop herself.

He smiled. "Fine. I'll be at J.J.'s Deli at seven o'clock tonight. If you decide to come, wonderful. If you decide not to…"

His voice trailed off, and she was surprised at the depth of disappointment she heard in it.

"If you decide not to," he said again, sighing heavily, "well, I guess I'll survive. Somehow."

She smiled back at him, but still couldn't quite bring herself to accept.

"But I think, Jayne, that if you do decide to come, we could have a very nice time, and a very interesting conversation. Seven o'clock," he repeated. "J.J.'s Deli. I hope you'll come."

And then Erik Randolph, eccentric, cute guy, potential multimillionaire, spun around and exited Colette without a backward glance.

And all Jayne could do was shake her head in mystification, and wonder what on earth had just happened.

Shortly after arriving home at five-thirty that evening—stumbling over Mojo as she did, because the blasted cat was, as usual, lying in wait for her, to trip her as she came through the front door—Jayne noted the flashing light on her answering machine indicating that she had received two calls. And she immediately sensed that her terrible, no-good, very bad day wasn't over quite yet. And, too, she wondered when she would learn not to jinx herself by being so bloody optimistic all the time.

The first message assured her that she was right, and it prevented her from playing the second message until she got the first straightened out. Because that first message, although short and simple—''Jayne, call me because there's something we need to discuss''—definitely had an ominous ring to it. A good reason for that might have been because the message came from her financial advisor.

What felt like hours later but must only have been a matter of minutes, Jayne hung up the phone again, having discovered that one of the ''sure thing'' investments of which she had been encouraged to take advantage hadn't been such a sure thing, after all, but that she shouldn't worry, because she hadn't lost *that* much money, really, and she *would* recover her loss, eventually, and that recovery would be possible in a very short time, say one or two years—three at the most—but in the meantime, her finances weren't going to be quite as fluid as they had been, so that might be a problem for a little while.

Jayne had had to laugh—albeit with a touch of hysteria—at that part about her finances not being quite as fluid as they had been, because they were barely a trickle as it was. Just what, she had asked her advisor, did ''not quite as fluid'' mean? Wherein he offered her a very detailed explanation that amounted, pretty much, to the fact that she wouldn't have enough money to pay any more college tuition for her brother and sister until the year 2003—2004 at the latest.

This, Jayne decided immediately, was going to present something of a problem. The current semester was covered, because she had paid that bill a month ago. Come spring, however…

Oh, dear. She really had been planning to give her brother and sister something for Christmas other than *the shaft*.

How was she going to tell Chloe and Charlie that they wouldn't be able to attend college after this, their first semester? She could still remember the joy sparkling in her siblings' eyes when they'd all said their goodbyes at Indiana University scarcely a week ago. The twins had been so excited about starting their studies, and over pizza and later brownies, the three of them had made such plans for the future. Jayne would do almost anything to preserve those plans, that excitement, that joy.

Almost anything.

She sighed heavily, gazing longingly at the telephone, wondering how on earth she was going to fix things this time. Because Jayne fully intended to fix things. She didn't know how yet, but she would figure out something. She wasn't about to tell Chloe and Charlie they'd have to quit school. She *would* fix things.

Because that was what Jayne did.

For the last four years, that was what she had been. Jayne the fixer. Since her parents' deaths, she had done whatever she could to ease the twins' grief along with her own. She had been there for the two of them no matter what. Whenever one or both of them had needed her, for whatever reason, Jayne had dropped what she was doing and remedied the situation, however she could.

Usually those remedies had consisted of a bandage on a sprain or help with homework or stretching a pound of hamburger into three separate meals. Whatever the problem had been, Jayne had somehow found a way to fix it. This time, though…

She sighed again. There was no quick fix for the loss of a large sum of money. Not unless one won the lottery, and Jayne—call her crazy—simply wasn't willing to put her faith in that. Not unless one happened to stumble upon another large sum of money somewhere to replace the loss. Not unless one stumbled upon some*one* who had a large sum of money to replace it.

Because you see, I myself happen to be a multimillionaire. Or, at least, I will be a multimillionaire. Once I get married.

Oh, dear, Jayne thought. That was the last thing—the last voice—she needed to be hearing in her head right now. Accepting Erik Randolph's proposal was *not* going to be the fix for this particular problem.

The marriage will be in name only.

That didn't matter, she told herself. There were all kinds of things that could go wrong in an arrangement like that. She wanted no part of it. Yes, she would do almost anything to keep her siblings in college. The operative word in that avowal, however, was *almost*. There was no way Jayne would marry a complete stranger just to keep her siblings in school.

Though she supposed she could argue he wasn't a *complete* stranger. She did know him by reputation. And they had enjoyed a nice, if superficial—and borderline surreal—conversation that afternoon. There were still a host of reasons why she couldn't—wouldn't—marry Erik Randolph.

Oh, certainly, we'll have to live together, to fulfill the terms of the agreement, but that won't be a problem.

And that was just the first of those hosts of reasons.

The arrangement will only last one year.

That was beside the point. The point was—

The flashing red light on the phone caught Jayne's attention again, and she was grateful for the interruption into her mental argument with Erik Randolph. Honestly, she thought, they weren't even married yet, and already they were disagreeing about things.

Not that she had any intention of marrying him, she

hastily reminded herself. It was just a hypothetical argument, that was all.

Oh, bother, she thought, pinching the bridge of her nose to ward off a headache that came out of nowhere. *Just play the next message, Jayne. Maybe it will be good news.*

She realized it was indeed good news the moment she heard the sound of her sister's voice. There was nothing Jayne liked more than hearing Chloe and Charlie's reports from the collegiate front, which had come pretty much daily since the beginning of the semester.

"Hi, Jaynie!" Chloe's voice chirped from the answering machine. In the background, Jayne could hear Charlie's voice, as well, a shout of "Hey, big sister, whassup?" and she smiled.

"Hello, Chloe. Hello, Charlie," she said, even though she knew they couldn't hear her.

"We just called to say hi and to tell you that we wrote a poem for you today in our Intro to Creative Writing class."

This announcement was followed by Chloe's clearing of her throat, Charlie's mimicking of an opera star warming up with a deep, resonant "Mi-mi-mi" and Jayne's laughter at both. Then her brother and sister began, in unison, to read their composition.

"*J* is for Jaynie, our sister so fair, *A* is for altruistic, unlike a bear." This was punctuated with giggling, and Charlie's murmuring of "I told you that line needed work." Then the twins began again, more soberly this time. "*Y* is for youth, which she gave up too soon. *N* is for niceness, by far her greatest boon. And *E* is for everything that she does for us, and also for everything she's given up for us.

"Okay, so the rhythm's off a little bit here and there, especially at the end," Chloe said hastily. "And the last rhyme wasn't so hot, either. It's our first poem, and we wanted to write it for you." There was a small pause, then Chloe and Charlie together said, "We love you, Jaynie.'' Charlie added, ''And we just want you to know how much we appreciate everything you've done for us. Everything is great here.''

''We *love* it at IU,'' Chloe added. ''Call when you can. Kiss Mojo for me. We'll talk to you soon.''

And then the soft buzz of the dial tone filled the air for a moment before going silent.

Only then did Jayne realize there were tears in her eyes. And not because she feared her brother and sister were going to flunk creative writing, either. But because she knew in that moment that she really would do anything to make sure they stayed in school.

Even if it meant marrying an eccentric—but cute—guy like Erik Randolph.

The least she could do, she told herself, was meet him for dinner as they had arranged, and listen to what he had to say. Maybe he wasn't as crazy as he sounded. Maybe what he was proposing would be the perfect arrangement for both of them. Maybe her encounter with him this morning was simple fate and everything would work out for the best.

And maybe, Jayne thought further, while she was sleeping tonight, the blue fairy would fly into her bedroom and turn her into a real boy.

Resigned to at least hear Erik Randolph out—and recalling that all of her matching clothes were in the laundry—Jayne picked up the phone again. This time it was to call her upstairs neighbor Lila, to see if she could borrow that cute little yellow dress the other woman had worn to the company picnic last month....

Four

She isn't coming.

The thought circled through Erik's head for the umpteenth time as he rearranged the salt and pepper shakers on the table before him for the umpteenth time. And even though Jayne hadn't actually promised to meet him at the restaurant, he was surprised by the realization that she wasn't going to show. Somehow he had been so sure that she would come tonight. She had seemed like she wanted to accept his invitation, even if she hadn't quite.

But it was now twenty past the hour, and Erik couldn't conceive of anything that would make someone run that late for an engagement—he smiled at his unintentional double entendre in spite of his gloomy mood—unless it was that the someone in question simply wasn't coming.

She isn't coming, he thought again. And his realization of that caused him to feel surprisingly melancholy.

Oh, sure, he knew that what he'd proposed to Jayne Pembroke earlier that day was unconventional, to say the least. She had been understandably wary. But by the time they'd parted ways, she had seemed amenable to at least meeting him tonight and hearing him out. And although he sympathized fairly well with what it must be like to be a woman in contemporary American society, where too many men were, well, pigs, Erik liked to think that he, at least, exuded an aura of allure and reputation that raised him well above the sty.

Still, he conceded, it probably wasn't every day that a woman was proposed to by a complete stranger. Even one as charming and irresistible as he. Especially dressed as he was in another of his best suits, this one a Brioni the color of bittersweet chocolate, to enhance what he cheerfully considered to be his dark, brooding good looks. Despite that...

She isn't coming.

He was surprised by the depth of his disappointment. He told himself his distress simply stemmed from the fact that he would now have to go back to square one in his hunt for a wife. But deep down he suspected his distress might well be the result of something else entirely. What that something else might be, though, he was reluctant to ponder. He only knew that at the moment he was unhappy, and that unhappiness had come about because he wouldn't be seeing Jayne tonight.

And that was a very odd development. Because it wasn't easy to make Erik Randolph unhappy, especially when it came to women. He had a naturally optimistic nature, a generally positive outlook on life, and it just took a lot to get him down. Women, in particular, had never seemed to him to be the kind of thing to lose any sleep over. Even the ones he found himself serious enough about to date for an extended period of time—like two months or so. Erik simply never got worked up enough over a member of the opposite sex to feel unhappy when that member wasn't around. But having had just one brief conversation with Jayne Pembroke that afternoon, he still found himself missing her this evening.

It was more than a little peculiar.

He sighed heavily and was about to stand—what was the point of staying?—when a flash of pale yellow near the entrance caught his attention. Erik turned his gaze hopefully in that direction, his heart rate accelerating to a rapid pace. But his hope was short-lived—and his heart rate slowed down again—when he saw that the woman who entered the delicatessen wasn't the one he had been expecting.

At least, he thought further, as a sliver of doubt wedged itself into his brain, he didn't *think* that was Jayne Pembroke....

The woman said something to the hostess, who nodded and said something back, then pointed in Erik's direction. And when the woman in pale yellow turned toward him, his heart nearly stopped beating entirely. Because it *was* Jayne Pembroke, he realized. And she *wasn't* the woman he'd been expecting.

And *boy,* was he glad he'd waited for her.

She grinned shyly when she saw him, then began to make her way toward the table he had chosen—one situated in the far rear corner, where, he had thought, they might have some degree of privacy. J.J.'s Deli was a basic delicatessen, small in scope, but with a high, bare-beamed ceiling, terra-cotta tiled floors and brick walls decorated with bright poster art of old movies. The front served carry-out clientele, but a handful of tables was scattered along the back for those who wanted to take their time as they ate. During the day, the place was usually packed, inside and out, situated as it was in the heart of Youngsville business district. At nearly seven-thirty on a Monday night, however, the place was fairly deserted.

As he watched Jayne approach, Erik told himself she shouldn't look out of place there, dressed in her simple, casual, yellow dress, with a pale-blue sweater tossed over her shoulders. But somehow he got the impression of European royalty as she drew nearer.

Had he been worrying about the impression he would make? he asked himself. Because if he was making an impression on her that was half as good as the one she was making on him, then he ought to be—speaking of old movies—in like Flynn.

"Hi," she said softly, when she came to a stop in front of him.

Her hair, which had been tersely bound that afternoon, was now piled loosely atop her head, held in place by some invisible means of support, with a few errant tendrils spiraling down around her face. Her violet eyes seemed even more violet than they had been that afternoon, and he was even more enchanted by the light dusting of freckles that dotted the bridge of her nose and her cheekbones. The only makeup he could detect was a soft pink applied to her lips, a color mirrored by the pale lacquer on the fingers that clutched a tiny, pale-blue satin purse in front of her.

Her most intriguing accessory, though, was a pin affixed to her sweater, an unusual but very lovely brooch that picked up on the color of her dress. Amber, he guessed, his knowledge of jewelry surprisingly good for a layman. But he couldn't quite place the designer or origin of the piece. Still, it was quite exquisite.

Okay, so maybe the fashion thing wasn't going to be a problem after all, Erik thought. Because at the moment she looked as if she had just stepped off the cover of a magazine, one devoted to ultrafemininity. Somewhere deep inside him, in a place he hadn't known existed, his testosterone levels fairly shot through the roof.

All in all, it was not an unpleasant sensation.

She was nervous, he noted, and the realization relieved him. Because it meant that the two of them were meeting on equal ground.

"Hi," he greeted her back. But he was damned if he could think of a single other thing to say.

Some latent sense of courtesy made him rise from his chair and move to the one beside it. He pulled it out for her, and she smiled before seating herself, another point in her favor. Erik was a firm believer in equality for both sexes, but it bugged the hell out of him whenever a woman rejected a perfectly good offer of common courtesy, citing the women's movement for her refusal.

When he seated himself again, he caught the waiter's attention and silently bid him come over. Then he ordered two glasses of pinot griggio and the focaccia bread and brie appetizer, and sent the man on his way.

"I was afraid you weren't coming," he told Jayne the moment their server was out of earshot.

"I'm sorry I'm late," she apologized. "I—" She stopped suddenly, as if whatever she'd intended to tell him had fled her brain completely. Then she shrugged philosophically. "I'm afraid it's been one of those days," she finally said.

Erik propped his elbow on the table, cupped his chin in his hand and eyed her with much appreciation. "Hasn't it just?" he agreed with a smile.

She smiled back, another one of those soft, shy smiles that set his heart to humming happily in his chest. Oh, yes. He was definitely glad he had waited for her. And he very much looked forward to whatever other surprises the evening held.

Somewhere at the back of his muddled brain, Erik realized that the conversation had stalled immediately after the sharing of greetings, something which made him a truly dreadful example of a host. With a swift, mental kick to his chat center, he straightened, wove his fingers together on the tabletop and tried again.

"So. Jayne. How long have you worked for Colette? I don't recall seeing you in the store before today."

"Oh, are you a regular customer at Colette?" she asked, her interest quite, *quite* piqued.

Hmm, Erik thought, backpedaling. It might not be a good idea to start off his wooing of a prospective wife—however temporary she might be—by telling her how often he was in her place of employment to buy gifts for other women of his acquaintance. "I, ah... I've been in a time or two recently. With my sister," he hastened to clarify. "Or my mother." He angled his wrist toward her as he added, "And not long ago I had my watch repaired there."

She nodded. She also seemed to be relieved by the benign choice of subject matter, because she continued to smile as she replied, "I've only worked there for about a month. But I've lived in Youngsville all my life. In fact, I moved into my own apartment just recently."

Erik's own curiosity now was quite piqued. "Why the move?" he asked. "Finally getting out from under your parents' thumbs?"

And why did the prospect of doing such a thing sound so appealing to him all of a sudden?

She shook her head. "No, my parents passed away when I was eighteen."

Oh, well done, Erik, he thought morosely. Nothing like bringing up a sad subject to set their conversation off on the right foot. "I'm sorry," he said.

She nodded. "Me, too," she told him. "But it's been four years. I'm coping." With one small sigh, she continued, "But my brother and sister, who I've been raising since my parents' deaths, headed off to IU this year—they're twins—so I'm on my own now, and I thought it was time for a change."

"And do you like having your own place?" Erik asked idly, trying to steer the conversation back into safe—ergo, not sad—waters.

"Oh, I love it," she replied enthusiastically. "But I do miss Chloe and Charlie."

"Well, I, for one, am glad you decided to stay here in town, instead of following them off to Bloomington."

That shy smile again—which really was so enchanting—then, "Thank you," she said. "I'm glad, too. Besides, Bloomington isn't so far away that I can't see them fairly regularly."

They eased into a comfortable chitchat mode for the next fifteen or twenty minutes, pausing only when their server returned with their wine and appetizer and to take their orders for dinner. Then it was right back into the small talk again, an activity that Erik found oddly enjoyable. Normally he wasn't the biggest fan of small talk, and viewed it simply as a means to an end—that end generally being an invitation into the woman's bed, or vice versa.

Tonight, though, small talk was taking on a whole new meaning. It was still a means to an end, to be sure, but suddenly that end wasn't so much being invited into Jayne Pembroke's bed as it was...getting to know her better. Not that Erik would turn down such an invitation, should she extend it, but that wasn't the primary reason for this exchange of information. Nor, he was sure, would such an invitation be forthcoming. Not yet, anyway. No, this exchange, he realized, was coming about because he genuinely wanted to know more about her as a person.

What a concept.

And my, but the big things he discovered about Jayne Pembroke as they talked small. He learned, for example, more about the struggles she had overcome while caring for her two younger siblings. Erik couldn't imagine taking on the responsibility for someone else—*two* someone elses—like that, especially at such a young age. Jayne, however, had done so without a second thought. She'd even postponed her own college education until her brother and sister completed theirs.

It was that last tidbit of information that Erik found most amenable to his needs. "And how have you been paying for all this, Jayne?'' he asked as he watched her stir cream into her coffee after the last remnants of their dinner had been cleared away. ''It must be expensive, sending two people to school, while maintaining an acceptable living standard for oneself. How do you manage it, on your paychecks from Colette?''

She stumbled in her motions when he posed the question, her hand nearly flicking the spoon right out of her mug. ''Well, I, um, I, ah… That is to say…'' She sighed fitfully and avoided his gaze most steadfastly. ''Well, I *do* make a nice commission,'' she finally told him.

''Oh, I don't doubt that you're a very good salesclerk,'' he conceded. ''But unless you're planning to unload the crown jewels on someone…''

She indulged in a bit more avoiding of his gaze, then, ''Actually,'' she said, ''until recently, everything was fine.''

Hmmm, Erik thought. This could be significant. ''How recently?'' he asked.

She continued to avoid his gaze as she said, ''Oh, until this afternoon.''

Oh, yes, he thought. This could be *very* significant. ''Before or after we spoke at the store?'' he asked.

''Um, after.''

Aha, he thought. Aloud, however, he only said, ''Ah.''

''I mean, I thought we were financially sound,'' she finally told him. ''I thought I had invested my parents' assets and life insurance settlement very well.''

''You *thought?*'' Erik echoed. ''As in past tense?''

She removed her spoon from her mug and lifted the latter to her mouth for a sip, and still avoided his gaze most steadfastly. Erik thought her evasion highly significant indeed. And not a little encouraging.

''Yes, well, I kind of got some bad news today,'' she said.

Well, this was good news, Erik thought. ''Oh?'' he asked.

She sipped her coffee experimentally, seemed to savor the flavor for a moment, replaced her cup on the table...and continued avoiding his gaze.

Yes, he thought, very good news.

"Yes," she said, "very bad news. It seems some of those investments I thought were so sound weren't quite as sound as I thought they were."

"No?"

She shook her head. "And now paying for Charlie and Chloe's tuition is going to be something of a hardship for me. In fact, it's going to be an impossibility."

Erik eyed her thoughtfully for a moment. So this was why she had come to meet him, after all, he thought. His proposal of a marriage of convenience seemed more convenient now to her than it had earlier. Perhaps fate really had stepped in, he thought. He'd already considered his meeting up with Jayne this afternoon to be serendipitous. Perhaps she was beginning to see things the same way herself.

"Well," he began, placing his own coffee mug on the table. He folded one hand atop the other and eyed her pointedly, silently willing her to look up and meet his gaze. After a brief moment of fighting it, she finally did. "Perhaps," he began again, "I can make that hardship much easier for you. Perhaps I can make that impossibility very possible indeed. And you, in turn," he added, "can help me out, as well."

"I'm not saying I'll marry you," she hastened to clarify.

"Aren't you?" he asked.

She shook her head slowly. "Only that I'll listen to what you have to say."

"Fair enough," he told her, confident that once he had outlined his plan, she would readily agree to the terms. Especially now that he knew her weakness—the twin siblings for whom she had been caring, for the past four years. They would be Erik's ace in the hole. First, though, he had to convince her that she needed him as much as he needed her.

"Well then, Jayne," he said with a smile. "Let me tell you exactly what I...propose."

Jayne listened to Erik's proposal as he outlined it, telling herself she was doing so with an *open* mind and not a *lost* one. Even so, a lost mind went a lot further toward explaining her desire to accept his offer than an open mind did. Because that was exactly what Jayne found herself wanting to do as she absorbed everything Erik told her. Accept his proposal. Marry him. Live with him—in name only—under one roof for a full year. And in exchange, take advantage of his fortune and allow him to pay for Chloe and Charlie's college expenses.

Because that was what he offered to do—take care of any costs incurred by sending two people to college for four years. Five or six years, if either—or both—of her siblings decided to go for their master's degrees. It was a very generous offer, she had to admit. Though, granted, with sixty million dollars in his wallet, the expense would be negligible to Erik. Nevertheless, it was the kind of offer a woman like Jayne would find very difficult to refuse.

And he would, of course, he promised, put it all in writing, in the form of a prenuptial agreement. He also offered what he termed "a substantial settlement" to Jayne, as well, once they dissolved their marriage, but she had declined that. Marrying for money seemed less tawdry somehow when she was doing it for someone else instead of herself. As long as she didn't benefit personally from the arrangement, then it didn't make her a gold-digger, did it?

Oh, way to justify, Jayne.

Besides, where was the harm in marrying Erik for a year? she asked herself. The relationship would be totally platonic. They'd share a roof, but nothing more. They'd have two separate rooms, two separate schedules, two separate lives. She wouldn't even have to change her name, she thought. Which, of course, she wouldn't, because what was the point when she'd just be changing it back in twelve months' time?

"If I do this," she said cautiously when he was finished describing his plan, "and I'm not saying I will," she hastened to add when she saw him smile, "there's one requirement I ask of you."

"Anything," he told her.

She hesitated only a moment before telling him, "I don't want Chloe and Charlie to know that I married you for your money."

He gazed at her thoughtfully for a moment. "Fine," he said. "Do you mind if I ask why?"

"I just don't want them to know the reason," she said, not sure she could fully explain her desire.

Maybe it was because she didn't want Chloe and Charlie to worry about her. Or maybe it was because she didn't want to tarnish their opinion of her. Maybe it was just because, as had been the case for four years, she wanted to protect them from those aspects of life that were less than stellar. And she didn't want them to know their financial difficulties were bad enough to warrant her doing something this desperate. Most of all, she didn't want them to think badly of her for doing it.

"I want Chloe and Charlie to think the reason we married is because we're in love."

Erik continued to study her in thoughtful silence for a moment, then, "Don't you think that will make it more difficult to explain things to them a year from now, when we file for divorce?" he asked.

"I have a year between now and then to think about that," Jayne said. "It won't be that bad. We can arrange it that you have little contact with them, so they won't end up liking you and missing you when you're gone."

"Oh?" Erik asked lightly. "Why, Jayne, you're hurting my feelings. I like to think I'm unforgettable."

She smiled. Oh, she was confident that was true. Something told her that fifty years from now, she'd still be looking back on her memories of Erik Randolph quite fondly. "If something comes up, and Chloe and Charlie come home for a visit, we'll just arrange for you to be traveling overseas or something."

"Fine," he conceded. "Fair enough."

"And just to be sure that Charlie and Chloe don't find out," Jayne added, realizing she sounded as if she'd already made a decision here, "my friends at 20 Amber Court have to think we're marrying for love, too. I don't want to risk anyone slipping up and saying something in front of the twins."

There was more thoughtful silence from Erik for a moment, then he asked, "And just what would we have to do to convince everyone we married out of love, instead of convenience?"

Oh, she really wished he hadn't asked that. Now Jayne was the one to eye him in thoughtful silence, as she considered her response.

Finally, she shrugged lightly and told him, "When we're around other people, we'll have to do the usual things that lovers do. Hold hands. Smile engagingly at each other. Address each other by terms of endearment. That sort of thing."

"That doesn't sound so bad," Erik said. "I can do that. And trust me. I can be *very* convincing."

Hmmm, Jayne thought. She wasn't sure if she should be worried about that or not.

"However," he added, "I won't call you Snookums, so you can put that right out of your head this very minute."

She chuckled. "Frankly, that suits me just as well. Calling me 'My darling, dearest, most perfect wife' will do just fine."

Then another concern wedged its way into her head. "You said we'll have to live together. Where, exactly, will we live? I don't want to move out of my apartment and have Rose lease it to someone else, then be without a place to live after the year is up. I really like it at 20 Amber Court.''

''Then we'll live at 20 Amber Court,'' Erik told her.

Jayne arched her eyebrows in surprise. She hadn't really thought he would suggest that. He didn't seem like the kind of man who would be comfortable in a small, two-bedroom apartment. Then again, she was just grateful that she had two bedrooms. She'd wanted two so that Charlie and Chloe would each have a place to sleep when they came to visit over the holidays—one could take the spare room, and one could take the hide-a-bed in the living room. Now it looked as though Jayne's guest room was going to be in regular use for the full year.

Which meant that she and Erik were *definitely* going to have to come up with some reason for him to be out of town when Charlie and Chloe came home. Because there was no way Jayne would be sharing a room with Erik, especially while her brother and sister were there to see it. She didn't want to set a bad example for them. Then again, she reminded herself, she would be married.

Still, it would be better to simply get rid of Erik whenever the twins were home. And seeing as how he'd described over dinner his love for traveling, Jayne didn't think it would be a problem convincing him to get out of town for a while.

Oh, dear, she thought. She really was going to take him up on it. She really was going to accept his offer.

Surprisingly, though, the realization of that didn't alarm her as much as she thought it probably should. Where was the harm? she asked herself again. It was only going to be for a year. It might be kind of fun, really. She hadn't been altogether comfortable living alone for the last month, having never experienced a solitary existence before. Her apartment felt so empty sometimes, having no one with whom to share it, except for Chloe's disagreeable cat—speaking of whom, Jayne did feel morally obligated to tell Erik about Mojo, so that he could make an informed decision in this marriage business. She wouldn't blame him if he wanted to call the whole thing off after meeting the cat.

But, if Erik did still want to go through with it after meeting Mojo, the situation could end up being ideal. Although Jayne had only known him for a short time, he was fun to be with. He had a good sense of humor, and he made her laugh. He was cute. He was kind. He was courteous. He really did seem like he'd make a good roommate. If it wasn't for that pesky Y chromosome he had, Jayne would feel totally comfortable with the arrangement.

Then again, if it wasn't for that pesky Y chromosome, she wouldn't be marrying him, would she? And Chloe and Charlie would have to quit school. So really, when she got right down to it, this thing with Erik was the perfect arrangement.

Except for its being totally nuts.

But then, what was the point of behaving reasonably if it couldn't even pay one's siblings' college tuition, hmmm?

As rationales went, Jayne realized hers wasn't the best. But the two most important things in her life were Chloe and Charlie. She'd promised her mother that she would take care of them, should anything ever happen to her parents. At the moment, the only way Jayne could keep that promise was by marrying Erik Randolph and being his wife for a year.

For one brief, final moment, Jayne told herself that what she was about to do was sheer madness. Then, in a quick rush of words she told him, "Okay. I'll do it."

He expelled a long, slow breath, and only then did she realize how much he had feared she would decline. Then again, there was sixty million dollars at stake, wasn't there? Of course he would be relieved.

"You won't be sorry," he told her.

Funny, Jayne thought, but she was already kind of sorry. For some reason, in spite of the pep talk she'd just given herself, she had a feeling this arrangement wasn't going to go as smoothly as she anticipated.

Immediately she shook the feeling off. It would be fine, she assured herself. Everything would be fine.

It would have to be.

She inhaled a slow, steadying breath and released it as silently as she could, then did her best to smile. "Well then," she said. "I guess there's nothing left for us to do except set a date, is there?"

Erik smiled, too, though his looked infinitely more sincere than hers felt. "Oh, there is one small thing we need to do before setting a date."

Jayne eyed him curiously. "What's that?"

He reached inside his jacket and withdrew a small, square box from his breast pocket. It was a box Jayne recognized quite well—the Colette Jewelry box. Ring-size, to be precise.

Sure enough, when Erik flipped it open, she saw a dazzling, square-cut solitaire mounted in white gold—two full carats, if she wasn't mistaken, and, it went without saying, she wasn't. The ring was one of the most exquisite ones they had in their collection. And Erik had bought it for his bride-to-be.

But instead of being delighted by the gift, Jayne felt sad for some reason. It was the kind of ring a man should give to the woman of his dreams, the woman with whom he intended to spend the rest of his life. And it was the kind of ring a woman should look upon as a symbol of her man's undying love for her. Her marriage to Erik was going to be a sham. Somehow Jayne felt as if she should wear a ring from a bubble gum machine instead.

"I remembered what you said about liking the square-cut diamonds and the white-gold settings best," he told her as he removed the ring from the box. "So I went back to Colette this evening, after your shift, but before they closed. If it doesn't fit, we can have it sized up or down.''

''I know,'' Jayne said inanely.

Erik chuckled again. ''Yes, I suppose you would.''

''I can't believe you remembered what I said about liking the square cut,'' she said softly. For some reason, she wanted to stall for time, wanted to delay putting on the ring. ''I mean, we barely had a chance to—''

''Well, now we'll have a whole year to,'' he told her as he reached for her left hand.

But before he could place the ring on her finger, Jayne withdrew her hand, curling it into a loose fist in her lap. ''I can't accept it,'' she told him.

He looked genuinely mystified. ''Of course you can.''

She shook her head. ''No, I can't. It's too much. Save that ring for the real thing, the real woman.''

''What? You're not a real woman?'' He smiled again. ''Is there something I should know before our honeymoon?''

Jayne gulped at his mention of a honeymoon, even though she knew he was only kidding. Then another thought struck her. He *was* only kidding, right? She considered his grin and decided that yes, he was. Of course he was.

She hoped.

''Of course I'm a real woman,'' she told him. ''But I won't be a real wife. Save that ring for when you get married for real.''

''Oh, I won't be getting married for real,'' he told her. ''Ever.''

His utter conviction in voicing the statement surprised her. ''How can you be so sure of that?''

He shrugged lightly, without a trace of bitterness or discontent—only absolute certainty. ''I just am, that's all,'' he said. ''I'm not the kind of man who can make a lifelong commitment to one woman. I like women—all women—too much for that.''

"Oh."

A cool feeling of something unpleasant settled in Jayne's midsection at hearing his matter-of-fact assessment of himself as a womanizer. Did that mean he would be unfaithful to her during their marriage? she wondered. Not that it would necessarily be infidelity, would it? Not if the people who were married didn't love each other. Still, the knowledge that he might see other women while being married to her didn't sit well with her for some reason.

"You look sad all of a sudden," he said. "What's wrong?"

"I was just thinking about what you said. About liking women too much to commit to just one."

He smiled. "Jealous already?"

"No," she denied. Though somehow, the denial felt like a lie. "I'm just not sure how much I'll like being cheated on while we're married, that's all."

"Would it be cheating if we're married in name only?" he asked.

"It feels like it would be," she told him.

"Then I won't see anyone else while we're married," he told her.

His ready concession surprised her. "You'd do that for me? Go without—" She halted quickly, blushing furiously, when she realized where the conversation was suddenly going. "I mean... Uh..."

Erik chuckled. "Yes, I'd go without," he said diplomatically.

"For a whole year?" she asked.

"Certainly. You're sacrificing a lot to help me out. There's no reason why I shouldn't make a sacrifice, too. Marriage is, after all—or, at least, should be—a fifty-fifty split with each party giving and receiving the same amount."

Jayne had always been of that opinion, too, and she appreciated that Erik felt the same way. Of course, they were talking about two entirely different things. Jayne was thinking more in terms of emotional give and take, where Erik was thinking more in terms of favors, but that was beside the point. The point was, her husband would be faithful to her, even if he wasn't making love to her. And for some reason that was a very big deal.

"At any rate," he began again, "once our arrangement has come to an end, and we divorce, I'll be through with marriage forever. So the ring is immaterial in that respect. It should be yours."

It should be hers, she translated, because it lacked meaning for him. Just as their marriage would lack meaning for him. Then again, she told herself, it didn't have meaning for her, either, did it? So they were even on that count, too.

Still, "You sound so jaded about marriage," she told him.

"Not jaded," he denied. "Just pragmatic. I'm simply not the marrying kind. Not the real sort of marriage, I mean."

Jayne nodded. Somehow, his assertion made her feel even worse.

"So come on," he cajoled. "Let me put it on your finger. Consider it the first of your lovely parting gifts."

Reluctantly Jayne lifted her left hand and extended it slowly toward him. Erik took her fingers gently in his, then slid the ring on her finger. It fit perfectly, she was surprised to see. She told herself it was a good omen. Somehow, though, she still didn't feel quite right about the whole thing.

Chloe and Charlie, she reminded herself. You're doing this for Chloe and Charlie. That's all you have to remember. That's all that's important.

Unfortunately, no matter how many times Jayne told herself that, she never did quite believe it.

Five

It was after ten o'clock when Jayne arrived home. Although Erik had offered her a ride in his outrageously expensive, low-slung, foreign sports car, something had made her decline. Citing the need to be alone for a little while, to allow the repercussions of their discussion to settle in, she had told him she wanted to walk home alone. It was a beautiful evening, as if in apology for the nasty weather during the day, and walking, she knew—she hoped—would clear her mind.

By the time she arrived back at 20 Amber Court, however, Jayne felt more confused and distressed than ever. She hesitated before going in, surveying her apartment building as if seeing it for the first time. Soon Erik would be moving in with her, and this would be their first home as husband and wife. All in all, she decided, they could do much worse.

The four-level apartment building was rather romantic, really. It had started off as a large mansion a century ago, but Rose had told Jayne that it had been converted into one- and two-bedroom apartments in the early seventies. It still claimed the original—and very beautiful—marble foyer, with a spectacular marble staircase that led to the second floor. Many of the apartments still claimed the original woodwork and fixtures and features of a bygone era, right down to the hardwood floors and old-fashioned lighting and arched doorways.

Jayne had been thoroughly happy living here alone for the last month. And she couldn't help wondering now if that happiness would continue while she was sharing her apartment with Erik.

He had told her he would have his attorney draw up the papers for the prenup the following day, and he would bring them by her apartment at seven o'clock the following evening, so that she could look them over. He'd assumed she would want to have her own attorney present for that, and Jayne had had to bite back a nervous laugh at how he thought everyone must have an attorney at their disposal the way he evidently did.

They really did come from two totally different worlds, she couldn't help thinking. Though she would certainly have someone look the document over before she signed it.

As she made her way across the foyer toward her apartment, Jayne heard the sound of feminine laughter coming from her landlady's apartment next door. She paused a moment to listen, and recognized the voices of her coworkers—Lila, Sylvie and Meredith—along with Rose Carson's. It sounded like they were playing poker. Over tea and biscuits. Again.

Jayne smiled, and just naturally gravitated in that direction. Since moving to Amber Court and starting work at Colette, she had been enthusiastically invited into the small trio of friends that had previous only comprised Lila, Sylvie and Meredith. Now they were a quartet. The Colette Quartet, she thought with a smile. And where the other three women had made it a practice somewhere along the line to have dinner with Rose once a month, they had immediately invited Jayne to partake of the evening, too. But September's dinner was still weeks away, Jayne knew. So tonight must just be one of those spontaneous girls-night-outs that came up every now and then, when the opportunity presented itself.

And Jayne discovered then, not much to her surprise, that out with the girls was very much where she wanted to be at the moment. So, without hesitation, she lifted her hand toward Rose's front door and knocked three times in quick succession.

Within seconds the door opened, and Rose smiled upon seeing the fourth member of the group. She was dressed in her typical hanging-out-with-the girls clothes—loose-fitting beige trousers and a lightweight, pale-blue cotton blouse. "Why, Jayne," she said, "you're home early."

This was news to Jayne. After all, how long could it possibly take to sell oneself out for a large sum of money? "Am I?" she asked.

Rose considered her thoughtfully for a moment. "Well, the girls did tell me you had a hot date tonight. We didn't expect to hear you come in anytime soon."

Jayne gazed over Rose's shoulder, down a long entranceway that opened up into her landlady's living room, and saw her three friends, all seated around the coffee table on Rose's couch and overstuffed chairs. And they had all turned toward the front door with identical—and very expectant—expressions etched on their faces.

Honestly, Jayne thought, they looked almost comical, making no attempt whatsoever to hide their outright curiosity. She would have laughed out loud if it weren't for the fact that she felt so strange inside.

"Is that Jayne?" Sylvie said sweetly. "So early?"

"Guess it wasn't such a hot date after all, hmm?" Meredith asked.

"How did the dress go over?" Lila wanted to know.

Then she glanced meaningfully down at her watch and back up at Jayne. "Or should I ask?"

"Very funny, everybody," Jayne said as she strode past Rose, who had moved aside in a silent invitation for her to enter. She strode down the corridor to the living room, and, as always, was vaguely surprised by the modernity of her landlady's apartment. In so many ways, Rose seemed like an old-fashioned girl. But her apartment was bright white, decorated with numerous, and very colorful, art sculptures and paintings. Jayne sighed heavily as she came to a halt near the coffee table, then said to her friends, "Actually, if you must know…"

"Oh, we must, we must," Lila said.

"My date went very well," Jayne told them. There. That was suitably nebulous, wasn't it? Let them make of it whatever they wanted to.

"Sit," Sylvie instructed as Jayne drew nearer to the table. "We want to hear all the gory details. You're the first one of us who's had a date in a long time. We want to live vicariously through you."

"Speak for yourself," Meredith said. "I'm perfectly content not to date."

"Yeah, yeah, yeah," Lila muttered. "Just wait till the right man comes along. You'll change your tune. Pronto."

Meredith opened her mouth to respond to Lila's assurance—probably in contradiction, Jayne couldn't help but think—but Rose interceded.

"Now, girls," she said, "maybe Jayne doesn't want to share all the, as you called them, gory details. From what I gather, this is a new man in her life. She may want to keep him to herself for a while."

Something about the way Rose offered her observation made Jayne think the other woman sympathized with her situation. There was someone special in Rose's past, Jayne realized then. She could tell by the way her landlady spoke. As far as Jayne knew, however, Rose had always been single. The idea that there might be one great love in the other woman's past piqued her curiosity more than a little. She would have loved to hear the story of Rose's love life, but she didn't want to pry.

Without thinking, Jayne lifted her hand to the amber brooch affixed to her sweater, the one Rose had loaned her that morning. She remembered her landlady telling her the pin had an interesting history. And for some reason, Jayne couldn't help thinking it was somehow related to the special man in the other woman's life. She had no idea why such a thought should occur to her, but there it was all the same. Someday, Jayne thought, she was going to ask Rose to tell her all about the amber brooch.

That day wouldn't be today, however, as was made quite evident when Lila suddenly—and very loudly—squealed, then leaped up from her chair with enough velocity to send it skidding backward.

"What?" Jayne asked in alarm. She took an involuntary step backward in response to the other woman's... exuberance. "What's wrong?"

"Nothing's wrong," Lila said. But she was pointing at the hand Jayne had lifted to the brooch and shaking her finger quite vigorously.

Jayne realized then, too late, that it was her *left* hand she had lifted to touch the brooch. Hastily she shoved her hand behind her back, even though she knew the gesture would be futile.

"That ring," her neighbor continued before Jayne had a chance to respond one way or another. "That humongous chunk of ice you're wearing. You weren't wearing that when you came up to borrow my dress earlier this evening," Lila added. "I would have noticed it. You had to have gotten that tonight. What's the deal, Jayne? If you ask me, that looks like an *engagement* ring."

Oh, dear, Jayne thought. She really hadn't intended to tell her friends about her impending marriage just yet. She'd hoped to have a day or two to get used to the idea herself. Not that she could have put off announcing it for very long, seeing as how Erik had to be married within two weeks' time. In fact, it really wasn't until this very moment that Jayne even fully considered the fact that she was going to have to tell *everyone*—including Chloe and Charlie—that she would soon be a married woman. And, seeing as how she hadn't even been dating anyone, explaining a sudden engagement was going to be just a *tad* difficult for her to do.

"Uuummm," she began eloquently.

"It *is* an engagement ring," Meredith said, grinning. "From the Colette collection, no less. I'd recognize that setting anywhere. I did, after all, design it."

"And a lovely design it is, too," Jayne said quickly, hoping to change the subject.

No such luck.

"Jayne, is there something you've been meaning to tell us?" Sylvie asked, also smiling. "Like, oh, I don't know... Maybe that you've been keeping some hunka hunka burnin' love under wraps somewhere? Is he a high school sweetheart you just never mentioned to us? Or is he a more recent acquisition? In which case, darling, we want to know *all* about this whirlwind romance."

"Hey, we want to hear about it even if he's someone you've known since preschool," Lila said. "Tell us all, Jayne."

Meredith nodded her agreement quite fervently as she said, "Pretty sneaky keeping him to yourself all this time."

Oh, boy, Jayne thought. How was she going to explain her way out of this one? She really should have thought a little further ahead before accepting Erik Randolph's proposal. Like, for instance, how doing so was going to throw her entire life into total upheaval.

Gee, hindsight really was twenty-twenty.

"Uuummm," she tried again. But again, no explanation was forthcoming. Probably because there really wasn't any way one might explain what she had done, Jayne thought. Not in any kind of coherent, socially and morally acceptable fashion, at any rate.

"Jayne?" Now it was Rose who was smiling, whose interest was quite piqued. "*Did* you get engaged tonight?"

"Um, sort of," Jayne said with much understatement.

"Sort of?" Lila echoed dubiously. "Look, with a ring like that, either you're engaged or you're not. This isn't one of those cute little engaged-to-be-engaged diamond chip sweetheart rings. This is one nice piece of jewelry."

"Yeah, this guy must be crazy about you, to drop that kind of money on a ring," Sylvie added.

"So what's up?" Meredith asked.

A barrage of questions followed that one, questions too numerous and too fast-coming for Jayne to even begin to answer them all, or to even identify who was saying what, for that matter.

"Who is he?"

"What's his name?"

"What's he like?"

"Where does he live?"

"What does he do?"

"Where'd you meet him?"

"How long have you known him?"

"How come we haven't heard about him before now?"

"Have you set a date?"

"Are you pregnant?"

"*Stop!*" Jayne finally cried.

And, surprisingly, everyone did.

"Of course I'm not pregnant," she said indignantly. "Erik and I just decided we want to get married, that's all." Then, reluctantly, because she knew it was only going to reinforce the pregnancy suspicion, she added, "We want to get married right away, as a matter of fact."

"Erik?" Lila asked, grinning. To the other women present, she added, "Girls, I do believe we have a name for Jayne's mystery man."

"How about a few other vitals, too?" Sylvie asked.

Jayne did some quick thinking. "I met him over the summer. At...at...at J.J.'s Deli," she finally said, the location of their meeting still fresh in her brain. "And we've met frequently over lunch." There. That would explain why she was home virtually every night—alone. "He, ah...he doesn't get out much at night."

"Well, then I guess we can all rest assured that he's not a vampire, right?" Lila asked playfully. "So then what does he do?"

Jayne realized then that she had no idea how to answer that. She didn't know what Erik did for a living. Only that he was wealthy. "He's, um, self-employed," she finally told them.

"As what?"

"As a, uh...as an entrepreneur." Yeah, that's the ticket, she added to herself. That was nice and vague.

"So you guys met and fell in love immediately, is that it?" Meredith asked.

Jayne nodded. "Yes. That's it exactly. There was just something between us right away, and the last month has been especially wonderful, and we both just decided tonight that we knew we wanted to be together." She swallowed with some difficulty. "Forever. So we're going to get married right away."

Lila made a soft tsking noise. "You virgins are always in *such* a hurry."

In response to Lila's remark, Sylvie chuckled, and Meredith blushed, and Jayne had no idea what to say.

"So tell us more about *him,* about Erik," Meredith said, presumably to change the subject, for which Jayne was grateful to her friend.

"I promise I'll give you all the details," she told them. To herself, she added, *Just as soon as I figure out what they are.* "Tomorrow," she added pointedly.

"Tomorrow?"

"Aw, come on..."

"But, Jayne—"

"Tomorrow," Jayne reiterated firmly. Then, truthfully, she added, "I'm really too tired to go into it all tonight. It was very unexpected. He surprised me with the ring." Oh, boy, was *that* the truth. "Everything happened so quickly. I'm still kind of dazed. Still getting used to the idea myself."

"Leave Jayne alone," Rose said mildly when the other women began to voice their objections again. "She said she'll tell you tomorrow, and so she will." To Jayne, she said softly, "I understand completely, dear. It can be rather dizzying when it happens quickly, can't it?" Her smile turned wistful as she added, "But there's nothing more wonderful than finding that special someone. Congratulations." And then she surprised Jayne by leaning forward and brushing a soft kiss on her cheek.

For some reason the gesture brought tears to Jayne's eyes. In such a short time Rose had become like a second mother to her, and in that moment all Jayne could do was wish that her own mother was here to share the news. Not that the news was anything special, she tried to tell herself. In spite of what her friends were thinking about a whirlwind romance, there was no romance, no love involved. This marriage was going to be a sham from the start. There was no reason to feel like it was something special. No reason to feel as if it were something to share.

But Jayne was surprised to discover that she *did* want to share. For some reason, her engagement to Erik *did* feel special. She wanted to share the moment, her feelings, her fears, her hopes. But in that moment she realized that there was no one in her life with whom she felt comfortable sharing those things. As much as she cared for Rose and her friends, she just wasn't comfortable opening up to them completely. And although she had family in Charlie and Chloe, there were some things she didn't feel comfortable sharing with them, either.

As her friends and neighbors clamored around her to

ooh and aah over her ring, Jayne realized she'd never felt more alone in her entire life. And all she could do then was wonder what it was going to be like, living under one roof with Erik Randolph for a whole year, and feeling so utterly alone.

They married the following Friday, with more than a week to spare before Erik's thirtieth birthday. Due to the circumstances, it was a small, informal ceremony held at Youngsville City Hall, presided over by a judge who had been a friend of the Randolphs for years. True to Jayne's request, Erik had told his family that he'd fallen in love with the young woman he planned to marry. And although the Randolphs had been somewhat surprised by their son's and brother's sudden change of mind where it came to romantic love—not to mention a little suspicious of the timing—they had been absolutely delighted by the announcement after meeting Jayne.

Strangely, they had also stopped being surprised and suspicious after meeting Jayne. Erik's father had even taken him aside at one point in the evening and congratulated him on making such a fine choice for a wife, concluding with, "Frankly, Erik, I didn't think you had such good taste."

Erik simply explained away his family's total and immediate acceptance of Jayne as being the result of their relief that they would be keeping Grandfather Randolph's oodles of money in the family. And he told himself that the reason Jayne hadn't informed her own family of their sudden engagement was a simple case of nerves and not because she was ashamed of him or herself.

Because she *hadn't* told her brother and sister of their engagement, Erik knew. He knew that, because she *had* told him that Charlie and Chloe wouldn't be at the wedding today. And had the younger Pembrokes known that their sister was getting married, they most certainly would have been present for the ceremony. Of this Erik was certain.

He and Jayne had spent as much time together this week as they could, getting to know each other and planning their meager wedding. And if there was one thing Erik had learned about her during this time, it was that family *always* came first. Even after such a brief exposure to the Pembroke clan—and his exposure to the twins had been secondhand—Erik could see clearly that they were a tightly knit trio. Considering the loss of their parents at such early and tender ages, he supposed that wasn't surprising. But Chloe and Charlie would definitely have come to Youngsville for their older sister's wedding—had they known about it.

He told himself he understood Jayne's reluctance to announce her engagement to her brother and sister. The circumstances were, after all, highly unusual. Probably, she was having trouble coming up with a suitable explanation for the rush and spontaneity. And he told himself it was her decision to make.

Still, something about her hesitation didn't sit well with him for some reason. Even with the highly unusual circumstances, Erik was a good catch, and his family was an honorable one. It wasn't as if he was someone to be ashamed of. On the contrary, any number of women would have jumped at the chance to be Mrs. Erik Randolph. He tried to forget about the fact that three in a row had declined the offer before Jayne, and that her consent had only come about in a moment of financial desperation.

That was beside the point.

The point was that Jayne, for whatever reason, was reluctant to tell her family that she was getting married to Erik Randolph. And, strangely enough that left him feeling a little hurt.

Ah, well, he thought now, as he glanced down at his watch and scanned the judge's chambers again and wondered where his blushing bride had got herself to. At least

Jayne had told her friends about their nuptials. Because three of them had arrived en masse and were seated side by side in a row of chairs against one wall, along with Jayne's landlady, whom Erik had met earlier in the week when he'd gone to Jayne's apartment to move in some of his things. So, clearly, Jayne wasn't *that* ashamed of him, if she'd introduced him to her friends and invited them to share in the celebration today.

Of course, seeing as how Erik would be living with Jayne at 20 Amber Court, and all of these women likewise lived at 20 Amber Court, she really hadn't had any choice but to tell them all she was getting married, and introduce them to her intended. That was beside the point, too. In fact, the point was—

The point was that here it was two minutes until post time, Erik thought frantically, and his bride was nowhere to be found.

Only when he couldn't put off facing that realization any longer did Erik begin to panic. Jayne would be here, he told himself. She would. She had promised. And she had signed an agreement, as had he.

More important, though, Erik knew Jayne was trustworthy. He wasn't quite sure *how* he knew that, only that he did. But she would keep her word. She would be here. He knew she would.

And no sooner had the reassurances formed in his brain than Jayne Pembroke entered the judge's chambers for her wedding, thereby ensuring that she was indeed going to keep her word. And not just about marrying him today, either, as evidenced by her appearance. But also about making the union look convincing—as evidenced by her appearance. Because she had dressed for her wedding as if…well, as if it were a special occasion.

Her suit was ivory and deceptively simple, with a slim skirt that fell to midcalf, slit on one side to just above the knee. The long jacket was cut to enhance her very curvy figure, with satin piping edging the lapels and two satin buttons closing the garment over a lacy camisole. Her pale red hair was knotted at her nape, and instead of a veil, she wore an old-fashioned pillbox hat with ivory netting that cascaded over half of her face.

And what a face. Her lavender eyes sparkled behind the netting, her cheeks were tinted with pink, and her mouth was kissed by a shade of berry he wasn't entirely certain was the result of cosmetics. Heightened awareness, he was sure, was as much responsible for her dazzling glow as was anything purchased at a department store.

All in all, Erik found her ensemble charming. Almost as charming as the woman who was wearing it. And out of nowhere, he experienced a sudden—and astonishingly intense—desire to help her take it off.

Well, well, well. It was going to be an interesting wedding day. And an even more interesting wedding night.

She crossed the length of the room to where Erik stood by himself, enjoying a final moment of solitude before joining his life—however temporarily—to another.

"I'm sorry I'm late," she said a little breathlessly. "I don't know where the morning went. Time just got away from me somehow."

"Well, you're here now, and that's all that matters," he told her. Then he smiled. "I have something for you."

She smiled back, her surprise—and her curious pleasure—obvious. "Something for me? What?"

He turned to the square white box he had placed on a chair behind him when he'd arrived, opened it and withdrew a bouquet of perfect white roses and sweetheart ivy. Then he turned and extended it toward Jayne.

"Oh, Erik," she said, her smile softening, her features turning even more lovely. "It's beautiful. I didn't even think about flowers."

He watched as she fingered the delicate blossoms with much care, then lifted the bouquet to her nose to savor the luscious, intoxicating aroma. The beauty of the flowers paled in comparison to her own, he thought. She really was quite sweet. He hoped he wasn't doing her a great injustice, marrying her this way.

Very softly he said, "I'm beginning to realize that there's quite a lot we didn't think about."

She glanced up from the bouquet, her eyes wide and startled. "Are you having second thoughts?" she asked.

He eyed her curiously. "Why do you sound so hopeful when you say that?"

She shook her head. "No, it's not that. Just... If you *are* having second thoughts about this, I certainly understand. And I certainly won't hold you to our agreement."

"I'm not having second thoughts," Erik assured her immediately, unequivocally.

Her expression changed not at all when he said it, giving him no indication of how she truly felt.

"Not about the wedding, at any rate," he added.

She said nothing in response to that, only nodded almost imperceptibly. So, with one final adjustment to the white rose he'd affixed to his own lapel—he'd opted for a dove gray suit himself, one that complemented Jayne's attire nicely—he crooked his arm in a silent bid for her to loop her own through it.

And before either of them had a chance to say another word, the judge began to hustle everyone into place. And then, before he even realized it was happening, Erik found himself slipping a different ring on the fourth finger of Jayne's left hand—a wedding ring. And then he heard himself saying "I do," and then he found himself waiting with barely contained anticipation to hear Jayne echo the sentiment herself.

She gazed intently into his eyes and smiled nervously as she slid a plain gold band over the ring finger of his left hand, then repeated the words to him. Only then did Erik realize how very worried he'd been that she would still back out of their agreement. And only then did he realize how very much he had wanted her to go through with it. And not just because it would net him sixty million dollars, either.

Then, as he and Jayne gazed into each other's eyes, wondering just what the hell they were supposed to do now, the judge was announcing them husband and wife and telling him he could kiss his bride.

In hindsight, Erik supposed it would have been a good idea to rehearse this kiss at least once at some point earlier in the week. Truly, though, he hadn't really thought about what it would mean to kiss Jayne in front of an audience this way. His head had been too full of so many other things, and he just hadn't given the wedding kiss much thought. So, with great care, and with both hands, he slipped the netting back over her hat to reveal her face. Then, clasping both of her hands in his own, he began to dip his head toward hers.

When he saw the look of panic that clouded her eyes, however, he promised himself that for this first time, he would make the kiss simple, swift and sweet. There would be time later for more, he told himself, if either of them decided more was what was wanted. And in that moment Erik knew that, speaking for himself at least, there would indeed be a want for more. For now, though, he only brushed his lips over hers once, twice, three times, before pulling reluctantly back.

And then a ripple of laughter and good cheer went up around the newlyweds, and they were engulfed in a sea of well-wishers.

Somehow Erik got separated from Jayne, and he was surprised at how perturbed he was by that separation. When he finally caught sight of her, though, it was to find that she was searching frantically for him, as well, and that made him feel better.

It was odd, really. Although he had initially gone into his wife hunt fully intending to marry someone, he hadn't for a moment planned for the arrangement to be anything more than a business transaction. He had been certain that he and his wife, although housemates, would both lead separate lives. He had known even then that he wouldn't stray or be unfaithful to his vows. He'd simply resigned himself to a year's…sabbatical, sexually speaking. Turning his gaze to Jayne again, however…

Well, suffice it to say his resignation wasn't quite as strong at the moment as it had been when he'd first proposed their marriage of convenience.

Jayne was a very attractive woman. To put it mildly. And, all modesty aside, he knew he was an attractive man. They were both unattached—or, at least had been, until a few moments ago. And now they were attached in the most traditional way a man and a woman could be joined. There was nothing—absolutely nothing—to prevent them from acting on whatever…impulses…might overcome them during the course of the next year.

Or the next week. Erik wasn't particular.

Because, speaking for himself, at least, he was already experiencing one or two of those impulses. And, speaking for himself, they were damned nice impulses to experience. It was going to be an interesting year.

Or an interesting week. Erik wasn't particular.

Jayne grinned at him, then her attention was diverted by one of her friends, and she shifted her gaze to the ring he had slipped on her finger. She turned it first one way, then the other, and smiled at the way the baguettes refracted and exploded and shone back in a brilliant array of color. It was a lovely ring, Erik thought. But not nearly as lovely as the woman who would be wearing it for the next year.

Oh, yes, he thought again. It was going to be a very interesting year indeed.

And an interesting week, too. He really wasn't particular.

Six

Jayne was *this* close to making a clean escape from the courthouse with her new—*gulp*—husband, when the other three members of the Colette Quartet caught up with her and gave her the very troubling news about her wedding present. Namely, that they had one they wanted to give to her. Because, quite frankly, the last thing Jayne needed or wanted at the moment was to act surprised and delighted with a gift chosen lovingly by her friends to celebrate her new life with her new—*gulp*—husband.

Then again, she noticed as the four Amber Court denizens gathered in the hallway outside the judge's chambers—and as she watched Erik wander off to chat with his family—that none of the women was actually holding anything. So maybe, Jayne thought, their wedding present wasn't going to be all that special, and maybe she wouldn't have to act surprised or delighted at all.

"So where are you and Erik going now?" Lila asked

in a voice that was the picture of innocence and immediately put Jayne's guard up.

"Well, ah," Jayne began, hedging. "Amy very generously offered to work my hours at the store this weekend, so I guess Erik and I will just go home, back to Amber Court, and, um…and, ah…and…you know…start our life together."

"Oh, you can't start you life together at Amber Court," Sylvie told her.

"Why not?" asked Jayne, thinking the question a very good one.

"As nice as Amber Court is," Meredith said, "it's no place for a honeymoon."

"Well, actually," Jayne said, "since we rushed the wedding the way we did—we did so want to be married right away—Erik and I kind of planned to take our honeymoon later." *Much later,* she added to herself. *Like a year from now. After we divorce. In separate cities.*

"Jayne, this is your wedding day," Lila reminded her unnecessarily. "It's special. You don't want to go back to your apartment."

"I don't?"

"Of course not," Sylvie said.

"Then…where do I want to go?" Immediately after voicing the question, Jayne regretted it. Because she was certain her friends were going to reply with something like—

"You want to go someplace *romantic,*" Meredith said.

—that.

"But…but…but…" Jayne began. However, no other words came to her rescue.

"And someplace romantic is exactly where you and Erik are going to go now," Lila told her. "The three of us took up a collection at Colette this week, and we got you and Erik something very special for your wedding present. It's all taken care of. One romantic honeymoon weekend, coming right up."

"What do you mean?" Jayne asked as a sinking feeling settled in the pit of her stomach.

"There's been a slight change in your plans for today," Sylvie said with a knowing little grin that Jayne decided right away she didn't like at all.

"From all of us at Colette to both of you," Meredith added—with the same knowing little grin. "A romantic weekend for two at the Sunset Inn Bed and Breakfast."

Uh-oh, Jayne thought. The Sunset Inn Bed and Breakfast was, hands down, the most beautiful, picturesque, *romantic* place within a hundred miles of Youngsville. Situated just outside of town, it was a sprawling Victorian farmhouse, which had been renovated several years ago to be a very lovely, very quiet, very peaceful—very *romantic*—getaway.

"And your chariot to take you to this romantic weekend awaits outside," Sylvie said.

"What chariot?" Jayne asked, liking this present less and less with every new remark she heard.

"The big stretch limo parked outside in front of the courthouse," Meredith told her.

Lila nodded. "The driver has instructions to take you and Erik directly to the Sunset Inn and to leave you stranded there until Sunday afternoon."

"But...but...but...I can't go now. I don't have anything packed," Jayne objected. "I can't go away for the weekend without luggage." There, she thought. That ought to settle it.

"We already packed a bag for you," Sylvie said. "And we put it in your room this morning. It has all the things you'll need for a honeymoon weekend."

"Which means hardly anything at all," Lila told her with another one of those knowing little smiles.

"But...but...but..." Jayne tried again. Oh, this wasn't good *at all*. "But what about Erik?" she asked. "He didn't pack anything, either."

''Oh, we took care of all of Erik's needs, too,'' Sylvie said. ''Don't you guys worry about a thing.''

And this wasn't supposed to worry her? Jayne thought frantically.

Oh, dear. What was she going to do? She couldn't very well tell her friends that she couldn't accept their gift. Not only would it be frightfully impolite, after all the trouble and expense they'd gone to, but how was she supposed to explain a couple of newlyweds—a couple of supposedly wildly in-love newlyweds, so wildly in love that they hadn't been able to wait a moment longer to get married— who didn't want to spend the weekend alone together at a romantic little getaway like the Sunset Inn, compliments of someone else?

''I, uh…'' Jayne sighed fitfully and gave up trying. What was the point? There was no way she was going to be able to talk her way out of this one. ''Thanks,'' she said, trying to sound convincing. ''Thanks a lot, you guys. It was very…thoughtful of you. And…and very sweet, too.''

She smiled, and somehow managed to make the gesture look sincere. She knew it looked sincere, because, strangely, it felt sincere. What Lila, Sylvie and Meredith had done *was* very thoughtful. Very sweet. It showed her how much they cared about her, even having known her only a month. Good friends, Jayne knew, were hard to come by. She wasn't about to risk losing them over a thoughtful, sweet gesture like this.

''Thanks,'' she said again. ''I'm sure Erik will be as surprised and delighted as I am.''

Oh, boy, was Erik delighted, Jayne thought as they entered their room at the Sunset Inn and he closed the door behind them. Way too delighted, in her opinion. When she'd told him what her friends had done, he had chuckled with what sounded like genuine satisfaction, and his expression had turned positively sublime. And now, as he looked around their room, his expression grew even more wistful, more wicked, more…wanton?

Uh-oh.

Oh, surely she was only imagining things in her nervousness, Jayne told herself. Why on earth would Erik look wistful? Wicked? Wanton? He barely knew her.

Though the Sunset Inn truly was romantic, Jayne had to admit. Romantic enough to generate wistful, wicked, wanton thoughts in anyone. Except her, of course. No way would she ever feel wistful, wicked or wanton. Not around Erik, at any rate. No, she'd only feel those things for the man with whom she fell in love someday. And that man most assuredly was *not* Erik Randolph. Because when Jayne fell in love, it would be with a man who could make a lifelong commitment to her. Erik had made clear his inability to do that. Husband—*gulp*—or not, there would be no wistful, wicked wantonness in this arrangement.

None.

What Jayne felt winding through her own body just then was something else entirely. Even if it *did* feel just a tad wistful, wicked, and—she might as well admit it— wanton.

It was nervousness, that was all, she assured herself again. With his silky sable hair and espresso eyes, and that way he had of looking at a woman as if she were the most desirable creature on the planet, Erik Randolph would inspire that kind of reaction in any woman. And Jayne, being the inexperienced sort that she was, would be in no way immune.

And besides, their room *was* awfully romantic. Situated on the second floor of the three-story structure, it overlooked the garden in back and a lovely pond beyond. After that came rolling green hills as far as the eye could see, beneath a flawless, bright blue sky. The furnishings within were turn-of-the century antiques, with a huge hooked rug spanning a good bit of the hardwood flooring. There was a mahogany chest of drawers pushed into one corner, with an ornate, scrollwork mirror hanging above it. A marble-topped table boasting a massive and sweet-smelling bouquet of flowers was situated beneath the window, an old-fashioned rocking chair placed beside it. A charming cheval mirror stood in another corner, and at the center of it all...

At the center of it all was a quite lovely—if rather troubling—four-poster bed.

It was at that last piece of furniture that Jayne couldn't help staring. Because it, too, was turn-of-the-century, and not even close to its more modern, queen-size counterparts when it came to accommodating two people. No, two people in that bed would definitely need to know each other *very* well. And care for each other *very* much. Because they'd be squished *very* closely together, whether they liked it or not.

And somewhere deep down inside Jayne, as she pondered the dimensions of that bed—and also as she recalled all that previously mentioned wistfulness, wickedness and wantonness—she realized she wouldn't quite be telling the truth if she said she wouldn't like being squished close to Erik Randolph. The problem was, she just didn't think she knew him well enough for...squishing.

Gee, she really wished she'd brought a book to read this weekend. Preferably one where there was absolutely no squishing going on.

"Wow, this place is incredible," Erik said, dispelling—for now, anyway—her less-than-comforting thoughts. "Your friends must care about you very much to give you a gift like this."

Jayne nodded. "It makes me feel even guiltier about not telling them the truth about our situation, and letting them think we married out of love."

He crossed the small distance of the room and placed his hands lightly on her shoulders. "It was your idea, Jayne," he said softly. "You were the one who insisted we make this look like the real thing."

"I know. And I will. But I didn't realize how hard that was going to be."

He smiled halfheartedly. "Maybe we can figure out some way to make it easier."

She eyed him curiously. "What do you mean?"

He shrugged, but somehow the gesture didn't look anywhere near careless. "We have a whole year to figure it out, don't we? And a whole weekend ahead of us to get a jump start on it."

Hmm, Jayne thought. She wasn't sure she liked the sound of that jump start business.

"And I do appreciate what you're doing for me, Jayne," he added. "Truly, I do."

Jayne sighed inwardly, hoping he'd still feel that way once he realized the full extent of what Lila, Sylvie and Meredith had done. Once he opened up the bag they'd packed for him, and realized that the two of them would be spending the weekend here like two newlyweds, he might not feel so appreciative.

Or, worse, she thought, he'd feel *very* appreciative.

As if reading her mind, he asked suddenly, "So... where are these bags that your friends said they packed for us?"

Jayne pointed to the two bags she'd noticed when they first entered the room. The two *small* bags. "That must be them over there."

Erik eyed the two—small—bags with much interest, then strode toward them. "I'll assume the flowered one is for you," he said, extending that—small—bag toward her. "And that the leather one is mine," he added, lifting that—small—bag into his other hand.

With no small reluctance, Jayne retrieved hers from him and moved to the bed to open it. And, just as she'd feared, she found it filled with the sort of things a bride would need for her wedding night. Assuming, of course, that the bride in question had married for something other than college tuition for her siblings.

Like maybe if the bride in question had married for love, for example, Jayne thought as she withdrew a bottle of very nice Merlot and two slender tapers fixed in two silver candlesticks. Or maybe if the bride had married for passion, she thought further as she withdrew a mere wisp of black lace that she suspected was meant to be a garment of some kind. Oh, yes. Her friends had certainly been thoughtful when packing this bag. There was no question what that little wisp of black lace was supposed to generate.

Thankfully, there were other garments in addition to the little black lacy one. However, few of them were any more substantial. The only one that would cover her reasonably well was a silky red number with spaghetti straps and virtually no back to speak of. It did, however, fall to ankle length—but everything between thigh and ankle was red chiffon and pretty much transparent.

When she turned to find out how Erik had fared, she saw that his own assortment of what was supposed to be clothing was no more abundant than her own. But where Jayne had misgivings about her collection, he was obviously quite pleased with is own, because he was smiling as he held up and considered a pair of brief boxer shorts made of paisley silk.

"Well, I must say, your friends have excellent taste," he said as he placed the boxers at the foot of the bed and reached into the—small—bag to discover what other surprises it might hold. When he glanced over at Jayne, he saw her standing with the racy red number held up before herself, and his smile grew broader—and more wistful, wicked and wanton, she couldn't help thinking. "Oh, yes," he added in a velvety smooth voice, his gaze scanning her from head to toe. "*Very* excellent taste."

Yikes, Jayne thought. What on earth had she gotten herself into?

She tried to laugh off the tension she felt winding through her body at the sultry way he was looking at her, but somehow the nervous little titter only made her sound sort of borderline hysterical. "Um, yeah," she agreed with some difficulty. "They're, uh...Lila, Sylvie and Meredith are nothing if not, um...tasteful."

Erik was about to comment on that, but he got sidetracked by the next item he withdrew from his—small—bag, one that rather countered Jayne's most recent observation about her friends.

"Well, now here's something you don't see every day," he said as he held up his prize. "Although I've never seen one up close like this, I've always wondered what a G-string for a man was really like."

Jayne shut her eyes the moment he identified the garment, in the hope that she might not get too good a look at it. But her effort, unfortunately, was futile. Because she did manage to catch a glimpse of the red silk...gee, *pouch* was probably the best word for it, but that somehow just didn't seem to do the item justice...before she closed her eyes. As a result, before she could stop herself, an explicit image of Erik wearing the...um, pouch...popped into her brain.

"But you know, as much as I appreciate your friends' thoughtfulness," Erik added, "I just don't think this is quite my..."

"Size?" Jayne heard herself blurt out before she could stop herself. Immediately she felt her face flush with embarrassment. Oh, how could she have said that? How inappropriate could she be?

Although, she thought further, truth be told, the G-string *did* seem to be a bit, oh...largish for...well, for what it was intended to contain. Mind you, not that she had any idea what the dimensions were of the average...well, the average thing that was supposed to be contained by the G-string. But still. Surely an average man wouldn't come close to filling that thing out. Would he?

"Style," Erik said. "It's not quite my style."

"Oh," Jayne replied meekly.

"The size ought to be just fine," he added. Not that he needed to add that, Jayne thought. Not with her overactive imagination running away with her the way it was at the moment. Not that that sort of thing was what a virgin's imagination should be running away with.

Or something like that.

Well, she thought succinctly. Well. Erik must not be...succinct, must he? He must not be an average man. And why, all of a sudden, did Jayne wish she knew more about average men? Or *any* men, for that matter? And why, all of a sudden, was she thinking that maybe, just maybe, this marriage business would offer her an opportunity to *learn* more about men? Or about one man, at any rate. Which, by default, would offer her infinitely more insight into the male animal than she had now. That way, when she did marry for love and passion someday, she'd know where to begin.

And just what on earth kind of reasoning was that? she asked herself. Honestly. One would think she was sexually attracted to Erik. Then again, she *was* sexually attracted to Erik. She'd be foolish to deny that. But being sexually attracted to a man was a totally different thing than being in love with him. And Jayne had decided long ago that her first time with a man would come about because she loved him. Not because he had beautiful espresso eyes and an irresistible grin and a charming way of making a woman feel as if she was the most desirable creature on the planet.

Because that was exactly the kind of man Erik Randolph was—one who had *a lot* of experience making women feel as if they were the most desirable creatures on the planet. In fact, Jayne wasn't sure she wanted to know how many creatures on the planet thought they were the most desirable, thanks to Erik Randolph. And she wasn't about to fall under his spell herself.

When she opened her eyes, however, she knew it was too late. He was smiling at her in a way he'd never smiled at her before, with a mixture of heat and wanting and longing that only a fool could miss. And she realized then that she was already under his spell. Because, heaven help her, she wanted him, too. She wasn't sure when it had happened, or why, but sometime during the week, as the two of them had gradually gotten to know each other, Jayne had begun to recognize needs and desires she hadn't realized she had.

Her heart began to race at the realization, rushing her blood through her veins at a dizzying pace. She inhaled a deep breath and released it slowly, hoping that might steady her some.

"Ah, well," Erik finally said with much resignation, tossing the G-string thankfully back into his—small—bag. "Guess I'll just wear the boxer shorts then."

He'd just wear the boxer shorts? Jayne echoed to herself. *Just* the boxer shorts? Nothing else?

Oh, it was going to be an interesting weekend.

"Even though I really am a briefs kind of guy," he added with another one of his toe-curling smiles.

This, Jayne decided, was information she didn't need. Because now she had yet another explicit image of Erik to add to the already ample assortment parading through her head.

"But I do like what they packed for you," she heard him say further.

She looked down to find that she was still holding the red silky see-through number up before her, and yet another explicit image exploded in her brain, one of her wearing it while Erik had on nothing but his little G-string, their slick, damp bodies squished together as they writhed in ecstasy on that little bed.

"But that little black number you held up a minute ago was nice, too," he added. "*Very* nice, as a matter of fact."

Oh, my, Jayne thought. It was definitely going to be an interesting—and long—weekend.

Seven

The thought came back to haunt her only hours later, as she exited the tiny bathroom adjacent to their bedroom, amid a plume of steam and wearing the red silk—and half transparent—nightgown. True to his word, Erik was wearing the paisley silk boxer shorts for which he had voiced his preference, but thankfully not just those. Because again, thankfully, Lila, Sylvie and Meredith had had the decency to include a matching paisley silk robe, and Erik had donned that, as well. He hadn't *tied* it, Jayne noticed uncomfortably, but at least he'd put it on.

Then again, it was an unusually warm night, she told herself. So maybe his state of dishabille was simply due to him being overly warm. Then again there were lots of reasons to be overly warm, weren't there? And seeing as how the Sunset Inn was air-conditioned, and seeing as how she herself had set their room thermostat at a very comfortable seventy-four degrees, and seeing as how she herself could hear the soft hum of that air conditioner purring right along, well...

Well, then it was reasonably safe to conclude that any sort of extra warmth in the room, whether Erik's *or* Jayne's was *not* the result of the climate control.

Which meant that the reason Jayne felt so overly warm at the moment, as she watched Erik—in his open robe and brief boxer shorts—pulling the cork from that bottle of Merlot, and as she noted the play and dance of truly spectacular musculature on his naked torso as he performed the task, not to mention the rich expanse of dark hair scattered across his broad, bare chest, and as she observed the capable fingers handling the bottle so gently, so tenderly, as if he were taking great, great care to touch it softly, caressing the glass as if it were the most fragile of lovers he intended to take a long, long time to satisfy, and...and...and...

And where was she? She'd quite forgotten what she had been thinking about...

Oh, yes. Now she remembered. She'd been trying to identify the reason why she was feeling overly warm. It must be because...because...because... Well, because she'd just had a hot bath, that was why. Yep. That must be it. Hot bath. No two ways about it. Nosir.

That was her story, and she was sticking to it.

Jayne sighed fitfully and tried hard to pull her gaze away from Erik. Truly, she did try. But for some reason she simply could not turn her focus away from the exquisite perfection of his nearly naked body, or from the too-handsome-for-his-own-good—or her good, for that matter—features. She was just too mesmerized by his beauty of movement to do anything but stare.

Oh, she really should have kept her suit on, she thought, crossing her arms awkwardly over her own scantily covered torso. Of course, if she'd done that, then she'd be feeling—and smelling—pretty ripe by the time the weekend was over. No, best to save the suit for when she and

Erik had to go home on Sunday. Which meant that, until Sunday, they were pretty much confined to this room. Thank goodness the Sunset Inn provided room service.

Of course, that meant they were likewise confined to these garments, Jayne realized. And there wasn't much room service could do about that, was there?

"Would you like a glass of wine?" Erik asked when he glanced up from pouring his own.

She nodded eagerly. Maybe a small glass would calm her nerves a bit and help her to sleep later. "Please," she said softly.

"Your friends have good taste in wine, too," he said as he tipped the bottle over a second glass.

"They know a good thing when they see it, I suppose," she agreed.

Erik hesitated a moment, then, very quietly he asked, "So then…what was their opinion of me?"

His question surprised her. Not just the query itself, but the way he asked it—as if he were genuinely curious about the answer. She was also surprised by the fact that he asked it at all. Really, what should he care what Lila, Sylvie and Meredith thought of him? He would be seeing very little of them over the coming year. And he wouldn't be seeing them at all, once this sham of a marriage was dissolved at the end of that year. Nevertheless, it was obvious that he cared very much.

"They like you," Jayne told him honestly. "Naturally they were surprised when I told them it was the celebrated Erik Randolph I was marrying—"

"Ooo, 'the celebrated Erik Randolph,'" he interjected with a chuckle. "I like the sound of that."

She smiled. "But once they met you, I really don't think it took much to convince them that I fell in love with you in a few months' time and wanted to marry you. Allegedly, I mean," she hastily added. "You're a very lovable guy."

He smiled. "Am I now?"

Oops. Maybe she shouldn't have gone so far as to say that, Jayne thought. Because there was just something about that smile…

"That's exactly how my family reacted to you," he said, chasing her observation away. "Until the night you came to dinner at the house, they all thought I'd just run out and grabbed the first woman I could find to marry."

This time Jayne was the one to smile. "Well, didn't you?" she asked.

"Certainly not," he replied indignantly. "You were the fourth woman I asked."

She gaped at him. "The fourth?" she demanded, feeling slighted for some reason. "I finished in *fourth* place?"

"Well, I hadn't met you yet when I proposed to the other three," he told her lightly. "Had I met you before them, I'm reasonably certain you would have been my first choice."

"*Reasonably* certain?" she squeaked.

"Very certain," he hastily corrected himself, smiling that teasing, toe-curling smile again.

"Hmpf," she said, feigning effrontery. She crossed her arms over her midsection and turned her head haughtily away, tipping her chin up indignantly as she closed her eyes. "Hmpf," she said again. "I'll bet you say that to all the girls who finish fourth."

He crossed the room slowly, the soft *swoosh* of his robe her only clue that he was moving toward her. But she felt his arm brush lightly against hers as he came to a halt beside her, and she could smell the clean, spicy scent of him, thanks to the shower he had taken prior to her bath.

Sandalwood, she thought as she inhaled the sweet-tangy fragrance. There had been a bar of the soap among the effects her friends had packed for him. His scent and his warmth both seemed to surround her as he approached, enfolding her, embracing her, but she told herself she must just be imagining that. Imagination or no, though, deep down inside of her, something began to purr with delight and anticipation in response to his nearness.

Experimentally she opened her eyes and turned her face toward him a bit, so that she might consider him more fully. "Fourth place," she said yet again, this time with playful indignity.

Erik continued to smile as he extended her glass of wine toward her and cooed, "Oh, come now, Jayne. Don't be like that. We don't need to be having a tiff on our wedding night."

She hesitated a moment, then turned her entire body back to face him and dropped her hands back to her sides. Then she reached for the glass he'd extended toward her, curling her fingers around the elegant stem. "I have a perfectly good reason for tiffing," she told him. "I feel quite tiffed."

His smile went positively indecent at that. "Then I'll just have to think of some way to...untiff you, won't I?"

Oh, my.

What on earth was she doing? Jayne wondered. She was actually *flirting* with Erik Randolph. In a scandalous negligee, no less. What could she possibly be thinking? That the two of them might spend the evening in a romantic fashion? That she might actually try to *seduce* him? Then again, he was her husband, so if she *did* decide to seduce him, it would be perfectly—

Nothing, she told herself firmly. There would be no seducing going on, tonight or any night. For heaven's sake, she didn't even know *how* to seduce a man, so who did she think she was kidding anyway? Which, on second thought, was probably actually all right, because Erik surely had no end of experience when it came to seduction, and he'd no doubt be able to talk Jayne into just about—

Nothing, she told herself firmly again. Erik would no more seduce her than she would him. End of discussion.

Probably.

"So now here I am wondering," he said in a soft, smooth voice as he lifted a hand to run the pad of his index finger lightly over her naked shoulder, "what, exactly, it's going to take to untiff my lovely new bride."

Uh-oh, Jayne thought. To put it mildly.

A thrill of heat shot through her where he touched her, becoming a veritable river of fire as it wound through her body from fingertip to toe. What was happening? she wondered. She'd never felt anything like this before. Oh, certainly there had been one or two times during the past week when she'd glanced up to find Erik looking at her in a way that made her feel all warm and tingly inside, but this...

This was different. A lot different. And whatever the sensation was, it had come out of nowhere, hitting her blindside, and now Jayne had no idea what to do.

In her nervousness she abruptly lifted her glass to her lips for a sip, but in her haste, she sloshed a good bit of her wine over her hand and fingers. She groaned her distress as she began to shift the glass from one hand to the other, but before she could make a move to remedy the situation, Erik caught her Merlot-drenched hand in his own.

"Allow me," he said softly.

And before Jayne realized what he intended, he lifted her hand to his lips and began to sip the wine from her sensitive flesh, dragging the tip of his tongue gently along her index finger, then to the delicate curve between it and her thumb, collecting the wine as he went.

The sensation that shot through her then was, oh...too exquisite for words. The sensuous glide of his tongue over her tender flesh, the sight of his mouth savoring her skin with such pleasure, the intimacy of the gesture itself... All combined to send a bolt of heat rocketing through her entire body. All Jayne could do was watch as he turned her hand one way, then another, taking each finger, one by one, into his mouth for an idle taste. The damp heat enclosing her hand gradually permeated her entire body, and, involuntarily, her eyes fluttered closed. She inhaled a deep, drugging breath, hoping to steady her raging pulse, then had to release it in a quick rush of air that made her dizzier still.

When she opened her eyes again, it was to see Erik turn her hand in his, until he could brush his lips lightly over her bare wrist, and up along the inside of her arm. His warm breath skittered over her delicate skin as he went, igniting little fires everywhere he touched her.

"Wh-what are you doing?" she asked breathlessly.

He grazed a few more light kisses along her skin, to the vee of her elbow, nuzzling the delicate flesh there with his nose. "I'm trying to untiff you," he said lightly. Then he glanced up at her and, as he ran the pad of his thumb over the soft, sensitive skin inside her arm, he asked, "Is it working?"

Oh, boy, was it working, Jayne thought. She'd never felt more untiffed in her life than she did in that moment.

"Um, yeah," she said a bit dreamily. "I, uh, I think it is, as a matter of fact."

"Good," he said simply, softly, before returning his mouth to the place where his thumb was driving her mad with slow, sensuous circles.

Jayne instructed herself—quite forcefully, too—to tell him to stop, that he'd gone far enough, that now that she was untiffed, they could spend the rest of the evening playing Hang Man or I Spy or something. Somehow, though, the words never made it out of her brain and into her mouth. Instead, she only stood there, growing more and more mesmerized—and more and more aroused—as Erik once again lifted her arm to his mouth and dragged his lips higher and higher, toward her shoulder.

Erik, however, didn't seem to be suffering from the same inability of speech as Jayne, because as he brushed his mouth gently along her arm, he whispered, "You taste even better than the wine, Jayne, did you know that?"

A little explosion detonated in her belly, spreading heat throughout her entire midsection. "Oh, Erik..." she murmured.

He rubbed his mouth lightly over the curve of her shoulder, then he nosed aside the minuscule spaghetti strap of her gown, urging it down over her arm. "And you are infinitely more intoxicating," he added.

"Oh, *Erik...*"

Now he reached for her wineglass, removing it from her nearly numb fingers just before she would have let it drop heedlessly to the floor. He placed it and his own on the dresser, then turned her fully around to face him. His expression indicated quite clearly what he had in mind. And Jayne told herself she was totally unprepared for that, not to mention completely unwilling.

Until he said, "I want to make love to you, Jayne."

And then she began to have second thoughts. And third thoughts. And fourth thoughts. And—

She shouldn't do this, she told herself. She'd never made love with anyone before, and she'd promised herself ever since she was a little girl that she would be in love the first time she gave herself to a man. But there was something about Erik that made her reconsider that decision, something about her response to him that made this suddenly seem like the right thing to do.

She wasn't a little girl anymore, in any way, shape or form. She had been robbed of her innocence with her parents' deaths and the ensuing responsibility of caring for two younger siblings. And the world was a different place now from the one where she had made that promise to herself. And she couldn't possibly have anticipated a man who made her feel the way Erik was making her feel at that moment.

She and Erik *were* married, she reminded herself. Not that the marriage was real in anything other than a legal sense, but they would be together as husband and wife for a full year. Living together under one roof. Day and night. And if this was the way she was going to be feeling about him, responding to him, during the course of that year, then making love was going to be inescapable. Of that, if nothing else, Jayne was certain. It was only a matter of time until it happened. So why not just let it happen now?

Nevertheless, did she want Erik to be her first? In spite of her response to him, she'd known him a very short time. Then again, some women made love with men immediately after meeting them. It was only sex, she told herself. The most basic human instinct there was. And her husband—her *husband*—was…oh. So attractive.

She was still wrestling with her decision when Erik, evidently taking her silence as acquiescence, dipped his head to hers and covered her mouth with his. Their light kiss at the wedding couldn't have possibly prepared her for the passion and fire that was so present in this one. It was a spectacular kiss, confident, coaxing, convincing. Erik kissed her as if she were the answer to every prayer he'd ever sent skyward, as if he wouldn't be able to take another breath without her. He consumed her. He crawled inside her.

And he made her want him *so much.*

So Jayne took him, at least for now, at least until she knew for sure what she wanted. She didn't have to go all the way if she didn't want to, she told herself. She could just do a little experimenting for a few minutes and see where it took them. If things got too scary, she could put a halt to them. Erik would understand, especially if she explained to him that this was her first time with a man. She may have known him only a short time, but she was certain he was honorable. If she asked him to stop, he would.

Of course, she didn't take into consideration whether or not she'd be able to stop herself….

Nudging the thought aside for now, and acting on instinct alone, Jayne melted into his kiss, opening her hands over his bare chest, marveling at the heat and bulk of the musculature beneath her fingertips. Erik was hard in all the places where she was soft, solid in the places where she was pliant. She skimmed her hands lightly over his chest and torso, urging them beneath the silk robe and up over his shoulders, where his skin was smooth and satiny and hot.

It was, evidently, all the encouragement Erik needed. Because as Jayne cupped her hands over his bare shoulders, he let his own hands go wandering. He opened his palms over her back, scooping one down over her fanny to push her body closer to his. She felt him swell to hard, heavy life against her abdomen, and a hot fire licked at her own belly when she realized the immediacy and intensity of her effect on him.

He wanted her. In the most basic way that a man could want a woman. And something about the realization of that thrilled Jayne deep down, in a place she'd never known existed inside her. She'd never understood what it meant for a woman to have this kind of effect on a man, never fully comprehended how she herself could actually change his body, simply because he wanted her. And having that knowledge now made her feel powerful, potent, in a way she never had before.

And bolder, too. As Erik skimmed his hands down her back and over her shoulders and arms, Jayne pushed at the supple fabric of his robe, until it fell from his shoulders. In one swift move he withdrew his arms from the garment, letting it pool in a forgotten heap at their feet. Then his hands were back, exploring, teasing, tantalizing, and Jayne had free rein to follow her instincts further.

She, too, let her hands go wandering, down along the warm, silky skin of his bare back, over the salient biceps and triceps in his arms, back to the dark, springy hair on his chest, then up to the rough skin on his jaw and throat. It was a journey of newly discovered sensations, because never had Jayne been even this intimate with a man. Oh, there had been passionate kisses once or twice, but never anything like this. And now... Now she wanted to take advantage of the experience. So she did.

Erik did, too, she quickly discovered, because with every eager move she made to learn more about his body, he responded in kind. He strummed his fingertips along her rib cage, then higher, beneath the soft curve of her breast. Before she realized his intention, he covered her breast completely, closing his hand over the fabric of her gown, grasping her in firm fingers. Jayne gasped at the contact, and Erik took advantage of that, too, thrusting his tongue into her mouth to taste her more deeply still.

The dual sensation of deep kiss and palmed breast was nearly Jayne's undoing, and it was only with great effort that she managed to keep her knees from buckling beneath her. Erik closed his fingers more possessively over her, pushing her breast higher as he moved his other hand to her back, down over her bottom, which he likewise claimed with eager fingers.

She tried to murmur something—something no doubt vague and incoherent—against his lips, but she felt the fabric of her gown begin to rise then, and she realized Erik was the one responsible. Gradually, he tugged it higher, up over her knees and thighs, until he had bunched it around her waist. The hand at her breast joined the one at her waist, holding her gown at the small of her back in one fist, as he urged his other hand lower again, over the satin bikini panties hugging her hips. The skim of his palm over the fabric was an exquisite, luscious torture, but it was nothing compared to the need that shot through Jayne when he dipped his fingers beneath the elastic and touched her bare skin.

She gasped again at the intimate contact, and Erik once more took advantage of her reaction by deepening their kiss. He cupped his palm more possessively over her bottom, pushing down her panties until he had bared her completely. The cool kiss of air on that part of her that

was so seldom exposed sent a delicious shiver of anticipation through her. In response to her shudder, he dipped
his hand lower still, creasing the elegant line of her buttocks with sure fingers as he bent her entire body backward and kissed her more deeply still.

Jayne's knees did buckle beneath her then, but Erik
held her firm until she righted herself once more. He
skimmed his hand over the soft curve of her bottom again,
then began to tug her panties down over her thighs. Acting
on impulse alone, driven by some unknown need, Jayne
aided him in his efforts, until the mere scrap of satin lay
in a neglected puddle on the floor near his robe. Then
Erik pulled her close again, this time skimming his hand
down over her thigh. He lifted her leg up, cupping her
knee in one hand, then, as the silk of her gown cascaded
down over her waist and his other hand, he moved his
fingers over her bottom, and lower, between her legs.

And then...and then...and then...

Oh.

And then he was pushing a finger against her, inside
her, caressing the damp folds of her flesh, moving through
her slick heat to penetrate her deeply. Never in her life
had Jayne felt anything so keenly, so acutely, and never
had she been more aroused.

Not until Erik dipped his mouth to her ear and murmured explicit, erotic promises, words that made her both
blush with innocent embarrassment and hunger to hear—
to do—more. A second finger joined the first, then a third,
until Jayne went limp with wanting him. But even then,
he didn't quite satisfy her, only chuckled softly with satisfaction and scooped her into his arms.

He carried her to the bed, pushing the covers to the foot
as he lay her on her back. As easily as he had scooped
the lower part of her gown up over her hips, he now drew
the upper part down over her breasts, until the red fabric
was tangled in a circle around her waist. He lay alongside
her, gazing down intently into her eyes before covering

her mouth with his again. As he did, he cupped a hand possessively over her breast, massaging with the flat of his palm before rolling the pad of his thumb over the extended peak.

For long moments he only kissed her and caressed her, then he pulled his mouth from hers and kissed her cheek, her jaw, her chin, her neck. Lower and lower he took his attentions, nuzzling the small divot at the base of her throat, sipping and savoring the line of her breastbone, until he moved to one side and opened his mouth wide over her sensitive nipple to draw her fully inside.

The damp heat, the subtle pull, the gentle fingers pushing at the bottom of her breast to press her more deeply into his mouth, all of it combined to send Jayne into a white-hot frenzy of sensation. Never had she imagined she could feel any of the things Erik was making her feel. Never had she realized it could be this way between a man and a woman. Never would she have guessed how intensely she could want something—want some*one*. And never would she be the same again.

As Erik gently sucked her, Jayne wove her fingers through his dark, silky hair and closed her eyes, arching her body upward to facilitate his ministrations. When she did, he moved his free hand back between her legs, parting her again for his—and her—enjoyment.

She didn't know how long they lay there so joined. Time seemed to dissolve into nothingness, and the world slipped completely away. It was as if only Jayne and Erik remained behind, as if there were no other experience for her to enjoy save the one he made her feel now. And just as she thought she would slip away completely, just when she thought she would go insensate with wanting him...

He moved away from her.

At her whimper of protest, though, he only smiled. Jayne saw him smile through a vague haze of longing that blurred her vision and dulled her brain. Although she didn't know when it had happened, he was gloriously na-

ked now, and she gazed upon his body with a fascination
that bordered on awe. He was beautiful. Totally. And he
was hers. At least for tonight.

"Don't worry," he told her softly in response to her
murmured objection.

And strangely, Jayne realized she wasn't worried at all.
She trusted Erik. She knew Erik. And she…cared for him.
A lot. What the two of them were about to do felt perfectly normal somehow, perfectly right. She was glad he
was going to be her first. Because she knew he cared for
her, too. And she knew he would be gentle. She knew he
would take his time.

"I'm not finished with you yet," he added playfully,
as if he sensed her thoughts. "Nor are you finished with
me. That, I promise you. But I just want to…take some
precautions," he added. "Your friends were kind enough
to see to that, too."

For a moment Jayne had no idea what he was talking
about, only knew that she wanted him back in the bed
beside her, touching her the way he had been touching
her, doing all the delicious things he had promised her he
would do. Then she saw him move to the bag her friends
had packed for him and withdraw a handful of little plastic
squares.

And vaguely, she was grateful that someone had had
the foresight to think ahead. Because there was no way
Jayne could have seen this coming.

"Hurry," she told him.

And, ever the gentleman, Erik was nice enough to do
as she asked. Because in no time at all, he was back in
bed beside her, dressed for success. He kissed her again,
rolling her body toward his until they lay on their sides,
facing each other. Instinctively Jayne hooked her thigh
over his hip, and Erik moved a hand to her bottom again.
And then he rolled some more, until he was on his back,
pulling her atop him.

In her surprise, she sat up, straddling him, her hair cascading down over her shoulders and arms and breasts. She gripped his shoulders fiercely, and met his gaze levelly. "What...?" she asked. But she couldn't bring herself to say anything more. For some reason, she didn't want him to know how inexperienced she was. She wanted him to think she was sexy and knowing and seductive. Still, she wasn't entirely sure what he wanted her to do. So she only gazed at him, her breathing ragged and thready, and waited for some kind of cue.

"I want you to set the pace," he told her. "For our first time, I want you to be in control."

Well, that certainly sounded promising, Jayne thought vaguely. And not just the her-being-in-control part, either. If Erik was thinking of this as their first time, then he evidently expected this to happen again. And as far as Jayne was concerned, she could hardly wait. Still, it didn't help her with the next step.

"Ride me, Jayne," he said softly, raggedly. "Put me inside you and ride."

Oh. Oh, boy. Oh, wow.

Now she knew what he wanted her to do. But she still wasn't entirely sure she was confident doing it. Slowly, she moved her body backward, until she felt the stiff length of him pushing against her bottom. Then she lifted her hips and scooted back a bit more, until she was positioned directly over him. He smiled a *very* satisfied little smile, then reached up to cover both her breasts with his hands.

"Do it," he whispered roughly. "Do it now."

Slowly she began to lower herself over him, pausing when she felt the ripe head of him separating the damp folds of flesh surrounding the heart of her. He was so big. She wasn't sure he was going to... That she was going to be able to... But where his body came into contact with hers, a sharp thrill of excitement shuddered through her, and she wanted to know more. So, inhaling one deep, fortifying breath, Jayne rose up on her knees once again, and, in one quick, heedless maneuver, she pushed herself down over him *completely*.

There was one tiny hesitation as the barrier to her virginity was broken, and then the pain was quite intense. So much so, that tears sprang to her eyes, and she cried her distress out loud. Immediately Erik rolled their bodies again, so that Jayne was on her back beneath him, and he hastily pulled himself out of her.

Even in her pain, though, she cried out her objection at his withdrawal. "No!" she said, reaching for him. She looped one arm around his waist, splayed the other hand open over his buttock, and urged him back toward herself.

"Yes," he countered instantly, gently. He cradled his pelvis against hers, and she could feel his hard length between her legs, but he didn't try to penetrate her again. "Jayne, why didn't you tell me this was your first time?" he asked her quietly. "You should have told me."

"I didn't think... I didn't know... I didn't realize... I didn't understand..." But no more words would come, because no more thoughts would form.

"Oh, Jayne," Erik said. He brushed her hair back from her damp forehead, then bent to place a chaste kiss at her temple. "I didn't mean to hurt you. I'm so sorry."

She shook her head weakly. "It's all right. Don't stop, Erik, please. Make love to me."

"But you're in pain."

"Only a little," she told him. "It will get better now. It will be easier now." She met his gaze levelly with hers. "Won't it?"

He grinned, but there was something in his expression she wasn't sure she liked. Something almost...regretful? Now wasn't the time to dwell on that, though, she told herself. Not when there was so much more at stake. They could talk later. They would talk later. They had all the time in the world. Or, at the very least, a whole year.

"I don't know if it will get easier now," he told her. "I've never bedded a virgin before."

She smiled halfheartedly. "Then this is your first time, too."

He grinned again, and again there was something in the gesture that disheartened her. All he said in response, however, was, "I suppose, in a way, it is."

"Then make love to me," Jayne said again. "Make this the first time for both of us."

He looked as if he wanted to say something else, and she was sure he was going to protest. But he only remained silent for a moment, gazing down at her as if he weren't quite sure what to make of her, of this moment. Then, just when she thought he would roll away for good, he moved, bracing himself on his elbows, one on either side of her head. Then he lifted his pelvis from hers and, positioning himself just so, he began to ease—very carefully—back into her.

Intuitively Jayne spread her legs wider, even lifted one to wrap it around his waist. Erik uttered a soft, contented sound at that, and, little by little, entered her more deeply still. She felt tight and close at first, but he took his time, and as he pressed even farther, her body opened and stretched to accommodate him. The pain lessened with each passing moment, until he had buried himself completely within her, and then suddenly, somehow, the two of them fitted perfectly.

For a moment he only lay still atop her, gazing down at her in that puzzling fashion again. Then Jayne nodded, whispered, "Please," and Erik began to move. Slowly at first, as if she were the most fragile thing he had ever beheld, and he didn't want to break her. Then, as his own passion mounted, he began to increase his rhythm. Jayne joined him, thrusting her hips upward with every downward stroke he made, until the two of them felt as if they were joined in a way that would prohibit them from ever parting. Again and again, Erik entered her, claimed her, took possession of her. And more and more he gave of himself.

Oh. She really would never be the same again.

And then she stopped thinking and let herself only feel. Feel the sizzle of heat that slowly built into a conflagration, feel the coil of anticipation as it grew more and more taut inside her, feel the explosion of sensation as Erik carried her to a place she'd never visited before. And then...

Oh. And then.

And then a veritable explosion of sensation unlike anything Jayne had *ever* felt before. Somehow, it was as if her entire body caught fire and burned white-hot to cinders in a matter of seconds. But when it was over, she was still there, still in one piece, shuddering in the aftermath as Erik pulled her into his arms. Unable to say anything, she only curled her body against his, draping one arm weakly over his chest, nestling one leg lethargically between his two.

For long moments they only lay silently entwined. Jayne, quite honestly, wasn't capable of speech, and she suspected somehow that Erik, although capable, had no idea what to say. Vaguely she registered the feel of his fingertips as he brushed them along one of her arms. Hazily she felt the rapid up-and-down of his chest slowly lessen and grow more regular. Little by little she felt her own heart rate become steadier.

Eventually she sensed that Erik had fallen asleep, and, with one quick, subtle glance at his face, she saw that he had indeed surrendered to unconsciousness. Something in his expression, though, was troubled even in slumber. Worse, something in Jayne was troubled, too. She just couldn't quite say what.

Finally, though, sleep overcame her, too. And for that she was grateful. All in all, this wasn't how she'd planned to spend her wedding night. And she couldn't help wondering just what kind of beginning she and Erik had journeyed upon.

Eight

Little by little, Erik awoke to some of the most exquisite sensations he had ever experienced in his life, and he battled consciousness for as long as he could in an effort to enjoy them more. As the pink-tinted light of sunrise crept over the windowsill, he registered vaguely that he was in a bed other than his own, that the bed was much smaller and softer than the firm, king-size monstrosity he normally slept in at home, and that...

Well, well, well. That he wasn't alone.

Still feeling hazy and only half-aware, he noted that there was a soft, warm, naked body nestled against his own, her back to his front, her legs tangled with his, her silky hair cascading over his arm and her torso. Whoever the woman was, she smelled sweetly of lavender and sandalwood and some other wonderful scent he couldn't quite identify. Her round bottom was nestled nicely against his groin—oh, boy, was it nestled nicely there—and one plump breast filled his hand. Instinctively Erik curled his fingers more intimately into her soft flesh, and the woman exhaled a sigh of unmistakable contentment.

Who could she be? he wondered, full consciousness still eluding him. Although he'd had some wonderful dreams the night before, he couldn't recall acting out any of them in the real world. Where had he been yesterday? he asked himself, still feeling a bit foggy. Where could he have met such a lovely creature as she? Perhaps she was a debutante he'd met at a party last night. Or maybe she was an artist he'd encountered at a Pace Street gallery opening downtown yesterday afternoon. Or a dancer from a local premiere. Or a salesclerk from Chasan's, his most favorite store in the world. Or even a waitress or bartender to whom he had taken a shine. Or she might even be...

His wife.

Erik snapped his eyes open, fully awake now. Oh, yes. It was all coming back to him.

He had gotten married yesterday. And then he and his new wife had come to this bed-and-breakfast for a phony honeymoon. Except that last night the honeymoon had ended up being not so phony. And now all Erik could do was wonder if their marriage was going to end up being not so phony, either.

Oh, boy. This was not good. This marriage of convenience was promising to be more inconvenient than he could have guessed. And not just because, after last night, it was going to be nigh on impossible to keep his hands off his wife, but also because Jayne, Erik remembered in a flood of graphic, erotic recollection, had been a virgin last night. And now...

Now she wasn't. And he was the one who was responsible for that. And virgins had a bad habit of taking sex way too seriously. They had an even worse habit of thinking that the first man with whom they made love was special. And now Erik was worried that Jayne was going to take their marriage way too seriously—and think it was way too special, too.

Oh, this was not good. Not good at all. Never in his illustrious sexual history had Erik ever deflowered anyone. Had he known that Jayne was an innocent, he never would have taken advantage of her last night—or any night, for that matter. Not that she hadn't been fully amenable to being taken advantage of, he recalled with a reluctant—and very lascivious—smile. Not that she hadn't taken a few advantages herself, he recollected with a less reluctant—and even more lascivious—smile. Not that either of them could have in any way anticipated the fireworks that had exploded between them, he reflected with the most lascivious smile of all. Not that they hadn't enjoyed themselves immensely during the conflagration.

Especially when they had awoken wrapped in each other's arms and let it happen that second time.

Still, how had this happened?

Twice?

Normally, Erik wouldn't have been in any way dismayed that he and Jayne had consummated their marriage. In fact, he would have rejoiced in the knowledge that now he wouldn't have to remain celibate for the next twelve months. He and his wife would be able to partake of the sexual joys and pleasures that were due any lusty, married couple, then say their goodbyes at year's end with clear consciences.

But not now. Not with Jayne being previously uninitiated with regard to those joys and pleasures. Virgins tended to recall their first times with some wistfulness. Erik knew this, because he recalled his own first time with some wistfulness.

Women, he knew, were even worse about that fond recollection business. And Jayne Pembroke definitely seemed like the kind of woman who would put much too much emphasis on her first sexual encounter. She was going to think that what had happened between them last night was *important*. Whereas Erik considered it to be…

Well now, just what did he consider it to be? he asked

himself. Not important, of course, but…perhaps significant. Yes, certainly what he and Jayne had shared last night had been significant to him. But important? Oh, surely not. Not in the way it had doubtless been important to her.

She stirred beside him then, murmuring the soft, sweet sounds of a woman who has spent the night in the arms of a man who has thoroughly satisfied her. Pride mixed with Erik's concern then, along with something else he was hesitant to identify. At least he'd made her first time good, he reassured himself. At least she hadn't lost her virginity to some brute who wouldn't have seen to her needs. At least she would recall this event fondly. Wistfully. Importantly. Specially.

Oh, no.

In spite of his anxiety that he was doomed now, Erik was shaken by a profound fear at the turn his thoughts had taken, at the thought of Jayne with someone else—for the first time or any time thereafter. Somehow the idea wove an inexplicable thread of sadness through the fabric of his soul. Why he should feel that way was beyond him, but there it was just the same. He simply could not tolerate the thought of her with another man.

Get a hold of yourself, Randolph, Erik told himself as he prepared for Jayne's awakening. *She may be sweet and gentle and beautiful, but when all is said and done, she's only a woman. No different from any other. There's no reason to be getting all sappy and sentimental over her.*

He watched as consciousness gradually spread through her, noted the way she sighed her contentment and curled her body closer to his as she awoke. She lifted a hand to her hair, that soft curtain of silk that had flowed over both their bodies the night before, pushing a handful away from her face. Her eyes fluttered open then—those lambent, lavender eyes—heavy and slumberous in what was clearly a state of mind as disordered and narcotic as his own had been moments ago. She smiled sleepily at him, and Erik

noted how her skin was rosy and warm and fragrant. And
he realized in that moment that all he wanted to do was
bury himself inside her again.

And again.

Oh, no. This most definitely was not—

"Good morning," she said softly. She launched her
body into a languid, though thorough, stretch, wrapping
her fingers tightly around the spindles of the headboard
the way she had done the night before as he'd... Well, as
he'd done so many things to her that were probably best
left simmering on the back burner for now. So to speak.

"Good morning," he returned softly. "How do you
feel?"

She inhaled slowly, deeply, and released the breath in
a long, leisurely sigh. "I feel wonderful. A little sore in
places, but..."

She blushed then, and Erik didn't think he could ever
recall such a reaction in any of his lovers. Normally he
bedded women who were as experienced as he was himself—or even more so. Never had any of them blushed
when recalling their adventures of the previous evening.
Purred with contentment, yes. Uttered erotic, explicit de-
mands for more, certainly. And he had always happily
accommodated them.

But something about Jayne's blushing now wedged its
way into a part of him where he would have previously
sworn he was incapable of feeling anything. It was at that
moment that he completely understood what Frank Sinatra
meant when he sang about having someone under his skin.
And Erik realized that none of the purring or demanding
had ever come close to arousing him the way simply gazing upon Jayne—all warm and naked and innocent and
blushing—did.

"You know what they say about that soreness, don't
you?" he asked.

She shook her head and blushed some more, and Erik
went hard as a rock at seeing it.

"They say you should just climb right back in the saddle again." He smiled. "To put it incredibly crassly."

She expelled a single little chuckle, and it was almost convincing. But he could see that she was no more comfortable with what had happened last night than he was himself. Though her reasons were probably not the same as his own.

"Are you all right, Jayne?" he asked simply, softly.

She hesitated a moment, then nodded. "I think so."

"But you're not sure?"

This time she shook her head. "I don't quite know how I'm supposed to feel. Or what I'm supposed to do. Or what I'm supposed to say to you now. It's very confusing."

Well, he certainly couldn't disagree with her there. He, too, hesitated a moment before asking, "Jayne, why didn't you tell me last night that you'd never been with a man before?"

She scrunched up her shoulders in something of a shrug, but there was nothing careless in the gesture. In fact, although she was adequately enough covered by the sheet, she tugged it higher still, to just below her neck, as if she were suddenly embarrassed by her nakedness. Funny thing was, though, Erik suspected it wasn't so much her physical nakedness that she was trying to cover as it was another sort of nakedness entirely. And sheets didn't help with that.

"I don't know why I didn't tell you," she said. "I just…I wanted you to think I was experienced. I was afraid you wouldn't want me if I was a virgin."

"Oh, Jayne…" he began.

But for the life of him, Erik had no idea what else to say. Because no matter how many times he told himself he *wouldn't* have wanted her if he'd known she was a virgin, he couldn't quite make himself believe it. Somehow the knowledge that he was her first lover, the realization that no man before him had touched her the way he had... Somehow that only made her all the more special to him.

And that, quite frankly, scared the hell out of him.

When he made no effort to finish whatever it was he had intended to say, Jayne asked, "Would you have? Wanted me, I mean? If you'd known I'd never...you know...before?"

He sighed heavily and rose to rest his weight on one elbow beside her, then gazed down at her face quite openly. Unable to help himself, he lifted a hand to her hair and brushed a handful of the silky tresses back from her forehead. Then he leaned down and placed a chaste kiss at her temple. When he withdrew from her, he saw that she was gazing back at him with stark curiosity, clearly puzzled by why he had done what he had just done.

"I think, Jayne," he said quietly, "that it would have been impossible for me to resist you, no matter who—or what—you are."

And that, Erik decided then, was what terrified him most of all.

She seemed not to detect his fear, however, because she smiled shyly in response to his statement. But she said nothing further, only snuggled her body closer to his. Erik let her do it, mostly because he liked the way she felt nestled there against him, even though that, too, scared the bejabbers out of him.

He wasn't a morning snuggler. He never had been. Normally if he spent the entire night with a woman—which in itself was a rare thing—he awoke before she did and, as she lay blissfully slumbering, he dressed, dashed off an affectionate note of farewell and left. There was no mess that way. There were no repercussions, no recriminations, no regrets. This morning, however...

This morning he couldn't just dash off a note and leave. And this morning there were most definitely regrets. Not for what he and Jayne had done the night before, really, but because Erik knew it was only going to complicate what was to come. He and Jayne had a year to spend together, living together as husband and wife, even if that union was based less on genuine emotion than it was financial convenience. And before last night it had been pretty much understood that the arrangement would probably be unconsummated, and would definitely be uncomplicated. Now, however...

Well, now Erik had no idea what the situation was going to be. Not where Jayne was concerned, anyway. Speaking for his side of things, the arrangement would continue to be what he had anticipated and hoped for it to be: a year-long union during which he and his wife would enjoy each other sexually on a regular basis, then part amiably at the end of that year, both of them richer— in more ways than one—for having undertaken the experience. That, he was certain, was the way it would be for him. All he could do was hope that Jayne felt the same way, too. Otherwise...

Well. Otherwise someone was going to get hurt. And that was the last thing Erik wanted to have happen.

"Erik?"

Jayne's voice, so soft and uncertain, scattered his thoughts, and he was grateful for it. There were infinitely better things to dwell upon than what might happen twelve months hence.

"Yes?" he replied.

"I, um, I don't think we should do this anymore."

That, however, wasn't one of the things Erik had hoped to dwell upon.

"What?" he asked, certain he'd misheard her.

"I don't think we should do this anymore," she repeated.

Not do this anymore? he then repeated to himself. After what the two of them had discovered they could create together? After what had been one of *the* most satisfying nights he'd ever spent with a woman? But he had been

looking forward to many months of doing this with Jayne.
How on earth could she be saying oh, so casually that
they shouldn't?

"Why not?" he asked, voicing his thoughts aloud.

She didn't pull back to look at him, only crowded her
body into his, as if she couldn't get close enough to him.
Contrary to her actions, however, she repeated, "I just
don't think we should do this anymore, that's all."

Maybe he was mistaken, Erik thought. Maybe she
didn't mean what he thought she meant. Maybe she meant
they shouldn't snuggle in bed in the mornings anymore.
Or maybe she meant they shouldn't sleep naked anymore.
Or maybe she meant they shouldn't get married anymore.
Or maybe she meant—

"I mean we shouldn't make love anymore."

Oh. Well. So much for that.

"Why not?" he asked again, telling himself he was
only imagining the panic that began to well up inside him.
"Was it that bad for you?" He had intended for the question to be a jest, but somehow it didn't sound funny at
all.

He felt her shake her head. "No," she said. "It was
wonderful. It was..." But she said nothing more about
the incident itself. She only added, "It's not that."

"Then what?"

But still she wouldn't look at him. "I just don't think
it's a good idea, that's all."

"But why not, Jayne?" he asked again, more emphatically than before.

She sighed restlessly, and this time she did push her
body away from his. Sitting up in bed, she clutched the
sheet tightly to her chest, obviously unaware that one
small dip in the fabric revealed the lower curve of her
breast, a curve Erik found himself wanting very badly to
taste.

"This is supposed to be a marriage of convenience,"
she reminded him.

"And you don't think it's incredibly convenient that the two of us are sexually attracted to each other? Jayne, we're married, and we enjoy each other. What could be more convenient than that?"

"But accidents happen sometimes," she told him. "What if I get pregnant?"

"I'm *very* careful," he rushed to assure her. "You won't get—"

"But accidents happen," she repeated more adamantly. Somehow, though, he got the impression that the anxiety darkening her eyes wasn't a result of her concern that she might get pregnant. Jayne, he suspected, was thinking about another kind of accident entirely. He just couldn't quite fathom what.

"Condoms aren't 100 percent effective," she pointed out. "Nothing is. Except abstinence. I don't want to risk getting pregnant, only to have my marriage ending after a year. Therefore, I think we should abstain from here on out."

This time Erik was the one to sigh restlessly. "If you get pregnant, which you won't," he hastened to add, "I'll accept responsibility and provide for you and the child. You'll lack nothing."

She expelled a single, humorless chuckle. "Really."

Erik was mystified by her concern. "Of course. You and he will have the best of everything that money can buy."

Her mouth dropped open slightly, as if she simply could not believe what he had just said. "You think it's that simple?"

"Of course it's that simple."

"What about the things money can't buy?" she asked softly.

Now Erik was the one who couldn't believe what she had just said. "What are you talking about? Money can buy everything," he told her.

She gazed at him as if he had just grown another head.

"If the baby is born after we divorce, will you come over at two o'clock in the morning to feed her, and change her diaper? Will you take care of her while I'm at work? Will you be there when she comes home from school and says, 'I made Daddy a Valentine in art class today'?"

Something about that last image she described made Erik smile—though, for the life of him he couldn't imagine why. There would never be a daughter to make Valentines for him, that much he knew. And truly, he had never once experienced any desire to have children. Strangely, though, where before that realization hadn't bothered him one iota, suddenly the thought of never having children left him feeling a little bereft.

How very odd.

"Jayne," he began patiently, "I really do think you're getting way ahead of your—"

"Will you be there, Erik?" she demanded. "Will you?"

"It won't happen," he reiterated decisively.

"But what if it does?"

He sighed again, even more restlessly than before. "Fine," he muttered. Anything to put an end to this conversation *now*. He and Jayne could talk again later, when the two of them weren't feeling so dazed and confused by all that had happened last night. "We won't make love again," he lied. "There. Are you satisfied? From now on, you can stay on your side of the bed, and I'll stay on mine."

She shook her head, and the action made the sheet dip lower, and it was all Erik could do not to tumble her onto her back and cover her breast with his mouth before he buried himself inside her again.

"No," she told him, "you'll stay in your room and I'll stay in mine. Just like we originally planned."

"What?" he asked, still not believing she would go this far after what the two of them had just discovered together.

"We'll do just as we agreed to do, Erik. When we get back to Amber Court tomorrow, I'll continue to sleep in my room, and you'll take the guest room."

He gaped softly at her. "And until then?" he asked, feeling more than a little affronted. Never in his life had a woman booted him out of her bed. And this was even worse. Because Jayne was booting him not out of her bed, but out of *their* bed. "Where will we be spending the rest of our time this weekend?" he asked her. "In case you didn't notice, this is a small room, and we have no spare clothing and no means of transportation. Unless you want to call a cab this morning and risk raising your friends' suspicion when we return from our honeymoon a day early, we are effectively stranded here."

Which, of course, wouldn't have been a bad thing at all if it weren't for this silly abstinence thing Jayne had brought up.

She shrugged again, and the sheet dipped lower still, and Erik had to squeeze his eyes shut tight so that he wouldn't have to look at the exquisite prize being denied him.

"You're bigger than I am, so you can have the bed," she told him. "The love seat will be fine for me." Her words came out a bit quicker and sounded a bit more anxious, though, as she added, "And room service has been very accommodating so far. Surely they'll send up a good book or two if we ask them nicely. And I read in the brochure that they have board games available. I don't know about you, Erik, but it's been years since I played Parcheesi...."

Jayne closed the bathroom door behind her, turned on the spigot over the bath, adjusted the temperature until it was ju-u-ust ri-i-ight, tossed in a handful of scented bath salts the bed-and-breakfast provided for her relaxation...

...and then sat down on the toilet seat and began to cry.

Oh, how could she have let things go as far as they had last night? she asked herself, not for the first time since awaking scarcely an hour ago. What had she been *thinking?* Of course, that was the problem—she *hadn't* been thinking. She had only been feeling. Feeling things she'd never felt before in her life, things she couldn't have imagined she was even capable of feeling. Her response to Erik last night had come out of nowhere and hit her blindside, and she simply hadn't been equipped to handle it. So she'd let that response overtake her. As a result it had completely overrun her. And now...

Now she was a different person, both physically and emotionally, because of that response.

She'd had no idea things could be that way between a man and a woman. She hadn't come close to comprehending what it meant to surrender oneself to another person—or to claim another person for oneself the way she and Erik had last night. She hadn't realized how much it would deepen the bond she'd already begun to forge with him. She hadn't known it would, instead of satisfying her curiosity and hunger, make her curious about—and hunger for—more. She hadn't known that making love with him the way she had last night would only lock him in a part of her she didn't think would ever release him.

And that was why she had told him they shouldn't make love again. Not because she feared getting pregnant—though, certainly, that was also something to consider. But more than anything else, it was because she knew—she *knew*—that if she let it happen again, her feelings for him would only grow stronger. Every time the two of them made love, she was going to fall a little bit more in love with him. And when it came time for them to part in a year—

She halted the thought before completing it, then backed up to the one that had preceded it. She was going to fall *more* in love with him? she echoed to herself. But that was impossible. She didn't love Erik, as it was, so how could she love him *more?* Or was that the problem? she wondered further. Had she indeed already fallen in love with him? Had last night simply been proof of that? She'd always promised herself she would be in love the first time it happened. So did that mean that last night...?

No, it couldn't mean that, she told herself. She hadn't known Erik long enough to fall in love with him. Had she? Just because she found him to be gorgeous and sweet and funny and kind, and just because it felt good to be with him, and just because he made her feel happy and fizzy and warm inside, that didn't mean she was in love with him.

Did it?

The tub was nearly full now, so Jayne switched off the water and snatched a towel from the rack, burying her face against it. She didn't want Erik to hear her sniffling. He might think she was crying over him. Crying over how much she wanted a man who had made clear he would never commit himself to anyone for any length of time—unless it meant claiming a multimillion-dollar inheritance. Crying over the fact that she had lost him before even winning him over.

Because she wasn't crying over that. She was too smart to fall in love with a man who would be leaving her in twelve months' time. A man who was so earnest about leaving that he had put it in writing and signed it. A man who made clear that he would never, ever marry for anything other than convenience, and only for as long as necessary.

Jayne wasn't about to waste tears over a man like that. She was only crying now because...because...because...Well, because that was what virgins did the morning after, wasn't it?

Oh, who cared why she was crying? Jayne thought. She felt lousy. She was entitled. She only hoped this feeling didn't last the whole year. Because every time she thought about Erik, every time she remembered what the two of them had discovered together, every time she realized that it wouldn't be happening again, every time she recalled that he would be leaving her in twelve months' time…

Jayne sniffled and palmed her eyes and buried her face in the towel again. Well, it was enough to make a grown woman cry.

Nine

The love seat will be fine for me.

Those words came back to haunt Erik late Sunday morning as he and his wife—yeah, right—checked out of the Sunset Inn. There was no way he would have allowed Jayne to take the love seat while he slept blissfully—yeah, right—in the bed. So, naturally, on Saturday night, after the two of them spent the day in awkward conversation about the stupidest things—and playing Parcheesi—he had given up the bed to make himself comfortable—yeah, right—on the love seat instead.

At this point Erik felt that he could honestly say this weekend had been both the most rapturous and most annoying of his entire life. And he couldn't help but think it was just the beginning of a pattern that would last for the entirety of his marriage.

Oh, it was going to be a long year.

Now, as he and Jayne retreated to their respective rooms in her tiny Amber Court apartment, Erik berated himself yet again. What on earth had he been *thinking?* That he could simply ask a woman he'd just met to marry him for a year, pay her a large sum of money for her trouble, move in with her, with a bit of luck make love to her, and then everything would move smoothly along from there?

All right, well, yes, as a matter of fact, that *was* what he had been thinking. But that was beside the point.

The point was... He expelled an errant breath of air as he lobbed his suitcase up on the bed in the spare bedroom and began to unlatch it. The point was that nothing was going as he had planned. Something he had thought would be so simple was turning out to be anything but. And the not-planned part and the not-simple part were both looking to become habits.

The point was that he couldn't stop thinking about Jayne.

Of course, that wasn't entirely surprising, seeing as how they were married and would be occupying the same home for the next twelve months. But that wasn't what he was thinking about. No, he was thinking about how she had smelled and felt and tasted Friday night. He was thinking about the erotic little sounds she'd uttered as he'd made love to her. He was thinking about the heat and fire she had roused in him, heat and fire that he seemed incapable of squelching.

And he was thinking about how much he wanted her again.

Might as well put that thought right out of your head, Randolph, he told himself. *Because she made it clear it won't be happening again.*

And true to her word, it didn't happen again, at least not during the week that followed. On Monday morning Jayne rose and went off to work the day away, leaving Erik alone to do battle with the fearsome creature known as Mojo. Allegedly a cat, the massive black furball was, Erik was convinced, at least half panther. And it followed him about all day, he was likewise convinced, licking its chops, waiting for him to...to...to hurt himself or something, so that it could consume him in his weakened state.

By Tuesday afternoon Erik was thinking maybe it was time he took his father's advice and went to work for Randolph Shipping and Transportation. He had resisted thus far, and his father had let him, because everyone in the Randolph family—including Erik—thought him too idle and disinterested for the job. Or any job, for that matter. Suddenly, though, for some reason—and not all of it was because he was feeling like Mojo prey—Erik found himself experiencing the strangest feelings. Feelings like, oh...a work ethic, for example. A sense of purpose for another. Even a feeling of duty, and a desire to provide. That was what husbands did, after all, didn't they? he told himself. They provided. Maybe it was time he tried doing a little of that himself.

So on Wednesday morning he began work as his father's newly, if temporarily—at least for now, until they saw how things would work out—appointed vice president in charge of vague things they put temporary vice presidents in charge of. And by Friday Erik had a revelation. He rather enjoyed the work. And he was surprisingly good at it. It gave him a sense of purpose, a sense of being needed, a sense of worth. Best of all, it gave him something to talk to Jayne about at day's end.

Because, truly, the two of them needed something to talk about after spending the first week of their marriage— save that brief, erotic interlude at the Sunset Inn—avoiding each other. Avoiding seeing each other, avoiding talking to each other, avoiding being in the same zip code with each other.

Well, not tonight.

Because tonight Erik had had enough of Jayne's avoiding him. He'd had enough of her fleeing in the morning before he even awoke. Of her staying at work late, and coming home too tired to do anything but escape to her bedroom. Of her impromptu get-togethers with her land-lady and her friends from Colette. He'd had enough of her being wherever he wasn't.

He missed her, dammit. There. He'd admitted it. He missed looking at her beautiful face, threading his fingers through her silky hair, inhaling the sweet scent of her that drove him to distraction. He missed listening to her voice, missed seeing her smile, missed hearing her laughter. Hell, he even missed playing Parcheesi with her.

He just missed *her*. Totally. Completely. Irrevocably. And he wanted her back, in whatever capacity she would allow. He could make do with separate bedrooms, if that was what she insisted upon. But he couldn't make do with separate lives. Not for twelve months. Not even for twelve days.

It was the strangest thing to realize. Never before had Erik missed a woman the way he missed Jayne. Never had he simply wanted to sit in the same room with some-one, sharing her company and idle conversation. Never had he thought that company and conversation would be enough to sustain his interest in someone. Yet with Jayne, his interest had not only been sustained, but had flour-ished. And with less than company and conversation, too.

Now he wanted more. And tonight, he decided, he would have it.

Oh, he wouldn't force her to do anything she didn't want to do. He wouldn't even encourage her to do any-thing she didn't want to do. But he wouldn't tolerate her avoidance of him anymore, either. There was something between the two of them that had been generated the mo-ment they met. And in the weeks that had followed, that mysterious *something* had only multiplied. Erik wasn't sure what it was, but he knew it was there. He knew it, because he saw it—he felt it—every time he caught Jayne looking at him.

And he *had* caught her looking at him over the last week. Several times, in fact. Looking at him as if he were the tastiest morsel on the planet and she were a woman hungering for the merest nibble. Oh, those looks didn't last long, because she glanced away the moment she realized he was watching her. But they had been present. And they had been plentiful. And they had been meaningful, too.

And tonight Erik was going to get to the bottom of them, one way or another.

"Jayne?" he called out as he entered the apartment at just past six o'clock.

He wasn't much surprised when he heard no answer, however. He had beaten Jayne home from work every evening. Probably because of that little avoidance issue she had. Nor was he surprised when Mojo came tearing down the hallway in a black blur and hurled himself at Erik's ankle. Erik simply stepped deftly aside so that the animal went sliding past him, out into the hallway of Amber Court, looking rather foolish, actually.

Naturally, though, being a cat, Mojo recovered admirably, hopping right back up again and, with a twitch of his tail and an I-meant-to-do-that expression, sauntered back inside, plopped himself down on the sofa, and began to give himself a bath.

Erik *was* surprised, however, when, just as he was pushing the front door closed, Jayne pushed it open again from the other side.

She wore her pale-red hair down loose today, something she didn't do often, though Erik wished she would. And she was dressed in typical work fashion, with a straight, pale-blue skirt that fell to midthigh, and a snug, cream-colored top with a scooped—oh, boy was it scooped—neckline. She was wearing the yellow pin that he realized must be some kind of family heirloom, so frequently did she wear it, an interesting piece unlike any he'd seen elsewhere. He kept meaning to ask her about it, but she always slipped away before he had the chance.

He wouldn't broach the subject tonight, either, though for entirely different reasons.

Tonight it was because he had other things on his mind.

"Hi," she said as she entered, brushing quickly past him in a wide path, to avoid touching him. Her next words came out in a nervous rush, as they usually did whenever she spoke to him these days. "Sorry I'm late. Again. But I'm only home for a little bit. I have to go back out again. Dinner plans. With Sylvie, Lila and Meredith. Promised I'd meet them at J.J.'s. Don't want to miss it. Very important. There's sandwich stuff in the fridge, or, if you want, you can order a pizza."

"Oh, I don't think so," Erik said mildly.

His objection clearly caught her off guard, because she turned to look at him full on, mouth agape. "Oh," she then said, shutting her mouth again. "Okay. Well. I think there's some chicken in the freezer. Or pork chops or something. You could—"

"No, I didn't mean 'I don't think so' on the dinner selections," Erik said.

"No?"

"No."

She arched her eyebrows in obvious puzzlement. Oh, she was just so cute when she was puzzled, he thought. "Then…what?" she asked.

"I meant 'I don't think so' on the you-going-out part."

She gaped softly again, then, "Oh," she repeated.

"You've been avoiding me for the entire week, Jayne."

She shook her head vehemently in response to his assertion. Too vehemently for the gesture to do anything other than identify that whatever she was going to say next was a lie. "No, that's not true." Yep, a lie. "I haven't been avoiding you. I've just been very busy, that's all. I have a busy, busy life. I'm a busy, busy person. Busy, busy, busy."

"You've been avoiding me," Erik repeated more emphatically. "And tonight, Jayne, that's going to stop."

*   *   *

Jayne gazed up at Erik and swallowed hard, and, as had been the case every day this week, she had to fight the urge to hurl herself into his arms and kiss him senseless. With each passing day it was becoming harder and harder to keep her hands to herself, because her hands instinctively wanted to go to Erik. The last week had been one of the hardest she'd ever had to get through.

And, gosh, she thought now, there were only fifty-one more like it that she'd have to survive.

It didn't help that Erik was working for his father now, so that every evening she came home to find him dressed in one of those high-powered suits that made him so utterly appealing. Today's selection was a charcoal pin-stripe, which was now in a state of elegant disarray. He had loosened his wine-colored silk necktie and unfastened the top two buttons on his white dress shirt, and she watched with unmitigated interest as he shrugged off the suit jacket and tossed it over the back of the sofa. Next, he unbuttoned his cuffs and rolled them back over surprisingly sturdy forearms, as if he were preparing to undertake some very serious and difficult task.

He settled his hands on his hips, shifted his weight to one foot and opened his mouth to utter what she was sure was going to be a very stern order. He was halted, however, by a series of quick, loud raps on the front door behind him.

Much to Jayne's astonishment, however, he ignored the summons and only continued to gaze at her.

"Aren't you going to answer that?" she asked.

"I don't want to," he told her frankly.

"Why not?"

"I made plans for us this evening, and they don't include anyone else."

Yikes, Jayne thought. Fortunately, the rapping sounded again. She pointed at the door. "Well, um…I don't think we're going to be able to ignore that."

Erik didn't alter his pose at all, only continued to gaze at her in that maddening way that made her think he had big, big plans for her. Very softly, he said, "Maybe, if we ignore the knocking, then whoever is at the door will go away and leave us alone."

The knocking sounded a third time.

"I don't think so," Jayne said perceptively.

With a barely restrained growl, Erik finally spun around. Just...not toward the front door. "You get it, then," he muttered as he stalked off toward his room.

The knocking was punctuated by the chime of the doorbell, and Jayne, much to her surprise, found that she wanted to ignore both and follow Erik back to his room, ask him what had gotten into him, and hope that maybe a little of it would get into her, too, because she really, really missed him, really, really missed being with him, really, really missed being part of him. That was why she came *this close* to not answering the door at all.

Until she heard Chloe's voice coming from the other side of the door.

And before her sister could get away, Jayne flung the door open wide and squealed with delight. Because Charlie and Chloe both stood on the other side.

"Surprise!" they chorused as one.

For one long moment, Jayne could do nothing but stare silently, mouth slightly agape, at her brother and sister. Chloe's pale-blond hair was pulled high atop her head in a somewhat ragged ponytail, a few errant tendrils falling softly about her face. Her blue eyes reflected laughter and good cheer at having caught her big sister off guard.

Charlie, too, was close to laughter, his own shaggy blond locks long overdue for a cut, his blue eyes reflecting his smug satisfaction at having the upper hand on his big sister. Both of them were dressed in their standard college garb of blue jeans, hiking boots and T-shirts—an oversize red one for Chloe that was decorated with the large, entwined letters *I* and *U,* a stretched-out khaki-colored one for Charlie.

All in all, they looked happy and fit and carefree, and Jayne suddenly found herself wishing she could feel exactly the same way.

What on earth were Chloe and Charlie doing here? she wondered, nudging her unhappy thoughts away for now. Truth be told, she was very glad to see her sister and brother. She just wished their timing could have been a little better.

"We came to help you celebrate," Chloe said, as if she'd read her sister's thoughts.

Something cool and uneasy settled in the pit of Jayne's stomach at hearing her sister's announcement. "Celebrate?" she echoed nervously. "What do you mean 'celebrate?' Celebrate what?"

Chloe rolled her eyes in a way that Jayne was sure must be endemic to eighteen-year-old girls the world over. "Your *wedding,*" she said pointedly. "Which you sort of neglected to tell us about, something for which you shall pay dearly."

"Not that it won't take a while for us to forgive you for running off and getting married without telling us," Charlie added, sounding sincerely hurt by her action.

Chloe nodded vigorously her agreement. "Or for not telling us about your special beau in the first place. Jaynie, how could you?"

Oh, dear, Jayne thought. This was going to take some explaining.

"H-how did you find out?" she stammered, stalling for time as she scrambled for something that might adequately account for what she had done.

Truly, she had intended to tell Chloe and Charlie about her plans to get married. In fact, she had initially intended to invite them to the wedding ceremony. But every time she'd picked up the phone to do so—and every time she'd picked up the phone this past week to tell them the deed had been done—something had made her stop. She just hadn't known what to tell her sister and brother that would convince them she had married Erik out of love. The three Pembrokes were so close. There was no way Jayne could have hidden a love interest from Chloe and Charlie, even if she'd wanted to. They would have known she was lying.

Still, she should have made some effort to explain before now. Because now, a week after her wedding, it was going to look awfully suspicious.

"I called you last weekend," Chloe said in response to Jayne's question, pulling her back to the matter at hand, "and your friend Lila answered the phone. And when I asked her what she was doing here, she said she was here feeding Mojo. So I'm like, 'Why are you there feeding Mojo?' and she doesn't say anything for a minute, then she's like, 'Didn't you know?' and I'm like, 'Know what?' and she's like, 'That your sister is on her honeymoon,' and I'm like, 'Honeymoon? Why would she be on a honeymoon?' and she's like, 'Because she got married Friday morning,' and I'm like, 'Married? What are you talking about?' and she's like, 'To Erik,' and I'm like, 'Erik? Erik who?' and she's like, 'Erik Randolph,' and I'm like, 'Erik Randolph?' and she's like, 'Yeah, Erik Randolph—I thought you knew,' and I'm like, 'Knew my sister was marrying a gorgeous millionaire? Of course I didn't know,' and she's like—''

"Stop!" Jayne interrupted, holding up a hand as if that might help halt the flow of words. Honestly. Once Chloe got wound up and chattering, there was nothing that would stop her short of shoving half a pizza into her mouth.

"So what gives, Jaynie?" Charlie asked. "What's this about you getting married?"

Chloe nodded. "And where's the gorgeous millionaire?"

"I'm right here," a voice replied from behind Jayne.

Oh, great. Just when she thought it couldn't possibly get any worse. Now, in addition to having to scramble for some reasonable explanation for her actions regarding her wedding, Jayne was going to have to be distracted by the hunka hunka burnin' love that was her husband.

As if Erik's comment wouldn't have alerted her to his presence, she could tell he was behind her by the way Chloe's expression suddenly changed—going from simple curiosity to stark-raving awe in a nanosecond. And if Jayne had looked even half that silly as she'd stood gaping in silence a moment ago, well... Thank goodness it had only been her brother and sister who saw her that way, and not Erik.

Because when she turned around to look at Erik, she saw him smiling at her sister indulgently, as if this were the kind of reception he experienced from women all the time. And suddenly Jayne realized that the reason for that might be because this was precisely the kind of reception he experienced from women all the time. There probably wasn't a woman on the planet who wouldn't succumb in a nanosecond to his good looks and charm.

She herself had been captivated by him, if not within a nanosecond of meeting him, then certainly within moments of meeting him. And she considered herself to be a very practical person. There was no telling how many women he'd made swoon, over the years. No wonder he didn't want to bother with a blushing little virgin—or rather *former* virgin—like her.

Because he *hadn't* bothered with Jayne. Not once all week. Not that she had encouraged any sort of bothering from him—on the contrary, she'd gone out of her way to avoid him. And, hey, it had been her idea in the first place that the two of them shouldn't be indulging in any sort of...bothering, so to speak, anyway. But she hadn't thought that Erik would let her get away with avoiding him—not for long. Or, at least, she had *hoped* he wouldn't let her get away with it. And she had hoped that he would, you know, *try* to bother with her. At least once or twice.

Then again, he had told her only moments ago that her avoiding him was going to end *tonight,* hadn't he? Hmmm... So maybe he had intended to bother. Of course, with Chloe and Charlie here, that wasn't likely to happen now, was it?

Erik smiled briefly at Jayne—a smile so sweet that it almost convinced her they hadn't just been having an awkward time of it a few moments ago—then turned his attention to Chloe. "Hello," he said in that charming, captivating voice of his. "You must be Chloe."

"I must?" her sister asked dreamily, her expression still reflecting her utter amazement that gorgeous—and celebrated—millionaire Erik Randolph stood only inches away. Then, after another moment of staring in awe, she shook her head once, as if to clear it, and replied, "Oh. Yes. Oh, yes. I must be. I mean, I *am*. I *am* Chloe. Chloe Pembroke," she clarified as she extended her hand toward him—as if clarification were necessary.

"And this is Charlie," Jayne threw in for good measure, knowing it would be another several minutes before her sister recovered enough to recall the presence of anyone else in the room.

"Hi," Charlie said, stepping forward. But where Chloe evidently had no qualms about the fact that Jayne was married to a man neither of the twins had ever met, Charlie was obviously more than a little wary. Nevertheless, he, too, extended his hand, and after Erik wrestled his own free from Chloe's possessive grasp, he shook Charlie's, as well.

"Erik Randolph," he told the twins.

"I know," Chloe said with a sigh.

Oh, she really was going to have to have a little talk with her sister, Jayne thought, if Chloe succumbed to the opposite sex this easily. Of course, she further recalled reluctantly, she herself had succumbed with record speed last weekend when it came to the opposite sex, hadn't she? Yes, she'd fallen right under Erik's spell, without a second thought. Then again, once he'd started touching her the way he had, she hadn't been capable of something so mundane as thinking, had she? No, she'd had other things—other responses—to occupy her then.

Best think about that some other time, she told herself. Like when she wasn't in the presence of her two younger siblings. She did want to set a good example, after all.

"Ahhh…come on in," she said when she remembered where she was, stepping aside so that Chloe and Charlie might do just that.

And when they did, she was somewhat dismayed to see that each of them was toting a weekender bag. Bloomington wasn't that far away—only a few hours' drive—so unless they were planning to stay over—

Uh-oh.

"So," Jayne began as her brother and sister made their way into the living room, discarding their bags by the door as they went. Charlie sprawled on the sofa in that way that only overly large teenage boys seem capable of sprawling, and Chloe made herself at home in the over-stuffed club chair. Leaving the love seat—oh, dear—for Jayne and Erik.

"So," Jayne began again as she took her seat there, squeezing as far to the left as she could, to put as much space between herself and Erik as she could. At this point she honestly didn't care if Chloe and Charlie found her behavior curious. "So I see you brought your bags," she finally concluded.

"Well, since the wedding was last week," Charlie said, "and since Lila told us you already had your honeymoon, we didn't think you'd mind if we spent this weekend with you." He gazed pointedly at Erik as he added, "You *don't* mind, do you, Erik? We wanted to get to know you, seeing as how we've never met you before."

Jayne sighed. Great. Now Charlie was going to be playing the part of the suspicious younger brother. This was all she needed. Especially since she had no idea how she was going to dissuade him of his mistrust when she didn't exactly trust this arrangement with Erik herself.

But Erik replied before she had the chance to, telling Charlie, "Of course I don't mind. We're family now. I totally understand your concern about me and Jayne, but I assure you, there's nothing for you to be concerned about."

Jayne nodded, hoping she looked convincing. "I know you guys are surprised. Erik and I were surprised ourselves when we realized how much we wanted to get married." Oh, she hoped God didn't strike her down for all these whoppers she was about to tell. "But it was something we'd talked about doing before, and—"

"And just where did the two of you meet, anyway?" Chloe asked, her own voice laced with skepticism, too, now that she was over her initial awe and captivation.

Jayne and Erik spent the better part of the next hour telling one fib after another in an effort to convince Chloe and Charlie that they were, in fact, wildly in love, that they fell wildly in love the moment they met and just didn't want to share that with anyone else, that they would be wildly in love until the day they died and that they didn't mind a bit if the twins wanted to spend the weekend with them, why the spare room was—

—filled with Erik's things, Jayne remembered suddenly. Oh, no. How was she going to get everything out of there and into her room without the twins seeing it? If they realized Erik was sleeping in the spare room, they'd know the marriage was a sham. And then they'd really be asking questions. And Jayne just couldn't bring herself to tell them that the reason she had married a virtual stranger was because they were all out of money, and she had been about to tell Chloe and Charlie that they couldn't go to school anymore, so sorry, but now they were on their own, good luck, and thanks for playing.

That wasn't something Chloe and Charlie needed to know about. Jayne knew they were adults, and maybe even capable of understanding why she had done what she'd done, but they were also both still kids in a lot of ways. In spite of the hard knocks they'd all suffered over the years, Jayne had managed to preserve an innocence and optimism in the twins that she didn't want to see torn away from them. Yes, she knew that they'd be entering the cold world of reality soon enough, and that she wouldn't be able to protect them from all of life's ills. But for now she could. And for now she would. Even if it meant keeping them in the dark about this arrangement with Erik.

"Um, Erik," she said suddenly, "why don't you take Chloe and Charlie out for ice cream?"

Three sets of eyebrows shot up at that. "Out for ice cream?" Charlie echoed. "Jaynie, we're not six years old."

"I know, but…but…but that would give the three of you a chance to talk and get to know each other better. And there's a Häagen-Dazs just up the street."

"But what about you?" Chloe said. "You should come, too."

Jayne shook her head fiercely. "No, I'll stay here. I have some, um, things to do. I want to *tidy up the spare room,*" she said, focusing her gaze intently on Erik's, "before Chloe puts her things in there."

"Oh, I'll help you," Chloe said, standing.

"No!" Jayne cried.

Again, three sets of eyebrows shot up, but where her sister and brother were gazing at her in outright concern, Erik, at least, was getting the gist of things. Because he nodded at Jayne and said, "Ice cream sounds like a great idea, kids."

Oh, great, Jayne thought. Now he sounded like Ward Cleaver. What next? Would he be smoking a pipe? Donning sweaters with elbow patches? Telling them what a bad influence that Eddie Haskell was?

"Well," Chloe said, clearly wavering.

"They have chocolate peanut-butter cup," Jayne said, knowing that was her sister's favorite.

"Okay," Chloe conceded readily.

"You, too, Charlie," Jayne said. "You guys will have fun, I know it."

Charlie didn't look anywhere near convinced, but he pushed himself up from the couch and strode after Chloe and Erik. "We won't be long," he told his sister as he went.

And for the first time that day, Jayne was confident that something, at least, was true.

Ten

It was after midnight when Jayne finally forced herself to go to bed. She used the excuse for as long as she could of wanting to catch up with Chloe and Charlie, and only when Chloe and Charlie themselves pointedly told Jayne that they were exhausted and wanted to turn in did she reluctantly retreat to her—her and Erik's, at least for the weekend—room.

He seemed to overpower the gentle femininity of the place with his utterly masculine presence, looking incongruous amid the Queen Anne style furnishings and the soft floral patterns, the lace curtains and the poofy cushions. He was already in bed when she entered, sitting on top of the turned-down, quilted coverlet with his pillow propped behind his back, reading a business journal of some kind. He wore only a pair of chocolate-brown silk pajama bottoms, and for some strange reason, Jayne found herself thinking his bare feet were very sexy. She smiled in spite of her nervousness.

Until Erik glanced up and saw her gazing at him. Until he dropped the magazine into his lap, threw her a decidedly lascivious look and patted the bed beside him. "Finally coming to bed, dear?" he asked in a voice that was also decidedly lascivious.

And Jayne was thankful then that she'd had the foresight to dress in a pair of massive flannel jammies that were decorated with various breakfast foods, in spite of the fact that she'd had to turn on the air conditioner, because it was unseasonably warm outside.

Hey, that air conditioner could get pret-ty chilly sometimes, she reminded herself. No need to go courting pneumonia. Among other things.

"I, ah..." she began eloquently. But no other words emerged to help her out.

"Come to bed, Jayne," Erik prodded gently.

Gulp.

"I...I...I... Okay," she finally said, knowing her only alternative was to flee back into the living room and/or points beyond, something that would surely rouse Charlie and Chloe's curiosity, if not their total alarm. "I'll, um...I'll just come to bed, why don't I?"

He smiled, then patted the mattress invitingly again. "Excellent idea. Wish I'd thought of it."

Slowly Jayne moved in that direction, but with every step she took the bed seemed to grow smaller and smaller. Finally she stood beside her empty half of the mattress and realized she had no choice but to sit down. Then lie down. Next to Erik. Who was half-naked. And had sexy feet.

Trying not to think about Erik—or his feet—she perched precariously on the bed, then pulled up her legs, first one, then the other, and tucked them beneath the covers. She scrunched herself over to the veriest edge of the mattress, as far as she could without falling off. Then she lay silently on her back gazing up at the ceiling, waiting to see what Erik would do.

What Erik did was toss his journal to the floor, tuck himself under the covers, too, then push his body way farther over the halfway mark than was even arguable. Jayne's heart began to beat a rapid-fire tattoo against her rib cage as he turned onto his side—arcing one arm over her head and balancing himself with his hand flat on the mattress beside her—then gazed intently down at her. She had to battle the urge to pull the sheet up over her head, and instead only gazed back at him, helpless to do anything else.

And then, very, very softly, he said, "You, um, you have cats on your sheets."

Somehow that wasn't what she had expected him to say. In spite of her surprise, however, she said "I like cats. Well, except for Mojo. But that's only because he doesn't like me," she added hastily in her defense. "He started it."

Erik smiled indulgently. "I've never slept on cat sheets before," he said. Then he eyed her attire—what little he could see, seeing as how she'd pulled the blanket snugly up over her torso—with clear amusement. "Nor have I ever seen a woman wear anything quite like that to bed."

"Hey, women wear stuff like this to bed all the time," Jayne assured him. "To their own bed, anyway. You've just never seen it with the women you've been to bed with, because the women you've been to bed with always have something else in mind besides sleeping in their bed when they go to bed with you." Realizing how hysterical she was beginning to sound, she added, "Or something like that."

"Don't tell me you don't have that in mind, too," he replied. Lasciviously, if she wasn't mistaken.

She blushed. Well, of course she *did* have that in mind—who wouldn't?—just not the way he thought she had it in mind. She was thinking how determined she was to avoid it, and he was obviously thinking how determined he was to—

"I like Chloe and Charlie," he said, surprising her again. "They're good kids."

She nodded, feeling relief wind through her body. Maybe Erik wasn't going to make this difficult, after all. Maybe he felt as awkward as she did. Maybe he was as disinclined to exacerbate the problem as she was. "Yes. They are good kids," she agreed.

"I can see why you're so devoted to them."

"They deserve the best," she said.

Erik's smile softened some. "Seems to me that's exactly what they have in you."

Something inside her melted and grew warm at the way he looked at her then. Not because the look was sexually charged, but because it was so affectionate. And that, more than anything, put Jayne on her guard. Sex was something she was sure—well, pretty sure, anyway—that she could avoid. Affection, however, was an altogether different matter. That wasn't exactly something she wanted to avoid. Actually, it was something she *couldn't* avoid. Because she herself already felt loads of affection for Erik.

He bent and brushed a soft, chaste kiss over her lips, then rolled back over to his side of the bed to switch off the lamp. In the darkness she could barely make out Erik's outline as he resumed his position beside her, again on her side of the bed. Only this time, after arcing one arm over her head, instead of balancing himself on the flat of his other hand, he lay down and draped his other arm across her torso. In an effort to brush him off, she turned on her side, too, with her back to him. But before she could voice an objection, Erik splayed his hand open over her belly and pulled her back toward him, nestling her body alongside his, spoon fashion.

And, *oh,* did that feel good. So good, she decided not to object after all. Not just yet.

"I was thinking," he said quietly, his voice a soft murmur just above her ear, "that since your brother and sister are here in town, maybe we could arrange something with my family on Sunday. It *is* my birthday, after all. Everybody could get to know each other that way. And I know my family would love to see you again.''

Well, this was certainly interesting, Jayne thought. Why would Erik want her family to meet his? Why would he want to encourage a relationship like that, when it was destined to end in a year's time? She was about to ask him if he thought that was wise when he began talking again and prevented her question.

''I'll call my mother tomorrow and arrange it. Let's plan for lunch at around one o'clock Sunday. That will give Chloe and Charlie plenty of time that night to drive back to Bloomington and finish any homework they might have.''

He sounded like a worried father, Jayne thought with a smile. Concerned that they might neglect their studies.

''All right,'' she told him, uncertain why she agreed so readily. Something in his voice was just so earnest, so eager to please. And maybe there was something in her, too, that simply wanted to agree. Something hopeful. Something she dared not think too much about. ''If you're sure,'' she added.

''I'm sure,'' he told her. After a moment's hesitation, he added, ''And there's something else I've been thinking about, too.''

Jayne wasn't sure she wanted to know what that something else was. In spite of that, she asked, ''Oh?''

He nodded against her hair, and the friction of the gesture set off a soft humming inside her. ''I've been thinking,'' he said quietly, ''about how much I want to make love to you again.''

That was what she had thought the something else would be. And she really wished now that she hadn't asked, and that he hadn't put voice to it. Because hearing him say it, so softly, so certainly, so seductively, only made her realize how much she wanted that, too.

In spite of her realization, however, she told him, "Erik, I thought we agreed—"

"It was an agreement made under duress," he interrupted her, nuzzling aside the collar of her pajama shirt to place a soft kiss on her neck. "I think we should talk more about it."

But he was clearly of the opinion that actions spoke louder than words, because instead of talking, he opened his hand more resolutely over her midsection, and began to drag the soft flannel across her sensitive flesh, up over her stomach, until he could tuck his hand beneath the fabric and open his fingers over her bare skin.

And just like that, Jayne was on fire. A conflagration exploded in her belly, racing to her heart, her brain, her every extremity. With that one simple touch, Erik made her want him. Then she realized that that wasn't really true at all. It wasn't Erik making her want him. She'd been wanting him all week long. She'd just managed to fool herself until now, because she'd run herself ragged every day to make sure she didn't have time to think about it.

Evidently interpreting her silence as acquiescence, Erik moved his hand higher then, up over her ribs and breastbone, until he caught the lower swell of her breast in the L-shaped curve of his thumb and forefinger. Jayne uttered a quick gasp of excitement at the contact, and she felt him swell hard against her bottom in response to the soft sound. She told herself she should object, should tell him to stop, but somehow she just wasn't able to form the words.

Probably because she didn't *want* to form the words.

And again he took her silence as consent. After only the slightest hesitation, he cupped his hand completely, over her breast, teasing the taut peak with the pad of his thumb. Jayne's eyes fluttered closed in the darkness, and she expelled a soft sound of surrender at the touch. Instinctively she moved her body back against his, growing warm and damp at the feel of his hard shaft stirring against her bottom.

She heard what sounded like a quiet chuckle, then she felt herself being rolled onto her back. Before she could say a word, though, Erik covered her mouth with his and kissed her quite thoroughly. Without even thinking about what she was doing, Jayne slid her arms up over his shoulders and around his neck, threading her fingers through his silky hair to pull him closer as he deepened the kiss.

For long moments they lay entwined, his hard weight pressing into her from above, his mouth plying at hers, his hands skimming up and down her bare rib cage and along the waistband of her pajamas. Then, vaguely, Jayne felt him unfastening the buttons on her top, and somewhere at the very back of her brain a little alarm went off, however faintly. She tore her mouth from his, gasping for air, noting only now how rapidly her heart was pounding. Just as he pushed the last of her buttons through its loop and spread her shirt open wide, she finally found her voice.

"Erik, it's not a good idea," she said, the words coming out in a ragged rush. But even she could tell she didn't mean it. Especially since she only wove her fingers more tightly in his hair and pulled him close again.

"It's an excellent idea," he countered softly before bending his head to her breast and flicking the tip of his tongue over her taut nipple. "Jayne, I want you," he whispered. Then he closed his mouth over her completely, pulling as much of her inside as he could, laving her with the flat of his tongue before sucking her hard.

"Oh…oh, Erik…" she gasped. "Oh, please…"

"Please what?" he murmured against her damp flesh. "Please do that again? Please don't ever stop? Please make love to me now?"

Jayne rolled her head from side to side as he turned his attention to her other breast, but she wasn't able to form the word *no,* which she told herself she really should say. Please…'' she only repeated, with more urgency this time.

Erik continued to suckle her as he dipped his hand lower, under the waistband of her pajama bottoms, then beneath the elastic band of her panties. Instinctively she parted her legs as he pushed his hand between them. Then she bent her knee and opened wider as he rubbed a finger between her damp folds, to facilitate his erotic exploration. Again and again, he touched her delicate flesh, penetrating her first with one finger, then a second, then a third. The friction of those movements was delicious, electric, and seemed to fill her up inside. She began to move her hips in time to his manipulation, until he growled out something incoherent against her heated flesh.

By the time Jayne realized Erik was tugging her pajama bottoms down over her legs, she was nearly insensate with wanting him. It was only with great effort that she managed to reclaim some semblance of sanity, recalling that her sister and brother were just a room or two away.

''But Charlie and Chloe…'' she said, the words emerging between ragged gasps for breath. She knew the protest was futile, seeing as how they were both too far gone to halt the inevitable, but somehow she felt as if she should make the attempt.

''Charlie and Chloe won't hear a thing if we do this carefully,'' Erik told her, pulling her pajama bottoms off her completely. ''Even if they do,'' he added as he went to work untying the drawstring of his own pants, ''hey, we're newlyweds. We're supposed to be at it like rabbits.'' He lay down beside her, gloriously naked now, and pulled her body alongside his. ''It will just convince them of what you want them to believe—that the two of us are hopelessly in love.''

Something about his statement sobered Jayne a bit, but not enough for her to pull away from him. She still wore her pajama top, though it gaped open and left her bared to him. Erik seemed not to mind, because he didn't bother to remove it. Instead, he bent to her breast again, dragging a few light kisses along the lower curve, before moving his mouth to her ribs, her belly, her navel, and points beyond.

Jayne was so overcome by the sheer pleasure of it all that she wasn't paying attention to where he went next. Not until he moved down to settle himself between her legs. Not until he shoved his hands beneath her bottom, and gripped one buttock in each hand. Not until he pushed her pelvis upward to greet his waiting mouth.

And then she couldn't help but pay attention. Because never had she felt such heat, such fire erupting inside herself. Erik tasted her leisurely, thoroughly, as if he were a starving man and she were the most luscious meal he had ever had laid before him. Over and over again, he savored her, consumed her, until Jayne could do no more than grip the spindles of her headboard and writhe beneath his ministrations.

Little by little, her breathing grew more erratic, harder and harder, until she didn't think she could keep quiet any longer. Erik seemed to sense her distress, because finally—*finally*—he moved his body back up along hers and knelt between her legs. At some point during her delirium, he had donned a condom, and now he wrapped her legs around his waist, holding her ankles firm at the small of his back. Then he slipped inside her, *deep* inside her, entering her again and again and again and again....

A tensely wound coil inside Jayne began to curl tighter every time he thrust himself inside her, clenching so taut, she thought it would never loosen. Then, as Erik increased his rhythm, as his penetration went deeper, that spring began to unwind. As he jerked himself forward one last time, as he spilled himself inside her, Jayne, too, felt a release unlike anything she had ever felt before, and she thrust her hips upward to meet him one final time. For long moments the two of them seemed to be suspended in time, then, as if the move had been choreographed, she reached for him, and he fell forward, collapsing beside her.

She wrapped her arms around his shoulders and held him close, and Erik buried his face in the curve where her shoulder met her throat. His breathing was as frayed and uneven as her own, his capacity for speech no better than hers. Neither of them spoke a word for some time. Each waited until their respiration had leveled, their heart rates had steadied, and their bodies had relaxed.

And even then neither seemed to know what to say. It occurred to Jayne, too late, that although they had taken precautions to protect her body, she hadn't done anything to protect her heart. And something she had begun to suspect earlier in the week, something she had absolutely forbidden herself to consider, became crystal clear in that moment. And it was a terrible, terrible thing to realize.

Jayne was in love with her husband.

And she had no idea what to do.

Jayne, Erik and the twins spent Saturday together, doing the sorts of things that families did on weekends. The four of them had breakfast together at a local diner, then Erik took them sailing on Lake Michigan. They enjoyed dinner at J.J.'s, where she and Erik had gotten engaged, and topped off the evening at an outdoor concert in the park. And through it all, Jayne had watched her siblings become as enamored of Erik as she was herself. And through it all, she only fell in love with him that much more.

The birthday lunch that Erik's mother organized at the Randolph estate on Sunday afternoon was even more fun, really more wonderful than Jayne ever could have imagined it would be. Mrs. Randolph—or, rather, Lydia, as she insisted Jayne and the twins call her—pulled out all the stops. The table was set with the fine Randolph china and crystal and silver, fresh flower centerpieces and place cards. There were elegant little sandwiches cut into crust-less triangles, fresh fruit and cheeses, cappuccino and mimosas. Never in her life had Jayne been a part of so grand an occasion. And it was for her and her siblings as much as it was Erik. They were guests of honor, too.

And, boy, were they made to feel like it, too. Erik's parents welcomed her and Chloe and Charlie with open arms, quite literally, hugging all three of them as they entered. Erik's sisters latched right on to Chloe, and Jayne noticed the three of them engaged in laughter and animated conversation every time she caught sight of them. Erik had made every effort Saturday to befriend Charlie, and now Charlie, her suspicious younger brother, was virtually Erik's best bud. By the end of the afternoon the two of them were chatting and laughing like old school mates.

It was nearly overwhelming for Jayne to see it all. For so long it had been only her and Chloe and Charlie, the three Pembrokes, you and you and me against the world. Now, suddenly, here was an entire family eagerly welcoming them into their fold, because Jayne had brought them into it by marrying one of their members.

Everything, truly, was perfect.

And Jayne entered a bleak, black depression as a result.

What next? she wondered. She hadn't anticipated this at all. It was bad enough that she had fallen in love with Erik herself. She hadn't expected for Chloe and Charlie—or herself, for that matter—to be so enthusiastically embraced by the rest of the Randolphs. She supposed she shouldn't be surprised—the Randolphs were known for being an outgoing, giving, warm family. And Chloe and Charlie were both utterly charming, captivating people.

Of course the Randolphs and Pembrokes would hit it off, she told herself. *Of course* they would all like each other. *Of course* they would all become friends. *Of course* they would all feel like family.

There was just one problem. They weren't family.

Not really. Not the way they all thought they were. Except for Erik and Jayne, none of them knew they would only be related for a year. And when that year was up, when Erik and Jayne dissolved their marriage, they would all be ex-family.

Would that make them all ex-friends, too? Jayne wondered. Chloe seemed to have hit it off especially well with Erik's youngest sister. She'd seen the two of them exchanging phone numbers and e-mail addresses, and promising to stay in touch regularly. They both had such a strong affinity for Marcel Proust and Gustav Klimt and obscure dance bands, Jayne knew the two of them would indeed forge a strong bond. If they hadn't forged such a bond already.

Chloe had never really had a best friend before. And she hadn't warmed up to anyone this way since their parents' deaths. And Charlie, whom Jayne had worried over for the past four years because he didn't have a strong masculine role model in his life, was already showing signs of looking up to Erik the way one would an older brother.

If things kept up like this—and truly, there was no reason to think they wouldn't, if the families were getting along this well—then it was going to devastate Chloe and Charlie to sever ties with the Randolphs when she and Erik divorced a year from now. And Chloe and Charlie *would* sever ties, that Jayne knew. They were too devoted to her not to. If—when—she and Erik divorced, even under amicable circumstances, the twins would side resolutely with Jayne. They would forsake the Randolphs completely, if for no other reason than to show their allegiance to their big sister.

A year, Jayne thought again. That was a long time for relationships to cement. By the end of that time, it really would devastate the twins to lose their newly discovered family.

Oh, what was she going to do? Jayne wondered as she

stood in the arch that separated the dining room from the parlor, where the luncheon party had retreated to enjoy coffee and dessert. She couldn't very well shout at them all to stop getting along so well, stop it right now, because they'd all be on opposite sides a year from now, could she? Even if the divorce was amicable, there were going to be some dividend loyalties. At best, there would be some awkwardness. At worst, there would be the complete severance of ties.

Chloe and Charlie had already lost so much, Jayne thought. They were just now getting to the point where they were rebuilding their lives and moving forward with them. She didn't want to see them embrace the Randolphs with wide-open hearts, only to lose them, too.

And *she* didn't want to fall any more in love with Erik than she already had, only to lose him, too.

"Nice party, isn't it?"

She spun around to find Erik standing behind her, as if he had been conjured from her thoughts. His smile told her he was quite pleased with himself for having succeeded in sneaking up on her. He looked very handsome in his khaki trousers and deep-purple polo, his dark hair pushed back from his forehead with a negligent hand. His clothes were a perfect complement to her own sleeveless lilac blouse and skirt. As an afterthought, she'd affixed Rose Carson's amber pin to her shirt, and now Jayne reached up to stroke it, feeling oddly comforted by its presence.

She'd taken quite a liking to the brooch over the last few weeks. But she was going to have to remember to give it back to Rose soon. Surely her landlady would miss so special a keepsake.

Erik's dark eyes sparkled with something Jayne was afraid to contemplate as he watched her, and she remembered how she had awakened in his arms the last two mornings, seeing an expression very much like the one he wore now. They had made love last night, too, she recalled as a warm, fizzy sensation bubbled up inside her, even more sweetly than they had on Friday. Despite all the misgivings she'd been having about their relationship, she hadn't been able to resist him when he touched her so tenderly. And this morning, when she'd awoken to find herself nestled in his arms, when she'd felt his heart beating in rhythmic time against her own...

She closed her eyes briefly now at the recollection. Because when she had awoken to all those things this morning, she had realized how irrevocably in love with him she was.

Her heart ached as she opened her eyes now to gaze at him. He was so handsome. So sweet. So gentle. So wonderful to be with. Why couldn't he fall in love with her, the way she had fallen in love with him? Why couldn't he just love her a little bit? Why was he determined that, in a year's time, they should part ways?

Because he *wasn't* in love with her, she immediately answered herself. Not even a little bit. Oh, certainly he cared for her—that she couldn't deny. But he'd made it clear that he simply did not fall in love, that he would never tie his life to another, that they would both be on their merry ways once their obligation to each other ended. And that obligation was legal, not emotional, she reminded herself ruthlessly. More than that, that obligation was temporary.

Would that her emotions could be temporary, too, she thought, there wouldn't be a problem would there?

"Yes. It is a nice party," she finally said in response to his question. "Your mother is a wonderful hostess. It was nice of her to put this together on such short notice."

Erik nodded as he scanned the room beyond. "Everyone seems to be having a good time."

"Yes. They do."

His gaze returned to hers, and he sobered. "Except for you. Why do you look so glum, Jayne?"

She met his gaze levelly, too, sobering even more than

he. And in that moment she made a hasty—but final—decision. "Erik?" she asked. "Can we talk?"

He shrugged lightly, but somehow the gesture seemed in no way careless. "Of course. About what?"

"Privately, I mean. Can we talk privately?"

Her request seemed to bother him, because he eyed her warily. "What's wrong, Jayne?"

"I just...we need to talk," she reiterated. "Privately. Please."

"All right. My father's study is through here."

He gestured toward a door on the wall closest to them, then proceeded in that direction without looking back. Jayne followed automatically, rehearsing in her head what she wanted to say to him, then reconsidering, then changing her mind, then resolving once more to go along with her initial decision with greater purpose. By the time Erik closed the door behind them, she was becoming so confused by the back and forth and circular motions of her mind that she wasn't sure what she wanted to say.

Erik seemed to sense her quandary, because he made no move to coax or cajole her. He only strode over to his father's desk and perched on the very edge of it, crossing his arms over his torso in a gesture that seemed defensive somehow. And he waited in silence for her to say whatever it was she needed to say.

He was so handsome, she thought again. And she loved him so much. Did she really want to end their temporary marriage before she'd had the chance to enjoy it to its fullest extent? But honestly, what other alternative did she have? Every day she was only going to fall more deeply in love with him. Every day her family would grow to love his more. By year's end, her heart—and Charlie and Chloe's hearts, too—were going to be so full, that losing the Randolphs and losing Erik would be too devastating to bear. If she ended this now, perhaps she'd at least be able to salvage something. A year from now, though...

A year from now she just might not recover at all.

"I can't do this," she said suddenly. She hadn't meant to just blurt her decision out that way, but once she had uttered it, she felt better for it. Sort of.

Erik seemed vaguely puzzled by the remark. "Can't do what?"

She hesitated a moment before clarifying, "I can't go through with our arrangement."

Still, though, he seemed not to understand. He only shook his head slowly in silence, his expression clearly puzzled.

"With our marriage," she added. "I can't go through with our marriage."

That had him on his feet in an instant. But he seemed not to know what to say, because he only stood there, staring at her, his mouth slightly agape, his hands hooked loosely on his hips.

"I'm sorry, Erik," she told him. "But it's just not going to work."

He did find his voice then, demanding, "What are you talking about? It's working beautifully. Better than I imagined it could."

Oh, sure, she thought. After all, he'd married a woman with whom he could make love every night of the week and never risk falling irrevocably in love with her... because he simply didn't have the capacity for such an emotion. But there was more to a marriage—even a marriage of convenience—than sexual compatibility. The problem was, Jayne was willing—eager—to embrace that *more,* while Erik wanted nothing to do with it.

"Erik, how do you feel about me?" she asked him impulsively.

The question seemed to stump him, because he looked vaguely puzzled as he asked, "What?"

"How do you feel about me?" she repeated.

He offered another one of those not-so-careless shrugs, shook his head in mystification again, then said, "I like you, Jayne. I think you're sweet."

"Nothing more?"

He expelled a soft, incredulous sound. "Well, of course there's more."

"Like what?"

"Like…like…like I think you have a good sense of humor. And you're nice. And I like how devoted you are to your brother and sister. And you make me feel good."

"Nothing more?" she asked again.

"Jayne, just what is it you want me to say?" Now his voice was faintly irritated, as if he were losing patience with her.

She supposed she couldn't blame him. She wasn't sure what she wanted him to say, either. Except, of course, that he loved her and couldn't live without her and never wanted to let her go. Oh, hey, but other than that…

She hesitated a moment before telling him, "I want you to say that there's more to our marriage than just convenience."

Once again he shook his head in that faintly confused way. "I don't know what you mean."

"I mean…" She inhaled a deep, fortifying breath and released it slowly. "I mean…" Finally she gave up trying to explain. How could she, when she scarcely understood it all herself? Instead she only reiterated, "I can't go through with our marriage. It's over, Erik," she told him softly. She twisted her wedding and engagement rings off her left hand, then strode toward the desk and laid them down on it. "I just can't do this for a year."

"But…but, Jayne…" he began. "You promised. You even signed a contract. We made a deal."

That stupid contract, she thought. After what she'd just told him, that piece of paper was what was uppermost in his mind. He was worried about losing his millions far more than he worried about losing her. If she hadn't already been certain that he didn't love her, this would have convinced her for sure.

"I won't file for divorce until the year is up," she told

him. "Not because I signed a contract, but because I made a promise to you. And I never break my promises. But you and I—" she swallowed with some difficulty "—we'll live separate lives for the rest of that time. Please don't come home...." She squeezed her eyes shut tight at her choice of words. "Please don't come back to Amber Court tonight," she corrected herself, opening her eyes again. "You can move your things out of my apartment tomorrow. I don't want to see you anymore after that."

He said nothing for a moment, only gazed at her blankly, as if he simply could not believe what she was telling him. Then very quietly he said, "You could be pregnant. What happens then?"

She shook her head vehemently. "We've always taken precautions."

"But nothing's 100 percent, remember?" he told her. "You said so yourself. What if you're pregnant?"

"I'm not pregnant," she told him decisively. "We took precautions, and the timing was totally wrong, anyway. So you don't have to worry about it."

"Who says I'd be worried?" he asked cryptically.

Jayne wasn't sure what he meant by that, or why he was clinging to an idea he himself had so disavowed only a week ago. But she did know one thing: his reaction to her decision now was cool enough that she was sure she was making the right choice. Erik didn't love her. And if he didn't love her after those extraordinary nights the two of them had shared, then he wasn't going to love her. Ever.

"Where is all this coming from?" he asked, still obviously baffled. "I thought we were doing great, Jayne. I thought we were both going to enjoy the year ahead. I thought..." He expelled a soft sound of frustration. "I thought you cared for me."

"I'm sorry," she said again, unable to tolerate the rush of emotion that was fast wringing her inside out. "I do care for you. More than you know. And I wish I could go along with our original plan. But I can't.''

''Why not?''

''I just can't go through with it, Erik,'' she told him again, unwilling to give him the real reason. ''I can't go on pretending to be your happily wedded wife when I'm not. I can't spend the next year letting everybody believe that we're wildly in love when that's such a bald-faced lie. I just can't do it. I thought I could, but I can't.''

''The pretending to be in love part was your idea,'' he reminded her.

She nodded, but the gesture felt jerky, awkward. ''I know it was. But it was a mistake. And it wasn't the first mistake I made about us, either,'' she added without thinking.

''Oh?'' he asked, his voice sounding sarcastic now, almost hurt even. She supposed that was only natural. She'd given him no preparation for this. No reason to suspect that anything was wrong. ''There were other mistakes?'' he asked further. ''Other than marrying me in the first place?''

She nodded again. ''Yes. There was another mistake besides that one, too.''

''And what other mistake did you make, Jayne?'' he asked coolly.

For one long moment she only looked at him, memorizing his features, imprinting him at the forefront of her brain, so that she could pull out the memory of him later in her life, when he was gone, and remember how wonderful he was. Then, very softly, she said, ''I fell in love with you, Erik. And that was my biggest mistake of all.''

And with that she spun on her heel and fled. She didn't think about how she must look running through the parlor with all those curious faces staring after her. She didn't worry about how she was going to get home. And she didn't fret about Chloe or Charlie, whom she knew could fend just fine for themselves among the Randolph clan.

For the first time in her adult life, all Jayne could think about was herself.

And about how empty her life was going to be without Erik.

Eleven

Dinner at Rose Carson's apartment was usually a lively affair, one Jayne, Lila, Meredith and Sylvie enjoyed on a monthly basis. Generally, the four women chattered amiably with their landlady about everything that was going on in their lives, both at work and at play. Tonight, however, the mood was decidedly bleak. Jayne, of course, was still reeling from her conversation with Erik the afternoon before, was still trying to weed through her emotions and figure out exactly what she was feeling. Mostly, though, she just felt numb. And she suspected that would be the case for some time to come.

For now, she had only told Chloe and Charlie that she and Erik had had a quarrel, and that was why she had fled the Randolphs' home the way she had. She could only assume that Erik had told his family something similar, because he hadn't returned to their—her—apartment last night. She hadn't spoken to him since then, but had left a message for him at work that he could come and collect his things this evening, while she was at Rose's having dinner. She hoped he would agree to do that. She wasn't sure she could tolerate having to see him face-to-face again.

In hindsight, Jayne realized that telling her brother and sister that she and Erik had quarreled had been inadvertently convenient. Over the next few months, whenever she spoke to the twins, she could tell them that she and Erik were having problems, and that the two of them weren't getting along. She could explain to her brother and sister that getting married so impulsively, the way they had, had ended up being a bad idea, and that neither of them had been prepared for the massive life changes such a union would bring about. Little by little Jayne could prepare Chloe and Charlie for the inevitable. And maybe, just maybe, it wouldn't be such a devastating blow to them when that inevitable came about.

So Jayne's ruminations over Erik were what had her so quiet and morose tonight. What made the others so quiet and morose was the fact that, earlier at work that day, the rumor of Collette, Inc.'s, hostile takeover had been confirmed. There was indeed someone who was making every effort to buy up stock in the company and force a merger of some kind. Unfortunately, at this point the actual details of the situation were sketchy. No one knew who was trying to hostilely take over the company. And no one knew why.

The general feeling among Colette's employees, however, was that the situation as a whole was not good. As a result, Lila, Sylvie and Meredith were feeling just as lousy as Jayne was tonight, if for entirely different reasons.

"I still wish someone was talking about the particulars of the takeover," Sylvie said from her seat across the table from Jayne. She, like the others, was dressed casually for their dinner, in khaki trousers and a pale-yellow knit top.

"Is no one saying anything?" Rose asked.

Their landlady had been surprisingly curious about the goings-on at Colette, expressing an interest in the takeover that Jayne found unusual. Still, she supposed the whole thing *was* kind of interesting. In a glitzy TV drama sort of way.

"No one's saying much of anything," Jayne told their landlady. "Just that there's definitely someone buying up stock, but no one knows who or why."

"Even some vague reference to the person or persons involved would be helpful at this point," Meredith concurred. She was dressed in her usual colorless, nondescript baggy style. "It's like nobody can find out *any*thing."

Jayne brushed a bread crumb from her sleeveless, white cotton shirt, only to have to flick it from her blue jeans when it landed there. "What about you, Lila?" she asked their other friend, who still wore her work clothes of beige suit and ivory blouse. "You're hooked up higher in the company than we are. Are you hearing anything from your boss?"

"Nicholas?" Lila asked, her voice sounding a little thready for some reason as she spoke the word.

"No, Santa Claus," Sylvie replied sarcastically. "Of course Nicholas. Nicholas Camden. Remember him? He's that yummy VP you work for."

"He *is* yummy, isn't he?" Meredith asked with a giggle.

"Very yummy," Jayne agreed, smiling in spite of her bleak mood.

Each of the women giggled after that. All except for Lila, who reacted by spilling her wine, leaping awkwardly up from her chair, and toppling her plate to the floor in the process. The other women watched with undisguised astonishment as Lila hastily began to clean up the mess. Then they exchanged sidelong glances.

"Why, Lila," Sylvie said as a look of discovery dawned on her face, "whatever is wrong? Was it something we said? Something like, oh…I don't know…about how Nicholas Camden is so yummy?''

Lila was attempting to right her wineglass when Sylvie offered the comment, but at the mention of her boss's name—*thump*—down went the glass again, this time rolling across the table toward Meredith, who scooped it up and set it down without incident.

"Well, well, well," Meredith said as she performed the gesture, grinning. "It would appear that our friend Lila becomes a bit…agitated whenever her boss's name is mentioned. Why is that, Lila, hmmm?"

Lila lifted a hand to brush her hair from her eyes, and Jayne saw that it was trembling ever so slightly. "I do not get agitated when you say…you know…his name."

"Whose name?" Sylvie asked, her own smile rivaling Meredith's. She deliberately waited until Lila was about to set her plate back on the table, then said, "Nicholas Camden's?"

And *crash* went the plate to the floor again. Muttering a growl of discontent, Lila stooped to pick it up.

"Oh, leave her alone," Jayne said, feeling for her friend. Hey, she knew it was no fun to want someone who didn't want you back. "Stop teasing Lila about Nicholas Camden."

Thump. This time the sound came from Lila's head as she banged it on the table while trying to rise from the floor.

"Oops," Jayne said, genuinely chastened. "I'm sorry, Lila. I didn't mean to say…you know."

"Nicholas Camden?" Meredith tried again.

But this time Lila was ready for it. She only flinched just the tiniest bit in response.

"Oh, Lila," Sylvie said in a voice of discovery. "You've got a thing for your boss. You've got a thing for Nicholas Camden."

"I do *not*," Lila said imperiously. "have a thing—*any*-thing—for, you know…him."

Jayne gazed at her friend thoughtfully for a moment, not buying a word of Lila's objection. She really did have a thing for her boss. Oh, my. Between that and the hostile takeover, the next few months should be *very* interesting. Both at Colette and Amber Court.

Rose opened her mouth to say something more, but was halted by a series of quick raps at her front door. She excused herself from the four friends, two of whom continued to needle a third about a certain VP for whom she worked, until Rose returned in a moment with a curious little smile curling her lips.

"It's for you, Jayne," she said softly.

"Me?" Jayne replied, puzzled.

Rose nodded. "It's your husband."

Jayne's eyebrows shot up in surprise. She had told her friends the same thing she'd told Chloe and Charlie—that she and Erik had quarreled and weren't on the best of terms at the moment. She hadn't mentioned to her friends that she had also asked him to move out of 20 Amber Court, but she knew the quarrel story would set the stage, and that she could explain his absence in other ways until the time came to tell everyone they had formally separated.

"I think he wants to apologize for whatever it was the two of you argued about," Rose said.

"But...but...but..." Jayne began. Unfortunately, no more words emerged to help her make sense of the tumult of thoughts wheeling through her brain.

"He certainly looks apologetic, anyway," Rose added, her smile growing broader.

"But..."

"I think you should go talk to him, dear."

"But..."

"He seems a bit...anxious."

Try as she might, Jayne could think of no excuse as to why she shouldn't go and talk to Erik. So, with the other four women gazing expectantly at her, she mumbled, "Excuse me for a minute," and went to see her husband.

Her husband, she thought morosely. Oh, that was a laugh. Funny, though, how laughter was the last response she felt like displaying at the moment.

Erik did indeed look anxious when Jayne poked her head around the corner to gaze down the long corridor toward the front door. He had his hands shoved deep into the pockets of his chocolate-brown trousers, and the buttons of his creamy dress shirt were misaligned, as if he'd been very distracted when he fastened them. His necktie hung around his neck in a careless manner that she'd never known him to display or possess. Erik was generally a satorial wonder, looking as if he'd just stepped out of the pages of *GQ*. At the moment, however, his appearance was obviously the last thing on his mind.

"Hi," he said softly when he saw her.

Jayne moved around the corner of the wall and made her way slowly down the corridor until she stood a scant foot away from him. She noticed then that it wasn't just his clothing that was in uncharacteristic disarray. He'd also obviously not been paying attention when he'd shaved that morning, because dark stubble dotted his jaw and chin. He also had dark circles under his eyes that were unmistakable, as if he'd spent a restless night without sleep. All in all he looked like a man who was deeply troubled by something.

"Hi," she said, just as quietly as he had.

"I, um, I got your message," he told her.

She nodded, crossing her arms over her midsection in a way that felt oddly defensive. "Good," she replied. When he said nothing to elaborate further, she added, "I'll, uh, I'll just wait over here while you get your stuff, if that's okay."

He eyed her thoughtfully for a moment, his dark eyes turbulent. "No," he said. "It's not okay." Then, before she had a chance to comment, he hurried on, "Jayne, we need to talk."

"I think we said everything yesterday that needed to be said," she told him gloomily.

"Oh, no, we didn't," he immediately countered. "We didn't even scrape the tip of the iceberg yesterday."

"What are you talking about?"

He gazed past her, down the corridor, up which drifted feminine laughter and conversation, then back at Jayne. "Can we go down the hall?" he asked.

"To my apartment?" she replied without thinking.

"No, to *our* apartment," he corrected her.

"It's not our apartment anymore," she told him.

He said nothing in response to that, only studied her with a ferocity of intent that she figured she was better off not contemplating. "Can we go down the hall?" he asked again.

She nodded, then strode in that direction, pulling Rose's front door closed behind her. She was about to fish her door key out of her pocket, but Erik already held his in his hand, and he opened the door quickly, gesturing for her to precede him. Jayne did so, performing a perfunctory search for Mojo as she went, so that the ill-tempered cat wouldn't trip her up. There was nothing more humiliating than being felled by a cat when you were about to have—

What? she wondered. Just what was it that she and Erik were about to have? Did he want to go over the details of the breakup the way he had gone over the details of the marriage? Did he want to reiterate that she couldn't file for divorce for twelve months, or else he'd lose $60 million and she'd lose years' worth of college tuition for her brother and sister? As if she needed reminding of those things. The only thing worse than leaving Erik was knowing she'd still be tied to him for twelve months before that break could be made clean.

He followed her into the apartment and closed the door behind them, then traced her steps into the living room.

Jayne had deliberately perched herself on the love seat, thinking Erik would move to the couch, but he joined her instead, seating himself close to her, with scarcely a breath of air separating them. She was about to object, or even move to the couch herself, but Erik took her hand gently in his and began talking.

"Jayne, you can't just tell a man you fell in love with him and then run off the way you did yesterday," he said.

She gazed down at their hands, at the way he was lacing his fingers loosely with hers, as if he weren't even thinking about what he was doing, but was doing it because it was simply a natural gesture on his part. "Why not?" she asked softly.

He said nothing for a moment, not until she turned her gaze back up to his face. Then very quietly he told her, "Because when you run off, it doesn't give the man a chance to respond."

Something fiery and intense flickered to life in his dark eyes then, and an answering blaze erupted in Jayne's belly in response. She was afraid to hope for what she was hoping for, was afraid to ask what she wanted to ask. Nevertheless, "And just how were you planning to respond?" she said, her voice sounding shallow, even to her own ears. Probably, she thought, that was because her breathing was shallow, her thoughts were shallow and, at the moment, anyway, her very perception of reality was shallow.

Erik swallowed visibly, then tightened his fingers with hers. "At first, I wasn't sure how to respond," he told her. "But after spending the last day and night without you, after thinking about the weeks and months to come without you, after visualizing my life ahead without you, now…"

"Now…?" she encouraged him.

"Now I realize…I don't want to live without you."

Jayne held her breath, held his gaze and tried not to

hope. Because he still hadn't said the words she wanted to hear, still hadn't told her what she needed to be told.

"After thinking about all that," he continued, "I know how to respond now." But he said nothing further, only continued to gaze into her eyes as if he couldn't quite believe she was real.

"Then…respond," she told him. "Please respond."

He smiled at that, having detected the urgency in her voice, she supposed. "I love you, too, Jayne," he said simply. "I didn't realize how much until you told me you couldn't stay married to me. Until I realized I was going to lose you. The past few weeks have been the best of my life. I never knew I could feel about anyone the way I feel about you."

"Oh, Erik…"

"I never knew there could be this…this…this satisfaction inside me. This contentment. This knowledge of how everything just feels right with you. And I like that feeling. I like knowing it will always be there."

"Oh, Erik…"

"I married you for money, Jayne," he said softly, covering her hand now with both of his. "But I want to stay with you for something that's worth infinitely more. I want to stay with you because I love you. And I want to stay with you forever."

"Oh, Erik…"

"Is that all you can say?" he asked with a chuckle. "'Oh, Erik'?"

"Oh, Erik…" she said once more, laughing with him.

"Tell me again," he said. "Tell me how…you know."

"I love you?" she asked.

He nodded. "Yes, that."

"I love you," she told him.

"Forever?"

"Forever."

"And you won't leave?"

She shook her head and smiled. "No. Never. You're stuck with me now."

"Even after twelve months is up?"

"Even after twelve months is up."

"Even when Chloe and Charlie graduate with their Ph.D.s?"

"Even then."

He smiled again, looking a little less anxious than he had before. Then he released her hand and shoved one of his into his trouser pocket. He extracted a small, square box and flipped it open, to reveal her wedding and engagement rings within. Silently he withdrew them, then, as Jayne watched silently, he took her left hand in his and slid first one, then the other back where they had been before. Back where they belonged.

"I do love you," he told her again, squeezing her fingers gently, possessively.

"And I'll never get tired of hearing that," she told him.

"I hope you never get tired of saying it, either."

She grinned. "I love you, Erik."

He grinned back. "That's what I like to hear."

He leaned forward then and covered her mouth with his, kissing her softly, sweetly, chastely. Right now wasn't the time for passion, but for promise. The passion, Jayne knew, would come later. Like maybe in an hour or so. Fifteen minutes, if they kept going the way they were now. At the moment, however, she only wanted to tell him, in so many ways, how much she loved, wanted and needed him. And she wanted him to tell her, in so many ways, the same thing.

For long moments they only sat on the love seat, hand in hand, kissing, caressing, loving, promising. Then Erik released her hand and trailed his fingers up along her bare arm, over her shoulder, along the collar of her shirt, then down lower, toward her breast. As his hand drifted down, he skimmed his fingers over the amber brooch Rose had loaned Jayne nearly a month ago and which she still wore.

She remembered then that she had meant to return it earlier, at dinner. Somehow, though, she'd gotten a bit sidetracked before she had the chance. Now she leaped up from the love seat and began to unfasten it.

"What are you doing?" Erik asked. "We were just getting to the good part."

Jayne smiled. "I have to do something before I forget."

Erik grinned lasciviously and patted the cushion she had just vacated. "Hey, I can make you forget anything. Just give me another minute or two."

"That's the problem," she told him. "And I need to give this back to Rose before you turn my brain into pudding." She unhooked the brooch, then cradled it carefully in one hand. "You are planning to turn my brain into pudding this evening, aren't you?"

"Oh, baby. You can count on it."

She grinned. "Then I'll definitely hurry back."

"You'd better."

Erik's seductive laughter hastened Jayne's speed as she jogged to her own front door, then to Rose's, where she rapped quickly three times.

"Hi, Rose," Jayne said as her landlady opened the front door. "I forgot to give this back to you earlier." She extended the amber brooch, still cupped gingerly in her palm. "I apologize. I didn't mean to keep your pin for as long as I did."

Rose smiled as she took the proffered brooch and cradled it gently in the palm of her own hand. Very softly she ran the pad of her index finger over each of the amber inserts, as if they were the most precious gems in the world. And Jayne supposed that in a way they were. At least to Rose Carson.

"Oh, that's all right, dear," the older woman said. "I wanted you to wear it for as long as you needed it. I thought it might bring you a lift."

Now Jayne was the one to smile. "Oh, it did do that," she assured her landlady. She glanced over her shoulder, toward Erik, who stood framed in her own doorway, as if he hadn't wanted to let her out of his sight. Then she turned her attention back to Rose. "And it brought me a lot more than a lift, too."

Jayne expected the other woman to look puzzled in light of the cryptic statement, but Rose only smiled knowingly, as if she understood completely. In response, though, she only said, "Perhaps I'll loan the brooch to Lila for a little while. After all the teasing she's endured tonight over Nicholas Camden, I think she could use a lift, too." Rose's blue eyes sparkled as she added, "Among other things."

Jayne figured she probably managed a little twinkle of her own as she replied, "Thanks again for the loan, Rose. Somehow, though, I think I can take things from here myself."

Her landlady turned her gaze first from Jayne, then to Erik, then back to Jayne again. "Oh, I don't doubt that for a moment," she said. "I'd say the two of you together can handle just about anything."

"Thanks, Rose," Jayne said again. "For everything."

"And thanks from me, too," Erik called from down the hall. He did sound a bit puzzled, though, as he added, "For...whatever."

Rose glanced at the amber brooch one last time before lifting her other hand to Jayne and Erik in farewell. Then she closed the door, leaving the newlyweds alone in the hallway outside.

"So what do you say?" Jayne asked her husband as she entered her apartment again. She halted in front of Erik, then circled her arms around his neck. "Since we're starting this marriage over, you think we ought to give that honeymoon thing a second go-around, too?"

Erik nodded. "Oh, yes. But this time we're going to do things the right way."

Jayne arched her eyebrows in speculation. "Oh? I thought they went pretty well the first time."

"This time," he said, "it will be even better."

"Now that's a promise I look forward to you keeping," she told him with a smile.

Erik smiled, too, then surprised her by scooping her up into his arms. So astonished was she, in fact, that all she could do in response was tighten her hold on him and laugh.

"I never carried you over the threshold the first time," he told her.

She thought about that for a moment, then nodded. "That's true. You didn't."

"So I'm going to start with that," he said.

"But I'm already inside," she pointed out unnecessarily.

"That's okay," he said. "We're not staying."

"We're not?"

He shook his head. "We have places to go, things to do, people to meet. We have our whole lives ahead of us."

She thought about that for a moment, then realized she couldn't wait to get started. "Wow. You're right."

"So what do you say, Jayne? Will you marry me again? The right way this time? For the right reasons?"

"Oh, yes. I will. I do," she said, hastily correcting herself.

Now Erik was the one to laugh. "I do, too. And I will. Just as soon as we get where we're going."

"And just where is it we're going?" she asked him.

He smiled. "I don't know. But it's going to be a wonderful journey getting there."

"It will be," she agreed. "I know it will."

And with that, Erik covered Jayne's mouth with his and carried her over the threshold, *out* of her apartment, and into their life together.

* * * * *

SOME KIND OF INCREDIBLE
by
Katherine Garbera

KATHERINE GARBERA

lives in Central Florida with her husband and their two
children. She wrote her first book to prove to herself
that she could do it and to have something to read at
work! She believes firmly in fiction that reflects the
reality of her life and the lives of those close to her. She
is a past recipient of the Georgia Romance Writers
Maggie Award. She loves to hear from readers, and
you can write her at PO Box 1806, Davenport, FL
33836, USA or e-mail her at kgarbera@yahoo.com

To secretaries everywhere who do an impossible job with very little thanks, but especially to those I work with at Disney Event Productions: Gina McTigue, Joyce Campos, Adele Swearingen, Eva Artimovich, Mary Leppich, Mary Baker, Becky Latourelle, Karen Satre and Kelly Darden. Also a special thanks to those women who mentored me when I was young and green! Vita Charles, Cindy Michener, Shirley Colebank and Jackie Mathews.

One

Late again, Lila Maxwell thought as she hurriedly closed the door to her third-floor apartment. She loved her home. It wasn't much, a four-room apartment in an older but nicely kept building. She'd spent the last two years carefully decorating each part until her flat of rooms had become her dream home.

She ran down the stairs at a rapid pace because she liked the exercise. As an administrative assistant at Colette, Inc., the world famous jewelry company, Lila spent most of her time sitting. The early morning was dark and Lila longed just for a minute for the warmth of her native Florida. Youngsville, Indiana, had a great community, but the weather was sometimes too cold for this Florida girl.

"Lila, can you stop for a cup of coffee?" her land-lady, Rose Carson, asked, stopping Lila in her tracks.

"Rose, I wish I could, but Nick's due back today and I'd like to be in the office before he gets there." Nick Camden was her boss. And the man of her dreams.

Not the girlish fantasies she'd entertained of a white knight who rescued her from the small government-subsidized duplex she and her mother had shared, but womanly fantasies of dark passion with a man who saw her for more than a nice collection of body parts. She flushed a little and hoped Rose didn't notice.

"I have something for you. Wait here for a minute," Rose said.

Lila loved her landlady. She was kind and caring and had made her feel at home when everything around her was very foreign. Rose's apartment took most of the bottom floor. Warm and inviting, it made whoever entered feel that a caring, successful woman lived there. Lila hoped to create that for herself some day.

"Here it is, Lila."

Rose handed her a beautiful piece of jewelry. A brooch made of amber and precious metal. It was almost heart-shaped and, though the term seemed inappropriate in the presence of something so precious, it was pretty. As Lila fingered it gently, she knew she shouldn't wear it. "I can't take this."

She handed it back to Rose, but the woman refused to take it.

"Just borrow it for luck."

"Thank you, Rose, but no. This is too valuable."

"I want you to wear it. It needs to be on a pretty young lady."

Rose brushed aside Lila's coat and fastened the brooch to her suit jacket. Lila loved the brooch but she knew better than to take something this valuable. She tried to remove it, but Rose's hand covered hers.

"Lila, it would mean a lot to me. It brought Mitch and me together. I like to think it brings love to the lives of those it touches."

Rose got that misty look she often had when she spoke of her deceased husband, Mitch. Though her black hair had a few shades of gray, Rose was still attractive. Her figure was slim but slightly rounded, giving way to a more matronly style of dress. Unwilling to upset her neighbor, Lila decided to keep it for today and return the brooch tonight.

"Thanks, Rose. It *is* lovely. I have to go," Lila said with a glance at her watch.

Rose nodded, and Lila hurried out into the cold. The sun was breaking over the horizon. It was nippy but not too cold for a walk to work. She lifted her face to the sun and pretended the high for today wasn't only fifty degrees.

She loved the parks and trees full of fall colors. Yellows, browns, oranges and reds filled every space. Halloween, her favorite holiday, was right around the corner, she thought, attributing the extra bounce in her step to excitement.

Usually she had some company on her walks to work. Sometimes Jayne and Sylvie walked with her, but Jayne had recently gotten married and hadn't been up so early in the mornings. And today she was too early for Sylvie.

Lila liked the fact that she had good friends here. It was as if she'd found the surrogate family she'd always been searching for. She really loved her life in Youngsville.

Not wanting to be late on Nick's first day back, she hurried. In her purse was the banana bread she'd baked last night. In fact, she'd spent every night for the last week baking.

Lila always felt in control in her kitchen. She was the executive there and she knew her way around. It was easy for her to fool herself into believing that Nick Camden hadn't almost kissed her while she was kneading dough and making sheets of sweet rolls.

A car slowed behind her. The low purr of an expensive machine told her it wasn't one of the other Colette, Inc. secretaries offering her a ride. She kept her head down and walked. She wasn't prepared to face Nick outside the office. In fact, he'd passed her a hundred times this summer and never once stopped to offer her a ride.

Men want only one thing from women like us, Lila. Her mother's warning echoed in her mind. Her ex-boyfriend, Paul, had proved her mother right. She didn't glance toward the car despite the warmth emanating from the open window.

"Want a lift, Lila?"

"No, thanks, I'm enjoying the crisp morning." If only she could stop shivering.

"Liar," he said, not unkindly.

He was right, she was lying. But that didn't mean she was going to admit it. A car honked, and Nick waved the driver by. Lila wasn't getting in the car with him, because after last week she didn't trust herself. She'd spent all of her time in Indiana adjusting to the new community and her home, learning to be proficient at her job and making some casual friends. But she hadn't been prepared for Nick Camden's sexy gaze when he had turned it her way.

She'd dreamed of him kissing her and touching her, but when he'd leaned closer to her last week in the office, she'd frozen. Paralyzed with the fear that she would disappoint him, she'd backed away. But he had a gleam in his eyes that said retreat wasn't possible.

Damn him. She tried to give him a reassuring smile and walked on. "Thanks, but no thanks."

"Suit yourself, Florida girl, but it's a cold morning and my car is warm and comfortable."

He was temptation. He hadn't been when she'd first started at Colette. But lately she'd been looking for a man who'd be serious with her. A man who wanted kids and a nice house. A husband who understood the importance of family.

Nick didn't even register on her scope because he

changed women every week. He wasn't a playboy, but he never seemed content to stay with one woman. He was like a hungry wolf eating his fill and moving on. Lila wasn't interested in being his next meal. If she thought there was even a remote possibility that Nick would stay with her, she'd give in to him.

But there wasn't.

Almost two years ago she'd decided that Indiana was a place for fresh starts. She wasn't going to get involved with any man unless she knew for certain it was right. Which meant no Nick Camden. No matter how heavy he made her blood run.

"Lila, I've been out of the office for a week. I need you to brief me on what's been going on."

Maybe she'd misinterpreted his intentions. She shrugged, and finally gave in. "Okay."

She prided herself on being a good secretary and before the episode last week she'd never have hesitated to get in his car. He didn't scare her on a conscious level, but her mind warned her to be wary of him. There was something about this very sophisticated man that wasn't very civilized.

She slid into the plush leather seat and hurriedly fastened her seatbelt. She closed her eyes, letting the heat seep into her bones. A warm masculine scent surrounded her and she imagined Nick leaning over her. His breath brushing her lips.

Wait a minute!

Her eyes flew open and Nick's face was a scant inch from hers. There was something electric in his eyes. Something that made her pulse race and her breasts tingle. Something masculine that called to every female instinct buried deep inside her. Made her want to indulge senses she kept firmly under lock and key, let them out and experiment with this very experienced man.

"Nick, what are you doing?" God, she could barely speak. She wanted to lean forward and taste him. To see if the sin his wicked mouth promised was as delicious as her fantasy assured her it would be.

"Fixing your seatbelt. It's twisted."

She couldn't breathe as his fingers brushed against her breast. Her nipple tightened and she wanted to thrust her chest out so that he'd have to do more than accidentally caress her hungry flesh, but instead she bit her lower lip.

"There we go," he said.

He pulled his hand away slowly and she wished she could see his eyes behind those dark sunglasses he wore. Nick was a master at seeming in control, but his eyes always gave him away.

Her pulse was still racing and she wanted to pull him back to her, wanted to feel his hard body pressed to her own softer one. Maybe Rose's pin was working its magic, spinning a spell around Lila and her dream man.

Lila shook her head. If Nick wanted her it was for business and not in the way a man wanted a woman. He was too savvy to mess up a winning partnership with old-fashioned lust.

Nick put the car in gear. Sweat broke out on Lila's body but it had nothing to do with the heat coming from the car. It had to do with the man sitting next to her. A man that she'd decided was off-limits. A man, she suddenly realized, who'd decided she was his next meal.

Nick knew that he'd unnerved Lila, but he couldn't just drive by and not stop for her. It bothered him that he'd probably passed by her this summer without noticing. But not that much.

He'd never paid much attention to her as a woman except to note that she complemented him nicely, being blond and built. She made them look good when he had visitors or when they attended meetings together. To him, Lila represented the perfect office assistant, someone who knew her job but was also pleasing to the eye.

All of that had changed after he'd returned from Paris in early September. Lila had seemed softer somehow. She'd chatted with him casually before taking a memo and he instantly knew something was different. Actually he knew exactly what had changed.

His reaction to her.

He'd gone on point like a hunting dog scenting prey, and he'd been unable to shake this damned attraction to her. And she seemed oblivious, which made him want to get a reaction out of her even more.

"You were going to tell me about your trip," she said.

Yeah, Camden. Now that you blackmailed her into your car, talk business. "I need you to prepare a presentation for the domestic guys with last quarter's financials. I have the data in my briefcase."

"I'll clear my desk and work on it first thing."

Nick nodded. Silence built in the car, and he realized he knew too little about Lila outside of work. He had no idea how she spent her free time. Lila was so homey sometimes he was amazed she'd chosen a career over a family. But she had. And now he wanted—no needed—to know why.

"You live at Amber Court, right?"

"Yes, why?"

"No reason. Do you like it?"

Oh, God, he sounded like an actor in a bad sitcom. He'd never tried to get to know someone he already knew. It seemed his MO needed a change but his focus on Lila was now purely physical.

"It's nice, but I've dreamed of owning a two-story house with—"

"A white picket fence, right?"

She bit her lip and stared out the window.

He knew he'd sounded sarcastic, hell, he couldn't help it. Reality was hard and cold when you spent most of your time in the dream world. And it seemed Lila Maxwell did a lot of dreaming.

Bothered that he'd hurt her, Nick changed the subject. He was not in the business of fixing hurts. He'd learned not to care after Amelia had slipped away from him into a drug-induced coma that was her only escape from the pain her cancer-ridden body felt—24/7.

"How was the office while I was gone?" he asked, trying to sound casual.

At first, he thought she wasn't going to answer. She glanced over at him. She fingered her scarf with her pearl-pink colored nails and the image of those fingers on his thigh imprinted itself in his head.

"Not busy. A few more rumors than usual."

Focus, man. "What kind?"

She smiled, and his inseam felt tight. Damn, but she caused a reaction that was close to nuclear in him.

"Oh, you know, the ones where we're all booted out the door."

"You think they're unfounded?" Nick asked. He'd been hearing similar things overseas.

"I work close to the top and we haven't heard anything substantial, have we?"

Nick sighed and grunted. The turn into Colette, Inc. was busy with employees all arriving at work, and though it didn't require his full concentration, Nick gave himself to the task. He didn't look at Lila again until he'd pulled his Porsche to a stop in the spot designated as his. He hoped for once that Lila's sharp mind would miss his non-answer.

A quick glance at her showed she hadn't. He pulled his keys from the ignition and reached for the door handle, but her hand on his arm stopped him.

"Have we, Nick?"

Lying went against the grain. Nick believed that life's little lessons were best served cold. But Lila's heart was in her big brown eyes and she looked scared. Though it had been a long, long time since he'd wanted to protect any woman, he suddenly didn't want to shake Lila's world.

He faced her and leaned close.

"Not yet."

"That isn't a no," she said quietly.

The confines of the car put them so close together that he could feel each inhalation of air she took as she breathed. Staring at her pink lips, Nick wondered idly if his breath was now filling her lungs, filling her body with life, and he had the urge to fill her with something more real. He didn't want to be satisfied with the fact that their appearance impressed vendors and visiting executives in the office. He wanted them to be together, physically.

Nick knew on a basic level that he was trying to hide from the fact that his safe haven, Colette, Inc., had turned into a battleground, but it was more than that. He leaned closer to Lila, not stopping until he could taste the air she was breathing, her lips softening under his, her hand on his arm clutching helplessly at his sleeve.

He knew that he was in for a world of hurt if he pursued her this way. But the world had gone crazy, and the carefully sheltered life he'd built for himself was crumbling. The only thing that looked solid was Lila Maxwell.

Lila moaned deep in her throat and opened her mouth under his. All thoughts of keeping things light and simple vanished. His blood roared in his ears, and his body screamed for more. Her mouth was soft, warm, wet…welcoming on this cold October day.

She clung to him as if the moment had taken her by surprise, too. Her tongue responded shyly to his. It had been forever since a woman hadn't thrust her own tongue into his mouth before he'd even wanted her there.

Nick pulled her closer, groaning when the gearshift ground into his hip. He pulled away. "Damn."

Lila stared at him as if she'd never seen him before. Her lips were swollen and her face was flushed. Tendrils of her perfectly styled hair surrounded her heart-shaped face. She was mussed and he wanted her more so.

He wanted that glorious hair spread on his navy pillowcase, those rosy lips swollen from his spent passion. He wanted his sweat and hers drying on their bodies. But he knew he couldn't put the car in Reverse and take them both to his home where they could spend the day in his king-size bed.

"Damn."

"You already said that."

"Some things need repeating."

Her hands trembled as she tucked the escaped

strands back into place. "What happened here, Nick?"

"I want you, Lila."

"Because of work?" she asked, not looking at him. Instead, she pulled her compact from her purse and repaired her lipstick.

Her armor was back and the dewy woman who'd been next to him just a minute before was gone. In her place was his ultra-efficient secretary. And he resented that. He couldn't pull out a mirror and makeup and smooth away signs of passion as easily as she had. "Because of you."

She gulped. "I'm not ready for this. I still think of you as my boss."

"Well, start thinking of me as your man."

He opened his door and got out. The air was cold but didn't cool the heat flowing through him. He wasn't going to be able to focus on anything in the office except that his wide cherrywood desk was big enough to support the weight of one slender blonde.

Lila met him on the sidewalk and brushed past him. He stopped her with a firm hand on her arm.

"What's the hurry?"

"I don't want anyone to see us coming in together."

"Don't be ridiculous. At least five people saw me pick you up this morning. And even more saw us pull into the parking lot."

"True. But I don't want anyone to get the wrong impression."

"Are you really that concerned with what others think?"

She nodded.

"Don't be. They aren't worth your time."

"You only say that because it's always the woman who comes out sounding like she's easy."

"Trust me, Lila, the last thing you are is easy."

"I know that, but other women…"

"If anyone says anything to you, tell me and I'll silence them."

She smiled. "Like Hannibal?"

"No. Like Dirty Harry."

"Death?"

"Intimidation."

"You're not as scary as you think you are."

"Neither are you."

"I'm not trying to scare you," she said and walked quickly inside the building.

But you are, he thought. Because a part of him was afraid she'd mean more to him than any of the brief affairs he'd had since Amelia's death two years ago, and that wasn't in the cards.

Two

The buzz around the office was that Colette, Inc. had a new board member who was planning on making some changes at the top. Lila returned from a quick clerical meeting led by Suzy, the Administrative Assistant in Human Resources, not feeling as upbeat about her job as she had a day ago.

She stowed her purse and tried to concentrate on her work, but the presentation she was creating couldn't hold her attention.

Dammit!

"Can you come into my office and take a memo?" Nick asked. Anger seethed around him in a cloud. He looked dark and menacing, not like the man who'd been keeping her at arm's length all day.

Lila saved the file she'd been working on and nodded. She tried not to glance at him as he hovered near her desk. The spicy scent of his cologne surrounded her and she breathed deeply to inhale his scent into her bones.

Bracing his big hands on her desk, he leaned over. His deep-blue eyes usually held boundless energy, but today anger simmered in their depths. She felt it radiating off him in waves. Concerned, she started to rub his hand, to offer him the most basic of human comfort, but then pulled back.

She watched as his eyes left hers to stare at her small hand now only a few inches from his right one on the desk. He'd spent the entire afternoon with the board of directors and, if his body language was correct, then the rumor that Colette was the object of a hostile takeover was true.

Colette, Inc. had proven a safe place for her to build her career and save the money she needed to buy her dream house. The rumored takeover reminded her how much she hated change.

When she'd packed up and moved to Youngsville it was with the intention of staying here forever. First, Nick had started acting like she was the most scrumptious woman he'd seen in years, and now her job was threatened.

It wasn't so much her role in Colette she worried about losing. It was her apartment. The homey place at Amber Court had given her the grounding she needed to find her own feet, to shape her own image

away from her mother. And suddenly that looked as
if it might be taken away.

"What's up?"

"I'd rather not discuss it out here."

Her stomach clenched, and she felt much the same
as she had on that day in high school when the guy
she'd been waiting for three years to be asked out by
had told her that he'd only done so because she was
considered easy.

"I'll be right in."

Nick straightened and then deliberately brushed his
fingertip over the back of her knuckles. Her breath
caught as electric tingles pulsed through her body.
She'd spent so many hours at her desk wondering if
she'd just imagined his attraction to her, but now she
knew it wasn't a fantasy.

For a tense moment they stared at each other. Lila's
breasts felt full and her lips were suddenly dry. She
licked them. Nick tracked the movement and started
to lean closer to her.

Down the hall an office door closed loudly. Nick
stood and walked into his office without another
word.

"Oh, my God!" Lila said. She had to transfer out
of this office before she completely lost all of her
common sense. She fingered the brooch Rose had
given her before she left for work. It was beautiful,
and Lila had found herself taking it off to look at it
several times today. In fact, it seemed to glow a little
more brightly whenever she touched it. Rose had said

it had always brought her luck. Lila had the feeling she needed more help than this brooch could bring her.

She signed out of the local area network, or the LAN, and removed her laptop from its docking station. Nick's office overlooked Lake Michigan. Tonight, the view was dark and menacing. Being a Florida girl she didn't care for all the cold weather, but the changing leaves had been beautiful. After a year and a half here, she still hadn't acclimated herself to the Indiana weather.

Lila set her laptop on the corner of Nick's desk. He was hunched over his own computer, probably checking e-mail, she thought. Tension radiated from him, and she wanted to touch him, to massage those broad shoulders until he leaned back in his big executive chair and smiled at her.

Of course, he never really smiled at her. Sometimes when they'd completed a really tough project, he'd give her one of his half-smiles, and she'd feel a deep longing inside to make him really happy. But she never did. Sleeping with the boss was the one thing she'd never do. Except this morning things between them had changed. Her dreams were slowly becoming reality. The actions she'd always longed to take were now presenting themselves to her.

"Ready, Lila?"

She swallowed and blocked her train of thought. "Almost."

She powered on her computer. "Should we close the blinds?"

"Why, afraid someone might see us alone together in here?" There was a biting edge to his words.

"Not afraid exactly." She'd never been afraid of any man since most of them turned and ran when life got tough. She knew she was strong and could take all they had to give. But she always tried to keep a part of herself secret. And Nick was harder to hide from than anyone else.

"Trust me, Lila. Everyone knows your reputation. Anyone who might see us will know we are only working."

Stung, she busied herself at the computer, pulling up the company memo template and readying herself to do her job. His words shouldn't have hurt, she thought. After all, their relationship was that of boss and secretary. But the words did hurt.

"I'm ready, Nick."

"Lila…"

She glanced up, hoping he'd attribute the tears in her eyes to the late hour.

"Never mind."

They'd been carefully treading around one another since that night two short weeks ago when Jayne had interrupted a moment that had almost gone too far. She'd wanted so badly to taste his lips on hers. To feel that rock-hard body that he worked at keeping in shape pressed against her own. To experience for once in her lonely little life the touch of real passion.

"The memo should go to all staff in the Marketing Division."

"Just our team or domestic, too?"

"Domestic, too. I'm handling this announcement."

"Promotion?" she asked hopefully.

"I wish it were."

"Subject?"

"Grey Enterprises," he said, pacing across the room and stopping in front of the Zen rock garden that he adjusted every day or so.

Uh-oh, she thought. Nick's deep-blue eyes reflected the frustration and anger in his tone.

"Dammit," he said under his breath.

"Nick?"

"Have you heard the rumors of a takeover, Lila?"

"Yes, but I'm sure they are unfounded."

"They aren't."

Shock rumbled through her, and for a minute she saw herself back in that duplex she'd grown up in. The government-subsidized housing that had been her world until she'd gone to trade school and accepted this job. She saw herself back in that world she'd struggled so hard to get out of. She saw her dreams slowly dying and vowed that she'd do whatever it took to prevent that from happening.

"What the hell should I say to the staff? Don't worry, we're not going to let you lose your job?"

"I don't know. Is that true?"

"Hell, I wish I knew."

Lila's hands started to shake and she realized that

this wasn't just change happening around her. This was the sky falling in. This was—

"Don't worry, Lila. Clerical staff is hardly ever let go. VPs on the other hand…"

"No one's going to fire you, Nick."

"Lila, sometimes you are naive."

She wanted to argue, but knew that to a suave sophisticated man like Nick Camden, she must seem a little small-townish. "But the board loves you."

"We might have a new board member."

"Grey Enterprises?"

"Yes. Marcus Grey, their CEO, has bought eight percent of the common shares on the market. He is now the fourth-largest stock holder."

"What are we going to do?"

"Whatever we can to survive. I've worked too damn hard to give this up without a fight."

He still stood with his back to her, searching, it seemed, for answers in his Zen garden. She stood, set her laptop on the chair and crossed to him. All her protective instincts told her to cradle this man in her arms. To comfort him and draw strength from the comfort he could offer her.

She knew it was dangerous, though. Nick held her dreams captive, what would happen if she gave him the keys to her reality?

"What can I do to help you?"

He pivoted on his heel and faced her. His deep-blue gaze brushed over her, and when he spoke his voice was huskier than usual. He moved a few paces closer. She could feel his body heat and started to back away. But something in his eyes challenged her to stay where she was.

"For me personally?" he asked.

For work, she wanted to say, but knew that wasn't true. Her words caught in her throat and she could only nod.

"Let me hold you."

She wasn't sure he'd really spoken. It was just like the dream she'd had the night before, in which he'd asked her to come into his office and then made passionate love to her.

"What?"

"I know all about sexual harassment and this has nothing to do with your job."

"Just hold me?" she asked.

"No," he said.

She waited.

"I'm going to kiss you, too."

She didn't hesitate to close the gap between them. She knew he was reaching out, as everyone in the office had been today. Just searching for some comfort in this time that had become troubled. But deep in her heart, as he lowered his head, Lila hoped it meant something more. Just a little bit more to him.

Nick knew that he was manipulating the situation, taking advantage of Lila because she was weak and vulnerable right now. But he'd wanted her for a long time. He didn't look too closely at himself because he didn't want to admit he had any of those feelings. The last time he'd felt this shaken was when Amelia had been diagnosed with cancer.

He brushed her lips lightly with his. She tasted like a bittersweet fruit and he wanted more. She sighed as his tongue slid past the barrier of her lips and teeth, learning the inside of her mouth.

Her hands clutched at the back of his neck and all semblance of control vanished. His groin hardened almost painfully. He clutched Lila's hips in his hands and held her closer to his lower body, feeling her move slightly. He thrust against her, sharpening the sensations in him.

He knew that Lila wasn't like the women he'd dated in the past, other executives from outside firms who were hardened by life and more cynical. No, Lila was different. She baked bread for the office when morale was low. She offered life, he realized, and though he knew he couldn't have it forever, he wanted a small slice of it for himself. He needed to believe for a few moments that he wasn't alone in the world.

Nick wanted to be a tender dream lover, but his body was on overdrive and he held on to his control by a string. His hands shook with the need to touch all of her. The low lighting in his office cast the room in a comforting glow. He loosened the buttons on her blouse, and met her clear gaze with his own.

No matter how badly he wanted this, he wasn't

going to push Lila to move too quickly. He didn't analyze why.

"Okay?" he asked, dipping one finger beneath her collar.

She nodded.

He released another button. Her skin was smooth and creamy, like the finest satin sheets. He leaned down to drop kisses on the flesh he'd exposed.

She shivered, her fingers tunneling in his hair and holding him close to her. He quickly opened the remaining buttons and stood back. Taking her wrists in his hands he held her arms away from her body. The bodice of her shirt fell open. A scrap of red satin and lace covered her breasts.

It enraged his senses the way nothing else ever had. It wasn't right that a bra meant for sin should be on her sweet body, but at the same time it was perfect. There was no other undergarment that could do this body justice.

He deftly opened the front closure of her bra. A quick intake of breath was her response. Deliberately, he bent and took the edge of the right cup between his teeth and slowly pulled the fabric away from her skin.

The stubble on his jaw scraped against her skin and she lifted her chest slightly. Her hands weren't as subtle, directing him to her nipple.

"Please," she said.

"Hell, yes."

He nibbled on her hardened flesh before suckling

her deep in his mouth. She held him tight to her body and blood engorged his sex, making him so hard and full he thought he'd explode before he moved on.

The slow pace he was trying to set evaporated. He took Lila's mouth as he planned to take her. Hard, swift but with infinite care, and he lifted her, carrying her to the cherrywood desk. He set her on its surface and slid his hands under her skirt.

He cursed when he found her warm, wet and wanting. Damn. He needed to fill her. To feel that humid heat on him. To revel in the fact that she wanted him as much as he wanted her.

His tongue thrust deeper into her mouth. Needing to deeply embed her essence on every one of his senses, he pulled her panty hose down over hips and legs. He wrenched his mouth from hers.

Urging her to lean back on the desk, support her own weight on her elbows, he spread her before him like a sensual feast. Her blouse fell away from her body exposing her flushed breasts with their hardened tips. Her skirt bunched at her waist revealing panties that matched her bra. His pulse jumped higher, and he couldn't breath until he'd tasted her intimately.

He sank back in his big leather chair and surrounded her hips with his hands. She glanced down at him, passion still in her eyes, but something else there, too.

"May I taste you?" he asked.

She nodded again.

He bent forward, resting his cheek against the lace

and satin that covered her mound. Then he slowly turned his face until he was surrounded by her scent. He couldn't wait any longer; standing, he ripped her panties from her body and carefully opened his fly.

Lila freed his long erection from his pants and brought him closer to her. The head of his manhood brushed against her and she moaned deep in her throat. She thrust against him, but Nick used his grip on her hips to slow the movement.

He slid carefully into her, slowly savoring each pulse around his hard length. She was small and tight, fitting him like a velvet glove. She tried to rush his possession, but he wouldn't let her. He was the master here. In her body he'd found the place where he should always be.

He seated himself to the hilt and paused for a moment.

"Keep going, Nick."

"Oh, I will," he said, but didn't move. Instead he bent to take her nipple into his mouth, sucking strongly until he felt her hips moving between his hands, felt the tiny tightening of her muscles against his manhood. Then he pulled out of her and started to thrust. Lila met him thrust for thrust, clutching his buttocks and pulling him to her.

The tension built inside him. He couldn't hold on another second, but he had to. He waited until he felt Lila's body clench around his, felt the extra warmth that hadn't been there before, and then let himself go.

Let his release take him to the stars and carry this sweet woman there with him.

He wanted to collapse against her but knew he couldn't, so he lifted himself away and sank back into his office chair. Eventually his pulse slowed and sanity returned. He zipped his pants and felt the stickiness of their joining. Damn, he hadn't used a condom.

Lila's descent to reality seemed to take a little longer, however. Nick knew the moment it happened because she grasped the edges of her blouse together and refused to look at him.

Some mistakes were the kind that took you years to realize, Lila thought as she fought to rebutton her silk blouse. And others stared you in the face from the moment the actions were taken. What had felt so right minutes earlier now felt horribly wrong.

Her heart ached and her stomach churned like a hurricane in the Atlantic. She tried to act calm but having had only one other lover in her life hadn't given her a lot of sophistication to call on in this type of situation. She slid off the desk and decided she could go home without panties or hose on because she sure as heck wasn't rooting around under his desk to find them.

With a calmness that she knew had to be some sort of protective shell, she smoothed her skirt, tucked her hair behind her ear and walked away from the man who'd just tilted her neat little world. First with the announcement that the safe predictable life she'd built at Colette was in danger, and then with the soul-searing intensity with which he'd made love to her.

Part of her thought the whole thing entirely roman-tic, but the forbidding look on Nick's face told her he wasn't going to get down on one knee and confess his undying devotion to her.

This heartache's on me, she thought, knowing that her fantasies about Nick had precipitated their love-making. She wanted to play it cool, but she was afraid if she tried to talk her voice would come out in a high-pitched squeak.

"Lila," Nick said. His voice was low and calm, washing over her like a warm breeze on a summer's day. She wanted to go to him and wallow in what he had to offer, but she knew it was a mirage.

"Yes," she said, picking up her laptop and pre-paring to leave, still refusing to look at him.

"We have to talk about what just happened."

Not if she lived to be a hundred would she ever want to discuss this with anyone. And certainly not with Nick. She made a noncommittal sound. Let him take that for whatever he wanted, she wasn't up for a post mortem right now.

She heard his footsteps and refused to glance at him. His body heat reached her in waves, and now that she knew how strong he was and how right it had felt to be in his arms, he was even harder to resist.

"Honey."

"Don't," she said, her voice cracking, as she'd feared it would. The way he'd pulled out of her body and sat in his chair waiting for her to recover told her more than words ever could. He did not think of her in an affectionate way, and she'd tolerate no lies from him.

"Lila, I didn't mean for any of this to happen but it did and nothing can change the fact that neither of us was prepared for it."

She became aware of the stickiness between her thighs. She knew immediately that he wasn't only concerned about health issues but about pregnancy. How careless could she be? she asked herself. Hadn't she learned anything growing up with her unmarried mother?

"I'm not on the pill," she said. She was one of the small percentage of women who were allergic to it. It had never bothered her because she wasn't swept away by desire. In fact, she had found the entire male-female lust-at-first-sight phenomenon to be highly overrated…until tonight.

"Well, hell," he said, then turned away from her to utter something profane and succinct.

His words cut straight to her heart.

"Yes, hell. This isn't the end of the world, you know." Chances were she wasn't pregnant.

Now he was the one avoiding eye contact. "It is for me."

"Why?" she asked.

"Because I made a vow never to marry again." His words affected her in a way she didn't want them to, and dashed her secret hopes once and for all. She'd been dreaming of Nick Camden for so long that she'd put him on a pedestal, and here he was revealing his very real clay feet.

"I don't recall asking you to marry me, Nick Camden."

His laser-sharp gaze pinned her to her spot. He didn't say anything in response to her sarcasm.

"If you're pregnant we can discuss the choices to be made."

"What are you insinuating, Nick?"

"That we will have to make some decisions once we know the full details of the situation."

"This sounds like the verbiage for a damned memo. This isn't about the job, you know. This is about life."

"My job *is* my life, Lila."

Truer words were never spoken.

"How soon until you'll know if you're knocked up?"

"Jeez, now that I've seen your charm I know why you're so popular with the ladies."

"Dammit, Lila—"

"Yes, dammit, Nick."

She walked out of his office and grabbed her purse from the bottom desk drawer.

"You didn't answer my question."

She sighed. She knew how dogged he could be when he set his mind to something. "A few days maybe. I'm not real regular."

She shut off her desk lamp and felt the heavy

weight of his hand on her shoulder. "I'll drive you home."

"No, thank you."

"It wasn't an offer."

"Was it an order?"

"Tell me you're not planning to walk home in the dark."

"I'm not planning to walk home in the dark," she said, feeling an edge that she normally tempered with lots of baking and a call to her mother.

"Smart-ass."

"Look, this is Youngsville, not Chicago. I'll be fine."

"You're not going without me and that's final."

"Okay," she said.

He grabbed his coat from the rack and reached around the corner to hit the light switch. Lila's discarded undergarments were under his desk. He stopped and pocketed them without a word. Then he closed and locked his inner office door. He took her elbow and escorted her down the darkened hallway.

Lila felt the emotions inside her swirling like a black mist and rising so quickly she couldn't control them. She knew she had to keep her mouth shut but somehow the words wouldn't stop.

"So I guess I shouldn't ask if it was good for you?"

Three

Nick had been at some low places in his life but never had he felt like this. The night was pitch dark and he was thankful that Lila was silent as they drove. He didn't think he could take much more conversation from her at this point. In his mind's eye he was surrounded by an image of Lila's wide brown eyes brimming with a sheen of tears.

Though his mind screamed for him to back away his body relived the incredible rightness that their joining had brought. And he knew that he should regret that he hadn't used a condom when they'd made love, but deep inside he was glad he hadn't. His groin still throbbed at the remembered feel of her around him.

Lila had been the fulfillment of his dreams, of what a woman could be. But she was his assistant, dammit. How could he have let this happen?

But he knew once hadn't been enough. In fact, as he came to a stop in front of her building, he knew that he wanted to come up tonight and mate with her again. To cement what was between them so that she didn't have to react with her sharp tongue.

"Well, thanks for the ride," she said and then a bitter laugh escaped her. "I meant the *car* ride."

"Lila, stop it. I'm sorry for the way that our first time happened, but I won't let you think it meant nothing to me."

"I'm sure you say that to all the girls, Nick."

"I don't have a stock of lines I pull out for the appropriate moment."

"I'm relieved."

She looked at him, but her expression was indiscernible in the feeble light of the street lamp. He knew his reaction earlier had made his comments seem, well, like a lie, but truer words had never been spoken. Lila meant more to him than the faceless ladies in his past and she deserved better than a burnt-out executive whose only emotion was cold, hard lust.

Except it hadn't felt cold or hard when he'd been with Lila. Buried in her sweet warm body he'd felt like he'd found the home he'd been forcing Colette, Inc. to be for years.

"Are you feeling better?"

She shook her head, the silky length of her blond

hair was illuminated by the light of the moon. He wished he'd taken his time with her. He wished they'd had all night to learn each other's bodies instead of a hurried explosion in his office. He wished that he could go back to the moment he'd pulled away from her and lie against her breast and comfort them both.

"I can't do this right now. I'm achy and not myself," she said.

"That's okay."

"No, it's not. I'm feeling mean, Nick. And I want to hurt you so deeply that you'll still feel it weeks from now."

"If it would make you feel better."

She looked out the window, and when she spoke again her voice was so soft he had to lean in to hear it. "My mother gave birth to me when she was only sixteen. I've never met my father."

Simple sentences. Simple words that summed up a life that was anything but simple. He hadn't realized how complex the situation was, but now he did.

"We're not in that situation."

"No?"

He wanted to do the right thing, to say he'd marry her if she found out she was pregnant with his child, but he knew he couldn't. The low points in his life were manageable because he'd found a way to guarantee they never happened a second time. He'd made the vow never to marry again because Amelia's death had cut through the layers of who he was and left him a quivering mound of insecurity. If there was one thing he wouldn't tolerate it was weakness.

"Well, you're not sixteen."

She reached for the door handle and Nick hit the locks.

"Let me out of the car."

"I can't."

"Don't be silly. You run a multimillion-dollar division for a large corporation, this should be a cinch for you."

"I want you to tell me that you'll stop beating yourself up about this. I seduced you."

"I had no idea you were this bossy in your personal relationships," she said, whipping her head around to face him. She leaned in close and he could taste her breath as it brushed across his face.

The leather seats and her scent teased his mind, tempted him to pull across the gearshift as he had this morning and kiss her until she was too exhausted to talk.

"You didn't seduce me."

He had. He knew he had. He'd been feeling out of control and had called on the one thing he could count on. Lila. She'd soothed him and comforted him and taken him out of his skin to a place he'd never really been before.

And he'd repaid her by possibly impregnating her. God, his technique could use some work. Except with Lila all those practiced moves didn't work.

"I'm not about to debate this with you. Thanks for bringing me home."

She manually unlocked the door and opened it. The chilly evening air swirled inside. It swept through the warmth and seeped into his clothing.

She closed the door and walked away without a backward glance. He watched the fluidity with which her limbs moved, while surrounded by the scent of her perfume and the chill of the autumn evening. The pain in his soul was unexpected but no less sharp than a knife to the gut.

Lila Maxwell already meant more to him than she should, but watching her walk away hurt. And knowing that he'd brought her pain added to the hurt that was layering through him.

Lila was tired by the time three o'clock rolled around. She'd been up since five in the morning baking pies and breads, which she'd dropped off at the Youngsville Nursing Home on her way to work. The route had taken her twenty minutes in the opposite direction, but she hadn't minded. She'd needed the therapy that baking had brought.

She'd tried leaving Rose's brooch at home but hadn't been able to. It complemented the deep-brown silk shirt she wore with a long black skirt.

Longingly, she fingered the piece of jewelry, then dropped her hands to her keyboard and forced herself to get back to work.

Nick had been out of the office all morning, which

meant she'd fielded a lot of calls from concerned staff on both the international and domestic teams. Lila didn't mind the extra time on the phone because it kept her mind busy. And busy meant away from that open door leading to Nick's office.

The phone rang as Nick returned to the office. Lila scheduled an appointment for Nick for the following week and pretended that he wasn't standing on the other side of her desk staring at her. Pretended that he was still just a casual acquaintance. Pretended that last night had never happened.

She concluded the call but didn't move. She was an efficient secretary until Nick walked into the room.

"Aren't you going to look at me?" he asked, taking the handset from her grip and depositing it in its cradle.

"Sure," she said, smiling up at him. All business, she reminded herself. "You need to sync your Palm Pilot. There are three urgent messages and an update to this afternoon's calendar."

"I'll do it right away. I'd like a few minutes of your time," he said. He was tired. He rubbed the back of his neck and loosened his tie. She wanted to pull him into her arms and offer him comfort. But couldn't.

She glanced at her day planner. Of course the afternoon was empty. But she wasn't ready to accommodate him. In the middle of the night as she lay in her bed staring at the cracks in the ceiling she'd realized that life gave you what you sought out. And she was seeking more than a man who couldn't commit to her.

"I'm in the middle of a proposal. Maybe later?" she suggested, knowing his afternoon was booked.

Suddenly she realized why people advised you not to get involved with someone at work. It made the atmosphere very tense and uncomfortable. Before, they'd been a team, and Lila had felt that she had his respect. But not anymore.

He put his hand on hers. It cut to the core. His big, warm hand surrounding her small one. Protecting, cherishing. His forefinger moving in a slow sweep from wrist to knuckles. "Lila…"

Not fair, she thought. But she nodded and stood, reluctantly tugging her hand from under his. "I only have five minutes."

"That's all I ask."

"I'll be right in." Lila waited until Nick left and forwarded her phone to one of the executive secretaries down the hall. The volume of calls today and the nature of them made her want to guarantee that someone answered the phone and reassured whoever called that Colette, Inc. was doing okay.

She entered Nick's office. Instead of seeing the plush surroundings she saw Nick sitting at his desk, looking a little lonely and very closed off. This was the man she'd hoped to reach.

"Have a seat."

She settled in his guest chair, trying hard to forget the incredible passion they'd shared on his cherrywood desk not even twenty-four hours ago, how his body had felt inside hers, how full and how right.

"I hope you're feeling better today."

"I wasn't ill yesterday," she said softly.

"I meant that smart mouth of yours."

"Oh." She wished she reacted to hurt the way others did, but she always lashed right back out. It was a holdover from her childhood, and she wished she could shake it but hadn't been able to yet.

"Well?" he asked.

"I'm fine."

"Good. I wanted to apologize for not protecting you."

She raised one eyebrow. "If you'd like me to keep my sarcasm hidden then please don't make any other comments like that."

"I didn't protect you, Lila."

"I'm just as much at fault. It wasn't as if we'd planned it. I'd have been surprised if you had pulled out a condom."

"I also wanted to reassure you that if there is a child, I'll offer you my full support."

Lila was surprised. "I thought you didn't want marriage."

"I meant financial and, of course, emotional support, but I won't marry again, especially not because of an unplanned pregnancy."

"Why not?"

Nick rubbed his eyes and stood, pacing to the window. "I was an unplanned child. My parents were forced to marry to give me legitimacy."

Lila's heart ached. She knew how it felt to know that your parents had conceived you by accident. But she'd also blossomed under the love of a mother who cherished her daughter and never allowed anyone to say that Lila was a mistake.

She walked over to Nick and slid her arm through his. She wanted to do so much more but didn't trust herself. "I came into the world the same way. My parents never married, though."

"Count yourself lucky. That kind of situation brings out the worst in people."

She wasn't sure what to say to that.

"I like you, Lila. You're funny, smart and sexy as hell. I don't want ever to wake up in the morning and see your face as my enemy."

His sincerity made her ache. She cupped her hand around his jaw, meeting his blue gaze squarely. "We're not our parents."

"I know. But we're already following in their footsteps."

"We don't have to."

"I'm not sure where we go from here."

Lila looked away. "We'll pretend it was a one-time thing. We can't make love again."

Both eyebrows rose, but he said nothing.

"You'll see. We'll get back into our groove here at work. Everything will work out."

"If you say so," he muttered.

"I do," she said and pivoted on her heel to leave.

"One more thing, Lila."

"Yes?"

"Let me know as soon as you've found out."

"I will." She walked away feeling as if she'd gone ten rounds with a title-fighter. But this was for the best. No matter how many nights she'd dreamt of Nick, she knew that he wasn't her reality man.

"Nick, do you have a minute?" Lila asked as Nick hung up the phone on a fruitless call to Grey Enterprises. He hadn't been able to get any information from the sales rep he'd been talking to. Maybe dinner and drinks would loosen the man's tongue.

Nick leaned back in his chair and glanced up at the woman responsible for making his life a living hell for the last two days. She treated him as a boss, and while he understood it was part of her plan, it wasn't helping.

Her red-and-black suit would have done justice to a power-monger on Wall Street, but on Lila it looked less threatening. He knew that she prided herself on her professional image and wondered how much of that attitude had to do with her wanting their relationship back on a business-only level.

If anything, her behavior had sharpened the desire coursing through his veins. Watching her try to keep her distance made him want to bridge the gap. He had the urge to needle her out of her work mode and make her react to him as a man, not as her superior.

Work usually consumed all of his waking hours. But lately, at the oddest moments, the image of Lila, her weight braced on her elbows and her skirt around her hips, would enter his mind. He'd gotten an erection in a staff meeting yesterday afternoon. Never had any woman interfered with his job.

"What do you need?" he asked, to get his mind off her tempting curves.

She entered his office, moving with the subtle grace of a confident lady. "It's about the annual charity event."

Every year Colette, Inc. sponsored a bachelorette auction that featured the new fall and winter jewelry designs. Calling on single women from Colette's many departments to be auctioned off for dates, they had the evening gowns donated from a local designer and then each woman wore a signature piece of jewelry that would be for sale during the Christmas season.

The money raised from the auction went to a local children's home and the event was a big community satisfier for Colette. Nick had even bid on one of the bachelorettes last year.

"What about it?" he asked. The administrative staff each handled different aspects of the event.

"Is it still on? I've been getting a few calls about it. And it's already October."

"Nothing has changed at Colette. We want the public to see that we're still strong. It's definitely on." The more Nick thought about, he knew they'd have to do an intensive marketing campaign in Youngsville and the surrounding areas. The community needed to believe that Colette wasn't taking the Grey threat lying down.

"Good. I'll get the ball rolling on the planning."

She stood to leave his office, and he knew he couldn't endure another day of pretending he'd never been more to her than the man who employed her. "Lila, would you like to join me for lunch?"

She tilted her head to the side. Her eyes said yes but from past experience he knew how carefully she weighed every decision she made. It still surprised him she'd made love to him that night in his office.

Unless she'd been thinking about it for a while. But he wasn't going to ask her that. Then he'd sound like some dopey guy who'd never had incredible sex before. And he'd had plenty of incredible sex. Lots of it. But never as good as it had been with Lila.

"I don't think that would be a good idea," Lila said.

He knew he should let it go. Let *her* go. But he couldn't. "Why not?"

She bit her lip and glanced over her shoulder at the open doorway leading to her desk. "I don't want people getting the wrong idea about us, especially since we agreed our business relationship is what's important."

A blush flooded her face and neck. He wondered where it started. At her pert breasts? Or higher? Did the warmth flooding her skin also affect other more intimate parts of her body?

"You're my secretary, no one would think there was anything else involved," he said.

"I don't know. You look at me sometimes in a way that's just not…"

She was too perceptive, he thought. He did look at her like he didn't know what to do with her. And he didn't. She'd managed to get under his skin and he couldn't decide how to get her out.

"We'll talk about the auction."

"I don't think so. I don't want to take a chance."

"A chance on what?"

She said nothing. He hated her silences. Hated that he knew he wouldn't be able to keep quiet because anger grew inside him. Hated that she was so calm and cool while he simmered with frustration.

"A chance that someone might think that we close the door sometimes late at night and make love on my desk?" he asked.

She glanced away. He knew he'd hurt her with his words, and he wanted to call them back. He was a bastard. He knew better than to talk to anyone when he felt this way. And it wasn't as if the situation with Lila was her fault.

"Not sometimes," she said, striding out of his office. She pulled his door toward her and before it closed, she said, "One time."

Nick picked up the crystal paperweight he'd been given when he'd gotten his first promotion at Colette and heaved it at the wall. Then he grabbed his coat and left his office, not glancing once at the woman who'd caused a roar inside him that couldn't be silenced with social niceties and childish games of do-overs.

He continued down the hall and took the stairs, fifteen damned flights of stairs outside to the fresh sunshine. Except that the darkness inside him threatened to black out the sunshine. His carefully controlled life had spun out of control and as it started to settle, none of the pieces fell where they belonged.

Four

Lila left her desk after Nick's departure. She knew Nick wasn't comfortable with their new relationship, but she was afraid to let her emotions get involved with Nick.

Suddenly she realized they already were. Even if she never touched him again, even if physically they lived in other parts of the world, he'd always be a part of her. If she never saw him again, he'd still haunt her dreams, not only as a phantom lover but as a man she cared about.

The sun shone brightly on this early October day. It was chilly outside and her suit, though lined and long-sleeved, was no match for the wind. If she ever moved again it would be back to someplace warm. Hawaii warm.

She scanned the parking lot looking for his car and saw him striding toward the park across the street. She didn't hesitate to follow him. But once he sat on a bench she was reluctant to approach. She had no idea what to say.

"Stop hovering, Maxwell."

She sighed, lowering herself to the wooden bench. She glanced around to make sure no one saw her sitting with Nick, but the lunch crowd was light at the moment.

"Why'd you follow me?" he asked.

"I wanted to clear up a few things." Darn, it was really cold by the lake. A stiff breeze ruffled her hair and she tried to tuck the escaping strands back into her chignon. She hugged her arms around her waist.

"Yes?"

"It's not you I don't want to be seen with."

"Yeah, right," he said.

"It's just I have a solid reputation here. You've probably always had one, having grown up in an intact family. But for me, everyone always said, like mother, like daughter."

"Are you like your mother?" he asked.

"Until two nights ago, no."

"Our intimacy changed that?" He shrugged out of his suit jacket and then draped it over her shoulders. She huddled into it. Still warm from his body, it was like being enveloped in Nick. She wanted that again. Not just the passion but the cuddling they'd missed out on.

"Yes. Mom was always…"

"Your mom's promiscuous?"

"No. She just doesn't care what others think. She lives by her own rules."

"Then what was the problem?"

"Honestly, Nick, look at me. I don't know why but I don't make friends easily."

"I think you should take your mother's attitude."

"That's easy for you to say. I've created a nice life for myself in Youngsville. People respect me and I'm a part of the community. I don't want to lose that."

He glanced away out over the lake. She wondered what he saw there. Wondered if it brought him peace of mind. She'd seen him at this bench a handful of times since she started working for him. It was where he cleared his mind.

She also knew that this bench was visible from all of the window offices. Subconsciously it seemed she'd made up her mind even if she didn't want to admit it. She wasn't going to let Nick slip away. She was going to have to face her fears. Was he worth the risk?

"I don't think you'll be ostracized for eating lunch with me."

She stared into his electric-blue eyes and knew she could easily lose herself in them. "You want more than lunch, don't you?"

"So do you," he said softly. He was right, she did want more. More than he had offered her. She wondered if she could settle for halfway.

She didn't say anything. His words went through her like a carnal kiss. Her pulse sped up and her breasts felt tight. A warmth penetrated her and forced her to admit the truth. An uncomfortable truth she hadn't been prepared for.

"Listen, we're under enough pressure at work with the takeover attempt. Why don't we try again?"

Lila wanted to say yes without thinking but that would be a mistake. "I'm not looking for a red-hot affair."

"That's all I have to offer, Lila."

"You have more, you just aren't interested in the wholesome, all-American family with me."

"No. I've just seen what marriage can do."

"I know," she said. "Face of the enemy and all that."

"Don't scoff. You're more concerned with other's opinions than you are with anything else."

"Maybe we both need to change a little," she admitted.

"I don't know if I want to."

"Our world is changing."

"One date? We might decide we don't like each other," he cajoled.

"Do you have a nasty habit you've been hiding from me?"

"Probably more than one. Will you have dinner with me tomorrow?"

"I have tickets to the symphony. They're doing an evening of Gershwin." She'd never been to concerts, theatre or the ballet as a child. But her mother had made her watch a lot of "Great Performances" on PBS and every Sunday they'd listen to classical music or opera after church. It had given her an appreciation for different types of music that many of her peers didn't have.

She loved that she could afford to hold season tickets to the symphony. Usually she invited Mrs. Tooney or Mrs. Appleton from the seniors' center. They were always looking for something to do outside the center. Or she took one of her friends from Amber Court.

"I'll take you to dinner first," Nick said.

"A lot of people from Colette will be at the symphony," she said.

"It's your call."

No guts, no glory, she thought. This was her chance to see if Nick Camden really was the man for her. "Yes, I'll go."

"Come on, let's get back to the office before you freeze to death."

Nick teased her all the way back to the building about the weather and her thin blood. The imprint of his hand on her lower back lingered long after he'd gone into his office and she'd called Meredith, her friend and co-worker, to talk about the details of the charity auction.

The next evening, Nick questioned his reasons for asking Lila out for a date. He knew nothing could come of it. Knew that he'd give anything for one full night in her bed. Knew that he wanted more with her than he'd had for a long time with anybody.

He'd made a reservation at Crystal's for the evening. The posh restaurant with its fireplaces and French food was the perfect place for seduction. In fact, he'd taken many women there before. He hadn't realized that until he'd exchanged looks with the maître d'. Pierre had seated him with many different women and it tainted the evening for Nick.

Lila seemed oblivious as she took her seat. They were close enough to the fire to feel its heat. Nick had never been nervous about a date before so at first he didn't recognize the symptoms. He'd graduated from high school when he was sixteen and started college early. He'd wanted to escape his parents so badly that he put everything else on hold. So sweaty palms weren't the norm for him.

Most of the women he'd dated had pursued him before he'd asked them out, so they'd eagerly accepted. Not Lila. She'd thought twice about the evening, had even doubled-checked with him before leaving the office to make sure he hadn't changed his mind.

Her question had roused a tenderness in him that he was unfamiliar with. He hadn't been able to shake it as he'd dressed and driven to her apartment. When she'd opened her apartment door, the tenderness had changed to lust. Not totally changed, as he would have liked, but lust was now the overriding emotion.

Dammit, it wasn't fair that she looked like an angel

and carnal sin at the same time. He didn't know how to handle her. In fact, she was the only thing in his life that had thrown him for a loop in a long time. Even the takeover attempt which was rocking his world didn't affect him the way Lila did. He knew he could find another job. Sure it would be a struggle, but so had his entire life. Lila offered a different view and he had no idea how to handle her.

Her sweater was pink and soft, hugging the curves of her breasts and making her skin glow. She wore pearl-gray trousers and tasseled loafers. It was the first time he'd seen her in something other than a business suit—or partially naked. These casual clothes showed him a glimpse of the woman Lila hid under her professional veneer. She had on an exquisite amber-and-precious-metal brooch. It was unusual for him not to recognize the designer. Having worked his way up in sales, he knew not only the "signatures" of the Colette designers but of most other designers in their field.

"Where'd you get that brooch?"

"Oh, Rose lent it to me."

"Who's Rose?"

"My landlady. It's so silly, but she said it always brought love to those who wore it."

Hell. "Are you looking for love, Lila?"

"I'm not searching for it, but if I find it I'm not going to run away."

"Well, I guess that piece is as good a talisman as any."

"Don't you believe in love, Nick?"

He shook his head. He wasn't ready to get into a discussion on what he'd seen done in the name of love. He knew for a fact that it didn't exist. Had never felt any great melting in his heart when he'd met his wife or thought of his deceased parents.

"I wonder who designed the piece?"

"I could ask Rose."

"Don't bother. I was just curious."

The waiter arrived and they both ordered. The sommelier stopped by next.

"Would you like a glass of wine with dinner?"

Lila nodded. Nick selected a French burgundy. One of the benefits of traveling in Europe was that he'd learned the difference between a gallon of grocery bargain wine and the French and Californian vineyards.

An awkward silence fell between them. Lila straightened her silverware and then glanced up at him. She blushed when she caught him staring at her.

"The atmosphere at work is getting pretty hairy," she said.

Nick grunted. The situation with Grey was getting worse. Rumors ran out of control like weeds in a garden and there was little the executive committee could do but smile and lie through their collective teeth. Nick usually felt calm at work. He knew the entire staff all worked hard and the company was solvent. This takeover attempt involved more than money, his gut said.

"What's the word?" he asked her.

"Rumors of unfair business practices. I couldn't run it down though. Even Paula in Human Resources was tight-lipped."

"A miracle has occurred somewhere if Paula was tight-lipped."

"No doubt. Maybe the second coming."

Tonight, though, he wanted to put thoughts of Colette on hold and focus on Lila. On him and Lila—together.

"Well, enough about work. Tell me about yourself, Lila."

"Why?"

"Because I'm interested in getting to know you."

"Pretty much what you see is what you get," she said, softly.

"I know there's more."

"What else do you know?"

"I know that your temper gets the best of you sometimes and you say things you normally wouldn't. I know that you bake when you are scared and that's probably why everyone on our floor took home a basket of cookies this afternoon."

"Is that all?" she asked, leaning forward. Her sweater hugged the curves of her cleavage. Nick stared at the creamy globes of her breasts and remembered the feel of her nipple in his mouth. Remembered the way it had hardened as he'd suckled. His mouth watered.

"I also know the sound you make when I'm buried

deep inside you. And I'd give ten years off my life to hear that sound again.''

Lila could think of nothing but Nick's words to her in the restaurant. For once the music of Gershwin didn't sweep into her soul and take her away from her mundane life. For once the thought of her peers seeing her out with her boss didn't bother her. For once she could only focus on the man next to her and whether she'd invite him in when they got home.

His voice, low and husky, brushed over her senses as he leaned closer and whispered something in her ear. She couldn't make out the words. His scent surrounded her and she closed her eyes for a moment, wanting this night to live forever in her memory.

She'd never flown by emotion before. Never given in to the urges that were now sweeping through her. The same urges that had led her to make love with him on his desk.

Wake up, Lila.

But she knew she wasn't dreaming. He was at once better than she'd dreamed he'd be and at the same time worse. Better because reality was warm skin and electric tingles, soft whispers and light, teasing kisses. Worse because he wasn't interested in the long-term the way she'd dreamed he would be. The way she needed him to be if she were pregnant with his child.

The orchestra played ''Someone to Watch Over Me.'' Lila felt the tears sting the backs of her eyes. She was transported back to her girlhood living room, to the battered Salvation Army couch and faded orange shag rug. Her mother holding her close and singing that bittersweet song along with an old Lena Horne recording. Her mother's voice wept with a longing that had always made Lila want to hide from the night.

Tonight the words seemed a warning, a reminder that love is blind. That what she felt for Nick was more like blind lust than love. She was throwing away her reputation for a man who was only looking for what she could give him in the darkest hours of the night.

Oh, God.

She searched through her purse for a tissue and found a snowy white handkerchief being handed to her instead. She felt trapped, like a vinyl record that had a skip in it and kept playing the same few bars of a song.

Was she doomed to be the same woman her mother was? She didn't look at Nick, just nodded her thanks and wiped her eyes. Exposed and vulnerable, she turned away from him and forced herself to the present.

The house lights came up and everyone filed out of the auditorium. But Lila didn't move. Her mind and body still hummed with the music she'd just heard. And, though it had brought her to tears, it had also enervated her body.

Also, she was honest enough to admit, she wasn't ready to get into that car again with Nick. His intimate, leather-smelling sports car that made her think of hot sex and steamy winter nights.

"Ready?" he asked at last. Most of the audience was gone by this time and Lila knew she was inviting the speculation that she'd always avoided.

"Yes." She started to hand back his handkerchief but decided she should probably wash it first. She slid it into her purse and followed him out into the night.

A harvest moon lit the evening sky and few stars could be seen in its bright glare. The air was cool and crisp but not unpleasantly so as Lila put her head back and looked up at the stars. She realized how small she was in the world.

She touched her stomach thinking of the child that could possibly be inside her. Nick's hand rested on top of hers. She looked up into his eyes and saw that something had changed since they'd entered the theater. She didn't understand it but there was no longer just lust in his eyes. Now there was something that looked more permanent. But Lila didn't trust herself enough to pursue it.

"I want to promise to watch over you," he said, so softly she barely caught the words. His earnest longing closed the back of her throat.

"But you can't," she said.

He pulled her close to him, holding her against that broad, strong chest of his that could protect her from any earthly threat, but not from the one thing that would hurt the most. Nick Camden.

Nick clasped her hand in his. "Let's walk down by the lake. There's a nice view."

Too tired and drained from the evening of Gershwin and feeling like she was in a fish bowl, Lila let him get away with changing the subject. "Really?"

"Yes. And a comfortable bench."

Trying for a lightness she didn't feel, she said, "You know, in Florida we have lakes all over the place. But Lake Michigan...it's so grand."

He smiled at her. "I learned to ski on that lake."

He never talked of his childhood, she realized. Except for that moment when he'd mentioned the war zone that his parents' marriage had been. "Who taught you?"

They walked in the dappled light provided by the trees. "Buster McKee's dad."

"Was Buster your friend?"

"Kind of. His dad was really great."

"Why?" she asked.

"He always had time for me. I mean I was a stubborn kid. I'd decided early on that I was the only one I could depend on."

"But he took the time for you?"

"Yeah, he did." Nick brushed his fingers through her hair and turned her face to his.

His eyes were half-closed, and she couldn't read anything in his gaze, but she wanted to. She wanted to know what he was feeling. To ascertain she wasn't the only one out of control.

"I'm going to kiss you."

She leaned closer and stood on her tiptoes.

"I take it you don't mind."

She smiled up at him. A kiss was just what she needed to end this evening. Because she knew that she wasn't going to ever have the opportunity to date Nick Camden again. She'd made a mistake thinking they could forget about that incredible sexual encounter they'd had. Made a mistake thinking that they could just continue on their merry way as if the world hadn't changed.

Because it had and it would never be the same between them again.

She kissed him. But in her heart she knew it was goodbye.

Five

—

Ah, hell, Nick thought. Lila's mouth under his was the sweetest fruit he'd ever tasted. Brushing his lips back and forth over hers only, he teased the both of them.

Hot breath was exchanged, and Nick swore to himself as he felt himself harden. Lila's hands held his head, as though she'd never let him go. He put his thoughts on hold and let his hormones take control.

Nick deepened the kiss. The inside of her mouth was warm and welcoming the way her body had been when they'd made love. He wanted to make love to her again. That night had been the last sane moment in his life. And it had been so far from normal that it shouldn't have been.

He thrust his tongue deep inside her and for the moment tried to quench a thirst that couldn't be quenched. Her tongue brushed against his, not shyly but like that of a woman who knew what she wanted. And what she wanted was within her grasp.

Nick slid his hands inside her coat and down her back, cupping her behind. He pulled her closer to his aching body. She moaned deep in her throat. Damn, he'd started something he couldn't finish here.

He wished they were at his place, on his big king-size bed where he could spread Lila out and take his time loving her. Because that was what they both needed. Especially him.

A cool breeze blew across the lake. Lila shivered in his arms and he pulled her closer. Lifting his mouth from hers he pushed her head against his chest and looked out over the vast expanse of water. It was a cold, lonely night, and having Lila in his arms should have assuaged those feelings, but it didn't. It sharpened them. He felt much the same as he had in his early twenties when he'd married Amelia and then learned she was sick. He'd had a glimpse of something he'd always longed for and then it was snatched away.

It wasn't that he was a cynic, he thought. He was a realist. He was meant to live alone.

Alone, he repeated to himself.

Why then did this one woman feel so right in his arms? Why then did her scent seem embedded in his soul? Why then did his body only feel alive when she was pressed intimately to him?

He breathed through his mouth, preparing to let go of her. *For good.*

"Let's get you home, Florida girl," he said, his voice sounding raspy to his own ears.

His erection still throbbed and for a minute he tried to figure out a way to make love in his two-seater sports car. The logistics wouldn't be bad if he was still a teenager, but he was a grown man. A responsible man...a horny man.

Damn.

"Mine or yours?" she asked.

Unable to believe she'd said the words he'd wanted to hear, it took a moment to respond. As much as he longed to spend the night in her bed he knew he couldn't. He wasn't the type of guy who carried condoms around. Though he'd dated a lot, he preferred planned seduction. But with Lila, there was no thought involved. Maybe he should start. He gave a harsh laugh, wishing for a moment that he could stop letting a certain part of his anatomy do his thinking.

"Yours, and then I'll go home to mine."

"Why? Despite my reaction to the song, Nick, I don't want you to watch over me. I'm a big girl, I can make my own decisions."

"I wasn't trying to watch over you."

"Yes, you were."

"The last time I stuck my tongue in your mouth

we made love on my desk, Lila. Give me a little credit for trying to do the right thing.''

''A little credit, that's all you want?''

''Hell, no. I want you on my bed, spread in front of me like a feast so that I don't have to rush. I want to savor every inch of you.''

''Then come home with me,'' she said.

He'd never had a harder time saying no. He shook his head.

''Face of the enemy and all that. Give me a break, Nick. This has to mean more than physical pleasure.''

He hated that she kept throwing those words back at him. Especially when he was doing the noble thing here.

''Nah, I'm just—'' looking to get laid, but he couldn't say that to her. Because he was afraid she'd hear the truth behind the words. What he really was, was needy. And she was the one thing he needed.

''Just what?''

Why couldn't she leave well enough alone?

''Nick?''

''Cut me some slack here, Lila.''

''I wish it were that simple. But you make me feel things so extremely that I can't help myself.''

''What can't you help?''

''Wanting you to be as vulnerable as I am.''

''What makes you think I'm not?''

''All you want from me is sex.''

''I wouldn't have stopped if that were true.''

''Dammit, Nick. What *do* you want from me?''

"I don't know." He wished he could say all he wanted was a night of their hot bodies writhing on his bed. That was something he could label and feel safely. But the emotions that Lila brought to the surface were neither safe nor easily labeled.

She said nothing. Just wrapped her own arms around her waist, protecting herself from the hurt he seemed to wield like a sword. It proved what he'd known all along. He brought destruction to those who cared for him. First his parents' marriage, then Amelia's life. He wasn't about to add Lila to the list.

Mrs. Charlotte Tooney had married her childhood sweetheart and spent twenty happy years with him until one day he'd had a heart attack at work, leaving her alone for the first time in her life. She had original artwork on the walls of her apartment and an electric organ on which she sometimes played Al Martino songs.

Lila admired the woman's resilience in the face of the fact that she'd spent the last twenty years essentially alone. She had no children but had a happy, fulfilled life. Lila wanted that.

But at the same time she'd put off taking a pregnancy test so that she wouldn't have to confront the fact that she might not be pregnant with Nick's child.

"Did you try that recipe I gave you for jalapeño bread?" Charlotte asked, interrupting Lila's thought.

Charlotte spent a lot of time watching TV cooking shows and jotting down recipes for Lila to try. And honestly, most of them were good. "Not yet. It was a cookie night last night."

The small apartments for the elderly at the nursing house shared an open common area. Lila had met Charlotte and her best friend, Myrtle, her first week in Indiana when she'd brought books to donate to the home's small library and had struck up a conversation with the two women.

To Lila, Charlotte and Myrtle were the grandmothers she'd never had.

"Tell me about Gershwin. Did you take Myrtle with you?" Charlotte asked.

"No, she didn't," said Myrtle Frye, who had entered the apartment without knocking.

"Who'd you take?" Charlotte asked.

"Charlotte, that's none of our business."

"Yes, it is. Was it a man?"

"Yes. But it's not what you think," Lila said. Unless what you're thinking is that I made mad, passionate love with him that one night and then found out the last thing he wants in his life is a wife and child.

"The concert was good. I had a nice time." Lila glanced at the cuckoo clock on the wall. "I've got to get going. Enjoy the cookies."

"We will, sweetie."

"Are you taking some to that man?" Myrtle asked.

"What man?"

"The one who got to go to our concert," Charlotte said.

"No," she said. She wasn't sure what to do about Nick, but she knew that bringing him cookies wasn't the right thing. She'd been thinking more about their relationship as she'd baked. He'd seemed so raw in the Colette, Inc. parking lot. Not in command the way he usually was.

She put on her coat and headed for the door. "Bye, ladies."

"Bye, Lila."

There was a bus stop at the bottom of the hill. Though Lila had driven her car from Florida to Indiana when she'd moved, she hardly ever used it. Especially not in the fall and winter. She really hated driving.

Standing in the sun, waiting for the bus, she realized two things. If she was pregnant, she wanted to share the upbringing of that child with a spouse. And the only person she could picture as her spouse was Nick. So that meant she'd have to hold her temper and convince him that love existed. That the face on the pillow next to his in the morning wasn't an enemy's but an ally's.

But how?

Before she could do that she needed to face the truth herself. She needed to get a pregnancy test and see if she was going to be a mom.

"Lila?"

She turned to see Nick standing behind her. He wore a pair of tight faded jeans and a cable-knit sweater that should have made him look like any other man on a Saturday. But he didn't. He looked big and strong and like the man whose voice had just made her heart skip a beat.

"What are you doing here?"

"Visiting Mr. McKee."

"The guy who taught you to water-ski?" she asked.

"Yeah, Buster lives in Hawaii."

"That's nice." It was something she'd never have suspected Nick of doing. He was solitary by nature. He kept boundaries between himself and those around him. Mr. McKee must have had a deep impact on his life.

It made her realize what kind of father he'd be. Because the type of person who'd spend a Saturday with the elderly was the kind of guy who could make a commitment.

He shrugged. "What were you doing?"

"Dropping off some cookies," she said.

"You want a ride home?"

She wanted to spend more time with him. The high energy he usually radiated was tuned down. "Um, I don't want to take you out of your way."

"I'm going in to the office. So I'll have to go right by your place."

"I have an errand to run. You better just go on."

"I'll take you wherever you need to go."

She glanced across the yard at him. The bus should be here any minute. "I was going to the drugstore."

"Condoms?" he said, almost teasingly.

Maybe it would be better to let him believe that. But once you started talking in half truths it was so hard to go back to honesty. "No, pregnancy test."

He thrust his hands in his pockets. "Can you take one this soon?"

Less than a week, she thought. Was it too early to tell? "I don't know. I was going to check and see."

"I'll go with you," he said.

"It might be weird." Especially if they saw someone from the office. She could conceivably explain going to the symphony with Nick but shopping for pregnancy test kits together was not something she wanted to talk about to her co-workers.

"I can live with it."

This was it, she thought. If she wanted to teach Nick about love and commitment she had to start here. "Okay."

He walked back up the hill as the bus approached and Lila followed him. The Porsche was warm from the sun and, as she slid into it, she realized that she could get used to this; get used to spending lazy Saturdays with Nick. And that idea comforted her deep in her heart.

Seeing Mr. McKee always brought back bittersweet memories of his childhood. Long, hot afternoons spent skiing and boating on Lake Michigan. The longing for the family that Buster had and that Nick never would.

He'd tried it once with his own family. He'd taken

three months of saved allowances when he was four-teen and rented a boat and skis for the afternoon. His father and mother hadn't spoken to each other the entire time they were on the lake. It wasn't what he'd been trying to find, and it had strengthened Nick's desire to leave Youngsville behind.

It reminded him as well that he'd promised to be the kind of father that Mr. McKee had been, not the kind Guy Camden had. Involved in his son's life, not removed. The kind of guy who'd coach Little League baseball and teach his own flesh and blood how to water-ski in the summer.

Nick realized that he didn't have the lifestyle that would enable him to be an involved dad. He was a total workaholic more concerned with his job than with anything else. His work was, quite simply, his life. He couldn't imagine it any other way.

Following Lila down an aisle in the pharmacy to procure a test kit seemed like the right thing to do. He knew marriage wasn't an option. Or was it? He'd tried it once and the decision never to remarry wasn't one he'd made easily.

Lila and this possible baby made him want to dream again. Dreams he'd had as a boy. Before life had shaped him into the man he'd become. But that man knew those dreams would never come true.

He needed time away from Lila to decide. He knew he wasn't going to be uninvolved in his child's life if there was a child, but a wife....

Lila stopped, glanced both ways and pulled a box

from the shelf, skimming the back quickly before once again checking the aisle for other customers. Though it sometimes annoyed him, her preoccupation with what others thought was kind of endearing.

She looked cute today wearing a pair of navy leggings and a bright-colored sweater. She had on a winter coat that was a little heavy for the fall weather, but he knew she was cold most of the time. For someone who'd chosen to move north she seemed ill prepared for it.

"I could stand watch at that end," he said.

"Ha-ha. This isn't like the symphony. I think that we should know definitely before we have to deal with any rumors," she said.

She looked so cute, though, the way she kept glancing over her shoulders, that he wanted to kiss her. But he couldn't. Not here, not now.

He watched her and thought of the night they'd made love on his desk. Thought of all the things he'd do differently the next time he had her in his arms. And he'd definitely make love to her again.

"Did you find one?" he asked, ready to leave the drugstore. Maybe she'd let him kiss her before she got out of his car. In fact, he wasn't going to wait for her permission to do so. He was just going to kiss her.

"I think so. But most of these aren't good until I've missed a period." Her full lips beckoned him. She'd used some red lipstick earlier and only a trace remained. He wanted to remove the rest of it.

"Have you?" He didn't think she had because, most likely she would have mentioned it. And besides, it had only been six days. Not that he was counting.

"Not yet, but I should know soon."

"Why don't we wait?" he asked. He couldn't believe those words had come from his lips. He dealt in reality, but for a few days he wouldn't mind living in the realm of maybe.

"Don't you want to know?" she asked. Her face was lined with worry, and it brought home again how he'd failed to protect her. Dammit, when was he going to stop hurting those around him?

He hugged her close. He couldn't help it. She was so tiny compared to him. Her bones were small and fragile under his arms and he nestled her close to his body. Surrounded her with himself and promised not to hurt her again. "Sure, but not knowing for a few more days isn't going to change anything."

She slipped out of his embrace. "I'm going to buy this one, so I'll have it on hand."

He followed her down the aisle towards the registers, plowing into her when she came to an abrupt stop.

"Oh, God. That's my landlady, Rose. I don't want her to see me buying this."

"Calm down, Lila. You go talk to her, and I'll buy the kit."

"What if she saw us together? What if she knows what we're purchasing?"

"It's not like she's going to make you wear a scarlet A."

"This is serious. Your reputation can be stained by the smallest innuendo."

"Florida girl, you worry too much. She's coming this way, so smile." Nick took the package from her hand and strode toward the drug counter at the back of the store. He'd pay for the damn thing there.

He couldn't help thinking that Lila was never going to want to have a child without a husband. It bothered him, because the opinions of others were so fickle, but her anxiety was genuine and he didn't want to be the cause of more.

He knew he should transfer her out of his department. Except, with all the turmoil at Colette, that would just cause rumors to spread. And he didn't want anyone else sitting at the desk outside his office. It didn't matter that right now they didn't have the smoothest working relationship. Lila was his. And he wasn't letting her go.

He didn't examine that desire too closely. Just paid for the damn pregnancy kit and asked for a brown bag. Lila's landlady eyed the bag when Nick returned, and he knew she thought he'd purchased condoms. He felt a faint blush steal over his face as the older lady winked at him.

He wasn't ready to be part of a community, and he suddenly realized that was one of the things that scared him about Lila. She had woven herself into the fabric that was Youngsville, and he'd never wanted to be any part of it.

Six

Two days later, Lila was back at the office and still not sure where she stood with Nick. Saturday had been a strange glimpse into his personal life, and she couldn't happily blend it with what she already knew of him.

He was calm, self-assured and focused on work. But the other man was very real. More faceted than the one-dimensional image she'd carried of Nick. It was the picture of a man who'd been hurt and whose life had been shaped by those pains.

She realized she wanted to influence the direction his life took. She'd spent half the night lying in the dark staring at the stars she'd painted on her ceiling and had realized that she didn't want Nick in her personal life only if she was pregnant with his child. She wanted him to be with her always, but he didn't believe he deserved happiness.

Even though he'd never said those words, she knew that he believed he deserved to be punished. Something about the way he'd focused solely on his career after his wife's death. Something about the types of women he dated. Something about his reaction to her and the possibility of her pregnancy.

She picked at the salad she'd brought for lunch. Nick had been in back-to-back meetings all day, and she'd heard more than one rumor about the takeover. To be honest, she was worried that her time at Colette, Inc. was running short.

"Working through lunch?" Nick asked as he entered the office.

"Yes. I wanted to be here when you got back. There's an emergency board meeting scheduled for this evening. They want to look at last year's numbers compared to this year's."

"Have you contacted Jill in our business office?"

"Yes. They're running the numbers now. Jill is meeting with you at 3:30. That gives you a half hour to get her information and assimilate it."

"Great."

"Did you eat at your meeting?" she asked. She normally didn't like to run out and get lunch. She felt it put secretaries back to the dark ages if they offered to bring food or coffee for their boss.

But Nick looked tired. Was he having a hard time

sleeping through the night? Did worry about her or
Colette keep him awake?

She hoped it was Colette, but at the same time
feared it might be her. Their relationship was like a
hurricane: stormy and out of control. They seemed to
be in the eye right now. Everything calm and smooth,
but still a tension underlay all their interactions.

"I'll grab a sandwich in the cafeteria."

"Before you go down there…"

"Yes?"

"I've heard some rumors you might want to be
prepared for."

He took a deep breath.

"Nick, let me get you something, okay?"

"Okay. Tuna on wheat."

"I'll be right back."

Lila hurried to the cafeteria and got Nick's sandwich, avoiding most of her co-workers by keeping her
head down and taking the stairs. Nick was seated behind his desk and was on the phone when she returned.

He hung up when she came in. She handed him his
sandwich. "Close the door and come in for a minute."

His serious expression worried her. "Is this another
bad-news scenario?"

"No. I'd like you to tell me what those rumors
concern."

Lila was used to being Nick's ears around the

building, but this rumor involved one of Nick's best managers. "Unfair hiring practices."

"Am I supposed to be involved?" he asked.

She shook her head. "I haven't heard your name, but Paul was mentioned."

"Damn."

"That's what I thought you'd say."

"Get me fifteen minutes with Paul and Human Resources."

"I've got them down at 2:30. That gives you about twenty minutes to scarf down your sandwich."

"Do you need anything else?"

"One more thing."

Lila moved closer to Nick's desk, prepared to grab a sheet of paper and jot down whatever he wanted her to do. But Nick stood up and leaned forward, his face inches from hers.

"I need something from you, Lila."

"What?" she asked, her voice a husky whisper.

His breath brushed across her face and she closed her eyes, enjoying the sensation, remembering the last time they'd kissed. It seemed like forever since they'd touched.

The moist brush of his tongue across the seam of her lips surprised her. She opened her eyes and met his sensual gaze. He rubbed his lips back and forth on hers.

"Will you let me kiss you?" he asked.

Her first impulse was to crawl over his desk and pull him into her arms, but she didn't. Bracing her weight on her hands, she leaned farther over. Tilting her head to one side, she licked her lips.

His eyes tracked the movement. "Don't tease me, woman."

"I'm not."

"Yes, you are. And all I can think of when you are in my office is that night when I took you on my desk."

"Me, too."

"Hell, Lila. Don't tell me that."

"Why not?"

"Because hearing you remember it too makes me want to take you again."

"Here?"

"No, not here."

"Then kiss me, Nick. And make it count."

Nick loosened his tie as he headed into the darkened parking lot toward his Porsche. He needed something to relieve the tension that had been riding him all afternoon. The meetings had not gone well.

All he'd been able to think of was Lila's sweet mouth as she'd kissed him with a carnality that had made his mind turn to mush and his loins painfully hard. He couldn't spend another night alone. He needed her, and it was past time for him to take control of this relationship he had with her.

Actually, it wasn't a relationship. It was more like on-going frustration. He couldn't sleep because he dreamed of the remembered tightness of her body clutching his. He couldn't work because the office smelled like her perfume, and he knew how much stronger it was between her pretty breasts.

He couldn't go to her because it would feed the need, yet, like a druggie, he couldn't resist one more hit. He told himself he could control it—the way he'd intended to this afternoon. Then the next thing he knew he was sitting in a meeting with a hard-on that wouldn't go away.

He turned down Amber Court and coasted to a stop in front of number twenty. He'd just talk to her. Talking wasn't touching. It didn't involve anything but voices. But he knew somehow he was going to finagle an invitation into her home.

With his decision made, Nick picked up his cell phone and had directory assistance connect him to her home phone. She answered on the second ring, breathless.

He wondered what she'd been doing. Would she welcome him tonight? It was past ten. Maybe he should hang up and just show up at her door.

"Hello? Is anyone there?" she asked.

He cleared his throat, feeling like a stalker as he sat in his car across the street from her building. "Hey, Florida girl."

"Nick."

"What's up?"

He didn't want to have to ask her if he could come over. He wanted her to say the words that might make him sound like he was in control. He'd prided himself on being the aggressive one in every relationship he'd ever had. But with Lila he was at her mercy, and, frankly, he planned to change all of that by taking back the control.

He needed to sleep with her one more time. Then he'd prove that what had happened in his office had been a fluke. The other kisses, they were part of his fascination with Lila that would end once he'd had her again.

"I've just finished up at the office."

"You sound tired," she said.

"I am." And lonely. But of course he wasn't going to admit that to her. In fact, the more he thought about it, he wasn't really lonely. He just didn't want to be alone tonight. Those were two very different things.

"I guess you're not calling for phone sex."

That surprised a laugh out of him.

"Why, have you always wanted to have phone sex?" he asked. For all her prim and proper ways, Lila had passion running deep inside of her. Even though she was afraid to let it out.

"Will it make me sound easy if I say yes?" she asked. There was a shyness to her voice that endeared her to him, though he didn't want to feel anything but lust for her. He realized suddenly that he wasn't ever going to be able to put Lila in one box and label her. She was already more to him than the women he'd dated in the past. She always would be.

He promised himself that he'd give her this. A belief in the beauty of expressing the passion she carefully hid from the world. "No. It will make you sound like just the girl I need tonight."

"Mmm. So you *were* looking for something from me."

"Yes, but not phone sex."

"Darn. Why not?"

"Because phone sex is essentially solitary and based in fantasy."

"Don't like fantasy, huh?"

"I'm ready for some more reality."

"Really?

Silence buzzed on the line. "Can I stop by?"

He sounded needy, which he hated, but there was no other option. He did need something that only she could give him. He only hoped she'd never realize how much he needed it.

"Sure. I just finished making lasagna for the next three weeks. I can heat some of it up for you. Have you eaten dinner?"

"No."

"Good. I'll feed you."

Feed my soul, he thought. He was suddenly starved. "I'll be right up."

"Where are you?"

"Across the street."

"Good thing I said yes."

"Good thing," he said, and disconnected the phone.

He crossed the street and waited for her to buzz

him in. He climbed the stairs to her apartment and her door was open.

She stood there illuminated by the light spilling from her homey apartment. Welcoming. Her long plaid skirt and long-sleeved creamy shirt created the image of vulnerability that he'd perceived the first time he saw her.

He knew he didn't deserve the sweetness that was Lila. Knew better than to believe that what she'd given him could last. Knew that he wasn't a man who'd ever be comfortable in such a homey environment because he didn't believe it was real…or that it could last.

But tonight it felt real, the way the cold did on a December morning. He saw her standing there and knew he wasn't going to be able to enter her apartment and seduce her. He wanted—no needed—for her to accept him in her bed. To want him there as much as he needed to be there.

"Lila?"

"Yeah?"

"I'm not leaving until morning."

She sighed and held out her hand. Her long fingers were warm and as she tugged him over the threshold, he heard her say, "Good."

Lila's apartment wasn't always clean, and tonight was no exception. She wished it could be like it was in the movies, where things just magically turned out right. But then real life seldom did.

It gave her pause. She wanted Nick. Had done nothing but think about him and the kiss they'd shared over his desk all afternoon, but now he was here in her cozy little place that hadn't been dusted in three weeks. Worse than that, it was laundry night and there was a pile of clean clothes on the couch.

"I'm sorry this place is such a mess."

He panned the room and she imagined the half-empty cups of tea on the counter were a bit off-putting.

"Why don't you have a seat, and I'll clean this place up?"

"Lila."

She glanced at him.

"I love your apartment. It's not messy. It's lived-in. Besides, I came to see you."

His words warmed her in a way that no one else's ever had. She didn't examine it too closely, though. Just wallowed in the feeling.

"I promised you dinner."

"Yes, you did."

She filled a plate with warm lasagna and gave him a bottle of beer. "I wish I had some bread, but I didn't bake tonight."

"This is great."

No, it wasn't. This was weird. She'd invited him in for dinner and…sex. It felt so strange. Too much pre-planning. The last time there hadn't been time to think. This time…this time, there was too much time to think.

What was she doing? She wanted to teach him to love and care. Show him that the people around him could strengthen, not weaken him. Make him believe that she was the only woman for him and instead she was hovering over him like some demented Martha Stewart wannabe trying to convince him that she was a good homemaker.

And she was failing miserably.

"Maybe you should go when you're done with dinner."

"Changed your mind?"

She shrugged. She wanted things to be perfect between them. In her head she had this image of how they should be. Her laundry didn't play into it at all.

Nick put down his fork and stood up. He came around the counter with a brisk stride, stopping only when a mere inch of space separated them. Every breath she took brushed her breasts against his chest.

"I'm not leaving unless you tell me to."

"I can't. But this feels so strange. So premeditated."

"Florida girl, you make me crazy."

He bent and kissed her. His lips brushing hers carefully, tenderly. Then the tone of his embrace changed. His hands settled on her hips, pulling her firmly against the cradle of his thighs. He rubbed his erection against her. An ache that could only be eased by Nick started at the center of her body and moved outward to every limb.

She forgot to breathe as his mouth devoured hers,

his tongue thrusting deep into her mouth. He tasted of garlic and oregano and something stronger. Something that her soul recognized as Nick.

Her entire body melted against him. He lifted her onto the counter, spreading her thighs to make room for himself. They were still separated by the barrier of her wool skirt and his pants. But she could feel the heat of him.

She rocked forward, rubbing against the hard ridge in his pants, needing from him something that was more powerful than words could describe. Something that only Nick could give, and it wasn't only physical.

His palms sliding up her thighs were rough against her skin. Her skirt bunched around her waist and he slipped his hands beneath her panties. His eyes closed and he tilted his head back, breathing harder than a racehorse that had won the derby.

Lila needed to be touching him. The emotions and sensations swamping her were too intense. She unbuttoned his shirt and caressed his chest and back. He shrugged out of it, struggling for a moment with his cufflinks, which made a pinging sound when they hit the linoleum floor.

"Take off your blouse," he ordered.

Their eyes met and held as she slowly freed the buttons on her shirt. She unbuttoned her cuffs first and then teasingly opened the front, giving him just a glimpse of the lacy camisole she wore underneath.

He bit her neck lightly and then licked the spot, sending fire shooting to her groin. She wanted to be his equal here. Wanted to tease and tempt him the way he did her. But she plain wanted him too much to wait too long.

The fire in his eyes convinced her to keep teasing. She let the fabric slip slowly down her shoulders, lifting one arm slowly out and then the other, then dropping her arms in one graceful, yet sexy, movement.

Sitting before him with only her camisole covering the top of her body and her panties covering the bottom made her feel sexy and bountiful.

"Now this," he said, stepping back so that he could watch her.

She lifted her arms above her head and slowly slid the silk and lace garment up her body. She heard his breath catch when her breasts were revealed, and by the time she'd pulled it completely off, he was back between her thighs, his mouth moving over her breast, kissing, licking and finally suckling her. She held his head close, weaved her fingers into his hair and held him to her.

He suckled both breasts in turn and the flesh between her thighs ached for his touch. Shifting forward, she rubbed herself against his hardened sex, felt him straining against the zipper.

"Lift your butt, sweetheart."

She did, and he slid her undergarment and skirt down her legs, crouching to finish removing them. Taking an ankle in each hand, he spread her legs open and stared up at her. Embarrassed, she tried to cover herself. But he stood and kissed her on the lips.

''Don't. You're so beautiful.''

He whispered in her ear the things he wanted to do to her. The ways he wanted to touch her and how that made him feel like he was going to explode.

''Okay?'' he asked, his voice deep and sexy.

Incapable of speech, she nodded.

He bent his head and touched her most private area with his mouth. At first just a soft touch of lips. Then he used his tongue and teeth. She rocked against his mouth, felt the tidal wave coming but didn't want to be washed away without him. Wanted to feel his heartbeat next to hers.

''Nick, come with me.''

He stood and grappled in his pocket while she freed his erection. He was hot to the touch. ''Not yet, Lila.''

''Do you have protection this time?''

''Hell, yes.''

He pulled a condom from his pocket, removed his pants and underwear, then sheathed himself and thrust into her, slowly, carefully finding his way until he was buried completely inside her body. She was so full of him. He rocked against her with building speed, his eyes watching hers, his hands gripping her hips, his chest rubbing against the aching points of her nipples.

''Come on, sweetheart,'' he said.

He bent his head and suckled on her neck, rocking harder and harder against her until everything in her body tightened and her body clenched around him. She couldn't breathe, couldn't think as Nick tilted her hips up and thrust so deeply she was sure he touched her womb. Then she felt him tense and watched as his climax washed through his body.

He cradled her close to him, held her as if he'd never let her go. And then, as they both came back down to earth, he lifted her high against his chest and carried her into her bedroom where he made love to her again before falling asleep in her arms. And Lila knew that he was on his way to falling in love with her. Knew that only a man who cared deeply for a woman would hold her so possessively, even in sleep. Knew that she'd found her man and her chance at happiness.

But could she convince him of that?

Seven

Lila wasn't really a morning person. That became glaringly apparent as she grumbled around her apartment trying to hurry him out the door. Nick took his time, kind of enjoying seeing this side of Lila.

He propped himself up on an elbow as she emerged from her shower. Her skin was still damp and waves of humidity filled the room. The scent of flowers surrounded him and he felt his morning erection harden even more. Damn, he wished she hadn't scurried out of bed when the alarm clock had rung.

She struggled into a red velvet robe that brought out the creamy freshness of her skin. She haphazardly piled her hair on top of her head and glared at him as she caught him smiling at her in the mirror.

He knew he should be worried about getting to work, but right now, he felt he had all the time in the world.

She left the bedroom and returned a minute later with a pile of his clothing. She tossed it on the end of the bed. "Aren't you going to get out of bed?"

He climbed to his feet and slowly put on his clothing. Aware of her gaze on him while he dressed, he glanced over his shoulder and she flushed before turning away.

"I don't have time to fix breakfast so you're on your own." She opened her closet, and he watched her careful selection. She pulled out several different outfits, held each against her body and then finally decided on one of her most severe suits.

He didn't like it. She'd chosen to wear full battle armor. The sharp black suit was one of his least favorites now that he thought about it. She always was a little harder to get along with when she wore it. He felt that it was akin to a cast-iron bra and spear. In fact, those things would seem tame next to the black suit.

It made him want to pull her back into his arms and tame her in a very masculine way. To stake a claim on her that the clothing couldn't cover and she couldn't deny. But he knew from the way she kept scowling at him that she wouldn't tolerate any sort of delays.

"I'll buy you something if you ride with me to

work,'' he said, slipping his cuff links into his pants pocket.

She frowned at him. "I can't."

He knew why. Despite the bonds that had been created between them, she still didn't want anyone to know that she was sleeping with him. Part of him, the callous part, didn't mind. If she were using him for sex, he'd take it. But another, deeper part minded.

''You rode to work with me last week and no one said anything.''

''That was different.'' She went into her walk-in closet to dress. She'd gone in the soft, sweet woman who'd welcomed him into her home and bed late last night and came out a superwoman. Capable of anything and not needing a mere man in her life.

''How?'' he asked.

''We hadn't…you know.'' There was the woman he'd held in his arms. The one who got flustered whenever she tried to talk about things like sex and pregnancy.

She blushed so prettily. Looked so sexy and tempting that he wanted to pull her into his arms and carry her back to bed. But he really had to leave if he was going to make it to the office on time.

''If we had the time, I'd tempt you back to bed.''

''Maybe I'd let you.'' The teasing look he received was unexpected but took the edge off what he'd been feeling.

He stalked closer to her, kissed her with the passion he'd been trying to redirect since she'd left him alone in her bed. She squirmed in his embrace, bringing her hands to the back of his head and standing on her toes.

"You'd let me," he said, coming up for air.

"I guess we'll never really know. You have to leave or you'll be late." He tried to tell himself she didn't sound smug, but he didn't believe it.

"If you hadn't spent all this time rushing me out of your bed, we'd have been able to make love again this morning."

She frowned at him until he reluctantly donned his suit jacket and headed for the door. She paced to the window and pulled the curtain back.

"Oh, my God."

"What's the matter? Did someone vandalize my car?"

"Why did you park it there?"

"Where else would I park?"

"I don't know. Not there. Everyone who drives by will see it."

"It's not like there's a big flashing neon sign over it, Lila."

"But some of the girls who live here work at Colette. They might recognize your car."

"So?"

"I like to think of them as my friends."

"My Porsche out front won't change that."

"Yes," she said, quietly. "It will."

"You have to stop worrying about what others

think. If these women give you a hassle about me spending the night then they aren't your friends."

"They won't have to say anything. But I'll know."

"Lila, believe in yourself and your choices. You're the only one you can please. Believe me, I learned that a long time ago."

"From your parents?"

"In an indirect way."

"Don't you ever wish you had someone else to lean on?"

"No. Then I'd have a liability."

"Caring about people isn't a liability."

"It can be," he said, and walked out the door. Lila would never understand how those softer emotions could chain a man until he couldn't stand on his own.

Lila was still shaken two hours later by what Nick had revealed on his way out the door. The office was still abuzz with rumors and speculation. Lila wished she'd called in sick so she wouldn't have to face Nick today. But he was busy in meetings anyway.

Caring is a liability. The words circled in her head like vultures, and she tried to calm herself, but she knew that they were pecking the heck out of her relationship with Nick. They didn't really have a relationship when you got down to it. What they had was hot sex once in awhile.

She leaned back in her chair and wrapped her arms around her body. She knew she was taking a gamble, hoping she could teach him to love, but she'd never realized how great the risk was. Until now.

Picking up the phone she dialed her mom's number. She needed to let the joy and love her mother felt for her wash over her. But her mom was at work and Lila got the machine. She didn't leave a message and hung up not feeling as if she'd resolved anything.

The brooch Rose had given her was pinned to her lapel. The gems shone brighter against the stark black backdrop. She'd worn the suit because it made her feel professional and in control. It also made her feel invincible.

Which hadn't helped at all when Meredith had mentioned hearing a man's voice in the hall last night. Was it someone visiting her or Mr. Parkes who lived in 3B? Lila pretended it was Mr. Parkes, but she'd hated lying.

Then again, she'd hate to lose the friendship she'd started with the women in her apartment building because she was having an affair with her boss. Damn, it sounded like a cliché but it felt real. Too real sometimes.

She wasn't ashamed of anything she'd done with Nick the night before, wasn't really ashamed to have others know they were seeing each other. But she was uncomfortable with the fact that he'd pretty much told her he'd never marry her.

The phone rang. ''Nick Camden's office, this is Lila.''

''This is the seniors' center. Is Mr. Camden there?''

"He's in a meeting. Can I take a message?"

"Yes, please have him call right away."

"What's this regarding?"

"Mr. McKee."

"What happened?"

"A minor stroke, but we couldn't get in touch with his son, and Mr. Camden is our second contact. Mr. McKee's at the hospital now. Having family around at his age can really make a difference."

"Yes...I'll let him know. Right away." She hung up the phone.

Lila's legs were shaking. She didn't want to pass the message on to Nick but knew she had to. He was in the building, probably on the executive level in the boardroom. She'd page him.

She typed a bland message into his alpha pager for him to call her right away and three minutes later he walked in the door. He looked hurried and stressed but not tired. In fact, a gleam entered his eye when he saw her. She thrilled at seeing it there.

Focusing herself on preparing to tell him bad news was hard. She never knew the right thing to do. "Sorry to pull you out of the meeting."

"I was hoping you would. What's up?"

"Oh, gosh. Nick sit down."

The gleam left his eyes and his shoulders straightened. He skimmed her body, staring for a minute at her stomach. "Just tell me your news."

Her news? She wouldn't page him out of a meeting

to tell him she'd started her period. "It's not *my* news, Nick."

"Lila, I'm tired because we didn't sleep much last night. I want you on my desk again and I have to get back to that meeting before tempers explode and irreparable damage is done. Just tell me why you paged me."

"The seniors' center called. Mr. McKee had a stroke. He's at the hospital."

His face didn't go ashen. In fact, no emotion was revealed there at all. Instead he shut down. Lila was ready to offer the comfort of her arms, but the man standing before her was a stranger. And not someone who'd welcome solace from her.

"I'm going over there. Call Judy, Xavier's secretary, and tell her I won't be coming back today. Then ask Phillips to call me in the car. I'll brief him on what's going on and he can attend the afternoon session of meetings with the board."

She picked up the phone and made the calls. She finished just as Nick came out of his office, briefcase in hand.

"I've got my pager and cell phone. If you need me, don't hesitate to call."

"Nick, is there anything I can do?" she asked, wishing she could go with him, even if only to sit next to him in the waiting room. But she had a job to do here.

"No," he said, with a finality that made her ache. She touched his arm as he walked by her. Nick glanced down at her hand on his jacket sleeve. "He'll be okay."

"No, Lila, he won't. He'll never be the same again even if he recovers."

"They said *minor* stroke," she said.

"But the message was the same," he said, taking her hand in his and pulling her closer.

"What message?" she asked. His eyes revealed the pain that he hid through confidence and disdain.

"Life is unexpected," he muttered.

Yes, it is, she thought. Because she'd never have expected Nick to be the kind of person who'd care so deeply about an elderly man. She'd never have expected Nick to want more than one night with her. She'd never have expected that Colette's problems would seem small compared to what was happening in her own life.

"That's not a bad thing."

"It's not a good thing, either."

"I know you don't believe that, Nick," she said, not willing to let him leave unchallenged.

"Yes, I do."

"What we have is unexpected," she said, and immediately wished she could call back the words.

He stared at her for a moment then moved to the door. "It's not lasting, either."

His words echoed in her mind as he walked away. She sank to her chair, telling herself that he was hurting right now. That the only adult who'd cared about him in his childhood was sick, and it was anger that made him react. But in her heart she feared that those words reflected feelings she couldn't change.

The luminous dial on his watch read eleven o'clock. Visiting hours had ended a few hours ago, and Nick had been relegated to the hallway waiting area. The waiting area was light, with big fluorescent lamps that seemed too bright for the ICU.

Nick rubbed his eyes and leaned back against the wall. Buster was flying in from Hawaii, but it would be about six hours until he arrived. Nick had assured his friend he'd stay. There were some debts that he'd go to any length to repay.

His life was such a jumble of confusion right now that nothing seemed normal. When he thought he saw Lila walking toward him it seemed surreal. He knew he must be hallucinating because after he'd told her what they had wouldn't last he'd expected her never really to talk to him again.

And who could blame her? He'd acted like an ass, the way he often did when he felt vulnerable. It always yielded the same results, injuring someone he'd never want to hurt. And causing Lila pain was a double-edged sword because it made him ache, as well.

She paused in front of him, and he knew she was no illusion. His body was on red alert, senses so attuned to her scent that they sent arousal rushing through him. She wore a plaid miniskirt and black tights that made her legs seem endless. But he knew they weren't. He was intimately acquainted with where they ended and met.

"Lila," he said. Just her name, hoping for some vocal confirmation that he wasn't having one hell of a daydream. After the day he'd had it would probably turn into a vicious nightmare that would scare the socks off even Stephen King.

"I brought you dinner," she said. Lila was so...homey. She reminded him of what he'd wanted his mom to be when he was growing up. The basket in her hands was wrapped in a towel and a tantalizing aroma filled the air. But at the same time she was a sexy siren who could make him forget about family and focus only on her.

"You shouldn't have."

He meant it. He didn't deserve her sweet caring. And he knew that she cared about him. Because if he'd learned one thing about Lila the woman, it was that she wasn't the type to sleep with a man she couldn't care about. More than just physical passion had brought her to him.

"I knew you wouldn't eat. Have you even left this hallway since he was brought in?"

"Yes," he said. He'd had to use the restroom earlier this afternoon.

"Why don't you sit down? I brought some cottage pie."

He started to say no, but there was a light in her eyes that warned against it. She was offering him an olive branch. He should take it and be happy that he'd gotten off so easily.

Except that he couldn't. He shouldn't be let off the hook that easily. And tonight had reminded him of some irrevocable facts, some truths in life he'd been conveniently ignoring while he'd enjoyed Lila. Today he'd realized he could bury his head no more.

"Why are you here?"

She shrugged and set her basket on one of the cloth-covered chairs. "I don't know. I tried to stay at home, but all I did was think about you."

"I'm not the right guy for you, Lila. Today made that brutally clear to me."

She propped her hands on her hips and tilted her head to glance up at him. "You can be so stubborn sometimes."

"I know."

"Don't you even care that this could be your once in a lifetime?"

"It's not. I already had that, remember?"

"Yeah. Sit down and eat before this gets cold."

"I'm not hungry."

"I don't believe you."

Suddenly, the knowledge that she wanted him and he couldn't keep her overwhelmed him. He reached out and pulled her close to him. He felt her rise on her toes. He bent his head close and rested his forehead against hers.

"I *am* hungry, Lila. There is a hunger so deep in my soul that I doubt even you could ever fill it. You keep pushing until I think maybe you could, but I know better. Today proved it. It was a careless comment, but I meant it. I'm not your forever man.''

''But you could be, Nick, and that's why I'm here.''

He didn't want to take the chance he'd hurt her again, maybe even worse this time. ''I don't know any other way.''

''I'm trying to show you.''

He sighed. She had a relentless streak that he'd never noticed before. It annoyed him. ''Lila, what do you want from me?''

She brushed her lips against his. ''A chance.''

Don't ask, he told himself. There were some things a man wasn't meant to know about. The inside of a woman's purse, the things she did in the bathroom and the secrets of her soul.

But he needed to know what secrets she was keeping. Needed to hear the words that would be like manna to his starving soul. Needed to know if what she felt was as real as she'd hinted.

''A chance at what?''

''Forever.''

Damn, that's what he'd been afraid of. He wasn't a forever kind of guy. Had tried it with disastrous results. He wasn't even sure he was a forever boss with the turmoil at Colette. He started to speak, planned to turn her down. But she put her forefinger against his lips and stopped the words before they could form.

"I'm willing to start with now."

"Now, I can handle," he said. In fact, now was what he needed from her. He tugged her closer to his embrace and held her for a long time, not letting go until Buster arrived. As Lila walked away, Nick felt for the first time that the future held something other than work and a cold, lonely existence.

Eight

According to Lila's somewhat unscientific calculations her period was a day late. Normally she would have been thankful, because she hated it. She loved it when she skipped a month or two, as was sometimes the case. But this month, with her new relationship with Nick as fragile as a porcelain Ming vase, she wanted it to start.

She couldn't stay with Nick if she were pregnant and he didn't want to marry her. Nick hadn't been kidding about never remarrying. There was something very serious in his eyes when he talked about the past, something he hadn't done since that night in the hospital.

But here she was on a Saturday morning in the

Home Depot, helping Nick pick out paint for his guest bedroom. She'd offered to help him with his redecorating when he mentioned how much he liked her place. The compliment had thrilled her and she'd eagerly volunteered to help him.

"They should be done mixing the paint in a few minutes. Want to come with me to get the supplies?"

"Sure." She followed him down another aisle admiring the way his faded jeans hugged his butt when he bent over to grab a pack of paintbrushes. Her fingers tingled with the need to pat him right there. To just reach out and feel his firmness, maybe give him a little pinch.

"Lila?"

"Yes?"

"Florida girl, what are you thinking?"

"Nothing."

"That's not what the blush on your face is telling me."

"You've got great buns, Camden. What can I say?"

Now he flushed, and she was pleased. "You were eyeing me?"

"Yes. And I was thinking of copping a feel."

Pivoting, he bent down again to pick up a paint tray. "Don't let me stop you."

This was the Nick she wanted to see more of. The man who forgot the pain of the past and let down his guard. Without even looking to see if there was anyone else on the aisle with them, she reached out and caressed his backside. Firm, taut and utterly masculine. She traced the pocket of his jeans and then lightly scraped her fingernail over the center seam.

"That's enough," he said, grabbing her hand and facing her. His erection distended the front of his jeans. She slid her fingers over the button fly.

For a minute he held her hand closer to his arousal, then he pulled her down the aisle after him. She felt a bit naughty and loved the feeling of power that came with it.

"What's the matter?" she asked teasingly.

"Nothing that you can't fix as soon as we get out of here."

"I'm not sure I can solve your problem. It looks hard to me."

"I am." She melted when he glanced over his shoulder, his eyes a promise of carnal delights. She loved the feel of him moving over her in bed. He always made love to her as if she were the most precious thing in the world to him. He also made her feel like the sexiest woman he'd ever held.

They rounded the corner and Rose was standing there at the paint counter. Lila forgot all about teasing Nick. Forgot all about how good he made her feel inside. All she could focus on now was explaining herself to Rose.

She tugged Nick to a stop but it was too late. Rose glanced up from the paint chips she was studying and caught Lila's eye. Lila pulled her hand free from Nick's and tried to appear circumspect but knew she'd failed miserably. Desire pumped through her veins and her pulse seemed to be dictating that all of her thoughts center on Nick.

"Lila, what a pleasant surprise."

"Hi, Rose."

"And who's this?" Rose asked.

"Umm, this is Nick Camden. My boss."

Nick gave her a sideways glance, but didn't say anything, just walked over to the counter to get the paint. She watched him leave knowing she'd disappointed him.

"Wasn't he with you at the drugstore last week?"

"Yes, he was, Rose."

"Has my brooch brought you luck then?"

"I don't know, Rose."

"That man doesn't look at you like he's only your boss."

Lila had hoped she could hide her personal life from the people who were important to her. Her mom, Rose, the women of Amber Court, Charlotte and Myrtle at the senior center. But she realized she wasn't fooling anyone.

"Please don't think that this is improper in any way."

"Honey, I was young once, too."

Lila looked at Rose. "I think you still are."

"Thanks, sweetie."

"I've been meaning to give you back your brooch. Will you be home this afternoon?"

"Yes, but you keep it for a while longer. Will I see you for dinner tomorrow night?"

Lila nodded. Rose had her, Jayne, Sylvie and Meredith over for dinner once a month. When she'd first moved to Indiana it had been a lifesaver, and in some ways it still was. Those ladies had become very important to her, just as Rose had. She thought about her relationship with Nick and realized she didn't want to lose him either. But she would if she kept pushing him away.

"Ready, Lila?" Nick asked. Lila nodded and waved goodbye to Rose. Nick didn't say anything to her until they'd gotten into his car. He stowed the paint cans behind her seat and then sat there without starting the motor.

"When are you going to trust me enough to stop pretending to others that I'm nothing but your boss?"

She knew it was a matter of trust, and it seemed wrong for him to question her trust when he was so lacking in it himself. "You're the one who said it wasn't forever."

"You're the one who said it could be. But apparently one of us was lying and one was telling the truth."

She slunk back against the seat. She didn't know what to say. She'd been urging him out of his shell, daring him to put his fears on the line while she'd stayed comfortably hidden behind her own. No guts, no glory, she thought. She couldn't ask him for everything and give only half in return.

"You're right. From now on I'm not hiding."

"You're sure?"

"Yes," she said. And to prove it she kissed him there in the car, in front of anyone who happened to be walking by in the parking lot. The act was freeing and Lila knew she'd never be the same.

The next evening, Lila hurried down to Rose's apartment. Of all the things she liked about her life in Indiana, the friendships she'd formed with Meredith, Jayne and Sylvie were perhaps the most important. To Lila it was as if she'd found the sisters she'd never had. Though she sometimes felt like she didn't fit in the group, she wouldn't miss their monthly dinners for anything.

She hesitated at the door. Her relationship with Nick played heavily on her mind. Would this be something she'd have to sacrifice if it became common knowledge that she was dating him?

She didn't want to think about that. She hoped that things wouldn't change, but the past had proven that life always did.

She knocked on the door and Meredith opened it. Meredith had the kind of natural beauty that most women would kill for, but she kept it carefully hidden. She could be a real knockout if only she'd dress a little better and maybe get some contact lenses. But Meredith's looks mattered little to Lila because underneath those baggy clothes was one of the nicest women Lila had ever met.

"Everyone else is here. I was just about ready to run up and get you." Meredith took the pie from Lila's hands and placed it on the kitchen counter.

"Sorry I'm late," Lila said.

"No problem," Rose replied, coming out of the kitchen.

Soon they were all seated around the table. Jayne kept the conversation going. She was her usual bubbly self and had even more energy than ever now that she'd found a solid man. Lila was envious of her friend, wondering if Nick and she would ever find a happy place in their relationship.

Sylvie brought the conversation around to work and no one really said much about the situation. Lila was glad because some of the things she knew were still confidential.

"Is the charity auction still taking place?" Rose asked.

"Yes. Nick said that the company wants the community to know that nothing at Colette has changed. The new jewelry designs are to die for. I almost wish I was going to be modeling this year. But I'm too involved in the planning."

"Yes, but you'd have to go out with one of those men," Meredith said.

"That wouldn't be too bad," Jayne said.

"Only because you have a man. The rest of us are fair game," Sylvie said.

"I don't think of myself so much as game as a lame duck," Lila said. She always felt a bit out of her element with these women. At her own level she was confident, but these three were very successful and she didn't even want to compare herself to Rose.

"Would you do it, Rose?"

"In a heartbeat."

"Well, it'll be lovely. I know that much since I'm in charge of the decor. So are either of you thinking of volunteering for the auction block?" Lila asked, looking at Meredith and Sylvie.

Sylvie shook her head and Meredith stood to collect the dinner dishes. "Who's ready for dessert?" she asked.

They shared the pie and coffee and then retired to the living room to chat for a little while longer. Lila left earlier than she normally would have, but she wanted to get home in case Nick had called her. He was out of town and she missed the sound of his voice. That was something she didn't want to think about too much.

Nick returned from a three-day sales trip to Boston. The office was still standing, but Lila wasn't at her desk. It was 4:30. She might already be gone.

Damn. He'd flown standby on an earlier flight just to get back in time to see her. He hadn't planned on stopping by her apartment on the way home. Though he did plan to spend the night with her.

He didn't want to upset her again by leaving his car parked on the street. But that was something they'd have to deal with. She'd said she wasn't hiding anymore and he was going to hold her to that.

Her phone was forwarded to Xavier's assistant and Nick found out from her that Lila was at a planning meeting for the annual charity auction. A surge of possessiveness flooded him, knowing that the women who worked for Colette were often the ones who volunteered for the auction block. Lila wasn't going to be one of them, he vowed. She belonged to him.

She hadn't convinced him that *forever* was meant for them, but he knew that *now* was. And next month would be too soon for him to let go of her. A weary part of his soul urged him to create more distance between them. But the hunger for her was too great. After so many years of emotional starvation he'd finally found a woman who could feed him, and he was needy enough to hang on to her whether it was wise or not.

Over the three days he was gone she should have gotten her period. He was torn. More than anything in the world he'd love to have a son to teach to water-ski and play baseball. Or a small daughter who'd be a reflection of Lila's sense of style and his own love of the outdoors. But with a keen sense of self-preservation, he hoped she wasn't pregnant.

Their relationship was like a leaky houseboat. On the surface it looked great, and each was careful to not rock the boat, but water was slowly seeping inside, and both of them were aware that sooner or later they were going to have to bail.

Yet every time they were together, he, who'd always prided himself on enjoying the peace that a life of routine could bring, enjoyed the tempest. Lila was by turns sexy and unpredictable, heart-touching and heart-wrenching. She was every woman and at the same time the only woman in the world for him.

And that scared him. He didn't like the emotions she brought to the surface. Didn't like the way she'd managed to make him care for her when caring was the last thing he needed. Didn't like that she was the first person he thought of when he woke up in the morning and the last face he saw before he drifted off to sleep.

He didn't think their working relationship would survive that obsession. He knew that Lila thought they could last forever but Nick was more cynical. He'd never known anything that had touched him to withstand life. He wasn't sure if this could even survive the turmoil at Colette. Sooner or later something was going to happen to drive a wedge through the crack already there. And the past had taught him that nothing would be able to repair it.

Nick entered his office and stopped to stare at his desk. In the center was a picnic-style basket and a thick brown blanket.

"Well, what have we here?" Nick muttered to himself. He dropped his briefcase on the floor and loosened his tie as he opened the basket.

Inside were food containers, a bottle of California merlot, two wineglasses and eating utensils. And, as he shifted around the contents, he realized there was a condom packet on the very bottom.

Seemed as if Lila had a surprise for him. He hoped he hadn't ruined it. He pivoted to exit his office. He'd wait for Lila by her desk.

"Who's in here?" Lila asked from the door.

"I am."

She flushed as she glanced from him to the open picnic basket. She was wearing a brown suit that should have looked dull but on her was vibrant. She was an all-American dream of home and family. Her blond hair was tied at the back of her neck. She was the end of summer and the promise of snuggling by a warm fire through winter.

"Welcome back," she said with a tender smile. It was the kind of smile he'd seen on her face only after they'd made love. His pulse beat faster, and his blood heated.

"Thanks. Did you get me a gift?" he asked, gesturing to the basket contents.

"Maybe. Maybe not," she said, walking into the room and closing the door behind her. Her hips swayed lazily with each step she took. Her skirt had a slit he hadn't noticed until she moved. It went halfway up her thigh. His fingers tingled with the need to touch her. And his groin strained against his inseam until he could feel his pulse in it.

"If not me, then who?"

She stopped next to him. Nibbling on her bottom

lip she pulled containers from the basket. "Maybe it's for Mr. McKee. Hospital food's not great."

Nick reached in front of her, deliberately brushing his arms against her breasts. Her intake of breath was his reward.

"I'm not sure he can eat all of this."

"You might be right."

Then Nick found what he'd been searching for and pulled the prophylactic from the bottom. "I'm sure they wouldn't let him use this."

"Well..."

He bent down to nuzzle her neck. "It had better be for me."

"And if it isn't?"

"I'll have to convince you I'm the only man you want to share it with."

"It might take a lot of effort on your part."

"I'm up for it."

She reached down and cupped his erection. "You certainly are."

She slipped her arms around his neck, and Nick took her mouth with the pent-up frustration of a man who knew that he was holding sunlight and winter was looming around the corner.

He made love to her on the surface of his desk and this time was so much better than the last. As he climaxed he clung to her with a desperation he would have denied, but in his heart he knew she was slipping away and he was helpless to keep her where he wanted her. *In his arms.*

* * *

The next afternoon, Lila grabbed a pre-made salad from the lunch counter and paid for it. The cafeteria was crowded but not noisy. The strain of the possible takeover had grown in the offices of Colette, Inc., but Lila realized it had also been spreading. A group of six men and women were talking about the takeover as Lila walked by.

"I heard that the executives are all cutting deals to save their own hides."

Lila paused to hear what the man had to say. She knew it was rude to eavesdrop, but she hadn't heard any rumors about the executives yet.

"Xavier's not going to be able to save himself. Grey probably won't keep any of the board."

"Nick Camden's been courting Grey," one of the women said.

"He has not," Lila interrupted.

"Who are you?"

"Nick's secretary. And I can tell you he's not interested in working for anyone who'd tear Colette apart."

"Yeah, right. What promises has he made you?" said one of the men.

"The same ones he's made to his entire staff. That he'll do everything in his power to make sure Marcus Grey is unsuccessful in his bid to take over Colette."

"And you believe him?"

"Yes, I do."

"I wonder why you're so loyal to him."

Lila told herself to leave. To just walk away before she said something she'd regret. But she knew she'd never regret defending Nick. He was a good, kind man and he didn't deserve to be talked about as if he were the villain in this scenario.

"Because he's an honest man, a good man. He won't go down without a fight."

"We're not doubting that. Just who is he going to be fighting for, himself or the company?"

"Colette is important to Nick." How could she convince them that Colette was the only thing that Nick really believed in? He'd dedicated his life to this company.

"Whatever you say. We'll just have to wait and see."

Lila spun on her heel and marched out of the cafeteria. Tears burned the backs of her eyes. She wasn't sure why she'd made such a big deal about Nick. She should have just kept walking.

But she hadn't been able to. She'd never spoken out for herself when she'd been picked on in school or unfairly judged because of the way she looked. But when it came to someone she cared about, she wouldn't let them be maligned.

When she got back to her desk she sat in her chair, anger vibrating through her. There was no way she was going to be able to work today. No way she was going to be able to see Nick and not tell him what had happened. Because she was still outraged that he'd been the topic of malicious gossip.

But more than outrage flowed through her. Though she didn't want to admit it she knew in the back of her mind those comments had raised some doubt. Why wasn't Nick more concerned about the takeover attempt?

"Lila, are you back from lunch?" Nick yelled from his office.

No matter how high up the rungs you climbed, the boss always liked to be able to yell for his secretary. She'd given up pointing out that he had an intercom on his phone, it was easier to call for her, he'd said.

"I'm here," she said, dropping her salad in one of her desk drawers. Maybe she'd eat it later.

"If you have a minute, I need you to take a memo."

"Sure." She went into his office and took the dictation. It was a policy change for international travel and when Nick was finished she hovered in the doorway unable to leave.

"What's up?" he asked.

She knew she should leave but she wasn't going to be happy until she knew. "Do you know Marcus Grey?"

He raised one eyebrow at the question. "I know who he is, but I've never met him. Why do you ask?"

His answer made her glad she'd spoken up earlier. She knew Nick wouldn't try to cut a deal. "I was just trying to figure out why he was doing this."

"Don't make it personal, Lila. He's a businessman

and Colette is a profit-generating company. I'm sure his interest is purely monetary.''

''Then why didn't he approach the board outright?''

''We're a tightly held company. You know that. He may have thought that was the only way.''

''Is that what you'd do?'' she asked.

He leaned back in his chair. ''Hell, no. I lack subtlety.''

''Yeah, you do.'' The last of her doubts melted away. Nick was more in-your-face than that. He wouldn't conspire behind her back or behind Xavier's.

''Thanks a lot.''

''I'm glad you aren't subtle.''

''Why?''

''A sneaky man wouldn't have seduced me on his desk and forgotten about protection.''

His eyes narrowed, but he didn't seem angry. ''How are we doing on that front?''

''No period yet,'' she said, flushing a little.

''Did you use that test kit?''

''Yes, but it didn't turn either pink or blue. I'm going to pick another one up on my way home from work.''

''I'll take you.''

''You don't have to.''

''I don't like you taking the bus after work,'' he said.

The possessiveness in his tone warmed her. "I drove my car today."

"I thought you hated to drive?"

"I hate the cold more. It was freezing this morning."

"If you'd stayed with me last night you wouldn't have had to drive."

"I know."

"Stay with me tonight," he said.

She hesitated. She had the feeling that her defense of him in the cafeteria was going to ruin any chance she had of pretending they were nothing more than co-workers, but that aside, she'd already decided to be open about her relationship with Nick.

"Please," he said.

And she couldn't say no.

Nine

Nick heard of Lila's defense of him as he was leaving the building later that day. Just a casual comment on the elevator from the Director of Domestic Marketing, but it changed Nick's world. No longer could he doubt even the slightest that Lila was committed to him. And she deserved the same commitment from him. She deserved to know that he wanted her in his life.

Her late period made him believe they were going to be parents. And he realized that was exactly what he wanted. He couldn't offer her marriage. Wasn't about to tempt those fates again by tying his name to a woman's, but he thought that he and Lila could have a good life without marriage.

Marriage was a piece of paper and what they had didn't require approval from the outside. Lila might be ready to accept that. He glanced at his watch. Lila wasn't due at his house until eight. That gave him two hours to make everything as perfect as he could.

Lila had been important to him for a long time. She helped him run his division by keeping him on track and balancing his wild impulses with a sense of sanity.

He knew she could bring the same thing to his personal life. And it was something that had been missing for a long, long time. Something he didn't think he'd ever had. It was as if he was alive for the first time.

He called his favorite restaurant and ordered a gourmet dinner. He stopped by the florist and picked up an exotic-looking bouquet that was as unique as the woman he planned to give it to. Then he drove to his house. The exclusive neighborhood catered to the up and coming. It was a posh area that made Nick feel as if he'd crossed a barrier and achieved something his parents wouldn't have believed he could attain. Maybe they would have changed their minds if they'd lived to see him graduate from college. But a drunk driver had assured they wouldn't.

The house was too big for a bachelor but would suit a family. He could easily see Lila having more than one child. His six-bedroom home would hold whatever her dream family was. He made a mental note to ask about her dreams of the future. The ones he'd never asked about before because the woman who didn't want anyone to see her with him wasn't someone he could build a tomorrow with.

His place was neat, thanks to the maid service he employed, and, after some scrounging, he found a pair of silver candlesticks and some long tapered candles. He'd never needed to seduce anyone before and had no idea how to go about it. But he knew Lila. Knew what it took to seduce her senses. She was a fantasy girl. She wanted the fairy tale, and tonight he'd give it to her.

He laid a fire in the fireplace and changed from his suit into chinos and a casual shirt. Lila arrived just as the delivery boy was walking back toward his car. She looked sweet and sexy and his heart lurched when she walked into his house.

She wore a silk blouse and slim-fitting skirt that ended mid-calf. She was a picture of respectability. Her powerful, feminine scent surrounded him, making him feel very masculine and primitive. The delivery boy smiled at her and Nick wanted to brand Lila as his. Wanted to mark her in some way that all other men who glanced at her would immediately know she belonged to him.

And that wasn't a comfortable thought. He didn't like the possessiveness. Didn't trust the emotions roiling through him like a thunderstorm gathering strength and wreaking havoc on the unsuspecting flowers and trees.

He pulled her to him, putting his arms around her.

She glanced up at him with a warm smile that made him hard. Her touches and gazes went through his control with an ease that would have been embarrassing if he didn't know that he affected her the same way.

She glowed in the moonlight and Nick was suddenly aware that they were alone inside his big empty house.

The heavy-metal emotion of Creed played in the background. Not exactly seduction music, but hey, Lila was early. She hummed along with one of the songs as she helped him set the food on the table. The feeling of losing control gained strength, and Nick motioned for her to sit down.

He lit the tapers and switched to a Harry Connick, Jr. CD, one he knew to be Lila's favorite.

The crooner sang of love and Nick knew better than to believe him, but tonight he liked the fairy tale. He filled both of their glasses with some French champagne he'd been given on a recent business trip. "To the most beautiful woman in the world."

She met his gaze, something that Europeans always did during a toast but he'd noticed most Americans didn't. It was a mark of the kind of woman Lila was. Whenever they were together, she created an oasis for him. A place where he could let slip the tight rein of his control and be himself, whether he wanted to or not.

Most of the time that bothered him, but tonight he felt safe. Safe from the prying eyes of his peers. Safe from the battle his parents had waged trying to use him to wound each other. Safe from the base emotions she called to the surface.

She tipped her head to the side. "I'm not good at toasts."

"Then just say, *Salud!*"

"If you give me a minute…"

"Tonight we have nothing but time."

She smiled. Her eyes glowed in the candlelight, and he saw in them something he'd never seen in a woman's eyes before. He couldn't define it, he only knew that it made him feel stronger and better than he was.

"To a man who embodies everything a man should be."

Nick knew there was no way he could live up to that. He didn't even know what she expected a man to be. Knowing that her father had left before she was born and that she'd been mistreated by the boys in her hometown, he feared he wouldn't be able to live up to her expectations.

"What are these qualities?" he asked.

"Just what you are, Nick. A noble man of integrity and truth."

Damn. Hard words to live up to. But he knew that for Lila, he'd try. No matter what, he'd always try to be truthful and act with integrity.

The champagne and rich French cuisine left Lila feeling voluptuous. Her senses were heightened and she felt as if her entire being was pulsing. The evening felt like a moment out of a dream and she reveled in it and in Nick.

"Ready for dessert?" Nick asked.

Lila nodded, afraid to trust her voice. Nick left the room for a minute and returned with a tray of coffee and French silk pie. Lila offered to pour the coffee but Nick brushed her hands aside.

She felt pampered as she ate the chocolate dessert and drank her coffee laced with Frangelico. She'd never felt like this before. The candles cast them both in a soft glow and it was as though they were in one of those dream sequences that you see sometimes in a movie or sitcom. Of course, in a sitcom it turns out to be a vicious joke. She'd never been able to laugh when the romantic scene turned to a nightmare, because it cut too close to her version of reality. It cut too close to the way she knew most men could behave. But not tonight. Tonight it felt like the real thing, and if she were deluding herself, she'd live with that illusion until tomorrow morning.

The Harry Connick, Jr., CD had switched over to Sade singing her lush songs of love and its sometimes bittersweet reward, but tonight Lila heard no warning. She felt the music in her heart, and, as she stared across the table at Nick, she felt as if he'd become part of her body as well. She felt as if their souls had intertwined to become one complete person, if only for this one night.

It was as if reality had ceased to exist and they

lived in a world of just the two of them. A sensual world, she realized, as Nick leaned forward and brushed his finger over her bottom lip.

"You had a crumb."

All evening he'd touched her in little ways that, taken separately, wouldn't have amounted to much. But together they were slowly bringing a heat to her body she'd never experienced before.

"Did you get them all?" she asked.

He leaned forward and stroked his tongue across her lips. His warmth, the taste of coffee and the pulsing of desire pounded through her.

"There we go," he said, and sat back.

She wanted to crawl across the table and pull his head to hers. To ravage his mouth in a way she'd never ravaged any man's before. Wanted to make him finish what these teasing touches had been leading up to.

He'd created something here tonight that she'd never sensed in him. She wouldn't have guessed Nick could find and light candles. Wouldn't have imagined he'd take the time to order a nice dinner.

Wouldn't have known that he'd be so good at seduction. Except that it felt more personal. Not like something he'd done for other women, but something he did only for her.

"Why all of this?" she asked, feeling like a fairy-tale princess who'd spent her life taking care of herself.

He finished his champagne in one swallow. ''I wanted to repay you.''

That stung—the evening of her secret dreams was a payback. She clenched her fingers into fists in her lap. Her nails bit into her palms, and she knew she shouldn't ask. Should just smile and thank him for the dinner. Should just pretend it didn't hurt but she couldn't. ''For what?''

''For defending me. I've always been alone and today...I don't know how to express what I felt.''

Disappointment laced with anger raced through her. When was she going to learn that men didn't go out of their way to seduce her? ''You mean at work?''

''Yes.''

She frowned at him. ''But that was a job thing.''

''No, it wasn't. It was because of what we have. It's because you had the chance to know me away from the office that you defended me. Thank you.''

His words made her believe that what they had was special and made her realize that she wouldn't have defended Nick the boss if she hadn't known Nick the man. Had she done something today that had far-reaching repercussions? Something she hadn't even realized she'd been doing?

''It was nothing. They were just spouting off.''

''But you did something I know is hard for you.''

She shivered to think he knew her so well. That he'd taken the time to look beyond the surface. She knew then that this evening wasn't a conscience gift but a gift from Nick to her. ''What was that?''

"You drew attention to yourself and to us."

She wasn't ready to deal with those consequences yet. She'd spent the afternoon sequestered in the office avoiding others, but she knew that couldn't last. "I couldn't walk away without saying something."

"I know." The quiet certainty in his voice touched her. She slid out of her chair and walked around next to him. Needing to touch him, she cupped his jaw and ran the ball of her thumb over his lips. His sharp intake of breath made her breasts feel heavier and her blood heat even more.

"What else do you know?" she asked.

He bit her thumb and held her flesh captive for a moment, nibbling on it. "That if I don't make love to you tonight I will go insane."

"Well, we don't want that."

"No, we don't. I've been imagining you on my bed since the first time we made love."

"Then let's fulfill your fantasy," she said.

"I hope we'll get to some of your fantasies as well."

Nick stood and lifted her in his arms. Lila knew that they'd already met and filled her fantasies. The man who'd orchestrated this evening wasn't a man intent on having a fling. This was a man who could make a lifetime commitment, baby or no baby. And that made Lila's heart pulse to life for the first time ever.

Nick had wanted Lila in his bed for so long that when he lowered her onto the navy counterpane, he

had to step back and really look at her there. The light
spilling from the hallway painted her in shadows. And
for a moment Nick wondered if she were really there
at all. Maybe she was only an illusion that would
disappear the first time he tried to touch her.

Her long blond hair contrasted with the darkness
of the bedspread and pillows. She flung her arms out
to either side and lay there before him. Legs slightly
parted, her skirt high on her thighs. She kicked her
shoes off and opened her arms, welcoming him.

Lust inflamed him, his sex had never felt as engorged as it did while he watched her on the bed.
Though he knew the secrets her body held, she
seemed to embody everything mysterious about
women. And in that moment she was the only woman
to his man.

He stepped out of his loafers, hand going to his
belt buckle. He wanted tonight to be special, a slow
seduction of the senses, but with Lila there was no
gentling. It was an intense rush that encompassed not
only his body but also his soul.

"Tonight is for you," he said, hoping saying the
words would give him the control he needed to make
this one of the slow and tender times.

"I hope it's for you, too."

"It is."

"Then come here. I'm lonely without you."

He let his belt fall to the floor and pulled his shirt
from the waistband of his pants, but otherwise left all

of his clothing on. Lila reached for the buttons on the front of her blouse but he stilled her hands.

"I've always enjoyed unwrapping my presents."

"A present, am I?"

The sweetest one he'd ever received, but he didn't say the words out loud. Instead he just unfastened her shirt and then slipped it off her body. She was heart-stoppingly lovely in the pale light of the moon. Her silk and lace bra cupped the alabaster globes of her breasts as a lover would. As he planned to. Her nipples beaded against the fabric and Nick couldn't wait another moment to taste her.

Bending down, he nipped lightly at her nipple before suckling her. She moaned and her fingers tunneled through his hair, holding him to her. He relished her touch. Her hands slipped from his head down his neck and then to the front of his shirt.

He leaned back and ripped it over his head. She watched him through half-closed eyes as he returned to her. He reached down and unfastened her bra. He slid it down her arms and she lifted a little to help but he left it at her wrists, effectively chaining her arms behind her.

"Nick?"

"Trust me?"

"Yes," she said, the word a sigh.

He rubbed his chest against her bare breasts with their hardened nipples, feeling the impact to his soul. He supported her with a hand under her shoulders so that her wrists weren't strained. Her hips rose from the bed, nestling against his hardness.

He bent and took her mouth, kissing her as if he'd never tasted her before. He nibbled around the edges of her mouth until she groaned and her hips ground harder against his erection. Then he plunged his tongue deep into her mouth.

Nick wanted her naked and writhing on the bed, to see her offered up before him like a virgin sacrifice of old. He propped two pillows under her shoulders and pulled back, stripping her skirt, hose and panties down her legs at the same time.

The sudden loss of his body heat and her clothing made her flinch and she tried to cover herself. "Let me see you, Lila."

"This feels…"

"Decadent?"

"No."

"Uncomfortable?"

"Uneven."

"Ah…"

"Take off your clothes, Camden."

"Not yet. I'm still in charge."

"Do I get a chance?"

"Yes."

"Five minutes?"

He nodded.

"I'm your willing slave."

"Spread your legs, Lila."

She moved them apart a little bit.

"Farther."

She did, but her hands still hovered over her breasts. She hesitated.

"Trust me," he said.

She did as he asked and lay before him as he'd imagined so many times. She was infinitely lovelier than any woman he'd ever seen. He wanted her so badly he knew he wouldn't last long.

He wanted to taste her from head to toe and lowered himself between her legs to do just that. He started at her left foot and worked his way slowly up her body, pausing to carefully bite behind her knee. At the apex of her thighs, he sucked on the skin so close to her center that he felt her humid warmth. He sucked until she moaned and lifted her hips from the bed.

When he moved on to sweeter flesh, he left behind a small mark. He wanted to leave more of them behind. He parted her silken flesh and bent to taste the pearl he'd revealed. Lila's breaths were quickening. Her flesh quivered when he blew across it and when he touched her lightly with his tongue, she cried out.

He felt her body's response to him, wanted to feel it on his most sensitive flesh. He thrust two fingers inside her and she welcomed him with a fierce clenching that made his arousal even fuller.

"I can't wait," he said.

"I can't either," she said.

He freed himself and thrust into her. She was still quaking from her earlier climax, and he waited for her to calm then began to build the tension within both of them again. He kissed her eyes and cheeks, the long length of her neck and the berry-hardened tips of her breasts.

He caressed her back and spine, finally cupping her buttocks in his hands and tilting her hips so that he could thrust deeper inside her. She lifted herself to him and he felt the minute contractions in her lower body around his most intimate flesh. It was like being caressed by the warmest, wettest glove. A red haze settled over him and he put his arms under her legs, bending them slowly back toward her body.

He stopped when she gasped. He could barely think, much less speak, but he had to know if she was okay. "Hurt?"

She shook her head. "Can you take more of me?" he asked.

She nodded and he pressed her legs back farther until she was completely open to him. He thrust deeper, deeper than he'd ever been before. He felt as if he were touching her womb and then he climaxed. He felt Lila's body clench around him again and their eyes locked as they shot together to the stars. It was a long, hard ride and it emptied him of his seed— rocking him to his very soul.

Ten

Lila knew that some dreams never came true. She'd spent her childhood searching for a father who never appeared. She'd spent her teenage years waiting for a white knight to rescue her from the cruel taunts of the other kids. She'd spent half her life waiting for Mr. Right—and he'd appeared out of the blue.

The lingering stickiness between her legs reminded her that Nick hadn't used a condom. She wasn't sure what that meant. Maybe he'd forgotten again, but she doubted it. The act of unprotected sex had to mean more to him than that.

She looked at the man lying still and quiet next to her in the dark. Their bodies were covered in a sheen of sweat and Lila didn't feel strong enough to move under the covers.

She shivered a little and Nick pulled her closer to his body, wrapping himself around her, cupping her buttocks in his palm and brushing his lips against her neck. She'd never felt so cherished, so vulnerable, so...loved.

But love wasn't something she trusted. It didn't lead to respectability but to passion-filled unions. Though his body protected her now, she'd never felt as exposed as she had earlier, when he'd been in control. Surrendering control had been difficult.

She stirred in his arms, needing their relationship to be equal. Needing to see if what he felt for her was on the same level as what she felt for him. Did he trust her enough to cede control?

Running her fingers down the line of hair on his chest, she tickled the spot right above his groin. His flesh hardened and she caressed him tenderly. His touch on her back changed from languid to inciting, sliding around to the front of her body, brushing his forefinger across her nipple until a delicious warmth gathered between her legs.

The sexual energy in the room rekindled, and she felt its pull. She knew that she was about to surrender to him once again. But she wanted, no, needed to be his equal tonight. She needed to know that this encounter wasn't going to be relegated to another affair with another woman in his mind. She needed to know that he felt for her what she felt for him.

She glanced up his long lean body. His eyes were

open and he studied her with an intensity that left her breathless.

"You rang?"

She wanted to feel what he did, that sense of surety in her partner that he had in her. She knew that the next few minutes would determine whether or not they'd both found something lasting. Knew that it was up to Nick to make the next move. Knew that she had to be brave enough to follow through.

"Nick, I want my five minutes," she said.

He stared at her, and her heart sank. He wasn't going to give up control for anything...not even her. He rubbed his jaw and looked away.

She felt what he wasn't saying. That her emotions were stronger than his. That she'd bared her soul, but his lay safely protected. That she loved him, but he didn't trust in that love enough to make himself vulnerable.

Suddenly her nakedness made her uncomfortable. She tugged on the sheets, trying to cover herself. She should leave. But she couldn't move right now. If she shifted in one direction she'd explode into a million pieces.

He touched her back, one finger moving slowly down the line of her spine. Then she felt the heat of his mouth in a slow, burning kiss just above the curve of her buttocks.

"Lila?"

She couldn't look at him. "Yes?"

"Okay."

At first she wasn't sure she'd heard him correctly, the word had been uttered so softly.

One glance at his eyes was all the confirmation she needed. She saw in them a light that she'd never seen before.

"On your back, Camden." She wanted to explore his body. Though they'd made love several times she'd always focused on her reactions. Loving Nick as she did, she wanted to find out what drove him over the edge.

"I'm yours to command."

The thrill of power went to her head, and she closed her eyes for a minute. But only a minute. She knelt next to him and realized that she didn't want him to be in the same position she'd been in. She wanted this to be equal, but different.

"On your knees."

He knelt next to her on the bed. She didn't need to tell him to spread his legs. The strength of his erection necessitated that. She drew her nails up the length of his thighs, teasing him by caressing him everywhere but on the hungry flesh that craved her touch.

If she'd learned one thing from Nick it was that waiting made the culmination so much sweeter. Leaning forward she bit his pectoral right above his flat nipple. He moaned.

She sucked lightly on his skin. His hands moved up to hold her to him. He rubbed his chest against her mouth. The hair over his muscles made her lips tingle. She moved down his body, tracing him with her mouth. He leaned back and spread his legs wider. She slid between them. She felt his hot erection brushing at her stomach and reached down to take him in her hand.

She stroked him a few times, then his hand on hers stilled the motion. "I'd rather be inside you when I climaxed."

"I'd rather have you there."

He lay back on the pillows and pulled her forward. Lila slid over him, bracing herself with her hands on his shoulders. Nick helped her to impale herself on him. She rode him carefully, unsure of herself in this position. Unsure of herself in the dominant role. But Nick, teeth gritted and eyes locked to hers, was letting her take the lead.

Each time she slid up on him, his hips rose slightly, when she slid back down, his fingers flexed on the bed and his hands moved toward her hips.

The slow sensuous moving was a delicious torture. But soon she wanted more and murmured, "Okay, control is yours again."

She realized she really only wanted his trust, not to take him as he'd taken her. Because, as he held her hips and thrust into her as if he couldn't get enough of her, she realized that what he felt for her was as intense as what she felt for him. She felt her climax coming, and then Nick's as he reached between their bodies to caress her more intimately.

Her entire body tensed, and she felt Nick's warmth deep inside her. As she lay down on his body, his strong arms wrapped around her, she knew she'd never sleep alone again. She knew that Nick was ready for a lifelong commitment. She smiled to herself and drifted off to sleep imagining living in his house as man and wife.

Nick felt as if every nerve in his body had been exposed last night. The sensuality exceeded even his fantasies, but the result was a shocking vulnerability he'd never felt before. He didn't like it.

Lila looked small and fragile in the morning light that spilled through the windows. Last night she'd been a match for him in the dark, but now she seemed too delicate for him and the life he'd led.

She stirred on the bed, and he climbed out before she awoke. Although his first instinct was to cradle her close and never let her go, he'd found that the things you held on to hardest were usually the ones that slipped most easily away.

He went into the bathroom, bracing his hands on the sink, and bowed his head. What had started out as one thing—seduction and thank you—had turned into a soul-baring experience that made him doubt his sanity.

He couldn't live with someone who brought him that close to his true self. He couldn't be with her night after night until she left and still survive.

It had been different with Amelia. She'd never breached his inner walls, and even if she'd survived the cancer, he'd never have been able to let her past them. He didn't think he could live with Lila seeing him at his softest, knowing the power she had over him.

He showered and shaved, and, when he emerged from the bathroom, he was no closer to figuring out what he was going to do next. One thing was certain, Lila and he could never live together.

He stopped as he entered his bedroom. Lila was sitting on the window seat overlooking the backyard. She wore only his discarded shirt. Her knees were held tight to her chest and her glorious blond hair fell in rumpled waves against her back.

She looked alone and scared. After last night, she deserved to wake up in the arms of her lover—not alone. But he'd been unable to stay. How was he going to tell her that they couldn't see each other anymore?

Wounding her went against the grain, but in this instance his own self-preservation won out. His survival had to be paramount. He cared deeply for Lila, but she would move on and love again. At least that's what he kept telling himself.

He walked across the room, stopping about ten feet away from her. She glanced over her shoulder. Her eyes were guarded, and there was no welcoming smile on her face.

"I'm..." He spread his hands. Damn, he hated these kinds of conversations. Not that he'd ever really had them. Amelia hadn't touched him as deeply as Lila did. His parents hadn't either.

"Scared?" she asked.

He shrugged. *Scared* wasn't a word he'd ever apply to himself and he didn't like hearing her use it. But he knew that he was running from her. Even rationalizing it didn't help.

Honesty seemed like the best option at the moment. "Not sure what to say."

"How about that we're great together and you can't imagine us living apart?" She stood up and the anger in those movements cut him deep. Carefully he looked at her, cataloging her features and her expression. This was his great gift to womanhood. Anger and disillusionment. He never wanted to forget this.

"That's not in the cards for us."

"It could be." She marched up to him and stood, arms akimbo, before him. The hem of his shirt lifted to the top of her thighs. His entire body tightened. He wanted to slide his hand up under that shirt, knowing she was naked and needing to touch her. He didn't know if he could stop himself.

He started to reach for her, imagining her soft skin under his touch. Imagining the return of the passion that had swept them away the night before. Realizing that nothing would ever again be the same between them.

She glared at his hand hanging in mid-air. He dropped it to his side, but Lila clasped it in her own. Her grip was cold and firm.

"Dammit, Nick. What happened?" Her eyes were

glassy and he knew she was fighting back tears. He felt like a big bully on the playground.

He didn't know how to put into words what was going through him. Didn't want to be vulnerable to her again even though he'd already been stripped to the soul in front of her. He owed her something, though, because he wasn't the only one who'd bared his innermost being last night.

"It was too intense."

"It *was* intense—and real."

"Not real. Life isn't made up of those moments. It's mundane living through a daily routine. Some of us are meant to make that journey together. Others are not."

She let his hand slide from hers. "I take it we're in the 'not' category?"

"I am. But Lila, you deserve a decent guy for a husband. I care about you so this isn't easy."

"What if I'm pregnant?"

"Of course, I'll do my duty to your child, Lila."

"Not marriage?"

"You know how I feel about marriage."

"Yes, I do. But I have to be honest here, Nick. It sounds like a cop-out."

"I wish it was. After Amelia died, something inside of me shut down. Work became my life and I'll tell you something, I don't think I'd ever want to go back to the way I felt those first six months after I buried my wife."

"If something were to happen to me would it hurt less if I wasn't your wife?"

He hated her perception. He couldn't answer this question. "I hope not."

"Help me understand this."

He took her hand and led her to the bed. He motioned for her to sit down but didn't sit next to her. "I've told you how it was growing up. My family wasn't much of one, but I'd always had this perfect image in my mind of what a family should be."

"The McKees?"

He nodded. "I had my shot with Amelia. But it wasn't perfect either. Our lives didn't mesh, and we never became a solid unit the way Buster's parents had been.

"After she died, I decided not to try again. I didn't just lose Amelia when cancer took her. Fate took my dreams, Lila. And you can't give them back to me."

"I'm not trying to."

"What do you want from me?"

"Not duty, for God's sake. You have to work at being happy. It doesn't just drop in your lap.

"Do you love me?" she asked suddenly, her eyes boring into him as if she were trying to reach his soul again.

"Lila…"

She stood and started gathering her clothing. She stalked to the bathroom door. "Fate didn't take your dreams, Nick."

He didn't say anything.

''You gave them away because you're too afraid of life to take even the simplest risk. Life is a rich morsel meant to be savored, not a fine meal put in storage until it's moldy and gray.''

She stormed out the door, and he tried to pretend that her going was for the best, but he didn't feel the relief he'd expected to feel. Instead he felt empty and even more alone.

Two days later, on Monday morning, Lila wasn't sure of anything except that she couldn't go into the Colette offices today. She'd woken up this morning to discover her period had arrived. No baby. Keen disappointment rolled through her. She knew it was for the best, but it didn't stop the tears from burning in her eyes.

A part of her would have always treasured a small being that was both her and Nick. Her dreams of happily ever after with Nick were dashed, but she knew in her heart that someday she'd try again, because she wanted a husband and a family. Maybe she'd try it without love. Maybe Nick was on to something, and it wouldn't hurt as much if she kept her emotions uninvolved.

She cleaned her apartment from top to bottom, washing all of the linens twice. She'd been unable to sleep in her bed because she remembered the night Nick had spent there, remembered his strong body wrapped around her own. Therefore, she'd spent Saturday night on the couch and last night in the kitchen baking.

She now had seven loaves of pumpkin, apple and banana nut breads, as well as enough cookies for the entire population of Indiana. But she hadn't felt in control last night while she'd been baking. She'd been like a mime going through the motions.

She had to shake off the lethargy that was plaguing her. Part of her said it had only been two days and it was okay to wallow, but the other part, the part that was trying to protect her, said to move on. Pack up her homey little apartment and start over somewhere else.

Because she didn't think she was going to be able to return to Colette, Inc. She wasn't even sure she was going to be able to leave her apartment now that she'd been so open about her affair with Nick. And it was over.

She called the office and told them she wouldn't be in today. She knew she was going to have to face Nick, would have to work with him day in and out. But not today. Today she was going to take the bread and cookies to Charlotte and Myrtle at the seniors' center. Then she was going to do some thinking and make some choices about the future.

As much as Nick had hurt her, she knew that she'd been expecting him to. Knew that from the first time they'd made love on his desk, she'd been waiting for him to leave. Had known deep in her heart that a vice president wouldn't settle for his secretary.

She checked her watch to make sure Nick would be in the weekly staff meeting before dialing his private line. She had to let him know that she wasn't pregnant.

His voicemail clicked on and Lila wasn't sure what to say. "Hi, it's Lila. I'm not—you don't—"

She hit the command to delete the message before he received it. This obviously wasn't something she could say over the phone. Maybe she'd send him an e-mail.

She finished getting dressed, realizing she still had Rose's pin. It hadn't brought her luck or love, she thought. It was probably time to return it to Rose.

She caressed the amber-and-metal jewel. The heart-shaped design drew her eye and romantic interest. She wondered who'd designed the brooch. It took a special person to design something that went beyond jewelry and became art.

Tucking the brooch into her coat pocket, she packed her baked goods in a large basket. She packed a smaller basket for Mr. McKee. She'd learned from Charlotte that he was back at home with a round-the-clock nurse. She didn't examine her motives too carefully, but she knew that although she was angry with Nick, right now she'd never be able to cut Nick out of her life. The people who were important to him would always be important to her.

The phone rang as she was leaving and she waited for the machine to pick up.

"Lila, are you home?"

Nick's voice echoed through her apartment, sending tingles of awareness down her spine. He sounded tired and frustrated.

He sighed. "I need to talk to you. If you don't pick up I'm going to come over and wait outside your window. I think we're too old for those kind of games but if you want to play I think you should know I always win."

His words didn't scare her. She was leaving. She could stay gone until he gave up and went home, but that was a childish thing to do. What she felt for Nick, what they'd had together, deserved more than that. She picked up the handset. "Nick?"

"Thought that would get you to talk."

"I'm not playing a childish game, Nick. I just need time to adjust."

"I know. I wanted to make sure you're okay."

"I am," she said, knowing she should tell him she wasn't pregnant, but the words wouldn't come.

"I've done some thinking since our discussion," he said.

"About?"

"What you said. I realized I'm not the only one who's running."

Damn, she thought. "I was willing to stop for you."

"It felt like you only slowed down."

"What's that supposed to mean?"

"Only that you never trusted me to stay, did you?"

"Hey, I loved you."

"Past tense already, Lila? It's only been two days."

"Well, being shown the door does that to a woman."

"Being judged and found wanting does that to a man."

"I didn't judge you."

"You sure as hell did. Why else all the secrecy and sneaking around?"

"I never asked you to sneak," she said, avoiding what she was beginning to believe was the truth.

"Not with words, but with actions."

Silence buzzed along the open line and Lila couldn't breathe for a minute.

"I tried to give you everything I had," she said quietly and hung up the phone.

It rang again almost immediately and Lila hurried out the door, but not before she heard Nick's deep voice once more through her answering machine. She knew she was running but realized that this time she wasn't running away. She'd made a good life for herself in Youngsville, and she wasn't about to give it up along with the only man she'd ever loved.

Eleven

The board meeting was long and boring, and Nick didn't pay much attention to anything that was said. Which concerned him. Colette had saved his life after Amelia died, and here he was letting his job performance slide.

The meeting adjourned, and Xavier stopped him in the hall. "I wanted to thank your secretary for defending the board and the choices we make."

Xavier had his hand in many pies at Colette and information was one of the areas that he exceeded at. But still, how could he have heard about cafeteria gossip? "Lila is very loyal to Colette. But how did you get wind of her actions?"

"My assistant was in the cafeteria. You know

many of our staff are playing the wait-and-see game, but she isn't. She's a fine woman.''

Xavier's words made him feel like a bastard because he knew they were true. ''You've never met her, Xavier. Maybe she was hedging her bets.''

''Do you think so?'' Xavier asked.

Nick had a brief idea that he should plant a seed in Xavier's mind and then go ahead and fire Lila. It wasn't a noble thing to do, but he was at a loss as to how to deal with her after she'd seen him at his lowest. But he'd also seen her at her lowest and that made him want to protect her.

Nick shook his head. ''No. She wouldn't do that. She's very loyal and involved in the success of Colette. I've never worked with a finer person—man or woman.''

Xavier put his hand on Nick's shoulder. The two men had known each other a long time and Nick knew that Xavier had helped save his sanity after Amelia's death. ''There's been a lot of tension around the office lately, and you've been putting in too many hours. Why don't you take the afternoon off?''

Where would he go? He had nothing outside of the office to turn to. He'd driven away the one woman who might have been interested in filling those empty hours. ''My work is my life, Xavier.''

His boss looked at him shrewdly and Nick thought he might have come up lacking. ''Maybe it shouldn't be.''

Xavier walked away, and Nick went back to his

own office. He knew that work wasn't his life anymore; that he couldn't let it be if he wanted to survive. But the leap he'd have to take to make that change seemed impossible.

And he knew he'd have to make a change.

Wishing wouldn't make his office situation any different. He and Lila were going to have to move forward and the more he thought about it the less he liked the idea of her not sitting in his outer office. But more than that, he disliked the thought of their lives not intermingling. Of her house not being his, her life not overlapping his, her children not being his.

Damn, he'd forgotten to ask her about the pregnancy test when he'd talked to her earlier. The way he'd acted he wouldn't have blamed her if she hadn't told him. Hell, he wasn't too sure he'd have told himself.

His office reminded him of Lila. Of them making love and more. Her spunk and attitude when he'd behaved in a way that no new lover should. She was his match on so many levels.

She was too good for him, for the bitter lonely man he'd let life shape him into. He thought he might want to be better for her, but those kinds of decisions weren't ones taken lightly. Maybe it was only the lust talking. He'd never had a lover to equal Lila. And it wasn't only physical. Something else happened between them when they made love.

She'd shared her dreams with him. Images of a

future where she lived in a large house with a white picket fence and had a family. A real family, with a husband and kids. Something he'd never offered her. He'd shared his lonely vision of the world where parents hated each other and the child grew up distrustful.

The very things she needed were things he'd never been able to depend on, but he knew that he was going to have to or he'd lose her forever. On Saturday morning, when they'd parked, he'd wanted only to get away from her, to hide in the dark until his protective skin had had time to regenerate. But now, with the distance of time, he realized that she hadn't peeled that layer away. He'd let it drop and invited her in without ever realizing it.

The threat to Colette had made one thing abundantly clear in his life. The job couldn't be all he had. He needed more. He closed his eyes. The only woman he could see by his side as his wife was Lila Maxwell.

''Damn,'' he muttered. Convincing her to stay with him was going to be hard. Could he change the habits of a lifetime? He didn't think so. But he knew he wasn't going to be responsible for making her cry again.

Nick remembered the night they'd gone to the symphony and his words, *I wish I could watch over you.* What an ass he'd been. Could he have tried any harder to push her away?

Even Xavier believed that his job wasn't important to him anymore. Of course, he wasn't going to let any hostile takeover wrest control of Colette without a fight, but his heart wasn't in it as much as it had once been.

His heart wasn't even his own anymore. It belonged to Lila. But he was afraid to give it to her.

He put his elbows on his desk and dropped his forehead into his hands, closing his eyes against the burn of tears. How could he love her? He knew nothing about happily ever after. But what he felt was so extreme it could only be love.

This should be the happiest moment of his life. His heart was pounding, and he knew he'd have to figure out a way to get her to stay without revealing his feelings. Those were words he could never say out loud. Never even intimate that he might have deep emotions for her.

He'd never survive if something happened to her and he didn't know what the future held. Didn't know what he was going to do because he couldn't live with Lila and he'd only just realized how barren life would be without her.

Lila left the seniors' center after a nice visit with Myrtle and Charlotte. Afterwards, she'd located Mr. McKee's apartment, but he wasn't up to visitors so she left the basket she'd made for him with his attendant. Seeing the elderly man lying pale on the bed made her heart ache. Not for herself, but for Nick.

As much as she'd wanted to cling to the bitterness he'd inspired in her, she couldn't. She loved him. At this moment it hurt like hell, but the pain reminded her she was still alive.

The day was gray, cloudy and cold. A light rain fell as she stepped outside. She pulled her gloves from her pocket and wrapped her muffler around her throat.

"Lila?"

She pivoted to see Buster McKee behind her. "Hi, Buster."

"Is Nick here with you?"

She shook her head. This was the beginning, she realized, the beginning of life without someone whom you'd made important. Though they had been together for only a month, she felt as if their lives were inexplicably entwined.

"I wanted to thank him again for all he's done for Dad."

"He wouldn't want your thanks. He did it out of kindness. Your dad is important to him," Lila said, though she figured Buster already knew that.

"I know. You had to see his parents to really appreciate your own."

"Tell me about them," she said, knowing she was using false pretenses to learn more about Nick. But maybe Buster could give her some insight that Nick simply couldn't.

"They looked like a perfect family on the outside, you know. I mean his mom was a CPA and his dad was a lawyer, and in public they presented this family that was straight out of *Saturday Evening Post*."

"And they weren't." Nick had said that the face of the enemy wasn't one he wanted to see in her.

"Maybe they were. But those two, they should never have had kids. They made Nick's life tough and I know he did whatever it took to graduate from high school early and go to college.

"His parents told him he was unlovable. That if he'd been a different child, his life could have been better."

Lila shivered in the rain, and she wished she could wrap her arms around Nick and hold him to her. To make him understand that he was so much more than his parents made him believe he was.

"When I saw the basket you dropped off for Dad, well, it made me realize that Nick had finally found someone who could love him as he deserved."

She could only stare at him, tears burning the back of her eyes. How could she tell him that she could love Nick with her heart and soul, but he'd never accept it? Now that she knew about Nick's past and finally understood what his formative years had been like, she realized that the secret hope she'd been harboring that he'd come back to her was self-delusion.

"I better let you get out of the rain."

Lila only nodded as she watched Buster leave. Her head down, she hurried to her car. The cold wet day was a perfect match for the weeping she was doing inside.

The key jammed in the door of her car, a domestic sedan that had seen better days and that she'd been reluctant to get rid of after it had made the trip to Indiana.

She sat in the parking lot for a few minutes waiting for the car to warm up. Her mind was full of Buster's voice telling her things about Nick's past. Nick's voice telling her that he never wanted to wake up and see her as his enemy. Her voice telling him he had to learn to love.

Turning up the volume on her radio to drown out the sound of the voices, she flipped channels, searching for the right song. Something loud, she thought. Not the Chili Peppers or Creed because they'd make her think. She found the local jazz station and raised the volume even more.

She put the car in Drive and realized as she was driving that it had started to snow. In Florida, snow had seemed romantic and fun, everything that fall and winter should be. Last winter she'd had a minor fender-bender while driving in the stuff.

She slowed her car and drove sedately toward town. The deejay introduced a recording of classic jazz...Lena Horne's *Someone To Watch Over Me*. Lila's foot slipped off the gas before she remembered where she was.

She put her foot more securely on the pedal and reached for the radio dial to change it. Remembering her own mother's melancholy reaction to that song was one thing, actually letting sadness seep through herself was something else.

She hit an icy patch on the road and her car did a

360°-loop. Everything spun so quickly. She tried to steer into it but she had no control. She slammed forward as her car rocked to a stop and impacted a tree.

Her head hit the steering wheel before the seatbelt yanked her back and the airbag exploded in her face. She slumped forward in her seat. The music still played in her mind and the voices continued to swirl around. Her heart felt heavy and her future looked dim as pictures of her life flashed in her mind. She had an image of herself and Nick as they'd looked the night they'd attended the symphony. Her mother and her at the beach. Nick and she in her bed, the desperate way he'd held her close. Nick's face as she'd seen it that last time.

Her head pounded, and she couldn't keep her eyes open. Pinpricks of light, so bright she couldn't focus clearly on them, floated around her and she gave up consciousness wishing for Nick and the life they could have shared.

Nick was leaving the office when the receptionist stopped him to take a call.

"Take a message," he requested.

"She said it was an emergency, Mr. Camden."

He took the phone from the receptionist and barked his name into it.

"I'm sorry to bother you. This is Kitty Maxwell, Lila's mother."

"Yes, ma'am?" Nick suddenly felt sick to his stomach.

"She's been in an accident. I'm on my way to the airport, but I won't be able to get to Indiana until late tonight. Will you go to the hospital and wait with her?"

"Don't worry, ma'am. I'll take care of her."

He hung up the phone and left the building as fast as he could. He drove as quickly and safely through town as possible, knowing that nothing could stop Fate. If Lila lived, she would whether he was sitting by her side or not. But he wanted to be by her side. Needed to be there so that he could give her some of his strength.

He parked and ran inside, not sure what he'd find. The emergency room was busy but not too crowded. He approached a reception desk, introduced himself as Lila's fiancé and was directed to a small curtained-off area. Lila sat on the side of the bed. A huge bandage covered most of her forehead and her fingers were laced tightly together.

"I'm going home, doctor," she said, her voice hoarse and small but determined.

"No, miss, you are not, not unless you have someone to take care of you."

"I will," Nick said. He wanted to make a vow to her there in the hospital because seeing her made him want to protect her always.

Lila glanced at him, but there was no welcome in her eyes. No wild emotions that called to his soul and made him want to react to her. Nothing that showed he was anything to her other than a boss.

"And you are?" the doctor asked.

"My boss," Lila said.

Her boss. Nick wanted to argue that he was so much more, but knew he'd forfeited the right. He'd forced Lila out of her comfort zone and challenged her to acknowledge him as her lover, and then pushed her away. Sometimes he really could be a bastard.

"She has a mild concussion. Here's a prescription for the pain, and she needs to be awakened every four hours," the doctor instructed Nick.

Nick pocketed the prescription. The doctor left them alone in the curtained room. It smelled of cleaner and antiseptic. Next door someone moaned in pain, and a doctor was paged over the loudspeaker.

"What are you doing here?" Lila asked. Her tone held a hint of accusation, almost as if she didn't believe he deserved to be there. Maybe he didn't.

"Your mom asked me to come."

"Well, you've fulfilled your duty. Thanks for getting rid of the doc but, I'm fine from here out."

"How are you planning to get home?"

"I'll take the bus."

"You are so stubborn."

"I'm not the only one."

He glared at her, realizing that she called to the extremes in him. Lila was never going to be a safe placid lover. She was always challenging him, not just to be his best but to be on his toes.

"Let's get you home."

She didn't say anything else. An aura of fragility

surrounded her, and he was afraid even to touch her. But he knew he had to. He wanted to feel her breath against his neck and her heartbeat under his hands to affirm that she was whole and fine.

He pulled her into his arms and held her for a minute realizing how desperately happy he was that she was alive and only concussed. She held herself stiff in his arms and then slowly, when he didn't let go, she wrapped her arms around his waist and rested her head on his chest.

He brushed her hair back from her face, placing the smallest of kisses right next to the white bandage. Her breath caught and she pulled away.

"I can't do this, Nick. Not now."

She was right. He needed to get her out of the hospital, and she needed rest. Then they could talk and touch. Because he wasn't going to feel as though she was safe until he could just hold her in his arms. Then he was going to have to convince her that what they had would last. He knew now that it would.

"Stay here, I'll see what we have to do for you to leave."

"Where am I going to go?"

"Don't be smart with me," he said.

She just shook her head, and he remembered the way she'd been after they'd made love on his desk. Her sass was her defense mechanism and he couldn't blame her for it. After all, he'd shown her that he was her enemy.

"I'm not your enemy anymore," he said.

"We'll see," she said.

She closed her eyes. Nick knew she wasn't up to a conversation. He walked out without saying anything else. He found the doctor, and Lila signed a few papers and then they left. He wanted to carry her, but she glared at him when he suggested it.

He seated her in his car. "Your house or mine?"

"Amber Court, please."

"My place is closer," he said.

"Nick, I don't want to go to your home."

He said nothing else, just drove quietly toward her place. He drove through the twenty-four-hour pharmacy and dropped off Lila's prescription.

When they arrived at her place, he parked on the street and came around to open her door. She was glaring at him again and Nick knew he'd made a big mistake, one that he was going to have to continue to pay for unless he made some changes.

He scooped her up into his arms, kicked the door closed and crossed the street. The rain had changed to a light flurry of snow and it dusted Lila's hair and clothing, making her look even more like an angel.

He entered the marble foyer and Rose Carson, Lila's landlady, came out, saying in shocked tones, "Lila, are you okay?"

"She has a mild concussion. I'm going to take care of her," said Nick.

Rose smiled slightly and murmured, "Good."

She went back into her apartment, and Nick felt as if he'd been given a seal of approval.

"Maybe I wanted Rose to stay with me."

"Looks like you're stuck with me," he said.

"Nick—"

"Not here in the hallway, okay?"

She nodded, and he carried her up to her apartment and placed her on the bed. Nick helped her remove her boots and coat. He wanted to help her change into her nightgown, but she was already asleep when he removed her second boot. He pulled the covers over her.

Lila's mother called to say that she couldn't get a flight until the next day, and Nick assured her that he was staying with Lila and she'd be okay. He hung up and took off his own coat, shoes and belt. He set his watch alarm for four hours and climbed into bed next to her, pulling her into his arms. He couldn't sleep, but holding her brought him a peace he hadn't realized he'd been searching for.

Twelve

Lila rolled over in her sleep, waking when she realized that Nick's arms were around her. She wondered where all of his protectiveness was coming from. Why did he suddenly seem not to want to let her out of his sight?

But she welcomed it. She felt puny today. The wound on her head throbbed, and her body had a bunch of bruises on it. She was acutely aware of every place their bodies touched and she snuggled closer to him while he was sleeping and couldn't see how much she needed him, needed his touch.

She stared at his face so close to hers. Even in sleep his intensity didn't wane. He looked fierce as he held her. She traced one finger lightly over his features.

She'd never noticed the small scar under his right eye. She memorized his features and the security his arms brought her, knowing that once he was awake and out of bed, she'd never touch him again.

She had to tell him there was no baby. Had to let him know that there was no reason for him to protect her. Had to make sure he knew his obligations to her were over.

His eyes opened and she found herself staring into his deep-blue eyes. They always reminded her of the Atlantic Ocean near the Keys where her mother used to take her every summer when she was a little girl.

"Lila? Are you okay?" he asked.

"Yes, I'm fine." But the words were a lie. She'd never be fine again. And she didn't know how to make his life right for him, knowing she wasn't the one who should do it anyway.

She glanced at the clock. It was 7:00 a.m. The sun peeked though the edges of her wooden blinds. It looked like it was going to be a nice day. She vaguely recalled Nick waking her throughout the night.

"Thanks for staying with me last night."

"No problem. I, um, had to sleep with you because the couch is too small."

She wanted to tease him about that, the way she would have a few days earlier, but now she didn't know where they stood. She knew she had a secret she had to share and that he'd told her she was running from life the last time they talked. So much was unsettled between them. She was almost afraid to settle it because then he'd leave and she'd be alone again, spending all of her nights dreaming of a man she couldn't have.

"Why don't you wash up and I'll fix you some breakfast?" Nick stood and she realized he'd slept in his clothes, too.

"Okay," she said, wanting to delay the moment when she had to tell him they weren't having a baby. Delay the moment when she'd sever the last bond between them. Delay the moment when he left for good.

She grabbed a change of clothes and walked to the bathroom. "Don't lock the door in case you fall."

"Will you catch me?" she asked before she could stop herself.

"I will," he said and walked to the kitchen.

She showered and dressed and joined him in her small kitchen. He'd made coffee and found some waffles she'd frozen the week before.

They sat at her counter to eat. When he finished his breakfast, he stood. "Ready to talk?"

She nodded.

"Let's go sit in the living room."

Her couch was comfortable, and Nick hadn't really spent a lot of time there. She didn't want him sitting on it now. Didn't want to have another piece of furniture or another room in her house that was overwhelmed by the memory of him.

But she sat next to him just the same. "I…"

"Lila, please let me say something first."

"Okay."

He swallowed and stood to pace the room. "You were right when you said that I was hiding from life and that Fate wasn't responsible, I was."

She wrapped her arms around her waist to keep from going to him and pulling him into her embrace. She knew it was duty that motivated him to speak to her.

"I've always known you were smart."

He didn't smile as she'd hoped.

"Lila, all my life I've been searching for something that was just out of my reach. Ambition in my career brought me close, my marriage to Amelia brought me closer, but neither of them touched the part of me that you did."

"I'm not sure that I really could reach you, Nick."

"I didn't know it either until I came so close to losing you."

"I was already lost to you. You said it. I was running away from love again."

"No, you weren't. This time I drove you away. I don't know about the past and I really don't care about it. I've always lived for the future and I want that future to include you and our baby."

Finally, he knelt at her feet, arms caging her hips and pulled her toward him. He lowered his head so that it rested against her stomach. She wanted to wrap her arms around him and hold him to her, but she knew he'd leave when she told him what she needed to say. Had to say it now.

"Nick..."

"Shh," he said, covering her lips with his fingers. "I know I've been cruel in the past, but as of this moment forward my life belongs to you. I can't live without you."

He straightened from her body and took her left hand in his. He caressed her fingers before lowering his head and brushing a butterfly-soft kiss against her hand. She shivered and watched him.

"Will you marry me?"

The words she'd always wanted to hear from the man who owned her body, heart and soul. The tears that had been burning the back of her eyes since he dropped to his knees in front of her began to fall.

"I can't," she said.

"Why not?"

"I'm not pregnant, Nick. There's no reason for us to marry."

Lila stood and stalked to the window. She stared blindly down at the street, wrapping her arms around herself and holding tight. Waiting for the inevitable sound of Nick leaving. Though she'd been expecting it, the sound of his footsteps still lanced through her, making the tears fall.

Nick knew he was probably going to rot in hell for what he'd done to Lila. He deserved to pay for the mess he'd made of both of their lives. All he'd really wanted to do was love her and yet that had gone awry.

Of course, he'd been hedging when he'd asked her

to marry him. Trying to protect himself and not give her a way out, and still she'd found one. An unexpected one that hurt him as much as it hurt her.

Lingering fear from his childhood made him believe that he was the wrong man for her, but sometime during the night as they'd slept close to each other in her bed, he'd come to realize that Lila and he were meant for each other. He'd dreamed of them in a house with a white picket fence and children playing in the yard. He'd dreamed of her pregnant with their third child and him holding her while a large group of their family and friends surrounded them.

He'd dreamed of a life he'd never had a shot at before her, and he wasn't going to let that slip through his fingers now. He'd waited a lifetime to find the woman of his dreams, not even realizing that he'd been searching for her.

He stepped out to Lila, and she stiffened when he touched her back. His hand seemed too big and rough for Lila in her pretty pink sweater. Should he leave? He heard the small catch in her throat as she breathed, knew she was crying and that he was responsible for those tears.

He pulled her into his arms. Her back pressed solidly to his front, he held her tightly and brushed his mouth against her ear. There were words he had to say, but he could do no more than whisper them.

She sniffled, and he reached for a tissue and carefully dried her face. She wouldn't turn in his arms, but in the window he saw their reflections. His big, dark shape behind her smaller one. They looked like yin and yang and he realized they were.

Man without woman, woman without man was not how nature intended humans to live. Until that moment he hadn't acknowledged why he needed Lila in his life, but finally he could.

"I love you," he said. They were words he'd never said before, not even to Amelia, who'd been a good friend and someone he'd cared deeply about.

She turned in his embrace. Her gaze searched his face and silent tears tracked down her pale cheeks. He brushed them away with a kiss, the salty taste of her tears bittersweet to his tongue.

He leaned back and she framed his face with her hands. Then leaning up on her toes, she pulled his mouth to hers. He kissed her with the care of a man who knows that he's finally found what he's spent his life searching for. Kissed her as if she were water and he'd spent the last years in the desert. Kissed her with all the emotion he'd been hiding from.

"Marrying you is about the only thing that can save me from a long, lonely life. Lila, you've been telling me that I threw my dreams away—but you've made me dream again."

"You're sure?" she asked, when he pulled back to breathe.

"Yes." He'd never been surer of anything. Even though he felt almost weak at the thought of putting himself in her hands. "Believe me, I love you."

"I love you, too."

Her words made him strong. And he realized that loving wasn't something that weakened you. It was something that made you stronger.

"I wanted your baby so badly."

"We'll have lots of babies," he said. He realized his dream last night hadn't only been a nice image of the future. It had been a warning that he was letting his destiny slip through his fingers.

"If this is a dream, don't wake me," she whispered.

Her words sealed it. "It's not a dream, Florida girl. It's Fate, and you can't escape it."

"I guess Rose's pin worked after all."

"What pin?"

"The heart-shaped brooch I've been wearing. Rose said it would bring me luck and love."

"Is that what it brought you?" he asked.

"It brought to life the desires I'd been hiding from."

"Which ones? Because I thought I had something to do with those physical desires."

"You did. This brooch woke me up and made me realize I'd spent all my nights dreaming of you."

His throat closed, and he hugged her fiercely to his chest. She held him with just as much strength. Nick brushed his lips against her ear and murmured, "Me, too."

"You're sure?" she asked.

"Positive." He knew that although she said she

hadn't been looking for someone to watch over her, she'd found someone all the same.

"Then take me to bed and hold me close."

Nick swept her up in his arms and carried her to the bed. "I'm going to make certain that you never have to settle for dreams again, Lila. You've got the real thing by your side for the rest of your days."

"The real thing is so much better than dreams."

"Let me prove it to you."

Her smile said yes. He laid her on the rumpled covers and placed himself next to her.

The intensity he always felt when he was with Lila was tempered with a new peace he'd never known before. Their mouths engaged in long, slow kisses, kindling a fire that burned through them both.

He joined their hands together and their eyes met, silently acknowledging the deep and lasting bond they'd made with their lives.

Two days later Lila returned the brooch to Rose. She and Nick had just returned from dropping off her mom at the airport. Lila had been pleased at how well her mom and Nick had gotten along. The minute her mother had seen Nick she'd hugged him close. When they'd announced their engagement, she'd told him to call her Mom.

"Thanks for loaning me this pin, Rose."

"You're welcome. Did it bring you luck?"

"It brought me more than that."

"Good, I think I may lend it to Meredith. She's a little nervous about going on the auction block."

Lila thought her friend was more than a little nervous. "Good idea."

"You look better today," Rose said.

"I feel incredible. You can be one of the first to know. Nick and I are getting married."

"Congratulations, dear."

"Thank you," Lila said.

Lila went back upstairs and found Nick sitting alone at the kitchen table. "What are you working on?"

He tugged her onto his lap and kissed her with an intensity that usually ended up with them both naked. But not today. They were going to drive out and visit Mr. McKee and Charlotte and Myrtle.

He pulled back and reached around her to show her a piece of paper. "I was thinking about Rose's brooch and I want to commission a similar piece for you."

Her throat closed. "I can think of nothing I'd love more."

"Not even me?" he asked, the words light, but she knew he still wasn't as secure as he should be.

"I love nothing more than you."

He pulled her close, his face buried against his neck. "I just want some of this luck for our children."

"Me, too," she said. They sat quietly talking about the future and the brooch. They knew that their bond would be strong enough to see them through the ups and downs of life and that they'd both found the one thing they'd never have had on their own...true love.

* * * * *

Turn the page for a sneak preview
of the next 20 AMBER COURT book,

The Bachelorette
by Kate Little

This is included in a two-in-one
volume with the final book in our
20 AMBER COURT mini-series

Risqué Business
by Anne Marie Winston.

On sale in December 2002.

The Bachelorette
by
Kate Little

The morning had been absolutely exasperating—
even for a Monday, Meredith decided. She'd missed
the bus and gotten caught in a downpour without an
umbrella. Not to mention a run in her panty hose that
was now as wide as the mighty Mississippi.

She scurried from the elevator to her office, opened
the door and slipped inside.

Usually, a little rain or a ruined stocking wouldn't
phase her. Her appearance was always neat, but carefully planned to blend into the woodwork. But she
was due to give a presentation this morning to just
about every high-level person in the company. Meredith dreaded speaking to groups, or any situation that
put her in the limelight. Having her hair and outfit
wrecked by the rain made the job even worse.

With her office door firmly closed behind her, she worked on some basic repairs, starting with her long reddish-brown hair, which was matted and damp, curling in every direction at once. She brushed it back tightly in her usual style, a simple ponytail secured with a clip. A bit severe perhaps, but certainly practical. Her complexion was fair, with faint freckles on her nose. She rarely tried to cover them with make-up. In fact, she usually wore no make-up at all. Which was just as well, she thought, since this morning she'd definitely have a bad case of raccoon eyes from melted mascara.

Her large blue eyes stared black at her in the mirror from behind oversize, tortoise-shell frames. She removed the glasses and wiped the damp lenses with a tissue. She often wished she could wear contact lenses, and had several pairs in her medicine chest. But her eyes never felt truly comfortable in contacts, especially during the close work required for jewelry design. Besides, she had no one special to impress.

A long floral skirt hid most of the run in her hose, she noticed. But her baize, V-neck sweater top, usually so baggy and figure concealing, now clung damply to her body like a second skin. Her mother had often told her that her ample curves on top were a blessing, but Meredith had never felt that way. To the contrary, she felt quite self-conscious about her busty physique and the unwanted attention it brought her, especially from men. Unlike most women she knew, Meredith did all she could to hide her curves, rather than show them off.

The large brooch pinned to her sweater pulled on the wet fabric and Meredith carefully unfastened the clasp. She took a moment to study the pin, holding it carefully in the palm of her hand. It was amazingly unique. Anyone would notice that. As a jewelry designer, it seemed even more remarkable to Meredith. It was a one-of-a-kind item you might come upon in an ''arty'' shop of handmade jewelry, or in a place that handled estate sales and antique pieces. Meredith's landlady, Rose Carson, had given it to her last night, when she'd been down at Rose's apartment having coffee. Rose was wearing the pin and Meredith had admired it. Then, without any warning at all, Rose took the pin off and offered it to her, insisting that Meredith borrow it for a while.

''Rose, it's lovely. But it must be very precious to you... What if I lose it?'' Meredith had asked.

''Don't be silly, you won't lose it,'' Rose had insisted. ''Here, put it on,'' Rose said, helping Meredith with the clasp. ''Let's see how it looks.''

Meredith had to agree it looked stunning. Yet she felt uncomfortable borrowing such a valuable piece of jewelry. But Rose, in her gracious, gentle way, wouldn't take no for an answer.

The design was roughly circular, a hand-worked base of different precious metals, studded with chunks of amber and polished gemstones. Staring down at it now in her hand, Meredith still found the composition fascinating, almost magically mesmerizing if one stared at it long enough, with the interplay of glittering jewels of so many different colors, shapes and cuts. The flickering shards of light thrown off from the jewels made Meredith feel almost lightheaded and she had to look away to regain her bearings. She had the oddest feeling each time she studied the pin, she noticed. But she couldn't quite understand why.

Brushing the question aside, she slipped the pin into the deep pocket of her skirt, feeling sure it would be safe there. Rose claimed the pin always brought her luck, and Meredith hoped that it would work for her today at her presentation, even hidden away in her pocket.

* * * *

Don't forget The Bachelorette *by Kate Little and* Risqué Business *by Anne Marie Winston will be on the shelves as a 2-in-1 volume in December 2002.*

1102/51a

DESIRE™ 2 IN 1

AVAILABLE FROM 15TH NOVEMBER 2002

THE BACHELORETTE Kate Little

20 Amber Court

Until she was 'bought' at a charity auction by delectable multi-millionaire Adam Richards, Meredith Blair no longer believed in falling in lust, let alone love. Could she overcome her past to forge a future with him?

RISQUÉ BUSINESS Anne Marie Winston

20 Amber Court

Sylvie Bennett was in danger of losing her job and the only family she'd ever known. She *had* to stop devastatingly handsome Marcus Grey from taking over the company, even if it meant risking her heart instead…

LUKE'S PROMISE Eileen Wilks

Tall, Dark & Eligible

Maggie Stewart's marriage to sexy-as-sin Luke West came with an expiry date—the payment of his inheritance. But if she pushed him to fulfil their desires, could she convince him that their love should last a lifetime?

TALLCHIEF: THE HUNTER Cait London

Tallchief

Adam Tallchief's first love Jillian O'Malley had returned—on a revenge mission to destroy his family. How could he convince the hot-blooded spitfire that he was not her enemy…but her answer to everlasting happiness?

STORMBOUND WITH A TYCOON Shawna Delacorte

Wealthy playboy Dylan Russell wanted solitude, but awoke to find his best friend's sister in his bed! Would Jessica McGuire be content with a few nights of passion when she really yearned for his love for a lifetime?

WIFE WITH AMNESIA Metsy Hingle

When Claire turned up with no memory of their separation, tycoon Matt Gallagher was determined to reclaim his wife—and protect her from her attacker. He could face any danger, but he couldn't lose her again…

AVAILABLE FROM 15TH NOVEMBER 2002

Sensation™

Passionate, dramatic, thrilling romances

BRAND-NEW HEARTACHE Maggie Shayne
JACK'S CHRISTMAS MISSION Beverly Barton
BANNING'S WOMAN Ruth Langan
BORN ROYAL Alexandra Sellers
A HERO TO HOLD Linda Castillo
ANYTHING FOR HIS CHILDREN Karen Templeton

Special Edition™

Vivid, satisfying romances full of family, life and love

BABY CHRISTMAS Pamela Browning
TO CATCH A THIEF Sherryl Woods
CHRISTMAS IN WHITEHORN Susan Mallery
THE MD MEETS HIS MATCH Marie Ferrarella
ALMOST A BRIDE Patricia McLinn
A LITTLE CHRISTMAS MAGIC Sylvie Kurtz

Superromance™

*Enjoy the drama, explore the emotions,
experience the relationship*

WHAT CHILD IS THIS? Karen Young
HUSH, LITTLE BABY Judith Arnold
A CHRISTMAS LEGACY Kathryn Shay
DECEPTION Morgan Hayes

Intrigue™

Danger, deception and suspense

LASSITER'S LAW Rebecca York
HOWLING IN THE DARKNESS BJ Daniels
GUARDING JANE DOE Harper Allen
ANOTHER WOMAN'S BABY Joanna Wayne

1102/51b

DELIVERED BY
Christmas

Linda Howard
Joan Hohl   Sandra Steffen

Available from 18th October 2002

Available at most branches of WH Smith,
Tesco, Martins, Borders, Eason, Sainsbury's
and all good paperback bookshops.

1102/128/SH41

THE COLTONS

FAMILY   PRIVILEGE   POWER

BOOK SIX
PASSION'S LAW
RUTH LANGAN

*Cynical police detective Thaddeus Law had
a mission: to catch the person trying to kill
famous millionaire Joe Colton.
This assignment would have been an open
and shut case if he hadn't been so distracted,
especially by Joe's niece—the smart and
beautiful heiress Heather McGrath.*

Available from 15th November 2002

THE
COLTONS

FAMILY PRIVILEGE POWER

BOOK SEVEN
THE HOUSEKEEPER'S DAUGHTER
LAURIE PAIGE

*Mighty Drake Colton could handle the Navy's most dangerous mission — but the housekeeper's daughter was a new challenge. The woman who'd worshipped him since childhood — who was now carrying his baby — had closed her heart to him. This tough and resilent SEAL was used to getting what he wanted. And Maya would be his — **whatever** it took!*

Available from 15th November 2002

COL/RTL/7

SILHOUETTE® DESIRE™

welcomes you to

20 AMBER COURT

*Where four women work together,
share an address...and confide in each
other as they fall in love!*

November 2002

WHEN JAYNE MET ERIK
by Elizabeth Bevarly

&

SOME KIND OF INCREDIBLE
by Katherine Garbera

December 2002

THE BACHELORETTE
by Kate Little

&

RISQUÉ BUSINESS
by Anne Marie Winston

SILHOUETTE®

DESIRE™

proudly presents

TALL, DARK
& ELIGIBLE

Eileen Wilks

*brings us three sexy, powerful,
exceptionally wealthy brothers...*

*Will three convenient marriages lead
to love for these bachelors?*

NOVEMBER 2002
JACOB'S PROPOSAL

DECEMBER 2002
LUKE'S PROMISE

JANUARY 2003
MICHAEL'S TEMPTATION

1102/SH/LC46

*Welcome to Montana — a place of passion
and adventure, where there is a charming
little town with some big secrets...*

SILHOUETTE® INTRIGUE™

and

HARPER ALLEN

present

THE AVENGERS

BOUND BY THE TIES THEY FORGED AS SOLDIERS OF FORTUNE, THESE AGENTS FEARLESSLY PUT THEIR LIVES ON THE LINE FOR A WORTHY CAUSE. BUT NOW THEY'RE ABOUT TO FACE THEIR GREATEST CHALLENGE—LOVE!

December 2002
GUARDING JANE DOE

February 2003
SULLIVAN'S LAST STAND

April 2003
THE BRIDE AND THE MERCENARY

1202/SH/LC48

SILHOUETTE®

SPECIAL EDITION™

presents

Patricia McLinn

with her exciting new series

Wyoming Wildflowers

These women are as strong and feminine
as the men are bold and rugged...and
they're all ready for...love!

ALMOST A BRIDE
December 2002

MATCH MADE IN WYOMING
February 2003

MY HEART REMEMBERS
April 2003

THE RUNAWAY BRIDE
June 2003

1202/SH/LC49

SILHOUETTE® SENSATION™

proudly presents

Ruth Langan's

fabulous new mini-series

THE LASSITER LAW

Lives — and hearts — are on the line when the Lassiters pledge to uphold the law at any cost

1002/SH/LC43